The Murder
of
the Maharajah

By H. R. F. Keating

The Murder
of
the Maharajah

H. R. F. KEATING

DOUBLEDAY & COMPANY, INC.

GARDEN CITY, NEW YORK

I

They were on their way. At the start of the first day of April, in the year of grace 1930. Under the Indian sun. Twelve people. Very different people, some from very different countries, all with very different ideas of the rules of the game. But on their way, in different fashions, to a meeting. A meeting with murder.

In the tangled jungle of the hills on the far outskirts of the State of Bhopore a man was on his way. He was an almost nameless man, and he was on his way to a man with as many names and titles as almost any other in the world. Clad only in a wisp of loincloth, he was on his way at a steady loping run to His Highness Maharajahdhiraj Raj Rajeshwar Lieutenant Colonel Sri Sri Sri Sahib Bahadur Mahapundit Mahasurma Sir Albert Singhi, Grand Commander of the Order of the Star of India, Grand Commander of the Order of the Indian Empire, Doctor of Literature (Benares), Maharajah of Bhopore. He was bringing him a gift, a rare gift.

It was a gift he had found deep, deep in the jungle that was his home, this almost nameless man from an almost nameless tribe living a life that seldom came into any contact with the great world outside. It was a very simple life, but it had its rules. And one of those rules concerned what the man had found hidden in the deepest green of the jungle. A piece of bark. Nothing more than a piece of bark, a chunky knot that had chanced to form on the trunk of a tree, the sapura tree, which normally had only the thinnest of skins.

But it was precious, this knot of bark, precious and very rare, found perhaps only once in every twenty years. It has a most curious quality. Detached from its parent tree and kept dry, it was soft and spongy, a startling orange in colour, with a faint sharp odour, somehow disturbing to smell and so staining to the touch that the hands of the running man would be coloured bright orange for days to come. But if it ever became wet it underwent a rapid process of hardening. Within minutes it became impenetrable as iron. And because of this any piece of it that any one of the remote jungle tribe ever found belonged as of right to His Highness the Maharajah of Bhopore, their distant overlord.

So the man who had found the sapura bark was running, running steadily through the dawning day on his way to the Maharajah's palace. There, he knew, he would be taken straight to the Maharajah to present this, his traditional gift. And, for all that it had no obvious use, when he presented it he would be richly rewarded. It was the custom.

Miles away on the borders of Bhopore at the other side of the sprawling state two very different people, the second and third of those going to meet murder, were making their way towards the Maharajah's palace. They were two Americans, coming as his guests. A fifty-year-old widow, Mrs. Elaine Alcott, and her daughter, Judy, both fresh from first a transatlantic crossing and then a tour of Europe. In Bhopore, Elaine Alcott's brother, Joe Lloyd, had finished supervising the construction of a mighty dam. To the opening ceremony, due in just a fortnight, the Maharajah himself had invited Joe's nearest kin, fares paid from Wisconsin. All the way to Bhopore.

They were on their way now by rail from Bombay. They had left the Broad Gauge network and had changed to a train on the Metre Gauge. Already, though the sun had not been up for long, it was appallingly hot. Judy, still a picture of fresh Wisconsin girlhood, lay flat out and gently sweating on one of the long leather seats in their compartment. Her mother, once almost as pretty, now much worried and nerve-shredded, lay flat out and gently perspiring on the seat opposite. Between them in a broad tin tray the remains of a huge block of ice, put into the compartment at the start of the journey, slid to and fro with a steady jerk-jerk of the wheels beneath. Above, a towel soaked in ice water hung in front of the blades of a slowly revolving fan.

"Judy," Mrs. Alcott said, "I don't think I'm going to be able to stand this."

"Oh, come on, Mother. It's going to be a great adventure. A maharajah. We're going to be guests of a maharajah. Why, he's so rich I guess he just has no idea how much money he's got. And jewels. And elephants. Only think."

"I don't want to have anything at all to do with elephants. Elephants ought to be in zoos. Behind bars. Where I'm safe from them."

"But, Mother, you'll be safe in Bhopore. The Maharajah isn't going to let any of his guests be trampled to— Well, be hurt by any of his elephants. And besides, there's Uncle Joe. He's been out in India years now. He's been all over. Remember those letters from the jungle we got when he was first prospecting for the dam? Well, Uncle Joe'll know when it's safe to go near an elephant. Honest, he will."

"Your Uncle Joe might know what's safe and what's not. But he never took the least itty-bit of notice, not from the time he could walk. As I know well."

"Mother."

"No, it's no use you saying 'Mother' like that. We should never have come. I knew it when I first saw that invitation card. All that red paper and that gold string. An invitation card should be black on white. Black on white and no more. 'Cept perhaps a very fine gold edge."

"Mother, take it easy. Relax. We're having fun."

Judy swung up from the stale heat of the leather seat, seized hold of the big basket of fruit that had been put in the compartment when they had changed trains, and thrust towards her mother its assortment of pomegranates, oranges, Cape gooseberries, and green figs nestling in their green leaves.

"Have some, Mother. It'll help cool you down."

"But they're all so dusty. What's the good of having that wire mesh over the windows so you can scarcely see out if the dust gets in just the same?"

"But you can peel an orange, can't you? Such dinky little oranges too. And so sweet."

"Well, I prefer California oranges. Good, big, clean California oranges. And I prefer American scenery too. Just look outside."

Judy peered through the close-mesh screen that covered the compartment's windows. Outside rolled mile upon mile of dry, yellow-grey desert, broken only by the occasional arid shrub.

But even as she gazed she saw something.

"Mother, Mother, look quick. It's camels. A whole string of camels. Isn't that just romantic?"

Mrs. Alcott heaved herself upright and came to the window.

"Camels," she said. "I guess they bite."

In the great new Indian capital of New Delhi, still a-building, three hundred miles and more away, the fourth of the twelve, the Viceroy of India no less, that superior being who represented George, King-

Emperor in this the richest part of his wide-spreading domains, was not yet on his way to Bhopore. But plans for his journey there to open the Maharajah's new dam were well in hand. A score of A.D.C.s had been working on them for weeks.

Because it is no simple thing for a viceroy to travel. His personal White Train, the only white train allowed in the whole Indian subcontinent, has to be got ready. The lists have to be drawn up of what personages are to accompany His Excellency. Provision on the train has to be made for each one of them. And for all the lesser servants without whom a viceroy cannot proceed anywhere. There are eighty-one of these lesser servants, and a place, however small, has to be found for each of them.

And thought, much thought and much studying of precedents, has to be given to what will happen when the Viceroy arrives in Bhopore. Will the correct procedure be adopted when his train pulls into the station? Will officials of appropriate rank be there to meet him? When he progresses to the palace will the Maharajah greet him at the exactly correct place? At the exact edge of the exactly appropriate carpet according to the number of guns fired in the salute granted that particular ruler? The more the guns, the less far towards the Viceroy must the ruler go. It all has to be studied. With care.

There is much, much, much to be done. Has the Maharajah's band been fully instructed in playing "God Save the King"? The day had not been forgotten when Lord Curzon, former holder of this great office, arrived for a state visit, to a much smaller state of course than Bhopore, and was greeted by a band who had only one Western tune to their trumpets, "Holy, Holy, Holy," picked up from the local mission harmonium. There may have been a certain appropriateness to the melody. But the incident had been something that was Not Done.

And when the Viceroy honoured Bhopore with his presence, in just a fortnight, there must not be the smallest shadow of anything that was Not Done.

On his way to the Maharajah's palace from yet another direction, mounted on as fine a piece of horseflesh as could be bought in the whole of Northern India, the fifth of the twelve on their way to a murder, Captain Ram Singh, A.D.C. not to the Viceroy but to the Maharajah, was travelling much more slowly than the speed his expensive mount should have brought him. It was not the horse's fault. It was the rider's.

The truth of the matter was that Captain Ram Singh did not want to arrive.

He was returning from a visit to his father, the Maharajah's cousin, the Thakur of Panna. But the visit had not been simply a few days' pleasant holiday spent in the old family home, a pause in the busy round of an A.D.C.'s duties, some days stretching perhaps into a week or even two. Captain Ram Singh had been ordered to go and see his father by the Maharajah himself. Revenues from the Thakur's wide estates had not been flowing in recent months into the Maharajah's coffers as custom dictated. Messengers from the Maharajah had not been treated well. Captain Ram Singh had been sent with a rebuke, a sharp rebuke and a demand.

But he had not been able to bring away the answer the Maharajah wanted. Captain Ram Singh, tall in his decorated saddle, moustaches defiantly curled, turban all gaiety and dash, uniform a splendour of peacock blue and cherry red, boots dazzlingly polished, was not digging his spurs into his horse's sides.

The Maharajah was urgently expecting him. But he did not want to come. He had been the Maharajah's favourite among all half dozen of his A.D.C.s when he had left. He very much expected he would retain his post with difficulty, if at all, when he got back. Yet he knew well he could not have remained at home either.

In his ears he felt he could still hear the words of the Thakur, his father.

"We are glad to hear Maharajah Sahib is well. It would be a sad day indeed if Maharajah Sahib were to fall ill. Or was to die even."

Captain Ram Singh, a dashing man on the polo field but not exactly a genius, allowed his expensive horse to drift to a halt in the shade of a huge rock towering over the dusty path.

Alone in his bungalow outside the town of Sangabad in British India some miles beyond the border with the princely State of Bhopore, District Superintendent of Police Howard, the sixth of the twelve travellers, had no thought in his mind at that moment of being on his way to Bhopore. He knew he had plenty to occupy him in keeping the King-Emperor's peace in the large territory that fell to his lot. It took him all his time staying abreast of all the thousand and one potentially troublemaking activities that might erupt there.

But, for all that, before very long he was to be summoned to Bhopore. And urgently.

In Bhopore the seventh of the twelve, the Maharajkumar, the acknowledged heir to the Maharajah's throne, the gaddi, was on his way to a murder too. It was his belief however, his fond belief, that he was on his way to his marriage. He was in love, hopelessly and passionately in love. And the fact that the woman he was in love with was English, and that this constituted a huge obstacle to his marrying her and afterwards in due course inheriting the gaddi, did not seem to him at this moment to matter one jot.

He let the detective story he had been reading—it was Agatha Christie's novel *The Seven Dials Mystery*—fall to the floor.

"Dolly," he said, his voice vibrating in rich emotion, "I love you. I love your eyes, your bright, bright blue eyes. I love you hair. Dolly, promise me one thing?"

Dolly Brattle, ex-member of the chorus at the London Pavilion and very much aware now that at thirty-one years of age her dancing days must be numbered, twirled the peacock feather with which she had been idly playing. She ran the tip of it down the Maharajkumar's somewhat fleshy nose until, with a little jump, it took off and lightly brushed his pouting lips.

"Porgy-poo," she said, "Dolly will promise. Really and truly, Dolly will."

Porgy-poo, more usually just Porgy, so called because he had been named George in honour of the King-Emperor and that name had been implacably sugared down by his specially imported Scottish nanny, altered the pout on his lips to a smile.

"Then you will never, never stop shingling your beautiful, beautiful blonde hair," he said.

"Shall if I want."

"Shan't ever. You've promised."

"What've I promised then?"

"You've promised never, never to stop shingling your beautiful, beautiful blonde hair."

"Beastly Porgy-poo. Beastly Porgy-poo to trap a girl like that. Now you've got to promise."

"I promise," said the heir to the gaddi of fabulously rich Bhopore.

Dolly jumped to her feet from beside the chaise longue against which she had been kneeling while Porgy reclined there. She whirled round on the smooth marble of the floor and kicked back a shapely thigh, cheekily as ever she had done in the Charleston at the London Pavilion.

"Now you've got to marry me," she said. "You've promised, Porgy. You promised to do whatever I wanted, and that's what I want. I want us to get married. Now, Porgy. Now. Next week. Right next week."

"But, my darling girl, we can't get married in a week."

"Yes, we can."

"No, we can't."

"Yes, we can. Why not?"

"Because when you marry me, little shingle-head, you're marrying the Rajkumar of Bhopore. There have to be ceremonies. There have to be guests. Hundreds of guests."

"Don't see why."

"It's the custom, my darling. A fellow's got to stick to the customs, you know. Proper wedding in the Old Palace. Brahmin priests and all that. Hundreds of guests there to see it all. Go back home and tell everyone Porgy Bhopore's got himself the most beautiful wife in all India. And the most attractive."

Porgy's full lips parted slightly.

"Come here, you attractive woman," he said.

Dolly made no move.

"But can't we send out the invitations now? Today?" she said. "Then we could be married the week after next or something."

"My darling, the week after next."

"Why not? Why not the week after next?"

"We've got a visitor, my darling."

"What visitor? Silly old visitor. What does a visitor matter?"

"But it's the Viceroy, my darling. Even you must remember the Viceroy is coming in just a fortnight. To open Papa's dam."

"Damn the dam. And damn that awful Joe Lloyd, always boiling up about it. You'd think he was the one who owned it. Instead of you."

"I don't own it, my darling. Papa does."

"Well, all right. But you're going to own it, aren't you? When you're the Maharajah and not silly old Maharajkumar."

"But that might not be for a long, long while, my darling Dolly."

"Well, I wish it were now. Yes, I do. I do. I know he's your father and all that, but, Porgy, if you were Maharajah you could do anything you liked. You could marry me tomorrow, Porgy."

"Oh, no, I couldn't, little shingle-head. We'd have to have the ceremonies. Can't go against the customs even when you're Maharajah."

"Bet you could."

"But I— Well, perhaps I could if I really wanted. There's one custom I've gone against even before I'm the Maharajah."

"What's that then, brave little boy?"

Porgy, Maharajkumar of Bhopore, gave a rich chuckle.

"It's a custom, I believe, for people who are going to marry not to go to bed together first," he said. "Come here, my little shinglehead."

"Oh, Porgy, it's so hot."

"Come here."

"Oh, Porgy."

It was hot too for the eighth person on his way to a murder in Bhopore. Although it was still quite early in the day, outside the immensely thick walls of the Maharajah's Summer Palace it was already blazingly hot. And through the heat, under the shade of a big black umbrella, the Maharajah's Schoolmaster was on his way to the palace from his humble home just outside the new City Palace in the town in Bhopore itself, twelve long miles away.

His task in life was the education in its early stages of the Maharajah's many sons, by his various concubines. It was a task which the Maharajah showed few signs, despite his sixty-odd years, of bringing to an end through lack of newcomers to the schoolroom. At just this hour of the day, indeed, five of his very latest offspring were making their way in procession back into the shade of the Summer Palace. Each was in a perambulator. Each perambulator had been supplied by Harrod's of Knightsbridge. Each perambulator was being pushed by an immense and bristly bearded Sikh of the Maharajah's personal bodyguard in a uniform of gorgeous green topped by a tremendous turban in magenta.

Beneath his black umbrella, a valued inheritance from a father who had been the first in his distant village to own such a marvel of Western technology, the Maharajah's Schoolmaster was plainly not regarding the day ahead with any pleasure. He was a slightly built man, notably bony about the shoulders, and he looked very much as if he might get easily blown away by any chance rush of wind. Or by some boisterous male offspring of a well-fed ruler.

Yet he was marching steadily forward along the dusty road. And, though his shoulders were a little slumped, his eyes were by no means cast down to the ground. They looked round him with a sharp interest in whatever was to be seen—a lumbering oxcart, its wheels squeaking out a desperate and uneven tune while its peasant driver slept his way to his destination, a four-year-old boy in charge of a nibbling goat and her thin-legged tottering offspring, even a lizard sitting stone-still on a rock in the sun till the moment came to flick out a tongue and bring death to a too careless insect.

At very much the other end of the social scale in the State of Bhopore the ninth of the twelve, Sir Arthur Pendeverel, His Majesty the King-Emperor's representative, the Resident Adviser (whose advice in all matters except those of family and religion smacked very much more of orders than suggestions) was not yet on his way to the Summer Palace. He was not due to meet the Maharajah until he responded to an invitation to dine that evening.

But he was more concerned about another visit to the palace, that of the tenth person to make his way there. Because this was the day chosen for an annual ceremony which the Maharajah had taken it into his head to make a custom of. This was the day the Maharajah was solemnly to entertain to tea the widower Resident's young son, Little Michael.

"Tell Ayah to bring you to see me before you leave," the Resident said, looking down from his gaunt height at the small figure of Little Michael, neat in white shirt and shorts with white socks just colour-banded at their tops drawn up unwrinkled to just below his knees.

"Yes, Father. She does that every year."

"Yes."

Sir Arthur seemed more than usually abstracted.

"It's April the first this year," he said at last. "I think perhaps I ought to give you certain advice, my boy."

Little Michael looked up at his father, straight-backed and firm of gaze, the way he had been taught to do.

Sir Arthur resumed.

"The Indian does not always possess our sense of proper restraint," he said. "You know what 'restraint' is, my boy?"

"I think so, Father. Isn't it what you've got?"

Sir Arthur looked, for an instant, surprised.

"Well, yes, my boy. Perhaps it is. Perhaps it is. However, the point is that today being the first of April, the Maharajah may well take it into his head to—ahem—play some April Fools' Day trick or other."

"But, Father, the invitation to tea is for four o'clock, and the rules say no tricks after twelve noon. Don't they, Father?"

Sir Arthur sighed.

"I'm afraid the Maharajah does not often take cognizance of rules, my boy. That's what I meant about 'lack of restraint.' I shall be quite surprised if you don't find yourself victim of some childish prank before your visit's over. I hope I can trust you to take it as an English gentleman should."

"Oh, yes, Father."

"And there's one other thing."

"Yes, Father?"

"How old are you now, my boy?"

"Nine, Father. Nearly ten."

"Yes. Off back home in August to school. Well, you are old enough now, Michael, for the Maharajah perhaps to . . ."

"To what, Father?"

Sir Arthur's mouth tightened in his gaunt-featured face.

"To consider it worth his while to question you about what goes on in the Residency, my boy. About any remarks you may have heard made. If he does try anything of the sort, I hope you'll simply ignore it. Remember the rule that was told to me when I first came back out to India as a young officer. 'Keep your mouth shut and your bowels open.' It's good advice, my boy. Think you can do it?"

"Yes, Father— I think so. I kept my bowels open already today in any case."

"Good boy. Then just remember the shut mouth, eh?"

Whether or not the eleventh person on his way to Bhopore had kept his bowels open history does not relate. But if failing to do that inevitably produces bad temper, as is widely believed, then this may be the explanation of the spluttering rage in which Henry Morton III, soft metals king of the American Midwest, was approaching the State of Bhopore.

Why in the hell has the Maharajah suddenly changed his mind and brought me all this way? he asked himself furiously as the Imperial Airways machine that had flown him from London in answer to an urgent cable glided down towards the airfield at Bombay.

And another damn flight when we do land, he thought angrily.

"Kindly accept invitation to dinner April 1. Shall be glad to discuss matter of zinc mining," the Maharajah's cable had said. But the guy's letter, not two weeks before, had turned down his proposals flat. Still, the chance was too good to miss. Too good to risk missing, the way things were.

But why the hell had the guy changed his damned Indian mind?

On the way to the palace along the same dusty road from the city as the Schoolmaster under his stiffly upright black umbrella, but a good long way behind him, there was coming, riding in a battered one-horse tonga, the twelfth and last of those going to meet murder, a plump figure well wrapped in a sari, head concealed by its folds. In her ample lap, clutched by both hands, hidden from all possible sight, there was an insignificant screw of paper.

Her destination was not the palace itself so much as one particular part of it, the zenana, the quarter restricted completely to women, from the Maharajah's two wives, First Her Highness and Second Her Highness, down through his various concubines, to all their daughters, their sons still under the age of seven, and the dozens of servants necessary to minister to them in their separate apartments. And of those servants none was at this moment more prized by her mistress, First Her Highness, the mother of Porgy, heir to the gaddi, than this plump creature moving steadily towards the palace from the mysteries of the bazaars in the city. She was one of the trusted "mamas," the elderly and respectable servants who alone are permitted to be seen if necessary in the male preserve of the palace, the mardana.

This was the one among the mamas that First Her Highness most trusted. And trust was necessary. In that screw of paper in her lap there was a small quantity of sharp, harder-than-steel diamond dust. Only a small quantity. But enough, should it happen that the need finally arose, to achieve a deadly purpose.

II

The Maharajah changed his mind. He had already taken his hand off the bishop which he had slid across the black and white marble chessboard to put his opponent's king in check. But without so much as a murmur of apology, he reached out now and drew the piece, which he would have lost at once, safely back again within the protection of a pair of pawns.

Opposite him Lieutenant James Frere, a guest at the palace for two months though playing his first game against the Maharajah, kept his gaze fixed levelly before him. He had kept it levelly facing his opponents in the boxing ring back at school at Haileybury. And would keep it, should the occasion arise, equally level facing an angry mob in some inflamed bazaar.

After all, he was a guest here, Porgy's guest, and a chap mustn't show open disapproval.

He waited for the Maharajah, that bulky figure in the extraordinary coat of pink and gold brocade, to find another move. Frankly, with those little sharp eyes of his embedded in those thickly fed cheeks, the fellow never ceased to remind him of an elephant. Not that he would ever allow the thought to escape his lips.

And he had a damned odd way of playing chess, too. To begin with, there were these extraordinary chessmen. Each one carved from ivory to represent people in the Maharajah's court, and no queens either, but viziers instead. The one the Maharajah had now— and there had been no question of his playing anything other than White—looked exactly like his chief minister, the Dewan, old Sir Akhtar. And with the man himself sitting so quietly a few respectful paces away, it was enough to put anybody off. Let alone the way the Maharajah had begun by attacking one pawn after another, regardless of what he himself had been doing. No wonder he had the old boy in such a fix now.

Still, he didn't seem worried about losing. Grant him that.

He'd half expected he'd have been told beforehand to see that he didn't win.

"Mr. Frere."

It was Sir Akhtar. The fine-featured old Muslim Dewan who ran the State so well.

"Mr. Frere, have you chanced to notice the carving of the ceiling of this room? It is particularly fine work. The masons came from Italy, you know."

James Frere obediently looked upwards, though he felt a little mystified as to why the Dewan should suddenly want to show him the carving. It didn't look particularly fine either, not compared with a lot of the other rooms in the palace.

"Yes," he said politely. "It's really very beautiful. Very."

"I'm glad it pleases you," said Sir Akhtar gravely.

James let his attention go back to the marble chessboard.

And, damn it, his knight was no longer on the square where it would have menaced the Maharajah's bishop if he had brought it up to put him in check. And, surely, it had been there a moment ago? Why else had the Maharajah abruptly taken back that move when he had already actually made it?

Could it be . . . ? Yes, it could be. The Maharajah had cheated. He had moved the knight while his own attention had been distracted. The fellow was a damn cheat.

James felt the hot flush mounting.

But, just in time, he pulled himself up. He was a guest here. And the Maharajah was supposed to be a great friend of Britain. Hadn't he sent troops galore to France from his own private army in '14–'18? Better just accept it.

He moved his king—the piece reminded him of someone; could it be the Viceroy?—out of danger's way.

So that was why Sir Akhtar had suddenly spoken about the ceiling. The old devil. His duties plainly ran to more than just keeping Bhopore running so well, though if what old Porgy had said was true he wasn't going to be allowed by the Maharajah to do that for much longer.

The Maharajah's plump, heavily beringed hand came out and rested on his other bishop. James Frere ran his eye along the diagonal the piece could take. Oh lord, now that he had lost the momentum of his attack by having to move his suddenly threatened king, he had left himself open to a nasty-looking fork. If the Maharajah brought that second bishop right up, it would check his king in one direction and take his queen in the other. What to do? Any way of countering the threat?

Damn it, yes, there was one. How about moving his king in the same illicit fashion as the Maharajah had moved that knight? Well, why not? Why not play the Maharajah's rules, if that was how the game was done here?

He leant well forward over the board, allowed his right hand to hover over his most advanced pawn, and then, quite blatantly, shifted his king with his left hand.

"I do not think you can do that, Mr. Frere," Sir Akhtar said at once.

"Do what?" he asked, innocently as he could.

Sir Akhtar smiled.

"You really must not move a piece in an unorthodox manner while your opponent can see what you are doing," he explained.

Checkmate, James Frere thought to himself with amusement. Evidently there are still rules here, even if they're rather different from the Queensberry type.

"Oh, did I budge my king?" he said aloud. "Frightfully sorry. I was concentrating on getting out of this nasty hole I'm in."

Scrupulously he restored his king to the place where the Maharajah could so neatly trap it.

Life in the palace must be pretty complicated under the smooth surface, he reflected.

Another complication of life in the palace was at that moment giving Sir Arthur Pendeverel, the Resident, cause for concern in this solid Georgian mansion planked on the crown of a small hill under the brazen Indian sun. Ever since the first of Little Michael's invitations to tea, to tea for two, he had wondered what His Highness's purpose might be. Of course, he reasoned, the first invitation could have been a mere whim. Heaven knows, the fellow had whims enough. To build a new palace, yet another. To lay out an airfield. To construct that dam of that American's. To have a new A.D.C. To alter the uniforms of his personal guard. To send his Dewan packing all of a sudden. To throw this damn dinner party tonight.

Why was he doing that? There was no real reason. The man Lloyd's sister coming to stay at the palace. Well, H.H. had taken little enough notice of guests before, even British guests.

One of these days his impetuosity was going to get him into trouble. Bad trouble.

But was that first invitation to Little Michael another example of the fellow's impetuosity? Or had it had some deep ulterior motive?

Because, no doubt about it, the Maharajah was just as capable of devious action as of acting on a mere whim. Look at the way he was suddenly wriggling over the matter of succession to the gaddi. It had all been decently cut-and-dried long ago when young Porgy had been officially declared the heir. And now H.H. was hinting about disinheriting. Of course, Porgy was a bit of a rake. But, damn it, there were worse evils in a ruler than that. No, there must be some devious reason for wanting to upset matters. There could be no doubt about that. And it wasn't as if there were any sort of adequate substitute for young Porgy either. Only that boy Raghbir, Second Her Highness's child. And he must be no more than twelve or thirteen. And a useless young lout at that, what he'd seen of him.

Better have Little Michael in now and warn him once more about the sort of questions H.H. was likely to try and ask him. Perhaps his aim all along had simply been to try and set up a sort of spy in the camp and this was the year it would begin to pay off.

He clapped his hands in a single explosive report.

At once a bearer, stiff turban on head, uniform immaculate, leather sash highly polished, bare feet slapping on the stone floor, entered and salaamed.

"See if Ayah has the Chota Sahib ready."

"Huzoor."

The bearer wheeled smartly out. A moment later Little Michael appeared, dressed even more neatly than in the morning, his ayah smiling tremendously and urging him through the door with little pats and pushes.

"Well, Michael, all ready?"

"Yes, Father."

"Haven't forgotten what I told you this morning?"

"About April Fools' Day tricks, Father?"

"No, no. April Fool nonsense. What else did I tell you?"

"My bowels, Father. But I said—"

"Michael."

"And to keep my mouth shut, Father."

"Yes. And I don't mean you're to sit there like a stuffed owl from start to finish. If His Highness asks you any reasonable sort of a question, answer up loud and clear. But if he gets onto the Residency and private matters, you just sit tight. Understood?"

"But, Father, can't I just say nothing all the time?"

"Certainly not. The Maharajah may be just waiting for an excuse to take offence. No, you're to answer up unless he starts asking about me. That's an order, Michael. Remember what old Rudyard says."

"About 'Obey,' Father?"

"That's the ticket."

Sir Arthur drew himself up. Facing him, Little Michael squared his shoulders. As one they declaimed:

> *"Now these are the laws of the jungle*
> *And many and mighty are they*
> *But the head and the hoof and the haunch and the*
> *   hump is Obey."*

"Good lad. Just remember. We're here, all of us, to see that things are done in this country in the right way. It isn't easy. We wouldn't have been put here if it were. So we've got to do our best, always. All right?"

"All right, Father."

Sir Arthur dismissed his son with a little, restrained nod.

But as the boy went out he called a last instruction.

"And, Michael! I didn't see your topi. Don't forget. The Hot Weather's begun officially now: never go out-of-doors without a topi on your head."

"Yes, Father. You get a punkah-wallah allowance from now on, too, don't you, Father?"

"Yes, my boy. Hot Weather drill from now on. You won't see me out without a topi on my head and a spine pad at my back while the sun's still up. So don't let me catch you bareheaded."

"No, Father. And 'the head and the hoof and the haunch and the hump is Obey.' "

In the Summer Palace, a few miles distant, His Highness the Maharajah was reclining at his ease. It was his custom at this time of day to have his Dewan read him suitable extracts from the newspapers.

So that each of them might be comfortable while this was going on, each had an ottoman to lie upon. But, so that the Dewan might recline without any disrespect to the Maharajah, there was always placed between them a heavily carved wooden screen. What the eyes did not see could be assumed not to be taking place.

"Enough, enough, Dewan Sahib. What must I be filling my head for with New York and its Red Thursdays? If they cannot control their Communists there, then they should be reading about Bhopore and the way we do things here, not me hearing about their riotings and *gol-mall*."

"Certainly we have so far avoided riots here, Highness. Allah be praised."

"Yes, yes. But to more important matters. You know I have received a piece of sapura bark this morning?"

"Yes, Highness. So I was informed."

"Oh, Dewan, Dewan, you take good care to be informed of every little thing."

"If the State is to be run smoothly, Highness, then it is necessary that I should know every little thing."

"Well, be careful that there isn't some big thing you don't know about one of these days, Dewan Sahib."

The Maharajah, slumped on his ottoman, huge belly lolling free, permitted himself a long chuckle.

On the other side of the screen, Sir Akhtar Ali permitted himself a look of sharp anxiety.

"But the sapura bark, Dewan Sahib."

"Yes, Highness?"

"I think I have got a use for it."

"A use for sapura bark, Highness? I had thought it singularly useless. Though, of course, precious because of its rarity."

"No, no, Dewan. You know that Little Michael, our upright, so English Resident's son, takes tea with me today?"

"Of course, Highness."

"Very good. The Resident will send him in his own car, will he not?"

"I imagine so, Highness. Although, of course, the car will not be flying the flag since the Resident himself will not be driving in it."

"No, no, that is a pity. But one cannot have everything. Alas."

On his side of the screen, the Dewan stirred uneasily.

"What is it that you are hoping to have then, Highness?" he asked with caution.

The Maharajah laughed. A long, rich, deep laugh that shook his elephantine belly like a wobbling earthquake.

"Dewan," he said at last, "imagine it when Little Michael is about to depart after we have had our tea. He comes out onto the steps in front of the palace. I am with him. Some other people are there also. Down at the foot of the steps Sir Arthur's car is waiting. Little Michael gets in. The Resident's chauffeur starts up the motor. And . . . And what?"

"I do not know, Highness."

"Dewan Sahib, come round the screen where I can see you. Where I can see you laugh."

Sir Akhtar rose from his ottoman and removed the expression of foreboding from his grave features. He presented himself in front of the Maharajah.

"The car is waiting, Dewan. The boy gets in, Dewan. The chauffeur starts up, Dewan. And then? And then? Then: Bang. Bang, bang, bang, bang, Dewan. In the exhaust of that car a piece of sapura bark. Wetted, Dewan. Hard as iron, Dewan. Not to be re- moved by any means. A wonderful April Fools' Day wheeze, Dewan."

Sir Akhtar brought himself to smile.

"Most ingenious, Highness. Most ingenious. Yet, if I may venture to remind you, Highness, the Viceroy himself is coming in exactly a fortnight and if Sir Arthur were to take exception . . ."

"Oh, pooh, pooh, Dewan. Sir Arthur will take it like a gentle- man."

"You want the Viceroy's visit to be a complete success, Highness."

"Of course, of course. It is imperative that it is the most complete success. How else will I hold up my head in the Chamber of Princes? But this little joke will spoil nothing, I tell you. If necessary I will apologise after. Like a gentleman."

"The Viceroy's visit brings me to another matter, Highness."

"Very well."

"It is the question of the Rajkumar, Highness. I feel that it is im- portant that while His Excellency is in Bhopore it should not be in any way evident that . . ."

"Is it Miss Brattle, Dewan? I tell you, I have already dealt with the matter. I have made it altogether clear to the Rajkumar that there can be no question of a marriage. Have you had replies to your soundings for a bride from a proper princely house yet?"

"Negotiations are continuing, Highness. But, as you know, these matters cannot be hurried. There are horoscopes to be matched. There is the question of dowry."

"Yes, yes."

"So if I could have your assurance, Highness, that while these negotiations are still in progress there will be no question of some hole-and-corner marriage, some dash by aeroplane to a London Register Office or to that Gretna Green place in Scotland . . ."

"Dewan, I have warned him. If anything of the sort happens I disown him from the gaddi. At once."

"Highness, that may not be so easy. The ceremonies of recognition have been gone through. The British, on the whole, approve."

"Pah. If I wish to disown, I disown. I can always declare that he is no son of mine, that he was merely a boy substituted for the girl actually born to First Her Highness."

"But— But was there a girl born? If I may ask."

"Of course there was not, Dewan. How can you be such a fool? There are times when I wonder how I put up with you one moment longer."

Sir Akhtar remained impassive, and before he could make any sort of reply the Maharajah spoke again.

"And that reminds me."

"Yes, Highness?"

"Captain Ram Singh. Is he back from Panna yet? He ought to have been here yesterday. I shall hardly have time to see him before four o'clock at this rate."

"He has not arrived yet, Highness. Perhaps he has experienced some delay. His horse may have cast a shoe . . . Anything."

"Dewan, you don't think he has stayed with his father? You don't think the Thakur will dare to rise against me?"

"Impossible, Highness. Your Highness's army is fully capable of dealing with anything like that. And my agents tell me the Thakur has very few armed men about him in any case."

"Then all the more reason why Captain Ram Singh should get back here when I am wanting him. That young man . . ."

"Shall I see that he is sent to you as soon as he arrives, Highness?"

"No, no. I will not have my tea party for Little Michael spoilt. One hour is to be allowed for that, and no one is to disturb us."

"Very good, Highness. But . . ."

"No, no, Dewan Sahib. I have said. Little Michael is a fine boy.

Loyal to his father, a good little Englishman. Whatever quarrels I may have with the English, I admire him. One hour undisturbed, and not a minute less."

"Very good, Highness. Then there is only one more thing."

"Yes? Speak up, man. I must go and be dressed in a minute or I shall not be ready."

"It is the question of the flooding of the jheels, Highness. As you know, Mr. Lloyd is most anxious that when the dam is opened it shall be allowed to operate to its full capacity. This will mean, almost certainly, that the level of the water in the lakes will rise and—"

"Dewan, I have spoken already. The water level in the jheels must not rise. The duck will not feed on them if it does. The Imperial sandgrouse will stay away if their usual haunts become unfamiliar. I cannot allow that. What would Bhopore be without its shikar for Imperial sandgrouse? Why, guns come for it from all over India. It is famous all over the world."

"Yes, Highness. But the extra flow of water will mean that a great deal more land will become cultivable. Mr. Lloyd has—"

"Dewan, I do not wish to hear any more of this. I know what Mr. Lloyd has explained. He has shouted and shouted. And he knows what I have explained. The Bhopore Imperial sandgrouse is famous the world over, and the Bhopore shikar for them will never be stopped. Never."

"Very well, Highness. If that is your final decision."

"It is final, Dewan. Final. The water level in the jheels will rise only over my dead body!"

The Resident's personal Rolls-Royce, not flying the little flag that indicated it carried the Resident himself, approached at a properly dignified speed the open gates of the immense wall that surrounded the Maharajah of Bhopore's Summer Palace. The Maharajah's guards, long alerted by the drone of the motor in the heat-stilled afternoon, presented arms with an explosive slap of white-gloved hands on oiled brown rifle butts. In the back of the car, sitting solemnly upright, Little Michael removed his pipe-clayed topi—it was of the approved pattern, well lengthened at the back to keep the sun off the neck—and held it strictly upright against his chest, as he had seen his father do.

The car swept into the palace grounds and on to the palace itself, coming to a halt under the shade of a small grove of neem trees.

Here Ahmed, the Resident's chauffeur, would be happy to leave it until, just one hour later, Chota Sahib would emerge from his tea with the Maharajah.

Little Michael waited until Ahmed had opened the door for him and got out. Alone and small in the scorching sunlight, he walked across to the palace and began to mount its wide flight of marble steps. The doors here, too, were wide open. Little Michael entered them, as he had done on three previous occasions so far, took off his topi, and set out. He allowed himself only swift, cautious glances to left and right at the possible mysteries that lay all around.

Down a wide corridor he went, through an empty, echoing purposeless marble chamber, towards the beaten silver doors of the Durbar Hall, the scene normally of the ceremonious occasions when the Maharajah gave audience. Beside these doors the white-breeched, blue-jacketed guards had not received advance warning of the visitor's arrival. Sleepily they scrambled to their feet and presented arms. At the sound two servants within drew back the heavy, elaborately decorated doors.

Little Michael entered.

The Durbar Hall was some fifty yards long. At its far end on a raised marble platform stood the gaddi, the throne of Bhopore, a magnificent piece of furniture, half carved and gilded wooden chair, half elaborate construction of cushions. Plumb in the middle of the gaddi sat His Highness the Maharajah. He was splendid now in lemon-yellow brocade with on his head an emerald-green turban fronted by a tall feathery aigrette fastened to the turban by a pigeon's blood ruby big as a bird's egg. Between gaddi and doors ran a long, long strip of deep red carpet.

Little Michael stepped out.

Back straight, shoulders squared, gaze level, topi firmly under his arm, he marched and marched along the red carpet.

Eyes fixed at a point somewhere above the beaten silver doors, the Maharajah of Bhopore sat still as a richly stomached god. Behind him his fan-bearer stood equally unmoving, the large peacock-feather fan on its thick ebony stick motionless in his hands. For, although this tea for two was to be strictly a tête-à-tête affair, naturally there had to be some servants present, the fan-bearer, the two at the doors, someone to hand Little Michael food from the table by his side (the Maharajah was forbidden by his religion to share food with an infidel and would not eat).

Little Michael arrived at the precise far edge of the red carpet. He came to a halt. He bowed.

"It is Little Michael," said the Maharajah, in a tone of mild surprise. "Come up, my dear fellow. Come up. Take a pew. Do have some tea."

Little Michael mounted the two low steps of the dais, went to the small but heavily laden table set just to the side of the gaddi, and sat on the small cane-seated chair next to it, under which he hurriedly slipped his topi. He looked at the table. It was exactly the same as it had been the other times. There were sandwiches in half a dozen different varieties. There were cakes, green-iced cakes, pink-iced cakes, violet-iced cakes, yellow-iced cakes. There was ginger beer, those thick stone bottles specially sent from Harrod's. There were Indian sweetmeats, gorgeous, sticky, and most of them silver-foil-coated.

"Eat, eat," said the Maharajah.

In silence Little Michael ate.

After a sufficient period had elapsed, the Maharajah asked him questions. But, to his infinite relief, they were only the usual questions. How he was, how he was progressing with his riding lessons, whether he had begun to play polo yet, whether he had yet been allowed to have a gun.

"Oh, yes, Maharajah Sahib. And I'm a jolly good shot, too. Everyone says so. Well, not my father, of course. But nearly everyone."

"Good, good. But you must eat, my boy. A youngster like you needs plenty to eat. There are jelabis there. Take some. Bearer, jelabis for Michael Sahib."

Little Michael accepted the proffered sticky golden balls dripping with rosewater syrup.

In a moment they would get on to the Maharajah's own young days. There was going to be no change. The problem of not letting Father down was not going to arise.

But suddenly there came an alteration in the routine, a shattering, altogether unexpected alteration.

There was the sound of abruptly raised voices from beyond the heavy silver doors. Then with a jarring crash the left-hand one was flung open and running—running!—down the length of the Durbar Hall came a lolloping, untidy, wild-eyed figure.

Little Michael recognised him at once. It was Raghbir, Second Her Highness's son, the big, awkward boy of twelve whom he had on occasion played games with, trying to conceal his dislike of the whole business.

He came to an untidy halt at the foot of the dais, half on and half off the carpet. He failed altogether to make a mujra, to bow low and touch his forehead three times with his right hand, as Little Michael knew it was proper for him to do when he came into his father's presence.

"Papa, Papa, why cannot I have tea in the Durbar Hall also?"

At last Raghbir had made himself intelligible.

Darting a quick glance at the Maharajah, Little Michael saw in those two small eyes deep in their layers of fat, the eyes that had only a moment before been twinkling at him cheerfully, a look of unbending rage that sent a chill right through him.

The look plainly chilled Raghbir, too. He stood, mouth open, one large bare foot twisted round the other.

"Raghbir, go to your rooms at once," the Maharajah said. "Did I not make it clear that I was taking tea with Michael Sahib and with no one else?"

"But, Papa . . ."

Blubberingly Raghbir seemed to have found his voice again.

"But, Papa, I want to have tea, too. With you, Papa. Papa, I am not feeling happy. I am not feeling well. Please, Papa."

Suddenly, blunderingly, he flung himself onto the steps of the dais and embraced his father's elegantly slipper-shod feet as they rested on their heavily upholstered fringed footstool.

The Maharajah, with the abrupt strength of an elephant, merely lifted one foot, and Raghbir in an instant went tumbling over backwards to lie snorting and sniffling on the marble floor.

"Bearer," the Maharajah called, "take the boy to his rooms."

The two servants from their places at the doors came hurrying to Raghbir. He lay where he was. Puzzled a little, they eventually picked him up bodily. He offered no resistance and made no attempt to get to his feet.

A look from the Maharajah was enough to send the pair of them scuttling off, their awkward burden, all arms and legs, somehow slung between them.

"Did I ever tell you about the first gun that I had?" the Maharajah said, leaning across towards Little Michael once more.

"No, Maharajah Sahib, you didn't," Little Michael boldly lied.

He recalled his father's voice from a confidential talk they had had once. "Of course, no gentleman ever tells a lie, Michael. You know that. But we are here in an alien land—you know what 'alien' means, I daresay—and there are times when it is necessary to say things other than what we mean."

From then on the occasion reverted to all its old comforting protocol. Nothing had changed. The rules were being kept again.

Until the very last minute.

The ancient black marble clock that stood on a little shelf on the wall somewhere behind the gaddi had in its usual way wheezed out the five strokes of the hour. Little Michael knew that at once, even in the middle of an anecdote, the Maharajah would get to his feet and say, "Well, Michael, it has been a great pleasure." And then he in his turn would get to his feet, even in the middle of a green-iced cake—only he was careful now to see that that didn't happen—and he would say, "Thank you very much, Maharajah Sahib," and he would pick up his topi, go down the steps of the dais, turn when he had just got onto the red carpet and bow, and then walk all the way back to the big silver doors.

Only this time instead of just getting to his feet the Maharajah stepped down onto the first step of the dais.

"I'll just see you out, my dear fellow," he said.

Little Michael gulped.

"But, Maharajah Sahib," he managed to get out, "you don't do that. You never do that."

He thought he saw a flash of that chill rage in the Maharajah's little elephant eyes. Only it was immediately replaced by an even more cheerful twinkle than before.

"Well, well. Sometimes we must do something that we have never done before, you know. What's the good of having rules, my dear fellow, if you can't break them every now and again, eh?"

"Yes, Maharajah Sahib," Michael said, though that was not at all what he wanted to say.

Together they walked down the long stretch of red carpet to the doors, which the bearers, returned from their task of carrying away the sobbing Raghbir—a fellow shouldn't blinking well blub—had hastened to fling wide. Together Maharajah and guest walked back through the wide, airy corridors and vacant antechambers to the main entrance to the palace.

Stepping out beside the substantial but easy-moving Maharajah and hastily donning his topi, Michael was surprised to see that there were several people standing on the broad flight of shallow marble steps despite the heat of the afternoon sun, which had hardly yet begun to diminish. There was the Rajkumar, the Maharajah's oldest son, the one whose mother was First Her Highness, called Porgy—only boys weren't supposed to call him that—and with him was That Person, Miss Brattle, Dolly, who was perfectly awful. And then there was Dewan Sahib, nice but a little frightening sometimes, only you weren't meant to be frightened of Indians. And he was talking to Lieutenant Frere. Lieutenant Frere was jolly nice, the times he'd seen him, a friend of Porgy's when he'd been in England. And finally there was Captain Ram Singh, the Maharajah's best A.D.C., and terrific at polo. He was all right, though jolly stupid really.

Michael noticed, however, that Captain Ram Singh had drawn back a bit when the Maharajah had come out, and the Maharajah had given him one of his looks, the ones that made you think of all those stories about the old maharajahs and tortures and things. But then Maharajah Sahib had looked away and the twinkle had come back into his eyes.

He seemed to be stopping himself laughing even.

"Good-bye then, Michael," the Maharajah said. "It's been most pleasant."

"Good-bye, and thank you, Maharajah Sahib."

Should he bow now? It was the right thing to do in the Durbar Hall, but was it right out here? I mean, with people just standing about, not in their proper places or anything.

He made a sort of bobbing movement that could have been a bow if it was the right thing, or could have been, well, just sort of bending forward.

Gratefully he turned and walked down the steps towards the car, managing not to run. Thank goodness Ahmed was waiting there at the wheel, though of course he hadn't started up the motor yet.

Ahmed scrambled out of his place and opened the car door for him. He clambered in and sat down, looking straight to the front. Better not wave. Might be a bit babyish.

Ahmed returned to the driving seat. He leant forward to pull out the knob for the electric starter. Much better than having to crank up the bally old engine.

But the smooth purr that only Rolls-Royces seem to produce failed to come. Instead the whole stately car gave a sort of bucking jerk. And then, from somewhere underneath, there issued the most tremendous bang.

Little Michael looked wildly round. Up on the steps, he realised, the Maharajah was roaring with laughter. And everybody else looked as if they were sort of tittering, even Dewan Sahib.

In front, Ahmed tried the starter knob again. And once more the whole car gave a lurching jerk and there came that tremendous constricted bang from underneath. Again Ahmed tried. Again the bang. Again. And again.

Now the Maharajah had come wobbling down the steps, laughing till there were tears in his eyes. He went round to the back of the car.

"Michael Sahib," he called out, "there appears to be something stuck in your exhaust pipe. An object, Michael Sahib."

"Go and look, Ahmed, go and look," Michael hissed.

Ahmed got out and went round to the car's rear. Michael could hear scraping sounds, as if he were poking about down there somewhere. Then he came round to the window.

"Sahib, it is blocked. Sahib, I am thinking it has been put in there. A something, Sahib. It has been put, and it cannot be moved, Sahib."

Abruptly the Maharajah's huge fat face replaced that of Ahmed at the window.

"Happy April Fool, Michael," he said. "Happy April Fool."

Father had been right. The Maharajah didn't keep to the rules.

He forced himself to turn and look that great laughing face straight in the eye. Take it like a gentleman, take it like a gentleman, he kept saying to himself.

He swallowed.

"Oh, jolly good joke, Maharajah Sahib," he said.

He opened the car door and got out into the hot sunshine.

"And now," he said to the Maharajah, "would you be so good as to have an elephant fetched? I'd like to get home."

For a moment the Maharajah looked as if he had heard something he hadn't expected. But almost at once he started laughing again.

"Yes, yes, of course, an elephant. Dewan Sahib, will you see to that."

The Maharajah put a podgy hand into a pocket somewhere underneath his splendid lemon-yellow coat and produced on the end of a short length of cotton twine a small piece of startlingly orange spongy stuff.

"This is what it was, my boy," he said. "A piece of sapura bark. Do you know what that is?"

"Yes, Maharajah Sahib. You told me about it last time I came to tea."

"Did I? Did I? Good, good. Well, while you were at tea this time, do you know what I had done? I had my bearer creep round and put the rest of this piece that came to me only this morning into the exhaust of your car and then pour some water on. So that it is now hard as iron, hard as iron."

"A jolly clever trick, Maharajah Sahib."

And after that there did not seem to be very much left for anyone to say. The Maharajah stood twirling the piece of sapura bark on the end of its cotton twine with his podgy, ring-glittering fingers and then suddenly called out to Captain Ram Singh.

"Here, you take this and look after it. It was jolly awkward in my pocket all the time we were having tea. It makes everything orange it touches, bright orange. And, Captain Ram Singh, I shall want a word with you when Michael Sahib has left."

"Yes, Highness."

Captain Ram Singh just managed to catch the piece of bark that the Maharajah swung at him. But he did not seem to Little Michael to be as clever as he usually was, grabbing at the little piece of bright orange stuff and getting its stain all over his fingers before hastily tucking it away.

Then at last the elephant came, lumbering its way from the hathikhana, the elephant stables, its mahout a small crouched figure on its neck. At the foot of the steps the mahout made the great creature kneel. Little Michael said good-bye to the Maharajah once again and shinned up the dangling blue velvet ladder on the side of the elephant onto its wide pad. At a quiet word from the mahout the huge beast lurched gently to its feet. It swung round, raised its trunk as if it were about to let forth an enormous bellow, dropped it quietly instead, and set out at a steady swaying pace in the direction of the palace gates.

Up on the pad, Little Michael, topi straight on his head, sat upright as a British grenadier, looking neither to left nor to right.

III

Very soon after the elephant bearing away little Michael Pendeverel, straight-backed under his topi, had turned out of the palace grounds another gently swaying beast could be seen approaching the sentry-guarded gates. Neither of its two passengers was particularly straight-backed. One of them, indeed, was positively crouching flat on the creature's cushion-covered pad, clutching at the ropes below with hands tenacious as two terrified claws. Mrs. Elaine Alcott.

"Mother," Judy said, for the ninth or tenth time, "there's really no need to lie down."

Yet she herself was keeping at least her right hand firmly holding a convenient piece of rope. And she was stopping herself ever looking downwards as the great grey-backed beast steadily swayed and swung.

"Why didn't Joe warn us?" Mrs. Alcott wailed, for the twelfth or thirteenth time. "I mean, don't they have any automobiles in this damned country?"

"Mother."

"Well, it is a damned country, and if I want to use bad language about the damned place I damned well will."

"But, Mother, we're on an elephant. An elephant. Just think."

"I am thinking. Do you think I can stop thinking I'm on an elephant? How I ever got up here I can't guess, but I certainly know I'm here."

"We didn't seem to have much choice, Mother dear. With this great thing just waiting for us there at the station, and none of the servants seeming to understand a word of English."

"But why didn't Joe tell us? And why wasn't he there to meet us? And why didn't he bring an automobile?"

"Well, I s'pose we're not strictly his guests. We're the Maharajah's guests, and I guess it was up to him to meet us. Or to send whatever he thought best."

"If you say so."

Mrs. Alcott ventured to lift her head for a moment, glimpsed the far sandy horizon, found it was moving gently up and down in an altogether unlandlike way, and plunged her face into the cushion below her once again.

Which had a terrible sort of spicy, musty smell.

"And that Maharajah," she muttered into the velvet, "I don't at all like the sound of him. I mean, Judy, why did he have to surround us with servants like that?"

"Well, I guess he has lots, and it seemed only right to send a good few to look after us since he wasn't coming himself."

"But, Judy, they're so sinister."

"I don't think so, Mother. Not sinister. Well, not very."

"And not a word of decent goddam English."

"I s'pose they speak only their own language, whatever it is. I guess it's too much to expect English from every one of them. And I'm even glad that this little guy right in front of us with that little hooked rod of his can't understand, after all you've said about the Maharajah."

"I don't take back a single word. He's sinister too, Judy. I know he's going to be. Judy, sinister things are going to happen to us. I know it. I feel it, Judy. Judy, can't we just turn right around and go back home?"

"No, Mother, we can't."

The last arrival in Bhopore that day was perhaps luckier in the mode of transport the Maharajah offered him. To meet Henry Morton III, soft metals king summoned by urgent cable from vital business dealings in London, His Highness had sent out to the Bhopore airfield, where his own private Fokker biplane had just made a safe, if bumpy, landing after its flight from Bombay, one of his most luxurious Daimlers, the one with the seats covered in tiger skin.

It did something to placate Henry Morton III. But not a lot.

What in the hell did the Maharajah want? All that had happened before when he made his proposals about the zinc in the guy's salt lakes had been that uppity snooty letter, "The Maharajah of Bhopore begs to state that Mr. Henry Morton's recent proposals are of no interest to him." Just that. In answer to Henry Morton III, soft metals king of the Midwest, and certified as such by the *Wall Street Journal*, no less. And then right out of the blue that cable. Come to dinner. All the way from London to India. What the hell did the guy want?

And what sort of an airfield was this, anyway? Just a big levelled patch of sand, and wind sock on a pole, and a damned tent. The guy ought to come out and take a good look at the way things were done in the U.S. of A.

Less unhappy with his lot was the man who had walked through the sun, black umbrella aloft, to the Maharajah's Summer Palace that morning. He was walking back now, through the slightly less scorching heat of the late afternoon, to his modest home near the Maharajah's City Palace and his wife and four small daughters. Four daughters; was ever man so unlucky?

It was twelve long miles to plod. But the Schoolmaster had walked them many times before, had walked, often as not, still smarting from the irrepressible bad behavior of the Maharajah's many illegitimate male offspring. So he accepted his lot now as nothing to be thought about in terms of complaint. Instead he glanced, sharp-eyed, from side to side under his aged umbrella. Whatever sights there were to be seen he quietly snapped up. A few new flower heads had appeared in front of a wayside shrine since he had passed that way earlier. At a fold in the ground some way from the road a shuffling queue of vultures indicated that some animal had come to its end. And, as at last he neared the sprawling city, another death came his way, a funeral procession going to the burning ghats, the dead man—the body was wrapped in white, not red, so was therefore male, not female—lying on the open flower-bedecked bier, borne on four sweating shoulders, the procession behind noisy with shouting and music.

Yes, he mused, not much disturbed, death comes to all. And comes suddenly, too, as often as not.

Captain Ram Singh, emerging from the conversation that the Maharajah had desired to have with him as soon as he had disposed of the important business of the Resident's son and the sapura bark, looked pretty much like death himself. His usually blankly impassive features were drawn. His shoulders, customarily carried with a jaunty swing, now decidedly drooped. He wanted, above all, to creep away to his apartments and to hide in the cool dark there until he had somehow built himself up again to a point where he could face the world. As well as to have yet another attempt to wash the sapura-bark stains from his right hand, vain though he suspected it would be.

So the last person he wished to encounter was the Dewan.

Cautiously he entered a dim antechamber, distinguished only by having hanging in it, in an enormously wide gold frame, a coloured reproduction from the *Illustrated London News* of the Delhi Durbar of 1903, the Maharajah's grandfather prominent among the assembled princes. He was halfway across to the far arched doorway when from the shelter of a large leather armchair pushed into one corner, who else but the Dewan should emerge, rising up like a ghost from a brown leather tomb?

"Ah, Captain Ram Singh. Just the person I was hoping to have a word with."

Captain Ram Singh came to a full stop. Intrepid on the polo field to the point of foolishness, he looked now, in face of the mild, grave figure of the Dewan, as if he wanted nothing more than to take to his heels and run. But he knew that he could not. The Dewan, after all, was the man in the whole State closest in most ways to the Maharajah. Or closest, Captain Ram Singh, corrected himself, up until recent months. For hadn't there been rumours in plenty of the Maharajah's increasing distrust of his chief minister? But, all the same, the Dewan was a person it was important, especially in his own present situation, to keep on friendly terms with.

"Dewan Sahib, I trust you are well. The heat is not too oppressive?"

"No, no. Thank you, Captain. My duties seldom take me out-of-doors during the day, so heat does not greatly affect me. But you? What about you? Did you find the sun too much for you on your journey back from Panna?"

"No, no. Why should I? I can stand the heat of the sun better than any . . ."

Captain Ram Singh's robust voice faded into silence as he realised why the Dewan might be thinking that he had suffered under the heat on his journey from his home. He had arrived a great deal later than he ought to have done. The Maharajah had just made him vividly aware of that fact.

"And your father?" the Dewan said smoothly. "I trust he is well?"

Captain Ram Singh found this simple inquiry unexpectedly difficult to answer. It seemed to him whatever he said about his father's state of health would be interpreted by the Dewan as providing a clue to what sort of answer the Thakur had sent back to the Maharajah about those wretched withheld monies. And, since the Dewan had so obviously lain in wait here to put just such a question, it looked very much as if relations with the Thakur of Panna were now one of those matters of State which the Maharajah, for deep reasons of his own, wished to keep from his chief minister. So it was up to him to give nothing away. His heart sank into his brilliantly polished boots and he clenched his orange-stained right palm more fiercely than ever.

"Yes. That is— Well, he is not in the best of health. That is to say, he is well enough. Yes, quite well."

"I am glad to hear he is well, Captain. I had feared that he had not perhaps been his usual self, that he had been forced to neglect some of his business, perhaps the gathering of taxes?"

"No. Yes. Yes, well . . . Well, it is good of you to interest yourself in affairs at Panna when you yourself have so much to do looking after matters that come directly under your hand."

Captain Ram Singh puffed his chest out frankly. He'd given the fellow as good as he had got. "When you yourself have so much to do." A dagger thrust there. A dagger thrust.

The Dewan sighed.

"Yes, there is a great deal to be done," he said. "But even events somewhere as distant as Panna have their effect on the life of the State itself, you know, Captain. We need every anna of revenue we can get if affairs are to be kept running smoothly."

"I am sure my father will never fail to pay what it is right and proper that he should pay."

"Of course, of course, Captain. No one could think otherwise. And I am glad to hear you say it. Most glad."

Captain Ram Singh found it now impossible to utter a word. He looked here, there, and everywhere in the dimness of the antechamber as if longing only to find a polo stick in his hand, a pony between his legs, and a well-placed ball lying just where it could be satisfyingly smashed between two goalposts.

The Dewan sighed again.

"You know, Captain," he said, "I have given twenty years of my life to making sure everything in Bhopore runs easily and smoothly. To improving the lives of the people, as far as there are resources to do so. And I hope with all my heart that I shall be able to go on doing that for a good few years still. Which is why I go to great lengths to make sure that I know what is going on. Without information there cannot be action. I am sure you yourself feel that."

"Yes, yes," said Captain Ram Singh, his mind hovering between the inviting prospects of a polo goal lying undefended in front of him and a good, heavily muscled boar standing at bay in the direct path of his pigsticking spear. "Yes, yes, without action no information. I must remember that. Excellent, Dewan Sahib, excellent. Without action, no information. Yes, yes. Good, good."

And he made his escape, happily convinced that the Dewan had learnt nothing that mattered about the result of his trip to Panna.

And the Dewan, contrasting those dejected shoulders he had seen coming towards him as he had waited in the depths of that tomblike leather armchair with the suddenly cocky swagger now departing, smiled a little. No need now to risk a rebuff by asking the Maharajah directly what message Captain Ram Singh had brought back from Panna. It had plainly been one that the Maharajah had not liked hearing. Poor straightforward Captain Ram Singh, snatching at whatever reassurance he could find to bolster up his deflated spirit, had told him so. It had been clear as if he had repeated every word of his doubtless appallingly stormy interview with His Highness. A small victory had been obtained.

Yet the Dewan sighed again.

And, before he had gone twenty paces along the high corridor from the anteroom on his way back to his own apartments, he had occasion to get hold of some more information that could lead, if necessary, to action.

A servant came scuttling along towards him, and something in the man's manner told him at once that he was on no ordinary errand.

He stopped him.

"Well, and where is it that you are going in such a hurry?"

"It is to Doctor Sahib, huzoor."

"To Doctor Sahib? Then someone is not well?"

"Yes, huzoor. It is Raghbir Sahib. He is in terrible pain. He is all the time being most terribly sick."

"Then hurry to Doctor Sahib. Hurry. It is so easy when the Hot Weather has begun to eat something that can be dangerous. Hurry, man, hurry."

And the delayed servant scuttled away to the palace Dispensary, bare feet slap, slap, slapping on the cool stone floor of the corridor.

The Dewan stayed where he was, impassive and thoughtful. To go to the Maharajah with this news or not? Perhaps not. The boy had created that ridiculous scene during the Maharajah's tea party for the Resident's son—not for nothing did the Dewan regularly pay small sums to the Maharajah's fan-bearer—and if the boy's illness was indeed no more than the effects of eating something not wholesome, then the Maharajah might well be struck with remorse for having bundled him out so unceremoniously when he was already not feeling well. And anybody who caused His Highness to experience remorse would not be thanked for it.

On the other hand, what if the illness was one that had not arisen from any natural cause? There were jealousies always in the zenana. So far as he knew, First Her Highness, the Rajkumar's mother, had no particular new cause for suspicion of Second Her Highness's ambitions for that little lout, Raghbir. But information from the zenana always took a little longer to come to him . . .

No, on the whole, say nothing still. Wait to see what events turned up.

It was perhaps as well for the Dewan that he did not choose that moment to go and tell the Maharajah of the sudden illness that had afflicted Raghbir. Because the Maharajah was having son trouble enough.

He was face to face with Porgy in the room called the Tiger Chamber, from the enormous circular rug that stood in its centre made from the skins of one hundred and one tigers, each shot by the Maharajah himself. And the look he was giving his heir was savage as that of any of the slain beasts in its prime.

"What do you mean 'marry Dolly Brattle'? What for is there a need to marry? Oh, keep her out of the palace while the Viceroy is here, send her to the hills, let her have a good time there. And when His Excellency has gone, bring her back, bring her back. But do not let me hear any of this nonsense of marrying."

"Father, this is 1930, after all. We are not Victorians any longer. You don't understand."

"Nonsense, boy, nonsense. Do you think your father does not know what it is to feel love? Why, I am feeling love at this moment. That girl from the South, I saw at that club in Calcutta, you know she is here, here in Bhopore?"

"That's got nothing to do with this, Father, if you'll excuse me."

"Nothing to do, nothing to do? What nonsense! I tell you it has everything to do with it. What you feel for this Dolly creature is just exactly what I feel for Kamakshi. It is love. Love. But that does not mean any marryings."

"Father, Dolly wants to marry me. I love her, Father. I can't think of life without her."

"No need. No need, I have told you a thousand times, to think of life without her if that is your real feeling. Let her stay here another week, even another ten days. Then the hills. Afterwards, when in a week the Viceroy has left, the dam has been opened, and there has been a most successful tiger shikar, then bring her back, then let her stay. And by that time Dewan Sahib will have completed his negotiations for your marriage to a suitable bride."

"But, Father—"

"Now, no more stupidity, Porgy. Do you think I was a celibate bachelor when I married First Her Highness? Good gracious, I was given my first concubine as a present from my father when I was sixteen. Marriage is nothing to do with love. It is a question of izzat, of prestige, of keeping up the position of the State. Love you can have anytime."

Porgy's full face was grey with rage to his very pouting lips.

"Father, Dolly will agree to nothing less than marriage. I have promised her, Father. I have given my word."

The Maharajah's little eyes burnt like coals in the heavy pads of flesh around them.

"Then you had no business to give your word. No business to make promises to a slut."

Porgy took a step forwards. The hand by his side flattened into a swinging instrument of outrage.

But his father stirred not a muscle.

"Do not forget yourself, my boy. You would not be the first son of this house to be thrown into a dungeon by his father."

For the time it took for the impassive fan-bearer behind the Maharajah to wield his instrument in two slow swishes the Rajkumar looked at his father in pure hatred. Then he swung on his heel and made for the doorway.

"Porgy."

The Maharajah's voice snapped with authority.

Porgy's step faltered.

"Since when, Porgy, has it been the custom for anyone to leave my presence without making mujra?"

The Rajkumar stood still, stock-still, his back to his father.

The Maharajah said nothing.

To left, to right went the heavy fan behind him. To left, to right. To left, to right.

Porgy turned. Slowly he bowed. His right hand went slowly up to his forehead. Once. Twice. Three times.

"And I think this is a suitable time for me to take a little shooting practice," the Maharajah said. "You will come out onto the back lawn and watch, Porgy."

To the left went the fan, to the right.

"Very good, Father."

It was the Maharajah's custom from time to time to stand out on one of the lawns at the back of the palace and give a semipublic display of his skill with the .22 rifle. He delighted to call these occasions "practice," but it was always well understood that he was not, like other people practising anything, going to begin badly and by dint of repeating his attempts gradually to improve. The Maharajah was going to begin splendidly and go on by getting, if possible, even better.

And for this he needed an audience.

It was one of the duties that fell to the Dewan, besides running the whole State, an area as big as a good many independent Balkan nations, to learn in whatever way he could that one of the Maharajah's "practices" was going to take place. Then he would ensure that a decently large audience came to see it. There were a good many people who could be briskly ordered to attend, and generally the loud-voiced Captain Ram Singh was entrusted with seeing that these volunteers were waiting, by chance, at the correct time on the lawn reserved for the Maharajah's displays. But there were other people in the palace who had to be cajoled into being present. Such as the Maharajah's guests.

It was a measure of the Dewan's dedication to this little task, as to his greater one, that when His Highness came out onto the lawn some twenty minutes after his decision to shoot, an interval filled by changing into a light khaki jacket and trousers suitable for the occasion, there were standing there, besides some twenty palace officials of various ranks, every one of the Maharajah's European guests, even those who had only just arrived at the palace.

So the "practice" had to be a little delayed until first Mrs. Alcott and Judy and then Henry Morton III had been introduced to their host.

"Joe." Mrs. Alcott directed a frenzied whisper towards the white-clad red-haired form of her little brother, builder of the largest dam yet to be constructed in India. "Joe, what do I do, for heaven sakes? Do I bow, Joe? Joe, I don't have to kiss his hand, do I, Joe? Do I?"

"I guess I didn't when I first came," Joe Lloyd replied, comfortably laconic.

"Mrs. Alcott, I am most happy to welcome the sister of the man who has built us a dam that will long be the pride of Bhopore."

Affability radiated from every inch of the Maharajah's huge frame. He joined his hands together in the namaskar greeting.

Mrs. Alcott shot out her hand, fixed rigidly in position for a good, old democratic American shake. Then, seeing that the gesture had not been reciprocated, she shot it back again.

"Oh," she said.

She jerked her head forward in a movement that might have been a bow, or might, had she been a bird, have been a particularly savage peck.

"Yes," she said.

The Maharajah smiled blandly.

"You will excuse me if I do not shake hands," he said. "Unfortunately, today I am untouchable. My astrologers tell me that I am in that state, and I must accept it. A religious principle, you understand."

"Relig—"

Mrs. Alcott's voice rose in an outraged squeak, came to an abrupt halt, turned into a screechy cough.

"Oh, yes, yes," she brought out at last. "I understand perfectly, Maharajah."

"And this is your daughter? Mr. Lloyd, you told me nothing of her beauty and charm."

"Guess I didn't know she had any," Joe Lloyd replied with the confident judgment of a score of backwoods ancestors.

"My dear young lady," the Maharajah went on, undisconcerted, "you must meet some of the younger people we have here. My son, the Rajkumar."

Porgy offered his hand.

"Delighted to meet you—er—Your Highness," Judy said.

Having succeeded in throwing off most of the boiling temper his father had left him in, Porgy was able to give a smile white-flashing as a film star's.

"No, no," he said. "You must call me Porgy. These are modern times. We can't always be standing on ceremony."

Judy contrived to raise an answering smile.

"Then hello, Porgy."

"And this is a friend of my son's," the Maharajah said. "The son himself of an old acquaintance of mine, who was kind enough to give Porgy some hunting when he was up at Cambridge, and whom I now have great pleasure in entertaining myself. Lieutenant James Frere."

Judy turned to the man the Maharajah had introduced. It would have needed eyes a good deal less sharp than the Maharajah's to have missed the look that came over the American girl. And to have missed the very similar look that swept the fresh-complexioned face of James Frere.

"Miss— Miss— Miss Alcott," James stammered. "I do hope, if you're going to call the Rajkumar Porgy, that you'll jolly well call me James."

"James."

Judy repeated the word as if in its single syllable it contained all the poetry that had ever been written in the world.

"James," she said again. "Yes. But you must call me Judy."

"Judy. Judy. Yes, I will."

The Maharajah did not consider it necessary after his first quick flash of comprehension to observe any further the meeting between these two young foreigners. He turned instead to the unmistakable figure of Henry Morton III, soft metals king of the American Midwest, square of shoulder, aggressive of chin, puggy of nose, his face marred, however, by a wide area of scar tissue all down its right side.

"But this must be Mr. Henry Morton. My dear sir, I cannot tell you how happy I am to welcome you to Bhopore. Dewan, Dewan, did you know that this is Mr. Henry Morton? The great owner of zinc concessions in America?"

He turned quickly to the grave figure of the Dewan. And, to his unconcealed delight, caught on that usually utterly impassive face a look of complete surprise.

"Dewan," he went on, his little sharp eyes alight with malicious pleasure, "surely you remember me telling you that I intended to ask

Mr. Morton to come and pay me a short visit? A visit combining, I hope, pleasure—and business."

The Dewan bowed.

"If Your Highness told me, of course, I remember," he said. "And I hope that Mr. Morton's visit gives him all the pleasure it possibly can."

"And the business, Dewan Sahib. And the business. Do not forget that Mr. Morton is first and foremost a businessman."

"No, Highness, you can be sure I shall never forget that."

Henry Morton III flicked his head from one to the other during this loaded exchange for all the world as if he were not standing on a lawn behind the Summer Palace at Bhopore but were transfixed in a seat at the finals of the Wimbledon lawn tennis championships.

"I shall be most happy to discuss that proposition I made to Your Highness at any time convenient," he said at last with determined emphasis.

"Yes, yes. Dewan Sahib and I will take steps to have the most thorough discussions with you as soon as possible," the Maharajah answered. "You will find the Dewan quite an expert on the matters. But not a word about it tonight. Tonight is for enjoyment. First, I myself am going to take a little shooting practice, an amusement for which of course you are under no obligation to stay. Unless, that is, you are interested. Then afterwards perhaps we should all play some Bridge, or, since you are here for the first time, possibly you would like to take a stroll on the palace roof. The view is extensive. Or there is the lake. Quite soon now the mugger-wallahs will take food to the muggers there—the crocodiles, as you call them in English—and perhaps you would be interested in seeing the creatures snap up the haunches of flesh thrown to them. Possibly even a servant will fall in. That has been considered an especial treat in the past."

"I guess I'm not much of a man for entertainment, Maharajah," Henry Morton said. "I guess I'll just go to my room and look over the figures I'll present to you and your advisers just as soon as I can."

"As you wish, Mr. Morton. As you wish. But I trust you will not go until I have managed to do a little shooting. Perhaps you also would like to try your hand?"

"No. No."

The tycoon's voice sounded suddenly loud, almost agonised, amid the subdued murmur of conversation from the courtiers assembled to watch the Maharajah. A hush fell.

Henry Morton bit his lower lip.

"No, to tell you the truth, Maharajah," he said in a more normal voice, "I'm just darned tired after that long flight from London. So if you'll excuse me, I think I'll take a rest before dinner."

"Yes, yes, of course, my dear chap. In any case I think you have met everybody here now, and so we'll see you at dinner. We dine at nine, with cocktails at eight-thirty. Your bearer will show you."

"Father, I think Mr. Morton has not yet met everybody."

Porgy stepped quickly forward between the Maharajah and the American tycoon.

"Father, he has not yet met Miss Brattle."

The Maharajah's face darkened at once with ready anger. But his son seemed to be undismayed.

"Dolly," he said, "may I present Mr. Henry Morton, from America? Mr. Morton, this is Miss Brattle, Miss Dolly Brattle, my very good friend!"

The Maharajah abruptly swung away, leaving Henry Morton to meet Dolly Brattle or not, as he chose. His whole big body rose and fell with the deep angry breaths he was taking. Even James Frere and Judy, who scarcely had eyes for anyone but each other, became aware of the tension.

Yet the Maharajah was not a man to be beaten by an access of rage, even his own rage. Less than half a minute had passed before he called to his gun-bearer, who had been standing patiently by all the while, a loaded Remington .22 in his hand.

"Bearer. Gun."

The Maharajah took the light rifle, weighed it for a moment between his two pudgy but firm hands, and then took his stance at the edge of the lawn. His feet were planted sturdily apart and, it was plain to see, his breathing now was no longer heavy.

"Bearer. Begin."

The gun-bearer stepped forward. From a pouch at his side he had taken a solid handful of silver rupees. Now, with a quick glance at his master first, he sent one of them spinning up into the sunlit air.

Crack.

At the very height of the throw a bullet sent the twirling silver disc flying far across the lawn.

But a second rupee was already in the air. And crack. Again at the moment when it hung between rising and falling a .22 bullet smacked full into it.

And again. And again. And again.

It was a remarkable display. James Frere, who had represented his school on the rifle range, acknowledged to himself that he would never in a dozen years get near it. Coin after coin went spinning up into the air, and never one of them began its downward fall. Ten. Fifteen. Twenty. Twenty-five.

"Enough."

A dutiful patter of applause came from the courtiers. A little sheepishly the European guests joined in.

The Maharajah ignored it all. Back towards the palace he strode, the purposefulness that was always in him now all the more apparent. Not a man to cross. Ever.

Some two hours later Mrs. Alcott, like all the other guests in the palace, was dressing for dinner. At half-past seven precisely a flock of servants had gone through the rooms, each bearing a smoking urn of elaborately chased silver. "It is what we call dhuan," Porgy had explained. "The aroma of the smoke discourages mosquitoes." And then it had been time to come up to the guest suite that had been allocated to her to prepare for the ceremonial dinner which was to take place at nine, with Sir Arthur Pendeverel, His Majesty's Resident in Bhopore, as principal guest.

Sir Arthur. Mrs. Alcott had found herself torn between two emotions. To be dining with a titled British gentleman, perhaps even sitting next to him: it made her heart flutter. To have to dine with a titled British gentleman, and perhaps—oh, God, what would she say?—to have to sit next to him: it made her heart thump.

Well, at least the bathroom nightmare had vanished away. Had that nice, handsome Lieutenant Frere been joking? He had looked solemn enough when he had said to her that in some of the guest suites in the palace you took your bath Indian-style, and he didn't know whether she had ever encountered the system.

A rapid sinking feeling had run through her.

"Well, no, Lootenant, this is my first time here."

James Frere smiled. A nice, warming smile it was too.

"Yes, I rather thought that. Some ladies are a bit disconcerted at first, you know. So I thought I'd just offer a word of warning. In case . . ."

"In case? In case, just of what?"

"Oh, just in case your suite should happen to have those arrangements."

"What arrangements?"

She hadn't meant her voice to rise up like that.

"Oh, nothing to be alarmed about. Nothing to be alarmed about at all. Rather nice, really. I've got an Indian bathroom here and I jolly well enjoy my bath."

"Lootenant, what is it? What happens?"

He smiled again. And it was kind, and reassuring.

"Quite simple. There's just a stone floor with a drain hole, you know. And a little wooden stool. You get undressed and sit there and in comes a servant with pots of water, jolly fine silver pots they are in the palace, too, and they pour them over you. Really great fun."

"A servant, Lootenant?"

A terrible quaking feeling had arrived in her stomach.

"Not— Not a man?"

James Frere's fresh-complexioned face burst into an irrepressible grin.

"Oh, good gracious me, no. I'm terribly sorry. Should never have given you that impression. Wasn't thinking. No, for you it'll be an ayah, a maidservant. And she'll help you dress and all that."

"Well, I've managed to do that for myself ever since I was three years old, thank you."

But again he had smiled in that nice, encouraging way.

"Oh, if you don't want her, I'm sure she'll just vanish away. But I'd have her if I were you. It's rather nice, you know. I haven't put on my own shoes once ever since I've been back in India."

"Well, I don't know about that. And I'm not at all sure I like the idea of being bathed like that either."

"No? Great fun, I promise."

But, mercifully, when she had entered the bathroom of the suite everything had been all right. There was a great big green bath, with proper taps, and a tall metal screen affair all round the top end that sprayed you if you wanted. And there was plenty of hot water, and both hot and cold ran clear as clear. No need surely to use the potash of permanganate crystals she had brought with her to disinfect contaminated water and risk finding her skin tinged with their deep purple afterwards.

Yes, the Maharajah certainly had things done well.

Only weren't they somehow done a bit too well? Wasn't there a nasty little feeling that if anyone could arrange the comforts of life so cleverly, they could arrange anything else cleverly as well? Anything else.

And it was strange, too. Things were strange here. Perhaps not exactly sinister the way she had expected. But strange, right enough.

The bed, for instance. Why was it out in the middle of the room the way it was? Beds should be up against the wall. That was the way they were meant to be.

A memory came back to her as she went over to the big bed standing all alone there and took off it her dining gown, which the ayah who had attended her had been perfectly happy, as James Frere had suggested, to leave for her to put on herself. Wasn't there a story she had read once long ago? A story with some Indian trappings to it? A kind of crime— Yes, that was it. It was Sherlock Holmes. The one about the girl in that big lonely country house and her wicked stepfather who had been—yes—in India, and who had come back with a deadly snake and had put it through the ventilator to murder her, only Sherlock Holmes had gotten on to it first.

Was that the reason beds in India were put in the middle of the room? So that no one got murdered by a snake creeping down the wall in the night?

A sudden knock came on the outer door. Elaine Alcott jumped a mile.

But when at last she brought herself to call, "Who is it?" it was only the gruff, American, blessedly American, tones of her brother's voice that answered.

"Elaine? Can I come in? Thought you might like to talk a bit before we get all formal."

"Joe. Joe. Come in, Joe."

It was certainly good to see him, standing there in a tuxedo which, although it fitted him well enough, he still managed to make look as if it had never been intended for his particular shape of body, nor even anyone else's. And one of the studs on his boiled shirt-front had popped out of its hole.

For a moment she was tempted to go over to him and set it to rights. But it was not a big sister that she felt the need of being now. It was just a plain sister, one who needed to be reassured.

"Joe, I'm sorry but I don't like this place."

"Honey, you don't have to like it. It's not a hell of a likeable place. But I thought you'd enjoy seeing it all."

"Well, I do, Joe. Or I will. I mean, afterwards when it's all over I'll be tickled to death I've done it. But right now . . . Joe. Joe, what was all that about that owl just when the Maharajah was going in?"

It had been a curious incident by any standards. Just as the Maharajah had marched away after his shooting practice, giving off that air of being a man who would always do exactly what he wanted, across the wall of the palace in front of him a sudden flapping shape had appeared. A bird. An owl, making a sudden foray as the light was beginning to go from wherever it had been roosting among all the pillars and arches of the palace wall.

But its appearance had brought a gasp, nothing less, from the Maharajah's assembled courtiers. And even the Maharajah himself had checked his stride for just an instant. Then, with a slight squaring of his immense, well-fleshed shoulders, he had marched forward once again and had disappeared into the building. And from the hushed courtiers there had come a swift buzz of conversation, of sharp questioning. Which had been as quickly brought under control.

"Joe, I asked that what-d'you-call-him, that Raj-whatever—"

"The Rajkumar. Porgy. Yes?"

"I asked him what that bird was, and why it seemed to have upset all those guys. And, Joe, he just said he hadn't noticed a thing. But, Joe, he did. I saw."

"Yeah, honey. Well, I guess that's something I know about. You can't have lived in this country as long as I have and mixed with the guys working on the dam an' all and not learn things like that."

"Like what, Joe?"

"Like omens."

"Omens?"

"Yeah, an owl crossing your path is a pretty bad omen to these guys."

"Even to the Maharajah? And that Porgy? Why, they speak English as well as we do."

"Most of all to the Maharajah, I'd say. Just because the guy sent his son to Cambridge University an' all, it doesn't mean he still isn't as superstitious as any of them."

"Well. Well, if it was only a superstition."

Relieved, Elaine turned to the huge dressing table with its three mirrors and glass top, plainly imported from London if not Paris.

She picked up a powder puff and began vigorously dusting her cheeks.

"What's it an omen of, an owl, anyhow?" she asked carelessly.

Joe Lloyd did not answer. He slipped out his cigarette case and busied himself tapping a cigarette on it.

It nearly worked. Elaine at that moment spotted a tiny flaw in her lipstick and looked round for the means to put it right. But Joe's silence just penetrated through her preoccupation, and she swung sharply round on the dressing table stool.

"Joe, what is an owl an omen of?"

Joe Lloyd sighed.

"Of a death, honey," he said. "Of a death coming soon, if you're hooked on that particular superstition."

At the dressing table, Elaine looked at herself in the mirrors. Three Elaines stared back at her, each a little bit pale under the powder.

"Well, I'm not superstitious," she announced. "Not about any Indian superstition, anyway. So there isn't going to be any death. Not one that I'm going to know about."

But the second knocking at the door of the suite made her jump even more than Joe's had done. And Joe himself had to ask who was there.

"It's me. Me, Judy. Is that you, Uncle Joe? Isn't Mother there?"

"Come in, kid, come in. She's here, all right. Only, you know your mother, always was a scaredy cat."

"I was not, Joe Lloyd."

"You were, Elaine Lloyd."

"But what are you being scared of now, Mother? The elephant got us here okay after all, didn't it? And everything's been fine since."

Her mother gave her a quick, shrewd look.

"Oh yes, miss. Everything's been fine for you since about six o'clock this afternoon."

"What do you mean 'six o'clock'? We've been here longer than that."

"But you haven't known a certain Lootenant James Frere longer than that, dear."

And Judy blushed. A hot, unstoppable blush right up to her pretty little ears.

"Mother, I've only just met him. He's nice. But, really, I've hardly spoken a word to him."

"No, dear. But all of a sudden everything's just fine. I may be your mother, my girl, but I can see what's right in front of my nose."

"But, Mother . . . Look, everything is fine. It really is. We're guests of a maharajah, a real big-shot maharajah. We're living a life you won't find maybe anywhere else on earth. Look, Mother, look what I brought in to show you. Maybe you haven't seen your copy. But look at this."

And she waved a stiff piece of paper, with thick black typewriting on it, under her mother's nose.

"What is it, dear?"

"*General Information for Our Guests,*" Judy read. "You're bound to have your copy somewhere around here, Mother. And listen. *Please send your servant to the Tea Pantry for your early morning tea. If you should require your afternoon tea in your rooms, this can be had from the same place.* Pretty different from getting up in the morning to a cold kitchen and putting on a kettle to make coffee. And listen to this: *Tennis, Squash Rackets, and Croquet can be had at any time.* Would you care for a game of Squash Rackets first thing tomorrow, Mother? Not like going out yourself to mark out the tennis court in the garden before folks come around on a Saturday afternoon, I guess. And how about *Whilst driving in cars Guests are requested on no account to load their guns.* They just about think of everything. It's wonderful. It's really wonderful."

But it was not her mother who answered to her enthusiasm. It was her Uncle Joe.

"Yeah, kid, they think of just about everything. It's the way you get, I guess, when you've got all the money you can use and more. But just remember this: they think of everything not for anyone but themselves."

"But, no, Uncle Joe. I mean, look, aren't they thinking of their guests in all this?"

She waved the sheet of richly thick paper under his nose.

"No, kid, that's just what they aren't doing. Why d'you think they put in that bit about the guns? So's no guest will hurt himself? Not on your life. It's so the game in the jungle won't be disturbed till it suits the Maharajah to disturb it."

"No, Uncle Joe."

"Yes, I tell you. Look at the way he's handled the dam. Yeah, have a dam built. But make it a bigger dam than any other maharajah's got. The pride of Bhopore. Didn't you hear him this afternoon?

And when you've got it, your biggest dam in India, what do you do with it? Do you let it do its job and irrigate more land than any other dam in India? Not if you're the Maharajah of Bhopore, you don't. Because that might cause your precious duck jheels to have a little more water in them than would suit your almighty Imperial sandgrouse when they come in to drink. And then you wouldn't be able to shoot more than any other princely house in India. That's what."

Judy had no answer to that. There had been an edge of cold anger in her uncle's voice, more anger even than what he had been saying seemed to warrant. It had left her simply not wanting to have heard it.

But luckily at that moment there came a knock at the door, another knock at the door. Yet this time soft and discreet, not at all anything to make even a nervy Elaine Alcott jump.

"Yes, what is it?" she called out, with a graciousness almost fit for the surroundings she had found herself in.

"It is half-past eight, Memsahib," a voice answered on the other side of the heavy teakwood. "Cocktails are served in the anteroom of the banqueting hall."

"Very well. Thank you. We're coming."

Elaine Alcott drew on her long white gloves.

It was while they were all taking cocktails that they learnt the news. There were champagne cocktails and there were, the Maharajah's favourite, Alexanders, a concoction of gin and crème de cacao topped with a frothy blob of whipped cream. And because of them an atmosphere of easiness had rapidly built up. Even Sir Arthur Pendeverel, magnificent in the undress uniform of a political officer of the Indian Civil Service, blue frock-coat faced with gold braid, long curvy sword hanging from the belt, tight blue trousers fastened under gleaming boots, white pith helmet with its gold spike and gold chain reluctantly abandoned to a servant, had been heard to utter something that could have been a laugh.

No one looking down from above would have thought that Joe Lloyd, not twenty minutes earlier, had been speaking of the Maharajah in tones so coldly angry that they had scared his niece, who did not scare easily, into silence.

No one would have thought that only that afternoon Porgy, Rajkumar of Bhopore, had quarrelled with his father more bitterly than he had ever done before.

No one would have thought that the Maharajah would have pre-ferred not even to see Dolly Brattle and her platinum shingle under the roof of any of his palaces and that he had set his face adamantly against any idea of her marrying his son.

No one would have thought that the grave figure of the Mahara-jah's Dewan, though he of course as a Muslim, had sampled neither champagne cocktail nor chocolaty Alexander, was anxiously turning and turning over in his mind the fact that the Maharajah had sum-moned Henry Morton III, soft metals king, to Bhopore to discuss mining the zinc beneath the State's vast salt lakes without having said a word about it to him, his supposedly trusted chief minister.

No one would have thought that the Maharajah's assiduous A.D.C., Captain Ram Singh, was counting the hours till he might expect no longer to be holding that influential and profitable office.

All was pleasant laughter and bright conversation. Outside on the lawn the Maharajah's band, gorgeously uniformed, was playing the latest, almost the latest, hits. Next day everyone was to go out early to shoot on the jheels. The prospect aroused much interested ques-tioning. When the Viceroy came in a fortnight to open the dam, a vast tiger shikar was to be organised for him. Again questions and excitement.

Till into the middle of it all came a soft-footed servant. Till, hav-ing stood for a little at the Maharajah's elbow waiting his chance, he leant forward and gave his master a swift whispered message. Till suddenly above the chatter and the tinkling laughter there came an anguished howl from the Maharajah's lips.

"Raghbir. Raghbir, my son. Dead."

IV

There had been a moment of sheer confusion, of horror too, when the Maharajah had lifted up his voice and bellowed his sudden grief at the death of his younger legitimate son. But it had not lasted long. The Maharajah had left at once, and immediately the Rajkumar had taken on the duties of host. He had begged the guests not to feel dismayed. He had pressed more drinks on them.

Within a quarter of an hour the Maharajah reentered, his face no longer contorted with sudden grief. He spoke briefly to Captain Ram Singh, who then at once went quietly round telling the guests what had happened.

"Sir Arthur, a most unfortunate occurrence. But Maharajah Sahib has asked me to say that you are under no circumstances to feel it necessary to cut short your visit this evening. The truth of the matter appears to be that the Maharajah's son—you had met young Raghbir, yes?—has become victim to food poisoning, to what His Highness's physician calls ptomaine poisoning."

The Resident's gaunt features went in an instant yet more stonily impassive. Poison. Was it truly ptomaine poisoning from food gone bad, or was it another sort of poisoning? He knew what could happen within the walls of an Indian ruler's palace. He knew what deadly intrigues could spread from rivalries in the zenana.

But Captain Ram Singh had evidently been prepared for just such thoughts to spring up in Sir Arthur's mind. He hurried on with his explanation.

"Yes, there can be no doubt, Sir Arthur. It was ptomaine. You know Dr. Sen Sahib, a damned clever chap, qualified in England and all that? Well, he is in no doubt. He says it is the classic symptoms."

The Resident made no answer. He simply stood and considered the situation. Then, at last, he pronounced:

"If Dr. Sen, who has prescribed for my son, Michael, on occasion, is satisfied in his diagnosis of the unfortunate event, then I think one must accept that it is as he says."

Captain Ram Singh sighed.

" 'Life is but a candle in the wind,' " he quoted, pleased to have found a ready-made sentiment.

Sir Arthur nodded gravely.

"Hygiene is so important in this country," he said. "And people will not realise it. Regular habits are vital. Vital."

"Yes, indeed, Sir Arthur. Yes, indeed."

And, as if to mark the closing of the subject, outside on the lawn under the overhanging canopy of the intense Indian stars the Maharajah's own band began to play once more. "Yes, sir, that's my baby. No, sir, don't mean maybe."

Sir Arthur allowed the smallest of winces to cross his gaunt face.

Mrs. Alcott was standing beside her brother when the discreetly circulated news reached them. She had not, in fact, dared leave Joe's side during the whole of the extra-prolonged cocktail session.

"Oh, Joe, Joe," she breathed when Captain Ram Singh had moved on. "The owl, Joe."

"Owl? What owl?"

Another stud had popped on Joe's boiled shirt-front, but he had not noticed.

"Joe, the owl omen. Don't you see, Joe? It's happened. And it's no one we know. Or not really. Gosh, I feel sorry for that poor kid. But it isn't as if it's one of us, Joe."

"Guess not."

"Well, I don't mind saying it: it's a terrible weight off my mind. I was convinced, Joe. Convinced something ghastly was going to happen. But now it won't. Now it won't."

It seemed as if the sudden death of the unfortunate Raghbir had indeed lifted a pall that had hung over the palace ever since the incident of the ominous owl, or even before that. Life, Captain Ram Singh had pronounced solemnly, is but a candle in the wind. And the sentiment appeared to be shared by everyone. To old India hands sudden death was no new thing. They were all of them used to the notion that the person you cheerfully shared breakfast with at the beginning of a day might not only have fallen victim to some swift illness by nightfall but have been buried or burnt on the funeral pyre too.

So the delayed dinner was as cheerful as the cocktail session had been before that soft-footed servant had come with his message for the Maharajah. And certainly if magnificence could make for pleasure, then nothing was lacking.

It had been only a quarter-past nine when the band outside on the lawn had abruptly brought "Dance, Dance, Dance, Little Lady" to a ragged halt and had struck up the British Army trumpet call summoning troops to the tables: "Roast Beef." At once each of the gentlemen had made straight for the lady whose name he had found in an envelope addressed to him as he had arrived. Her it was his duty to take into dinner. And, if wise in the ways of the world, he had taken the opportunity, too, to consult the table plan set up on an easel so as to see where he ought to lead his lady to among the fifty covers laid in the banqueting hall. Or so he had done if he had been given the honour of escorting one of the European lady guests to the table. Naturally, none of the palace ladies was going to leave the concealment of the zenana to dine in company, although from a stone-screened balcony at the far end of the banqueting hall they were able to share in the festivity at second hand.

So down towards the lower reaches of the immensely long table, with its huge starched white cloth, its spaced decorations of crystal candelabras of gold dishes piled high with fruits, of gold and crystal vases filled with flowers, there was nothing but lean brown Indian faces cheek by jowl under gorgeous turbans. While up at the head of the table, on either side of the Maharajah himself, there were male and female countenances in proper alternation, some white, some brown.

Behind every two guests, standing straight as a pillar, was a bearer, white-gloved, white-uniformed, starched white turban on his head. In front of each guest was a printed copy of the table plan. No one was to be left in the dark about who anyone else might be. For each lady guest there was a small gift from the Maharajah, an elaborately wrapped bottle of perfume bearing the name of a famous Paris house, and not so very small at that.

Hors d'oeuvres were served. Only the Maharajah, portly and magnificent in scarlet and gold, was not offered the huge gold dishes with their great circular patterns of appetizing titbits, caviar and curried shrimps, potato salad and cucumber salad, tomatoes garnished and beans garnished, olives and anchovies, little beetroots stuffed with capers, smoked salmon and oysters—everything that the Western world had put into tins and India had preserved in spices.

The Maharajah did not share the food he offered so generously to his guests. At a later stage in the proceedings a huge golden salver hidden under a huge golden cover would be set before His Highness. At one end of the cover there would be a stout golden hinge, and at the opposite end there would be a stout golden padlock. The Maharajah's only trusted personal bearer would turn the sole key there was for that padlock. Then the Maharajah would eat, safe in the knowledge that once more he had evaded poisoning.

Yet, for all that he began by taking nothing and for all that he had, so few minutes before been devastated by the news of Raghbir's death, there was nothing of the melancholy about him now. He chatted animatedly, if a little overbearingly, to the guests. Nearest him was Mrs. Alcott, with beside her—"but what shall I say, Joe, whatever shall I say to him?"—Sir Arthur Pendeverel, gold-braided blue frock-coat, long curvy sword adroitly not allowed to impede his intake of food. On the other side there was Judy Alcott, with next to her Henry Morton III, determined of chin, puggy of nose, mysteriously scarred down his right cheek.

"Now, Mrs. Alcott, do you see this little silver train that I have resting here before me? And the rails? The rails which go all the way round the table?"

"Why, yes, Maharajah. And are the rails silver, too? I believe they must be."

"Yes, yes, of course. Silver, all silver. It is best."

"But does the train go then, Maharajah? Back home in the States children's toys are made of tin. They go all right, but will a silver train actually move?"

"But, of course, of course. Why would I have a train made that did not go? This has an engine made for me by Hornby and the rest is by Asprey's of London, you know."

"Oh, yes. Asprey's."

Elaine Alcott felt pleased with the way she had tossed that off.

"So when we get to the dessert, you will see. I press this little silver knob beside me here, and off she goes, my little train, on her great journey, all the way round the table. And if you yourself or anybody else wishes to take something from the trucks that the servants will fit onto it later, some sweets, some port, some liqueur—I have excellent crème de cacao, delicious—then you have only to lift up the dish or the bottle while the train passes and automatically it stops until you have helped yourself."

"Pretty clever," Henry Morton III grunted. "Only if there are all of fifty people around the table, it's sure going to take a hell of a long time till it reaches me."

The Maharajah laughed, a great rolling laugh.

"Oh, do not worry, Mr. Morton. It will reach you in good time, I promise."

"Well, I can't see how. I guess having a squad of well-trained waiters like we do back in New York would be a sight more efficient."

"Oh, ho. Your American efficiency, Mr. Morton. But do not worry, I tell you. The train will come to you perhaps sooner than you desire."

"Not if it can be stopped by all fifty people around this table."

Porgy, sitting a little down from Henry Morton, leant across.

"Ah, but you see, Mr. Morton, it will not be stopped by fifty people. Forty of the guests here tonight know much better than to stop Papa's train when he has set it going."

The bearers, deftly working as if they too were clockwork made in London by Hornby, started to serve the soup, white asparagus. Outside in the gardens the band was playing "I'll See You Again."

The Maharajah began recalling his last year's visit to Delhi for Delhi Week, the Cold Weather round of festivities presided over by the Viceroy while the Chamber of Princes held its meeting.

"It so happened, you know, that I had the honour of being the prince selected by the Viceroy to walk back with him all the way up the lawn into the Viceroy's house when he had spoken to all the necessary people at the garden party. It is the greatest honour of the whole Week, Mrs. Alcott."

"I'm sure it is, Maharajah."

Elaine felt almost as if she had been there, had walked among all the princes in their finery and the chief men of the British Empire in their more sombre best, among the turbans and the top hats.

"Yes, that was when I took the opportunity of asking His Excellency to open our dam. And he at once agreed."

The Maharajah leant back with a tremendous air of satisfaction. And that was when Judy decided to try to put in a word for her Uncle Joe.

"I think it's marvellous the way you're having that dam built, Maharajah," she began.

"Well, well. One must do one's best for one's people."

"Yes, I'm sure you do that, Maharajah. But I was wondering . . ."

"Yes, yes, my dear young lady?"

"Well, why don't you go right ahead and let Uncle Joe make full use of the dam? Why don't you let the water irrigate just as much as it possibly can? Think of the extra good it'd do. All those poor people who are starving and who'd be able—"

"Mr. Lloyd."

The Maharajah cut across Judy's innocent plea like a giant liner majestically swamping a bobbing little sailboat. The look in the two little eyes so deep-set in his heavily fleshed face was savage.

"Mr. Lloyd, have you been teaching this young lady to put these views to me? I have said already, and I will not say again: only over my dead body will the water levels in the jheels rise one inch above what they have always been. Is that understood? Is it? Is it?"

Into Joe Lloyd's sun-reddened face a deeper flush spread quickly as a prairie fire.

"Maharajah, I have not put a single damned word into the girl's mouth. I tell you right now I'd scorn to do such a thing. And I'll tell you one more thing. And that's this. You're wrong not to let my dam work to the full. You're damned wrong, and I don't care who hears me say it. What you're doing is murder. Yes, murder. You're killing all the poor guys who would benefit from the water flow. Killing them, Maharajah."

He began to push back his chair, preparatory to storming out. But a cool voice stopped him as if he had suddenly come up against a sheeted barrier of ice. It was the Dewan.

"Mr. Lloyd," he said, "you know, you have not taken all the facts into account."

Joe Lloyd slumped back in his chair. But he still looked furious and suspicious.

"What d'you mean, Dewan?" he said. "I ought to know as much as anyone about what the dam can do, and what it should do."

"Of course, of course. But do you, I wonder, know quite as much about what our poor peasants of Bhopore can do? As much as I do?"

"Well, I don't know."

"No, I think you have not taken the human factor enough into account, Mr. Lloyd. Each of those people, I can promise you, would cheerfully lay down his life, or her life, for their ruler. For his slightest whim, even. It is in their blood, Mr. Lloyd. Haven't you seen how they will walk for miles in the heat just to catch one glimpse of His Highness? They know that with that they will have blessings for weeks and months to come."

"I guess you know best, Dewan. But . . . Oh, hell, let's leave it."

Joe Lloyd subsided completely, and the bearer quietly waiting at his elbow removed his soup plate and replaced it with a plate of elegant little fillets of fish covered with prawn sauce.

For a while conversation was general. The fish was eaten and the bearers put onto the long table the side dishes of the day, chicken in cream sauce with cucumber, or roast duck with green peas and mushrooms. At a table behind the Maharajah's ornate chair the carving of the roasts, roast turkey and roast saddle of buck, began.

The Maharajah reverted to the subject of the Viceroy, his cordial relations with him, the honours that had been bestowed by him during Delhi Week, and the great man's forthcoming visit with his consort to Bhopore.

"Dewan, for the Vicereine we must have Sitara and her rose petals."

"But, Highness . . ."

The Dewan looked a little put out at this announcement. Judy, puzzled, leant forward.

"Maharajah, who's Sitara?" she asked. "Is she some sort of dancer? Does she toss a handful of rose petals over a special guest?"

To her surprise her questions were greeted by a burst of laughter.

"Oh, no, no, my dear young lady," the Maharajah answered at last, wiping tears from his enormous cheeks. "No, no, that is not it at all."

"But what then? Am I making some kind of a fool of myself?"

"No, no. My dear beautiful young lady, if anyone were to make a fool of you, I should have him thrown to the muggers in the lake, I assure you."

Judy looked as if she weren't sure whether this pleased her or not. But she put her question again.

"Then just who is this Sitara, Maharajah?"

"Sitara is . . ."

The Maharajah grinned.

". . . is nothing other than an elephant, my dear. And it is not a handful of rose petals that she flings towards an honoured lady guest. It is a cloud. A cloud of rose petals, blown from her trunk. Rose petals brought from all over India. A truly magnificent sight. A truly magnificent sight, I assure you."

"And a truly expensive one," murmured the Dewan.

It was a foolish thing to say, and uncharacteristic of the cautious Dewan. But evidently he had been driven into unusual exasperation by this new example of the Maharajah's extravagance, a final straw, coming on top of his mysterious talk about a huge business deal with Henry Morton III. So he had allowed the thought that had come into his head to voice itself as a murmured rebuke. It was a rebuke he must at once have hoped had been lost in the clatter made by the bearers as they exchanged the plates on which the roasts had been eaten for those to be used for what was called the "Second Course," a choice between caviar served on biscuits and mounded rice pilau with curry accompaniment.

But with servants as well trained as the Maharajah's there was no clatter at all as plates were swiftly whipped away and others put in their place. So the Dewan's words, though low-voiced, had come clearly to the Maharajah's ears.

For a moment it looked as if there were going to be a second explosion of rage, to cap that which had so lately descended on Joe Lloyd. But the Maharajah was not a man to do the same thing twice. Instead, after just that short interval in which his face had darkened as if a thundercloud had abruptly swept up into it, he turned not to the Dewan but to Henry Morton III. And he turned to him with a smile of great sweetness.

"Mr. Morton," he said, "earlier today I forbade any talk of business. I said that this evening must be for enjoyment only. Mr. Morton, I thought then that the efficient American businessman in you was not quite content with that. Was I right?"

The pudgy-nosed, scarred-faced tycoon gave him a shrewd glance.

"I guess you were, Maharajah. I guess I don't altogether hold with oriental subtlety. If there's a deal to be discussed, Henry Morton wants to get down to business right away."

The Maharajah smiled, smiled like an innocent baby elephant.

"Then shall we talk over that deal here and now?" he said. "I am sure my guests will forgive us."

"Guess the sooner we begin the sooner we get to where we shake hands on it," Henry Morton replied.

The Maharajah smiled.

"In my case, I am afraid, the handshake, if it is reached tonight, will have to be merely symbolic," he said. "Today is one of those unfortunate days when I am untouchable. A religious dictate, you understand."

Henry Morton turned his eyes up to the heavens. What a way to run a business.

"Dewan Sahib," the Maharajah said sharply, "I want you to listen to this most carefully. You may have considerations to bring to bear which I have not thought of."

"Highness," the Dewan acknowledged, biting off the two syllables.

"Now, Mr. Morton," the Maharajah went on, "I understand that you wish to exploit the zinc lying in large quantities beneath the salt lakes of the State?"

"More than that, Maharajah," Henry Morton said. "I want to use the labour you have here. I saw quite enough just on my way from the airfield. There are guys by the hundred here doing nothing but peck at the earth with tools that have been in use since man was little more than a monkey."

"Well, well, Mr. Morton," the Maharajah said, apparently unperturbed by the clear note of criticism in the tycoon's voice. "Well, well, do you think we should provide them with tractors? I am afraid they would not know how to employ them, you know."

"Tractors, hell. No, I want to provide those guys with work for their hands. I want to build factories here, Maharajah, and get those guys into them where they can work on the ore they dig from your lakes. I've had trouble back in the States, I don't mind telling you. Union trouble. Nobody there wants to work anymore. So what I propose to do is to bring my whole operation over here to Bhopore."

He leant back with a look of fierce delight on his face.

"Labour is what you've got for me, Maharajah," he said. "Labour that'll do some work. I guess you know how to keep your guys hard at it still, eh? No nonsense of union hours and union rates here."

The Maharajah looked at him, and then at his Dewan.

"Oh, I am sure that if I were to order men to work for you, they would do it," he said, a little enigmatically.

"Highness."

The Dewan no longer made the two syllables a bitten-off polite reply. Instead there was a whiplash of anger in them.

"Ah, Dewan Sahib. You have some suggestion to make? You can

see a way of providing our good Mr. Morton here with even more workers?"

"Highness, I remember Mr. Morton's letter to you in the first instance. I remember then that we decided that any such proposition was unacceptable."

"Did we, Dewan Sahib? I am sure I do not remember giving any such answer. Why should we think such a scheme unacceptable?"

The Dewan plainly had more than a little difficulty in containing himself. If what the Maharajah had said was in some way punishing him for his rebuke about the expense of entertaining the Viceroy so lavishly, then the punishment more than fitted the crime.

At last he managed to reply.

"Maharajah, the traditions of the State. To make your people into slaves to this—to this gentleman."

"Oh, come, Dewan, come. American workers are not slaves. Why, if we allow Mr. Morton to bring his American methods to Bhopore, should we believe he will make our people into slaves?"

"I guess I'd hope they'd work pretty hard all the same, Maharajah," Henry Morton intervened.

"No, no," the Maharajah went on. "It is modern methods we are bringing in. Isn't it, Mr. Morton? Modern methods. People are always saying that it is Porgy who is the modern one and that I am only an old stick-in-the-mud. But here I am being good and modern."

The Maharajah allowed his two little eyes to slide from his son and heir along the table to where, well separated from Porgy by deliberate decision, Dolly Brattle sat, her peroxide shingle gleaming even among the vividly colourful turbans on either side of her.

But it seemed that his sudden unveiling of his plan to take advantage of the industrial experience of the American tycoon had been a sharper torment to the Dewan than perhaps even he had realised. Because that usually grave and reserved figure now favoured him, and the whole table within earshot, with something of a tirade.

"Highness, you talk about modern methods as if they were something that can only be good. But, Highness, you know that that is not so. How many times have we congratulated ourselves that Bhopore is escaping at least the worst of the dangers of the modern world? That our people, though poorer than many in the West, are content? But what you are proposing to do now, Highness, is to bring in that very poison we have so far fought to keep out. If the people of Bhopore are crowded into factories and made to work long, long hours in conditions hardly fit for any human being, do you believe that it will be long before we have trade unions here? Trade unions in Bhopore. Agitators. Terrorists. Think, Highness. Think, I beg you."

But the Maharajah had not finished with his Dewan yet.

"Dewan Sahib," he replied, his voice quiet, dangerously quiet, "are you suggesting that I have entered into business transactions with my guest, Mr. Morton, without having given the matter due and proper thought?"

"Highness, if you have given the matter thought and if you are still intent on agreeing to this pernicious scheme, then I am afraid I must give you a warning. I must warn you that you are putting yourself into danger, into the very gravest danger."

The Dewan sat back then, waiting for the thunderbolt to strike.

But it did not.

Instead of flashing out anger, of dismissing his long-in-office minister with a single word of fury, the Maharajah politely agreed with him. Or at least agreed as politely as it was in his nature to do.

"Dewan Sahib, I see that, for reasons of your own, no doubt, you are finding objections to Mr. Morton's most interesting proposals. Perhaps in that case you and I better thrash the whole matter out together at some convenient time before I proceed any further with Mr. Morton."

"Certainly, Highness," the Dewan said, guardedly.

"Alas, Mr. Morton," the Maharajah continued, "tomorrow I have arranged for shikar on the jheels first thing, so these discussions will have to be postponed till late in the morning. But perhaps sometime tomorrow afternoon you and I can bring our deal to a conclusion."

His little eyes twinkled at the tycoon.

"And tomorrow, since then I shall be touchable once more, we can conclude in the best American tradition by shaking hands."

"Just so long as the deal goes through," Henry Morton said. "I don't care who or what touches you, Maharajah."

"Oh, but why should you think that the deal will not go through?" the Maharajah replied. "Remember, I am a very, very modern man, altogether as modern as my modern son. And I always carry out what I say I will."

He turned then to Elaine Alcott.

"But, my dear lady, I have been neglecting you. Let me tell you about this shikar—that is our Indian word for hunting, you know— which I hope you will accompany us on tomorrow morning."

"I hope I don't have to shoot any guns myself, Maharajah."

"Oh, but we must teach you to shoot before you leave Bhopore, Mrs. Alcott. We will teach you to shoot as well as—as well as—oh, let us say, as well as a viceroy."

And the Maharajah laughed long and loud.

On Mrs. Alcott's other side Sir Arthur Pendeverel's grave face became yet graver and stonier. Was the fellow cheeking His Excellency? It was pretty well common knowledge that not every viceroy had always hit the tigers that were manoeuvred towards the tree where, safe up on a machaan, he had waited for them, although great care was taken to announce at once that the first shot to wound the beast had come from the viceregal gun and that therefore the kill was to be credited to His Excellency. But, damn it, it wasn't proper to mention things like that, even obliquely. Pity young Porgy hadn't come to the gaddi. There was a straightforward type for you.

"Let me tell you a little of what will happen tomorrow, Mrs. Alcott," the Maharajah went on, smoothly as if nothing of any import had just been said. "We leave very early in the morning. But I am sure you will not mind that. Dawn is most beautiful seen over the still waters of the jheels. There will be quite a large party of us, all my guests, I hope, and—"

But Henry Morton interrupted.

"Maharajah," he said, "I trust you'll excuse me, but to tell you the truth, I won't be going along. You see . . ."

His voice, unexpectedly, faltered. Then abruptly he put up his hand and touched his scarred cheek.

"Well, to tell you the truth, Maharajah," he said, "I used to like hunting a hell of a lot. But, one time I was out, a rifle got something jammed in its barrel, and when I fired with it, it exploded in my face. It was an absolute miracle I wasn't killed. So since then I've never used a weapon again and I never will."

"Of course, Mr. Morton, I understand. A terrible thing to have happened. As you say, it was a miraculous escape. It makes me swear to speak to my gun-bearer myself tonight, to tell him to double-check each and every one of my guns. I was looking forward to a new pair of Purdeys that have just arrived from London. But now I am not so sure that I shall use them. But let us see what the omens tell us. Some bird droppings falling on any member of the party and I will send the guns straight back to London. On the other hand, if we see a mongoose, then I think we need have no anxieties."

"Well, I'd rather trust to taking a good look myself along the barrel of those guns," Henry Morton said. "Yes, sir."

"Oh, I trust my gun-bearer totally," the Maharajah answered. "That post has come down from father to son as long as there have been guns in Bhopore. Thank goodness, there are still some things you can rely on in this world."

And, as if reminded of what was reliable and what was not, the Maharajah, having noted that the cabinet pudding and the sweetly sticky almond badaam kheer had been disposed of by his guests, clapped his hands and ordered his own meal to be brought under its padlocked cover of gold.

It must have been ready and waiting for him, because within a minute his personal bearer, whose hands were noticeably orange-stained from his activities with sapura bark and the Resident's car that afternoon, was solemnly placing the huge dish in front of him. Then from the folds of his cummerbund he extracted a small key, inserted it in the padlock, turned it, and drew back the cover of the dish.

If the Maharajah's guests had done well at the meal he had had served to them, it was at once apparent that he himself was going to do no less well. There were not three or four separate courses on the big gold platter, but instead there was a mound of rice that was truly enormous, all glinting with the good things buried in it. And on top of it there were no fewer than three chickens awaiting their fate.

The Maharajah extended a podgy hand towards the high pile. But before he took a first mouthful he paused and unexpectedly broke into a long chuckling laugh. Politely his guests waited to hear what it was that had suddenly amused their host.

"Oh, we have had such fun today," the Maharajah said at last. "It has been the best April Fools' Day that I remember. Poor Lieutenant Frere, did you enjoy your morning tea?"

James Frere let a sheepish grin spread across his open, cheerful countenance.

"I might have done, Maharajah," he said, "if there hadn't been so much salt in it."

The Maharajah burst into renewed laughter. Then he went on to luxuriate in every joke he had played on his courtiers during the day, false errands of all sorts, food of various kinds replaced with china imitations, delicious drinks of chilled buttermilk laced every one with soap.

In the meantime the great platter of food went untouched. In front of the Maharajah half a dozen servants under the supervision of Captain Ram Singh busied themselves in bringing to the table the silver goods trucks that belonged to the dessert-carrying train. One by one they attached them to the waiting locomotive.

"Sir Arthur," the Maharajah continued, "how about you? Did you by any chance receive a telegram from the Viceroy this morning?"

The Resident allowed a faint smile to hover on his face.

"Why, yes, Maharajah," he said, "a most disquieting piece of news. Summoned back to see His Excellency at once, told that I was to be sent home in disgrace. It gave me a bad quarter of an hour, I can tell you."

"And then you realised that the address on the form was my palace and not the Viceroy's House? Isn't that it? Isn't that it?"

"I did indeed, Maharajah. You can count me as one of your victims."

The Resident leant well back in his chair and permitted himself a discreet and weary sigh.

Only one jape went unmentioned in the Maharajah's catalogue. He made no reference at all to Little Michael and the Rolls-Royce that had not started. Opinion among the select circle who had watched this particular April Fool effort was divided. Some thought that it had been blotted from the Maharajah's mind. Had not Little Michael, so calm and dignified, in his simple request for an elephant to convey him home actually had the last laugh? The more charitable put the omission down to the fact that the Maharajah perhaps would prefer the Resident not to know what had been done to his car on the eve of the Viceroy's important visit.

The laughter rang on round the table, even down to the farthest end, where hardly a word of the Maharajah's exploits was audible. But those lucky enough to scrape their way to sit at that remote end of the table knew well that when the Maharajah was seen to be laughing it was time to laugh themselves.

So when His Highness gave a yet louder roar no one at first believed it was anything other than at a new practical joke.

V

Amid the sycophantic laughter down at the farthest end of the table the roar that the Maharajah had given had certainly passed as just another explosion of April Fools' Day laughter. Even many of the guests at the top end of the long table thought for a little that nothing untoward had occurred. Only those sitting closest to the Maharajah, Mrs. Alcott, the Resident on the other side of her, Judy Alcott opposite, and Henry Morton at her side, actually were able to distinguish the single word that the Maharajah had bellowed out.

"Poison!"

He had a moment earlier, amid the still echoing laughter, carelessly plunged the strong fingers of his plump right hand into the huge mound of richly spiced rice on the golden platter in front of him. He had lifted a deft mouthful towards his lips. And then, at the last second, some whiff of something not quite right must have come to his nostrils.

And the neat little gobbet of rice had been shot from his fingers to fall back at the edge of the softly glinting gold platter, a disfiguring dripping mess.

But soon the import of that single shouted word spread from the four of them who had heard it distinctly along to those nearby. A shocked gasp began to run like a dart of zigzagging lightning all down the length of the huge white-damasked table till it reached the very end. To be succeeded by silence.

A cold, waiting silence that hung in the air. Only from out on the lawn came the steady beat of the brass of the Maharajah's band as the musicians beat out their tune, "A Room with a View." "With no one to worry us, no one to hurry us through."

But the Maharajah had not finished yet.

Slowly he turned in his chair, his two little eyes beadily passing from person to person. For long they rested on the carved stone screen of the balcony at the far end of the long hall. But at last they moved on. On and on they moved, balefully examining.

And then the Maharajah spoke.

"Captain Ram Singh."

The tall A.D.C., immaculately uniformed from the very top of his much pleated turban to the very soles of his dazzlingly polished boots, attempted to keep his full, handsome features masked in total lack of meaning. But he could not. All too plainly to see, for those near where he was standing at the head of the table not two yards from the Maharajah's huge golden dish, a look of fear came into his dark brown eyes. A look of abject fear betrayed itself in a tiny slackening of that full-lipped mouth.

"Captain Ram Singh," the Maharajah repeated, "what are you doing here, at this end of the table? Why are you standing there, so near to me, so near to my food?"

"But— But— But, Highness . . ." The A.D.C. was stammering appallingly. "Highness, it is my duty."

"Duty? What duty?"

"But, Highness, it is always my duty when I am your A.D.C. in attendance and there is a dinner party."

"What are you saying? You traitor. You liar."

"But, Highness, you yourself have seen me many times. It is always my duty to make sure that the trucks on the silver train are coupled on in the right order. It has been my duty for a long time. Your Highness yourself gave orders."

Whatever his bravery confronting a tiger on a jungle shikar expedition or, perhaps yet more vicious, a wild boar goaded beyond endurance by the pigsticking hunters on their dancing ponies, Captain Ram Singh, faced with the wrath of the ruler of Bhopore, had plainly gone to pieces.

That man did it, tried to poison the Maharajah. The thought flashed inexorably into Judy's mind as she sat watching the scene, stunned. I am seeing a crime, a terrible crime. Poison. Murder. I shall remember this as long as I live.

"No, Captain Ram Singh," the Maharajah pronounced. "Whatever excuses you make are as nothing. Nothing. A puff of wind. I know now, clearly as if I had eaten that rice and was writhing on the ground here in agony, that you have tried to kill me. The poison is on your person still. The poison. The little bottle. The flask. It will be there. The evidence."

"But, Highness . . . No. No. Please listen. It's not so. I promise. I beg. Highness . . ."

Captain Ram Singh began then at last to pull himself out of the wild panic that had assailed him.

He licked his dry lips beneath his luxuriant moustache.

"Highness, if I am guilty, if I have the evidence on me still, search me. Highness, have me searched."

"Yes," said the Maharajah. "Yes, that is what we shall do. We shall have you searched, and then we shall have proof."

He stood for a moment beside the cooling mound of rich spiced rice on its gold dish and he glared at the A.D.C., a figure of massive menace.

"But who shall search him?" he said at last. "Who can I trust not to lie to me, not to try to deceive me?"

He swung round and looked at the guests still seated or half standing round the long table.

"Nobody," he muttered. "Nobody will tell me the truth and no more."

Then his still travelling gaze stopped.

"Yes," he said. "Yes, there is one. There is one I can trust to tell me without a shadow of a lie just what he finds on Captain Ram Singh's person. Lieutenant Frere, would you be so kind as to do me a small favour?"

James Frere got slowly to his feet. His fresh-complexioned face paled a little. But the gaze of his bright blue eyes was steady. Steady as he would be facing a charge by wild tribesmen on the Northwest Frontier.

"Of course, Maharajah," he said.

"Very good. Lieutenant Frere, would you take Captain Ram Singh out, perhaps to your rooms, and would you be so good as to search him? To search him, Mr. Frere, from top to toe, so that you will find even the smallest phial."

"Yes, Maharajah. I understand."

James Frere's fresh face was white now as paper. But his gaze was level still.

He pushed back his chair, stepped away from the table, and walked over to where the A.D.C. was still rooted to the ground.

"Captain Ram Singh," he said, in a tone that well mixed polite inquiry and a stubborn authority.

"Of course, Lieutenant," Captain Ram Singh answered, matching his tone to the young Englishman's.

Together the two of them went, marching with stiff military precision, all the way down the length of the banqueting hall and out through the far arched doorway.

In James Frere's set of rooms, conveniently close to the banqueting hall, the two of them went in complete silence into the Indian-style bathroom.

"I'll have to ask you to take off your clothes," James Frere said, in scrupulously clipped tones.

"Yes. Of course."

Captain Ram Singh was as clipped.

Carefully and precisely he undressed, handing each garment as he took it off to the Englishman. James Frere examined each one with complete care. Not a fold, not a tuck escaped him. Every pocket was emptied of its contents. A penknife with blade for extracting stones from horses' hooves, five rupees, and one two-anna piece, an old and very crumpled letter, of which James Frere scrupulously avoided reading even so much as the address. Each he laid out carefully on the small wooden stool on which ordinarily he sat while his servant poured deliciously cool bath water over him. A handful of little miscellaneous bits was added.

"The golf tee belongs to the Willingdon Club in Bombay, I am sorry to say," Captain Ram Singh murmured as that final humiliating scrap was laid down.

"I'm afraid I'll have to carry out a body search now," James replied, hardly muttering less.

"Yes. Of course."

But the most rigorous search revealed nothing in the nature of phial, bottle, pillbox, or any other possible container of poison.

"That's all then," James said at last. "And may I add that I'm delighted myself that nothing's come to light. Of course, I never believed it would."

"Thank you," said Captain Ram Singh.

He got dressed again, crammed into his pockets at least his major possessions, as well as the Willingdon Club's golf tee, and then the two of them marched out and along the wide and echoing marble corridor back to the banqueting hall. They marched, footsteps smartly cracking down, all the way up the length of the long room, watched by guests silently setting down coffee cups on saucers. They came at last to the Maharajah, just finishing consuming a fresh dish of rice and three freshly served chickens, miraculously brought in hardly any time at all from the kitchens.

"I beg to report, sir," said Lieutenant Frere, "that I have searched Captain Ram Singh with the utmost thoroughness and that I found nothing whatsoever of an incriminating nature."

"Thank you, Mr. Frere."

The Maharajah turned towards his A.D.C.

"Do not believe, Captain Ram Singh," he said, "that you have escaped me. Perhaps you did not have any poison on your person. Perhaps even my food was not poisoned at all."

His little eyes flashed as they darted here and there over the tall A.D.C.'s person.

"But nevertheless I am not letting any enemy of mine go free to plot against me. Do not believe that."

He barked out a sharp command to the two immensely tall Sikh guards at the doorway behind him. They came up at a run, seized Captain Ram Singh by the elbows, and before anyone could express any reaction at all, they had hustled him out.

The Maharajah clapped his hands.

"And now," he said, "we must start the little train. Departure has been disgracefully delayed. All is loaded, yes?"

A servant uttered a respectful, "Huzoor."

"Very well," the Maharajah said, his face beaming with all the benevolence of a shining golden full moon. "I press the button."

He leant forward and put a firm finger on the silver button in its silver mounting just in front of him. The delicately modelled silver locomotive gave a sharp little whistle-shriek and the train moved sedately off.

"Quick, Mrs. Alcott, quick," the Maharajah shouted. "Lift something off. Lift off some nuts, some crystallised fruit, some port perhaps. Lift, or you will miss the train."

"Oh. Oh. Oh, dear. What? What shall I—"

"Mother, the nuts. You love nuts," Judy called.

Mrs. Alcott seized the two silver handles of the nut dish inside its silver goods truck. At once as she lifted it the little train came to a halt. She helped herself.

"Now, if I put it back, does it go off again, Maharajah?" she asked.

"Yes, yes. Just see. Just see."

Captain Ram Singh, accused without evidence, hustled away to some dark, appalling dungeon, was forgotten as the little elegant silver train ran down the length of the table, encouraged by shouts and commands from the broadly smiling Maharajah.

"Halt it, halt it, Porgy. Take something. No. No, don't take that. Don't take the crème de cacao. Take port. Take port."

Before long the line of silver trucks reached the outer territories, where it was not done to arrest their progress by taking any of the goodies they carried, no sweet nuts, no consoling port, no sticky chocolaty crème de cacao, no sugar-coated chunks of crystallised fruit.

Watched by fifty pairs of eyes, the little train rounded the curve at the far end of the table and made its way steadily back towards the parts where it was permitted to lift out the interior lining of a truck, to bring the small toy to a halt, to select something to eat or drink, to replace the basket and send it on its way again.

"No, Miss Brattle, take port. Take port."

The Maharajah seemed to resent Dolly's attraction to the truck with its squat bottle of dark crème de cacao—she loved everything really sweet—as much as he resented the possibility of his son and heir sneaking off somewhere to marry this low-caste Englishwoman.

"Now, Mr. Morton, it is you. Take. Take."

"Oh, I think I'd prefer just a cigar."

"No, take, Mr. Morton. Take while you can. Take crème de cacao."

With a shrug the scar-faced American reached forward, grasped the heavy opened bottle of crème de cacao by its neck, lifted it, began to bring the silver train to a halt—and released a well-concealed powerful spring which sent the whole bottle shooting up towards him like a jack-in-a-box.

A thick stream of dark, chocolaty, sticky liquid spurted all over white starched shirt-front, immaculate white tuxedo.

"April Fool, April Fool," trumpeted the Maharajah. "Oh, Mr. Morton, what a good one, what a beauty! It was worth bringing you all the way from America for that."

He sat in his huge chair at the head of the enormous table shaking with laughter like a huge jelly.

Henry Morton III took it pretty well. He did not manage to laugh. But neither did he curse.

He had leapt back from the table as the thick chocolate-coloured jet had swooshed up at him, and he stood now with the sticky liquid trickling heavily down his white tuxedo and slowly brought onto his scarred face a sort of smile.

"Guess I ought to have seen that one coming, Maharajah," he said.

Next to him Porgy, too, had got to his feet. His features wore an expression of sharp irritation bordering on anger.

"Father," he said, "really this time you have gone too far. What will a progressive person like Mr. Morton think of us?"

"Pooh, pooh," said the Maharajah. "It is not everything to be progressive, Porgy. You will learn that in time. And besides, April Fool jokes are a very old tradition, a very old Western tradition. It is right that we should keep up things like that."

Porgy plainly despaired of bringing his father to a sense of the outrage he had committed. He turned instead to the American tycoon.

"Mr. Morton, please accept my apologies. On behalf of my father. You are really in a dreadful mess. We must get that dinner jacket off before the stuff ruins your trousers too."

"Well, I guess I'm not going to be able to wipe it up any," Henry Morton answered, still outwardly not too much perturbed.

"Don't worry. Don't worry. The bearers will cope. I'll find you somewhere to wash."

And so Porgy, making deliberately heavy weather of their departure by way of silent rebuke to his father, escorted the tycoon all the way down the length of the banqueting hall. It was a tribute to the power of the fuss he was making that hardly anyone dared to raise his voice above a discreet murmur for the whole of the time that it took the pair of them to make their way out. And even after they had passed through the far doorway Porgy's voice, perhaps raised a little on purpose, could be heard offering excuses and explanations.

". . . every April the first . . . same thing every time . . . only this afternoon he . . ."

Abruptly up at the top of the table the Maharajah lumbered to his feet, holding in front of him a glass charged with champagne. Outside, where the bandmaster had been anxiously peering in, awaiting just this signal, the crash of the opening bars of "God Save the King" sounded loud and brassy from the lawn.

"Your Excellency, ladies and gentlemen," the Maharajah proclaimed, "I give you a toast. Your Excellency, ladies and gentlemen, the King-Emperor."

They stood, they drank, they murmured their loyalty. Dinner was over. The Maharajah, more splendidly alive than ever, strolled among his guests, speaking with happy expectation of the morning's shooting on the jheels that awaited them next day.

"It will delight you, I promise. It will be a most wonderful day, the most wonderful day of my life."

VI

For breakfast they ate bacon and eggs washed down with either whisky and soda or hock and seltzer. The Maharajah's cellars had a particularly good range of hocks, Johannisberg Originalabfallungs, Erbach Kabinettweins, Rudesheim Goldbeerenausleses. So they were a lively party as they set out in the still dark night before the sun had begun to whiten the distant horizon.

Even Mrs. Alcott felt happy, though she had woken dreading the day ahead with all the complications of an unknown experience, of perhaps being made by the Maharajah—he could force me to do anything, if it entered his head, I know he could—to use one of his new guns. What were they called? Pearlies? Birdies? And of ending up by shooting dead some poor innocent peasant.

Judy, of course, was simply tingling with delight even before she had drunk her half glass of hock and seltzer. She was living in a palace, a real palace. She had sent her servant—well, one of the Maharajah's bearers—to the Tea Pantry for her early morning tea, and then there had been that breakfast long before light with—with him there. James. Lieutenant James Frere. Oh, my gosh.

Joe Lloyd was not quite so ecstatic. How could he be? But he felt pretty good, on the whole. He had been out on these shikar expeditions to the jheels before, and setting everything else aside, they were great. The still water of the lakes with the dawn light coming onto them here in India slows for just a little and then rushes in and brings with it the birds. More birds than you could count, and great sport. Great sport. So think of that, and don't think of anything else. Anything else at all.

Porgy was of much the same opinion. It went back to his earliest boyhood, to the time when he had loved and reverenced Papa above all else on earth. To before the quarrels. To before the time he had realised just what sort of a man his father was. So now, forget everything else; just think about the Imperial sandgrouse coming winging their way in—in their thousands, and of getting the rhythm of shooting just right, the way he had learnt long ago by watching Papa. Think of the birds and bringing them down. Think of nothing, nothing else.

Dolly, standing close to Porgy the whole time and having downed several whisky and sodas rather fast, had at least begun to feel more cheerful than when she had been woken in the dark. Go through with it. That was the answer. Go through with everything.

The Resident had arrived after the Maharajah's breakfast was over, driving to the Summer Palace in his car with Little Michael. He was in good spirits. In a reserved manner.

Thank goodness, he thought, Ahmed had managed to deal with that minor breakdown yesterday, whatever it was. Not like a Rolls to play up, but even a Rolls couldn't be faultless in this damned climate. But he was here. That was the main thing. Here for a grand morning's shikar. After all, sport was the great thing that united people. This was where they could be equals, almost. Old Rudyard was right. "But there is neither East nor West, Border, nor Breed, nor Birth. When two strong men stand face to face, though they come from the ends of the earth." Hope young Michael won't make a fool of himself.

And Michael, though like his father only tea and porridge had crossed his lips that dark early morning, was bubbling over with delight to come out on the shikar. With Father. Even if he didn't succeed in bagging a single bird, what could be more marvellous? To be doing what Father did.

Lieutenant James Frere, though he could give Little Michael some sixteen years, was almost as excited. Shikar. The light in the far sky, first pale yellow, then soon tinged with red. And the lakes coming into view, and then— Then the birds coming beating and pouring in, if only half what old Porgy had told him was true. It was going to be a day's sport to tell his grandchildren about. And Judy to watch him. Judy. Would she . . . ? Was it possible that Judy was going to be the grandmother of James Frere's grandchildren? Judy, who . . . It was too overwhelming even to think about.

Even the Dewan felt a sense of quiet pleasure although, good Muslim that he was, not a drop of hock, not a drop of whisky, had crossed his lips. He was not going to shoot, though he felt it his duty to be present, and he had never shirked doing what he knew to be his duty. And the beauty of the morning, the beauty of beautiful Bhopore, would be compensation for many, many things that had to be compensated for. The beauty of Bhopore, it was worth a lot, a very, very great deal.

Even Henry Morton III, despite the revelation at dinner the night before of why his face was scarred and why he would never use a gun again, had turned up. Perhaps it was by way of showing the Maharajah that he bore him no grudge for the crème de cacao incident. Nobody had liked to ask him exactly what had made him change his mind. But the Maharajah—he was touchable today—had pressed whisky and soda on him with his own hands.

And the Maharajah himself? There could be no doubting that he was in the very best of spirits. He went from guest to guest, joking, cajoling, encouraging, boasting. He supervised with a great many shouted orders the safe departure of his many guns. They were carried in a special large wooden rack, each gun in its allotted slot, the whole carefully locked with a wooden bar secured by a padlock to which only the Maharajah's gun-bearer, a dark, silent individual wearing a much darned khaki shirt and shorts, had a key.

"Well, well, are we all ready? Shall we go? We must be at the jheels before it gets light. The cars are waiting. Come. Come."

He bustled them cheerfully out. The cars were all there, neatly lined up, Rolls-Royces, Daimlers, and several lesser breeds, a Marmon Straight Eight, a Vauxhall Richmond.

"Mother, I hope you've 'On no account loaded your gun,'" Judy whispered.

"My gun? My gun?" Mrs. Alcott looked wildly round her.

"Mother, I was only quoting from *General Information for Our Guests*. Remember? We don't have any guns. They're all being safely looked after by the gun-bearers."

"Well, thank goodness for that. We don't want any nasty accidents like the one that happened to Mr. Morton."

"Oh, Mother, don't be silly. That must have been carelessness, and no one's going to be careless today."

James Frere, standing close to Judy—where else?—chipped in.

"I should jolly well hope not, Mrs. Alcott. I mean, there are Englishmen here, I think you can count on decent standards being kept up."

"But what if the Maharajah doesn't see a mongoose?" Judy said.

"Mongoose? What mongoose?"

"Oh, James, don't you remember? He said if he saw a lucky mongoose this morning everything would be okay. But what's a mongoose look like, anyway? That's what I want to know."

"Oh, they're jolly little beasts. Furry, you know. But I can't imagine how His Highness is going to spot one now. Too dashed dark."

And, indeed, it was still much too dark for anybody to have seen anything by the wayside, even the Maharajah's keen-eyed Schoolmaster, had he been among the distinguished guests instead of being in his humble home in the twelve miles' distant city of Bhopore itself having the last of his night's sleep. But if the Maharajah thought of his hope of a good omen and was disappointed, he said nothing.

The cars came to a halt and the party got out and were directed by flashlight and lantern to their butts at the edge of the great calm expanse of the jheels.

The little predawn wind felt almost cold, but they did not have long to wait. Hardly had the gun-bearers seen that every marksman had his weapon with the loader in position, with the second guns behind them, when the first faint pale lemony streaks of day appeared on the distant horizon. A moment later they were reflected in almost invisible pale streaks on the still water.

Then, quite suddenly, the sky took on its first tinge of pinky-red. And the whole huge dome of the heavens above, which when they had set out had still been pricked with pale stars, moved imperceptibly from blue-black to an overarching pallor. The shape of the land round the unmoving water of the lakes began to be just discernible.

And then, after a single long hush, the first heralds of the sandgrouse could be heard as a tiny insistent drumming of wings.

For three days before the birds had been prevented from drinking. Every tank where water was stored for the villages, every pond, every stream had been patrolled by village boys with just this object. Sticks and stones and shouts and dancing up and down had disturbed any bird that had sought to drink anywhere. The Maharajah had had a considerable sum disbursed with this sole object. So now the thirst-crazed birds came down towards the still and unmolested jheels in their thousands. Elsewhere, wherever they were likely to descend for miles and miles around, the boys were there as usual, shouting and threatening. But here, to the birds, it must have looked as if at last they had found somewhere to slake their thirst to the full.

In a dense cloud that stretched out for hundreds of yards as daylight flooded in, they came. And as they skimmed the water, the sound of the guns broke out. Bird after bird fell and floated to await the little electric boat which the Maharajah would have sent out later to pick them up. Traditionally they would be taken then to the magnificent flight of marble steps in front of the Summer Palace. There they would be laid out in long rows. The people who had taken part in the shikar would be told that all was ready. They would come and stand in a somewhat self-conscious line all along the top of the steps with the Maharajah, massively outtopping them all, in the centre. And the palace photographer would duck under the dark cloth of his heavy instrument on its solid tripod and the photograph would be taken.

Then in the evening the cooks in the palace kitchens would take the pick of the birds, the plumpest out of as many as three thousand shot in one morning, and they would plunge each one into a huge vat of boiling oil, removing in an instant feathers and skin and cooking the flesh to perfection. There would be great eating in the banqueting hall that night.

But now the business of getting the biggest bag possible was in full swing. Judy, not trusting herself with a gun any more than her mother did, had stepped back from the butt to which she had been ushered with the intention of watching James. For a little she had done so, indeed. She had watched his crown of unruly fair hair and had admired his profile as his gun had swung up, steadied, fired.

But before long her eye had been caught by another sight. The Maharajah in action.

Much as she admired James, she saw that his skill was only rudimentary compared with that of this hulk of a man, apparently so ungainly. But ungainly with a gun in his hands he was not. He worked to a rhythm that was as appealing to the eye as that of any dancer. As the sandgrouse flew in their hundreds over him he swung his gun in time to their flight, fired one barrel, fired another, tossed the gun to a waiting loader, reached out to his gun-bearer for a second gun, fired just one barrel of that, and still swinging round in time to the flight of the birds above him, took a third gun, fired its first barrel, fired its second. And so far as Judy could see, looking from the rhythmically moving man to the bird-crowded sky above, each shot brought down a victim.

It was magnificent.

She was not at all sure that she liked the notion of the birds being massacred in this way. When one of them had fallen at the edge of the lake quite near her she had seen how beautiful it was, and had experienced a momentary pang. But the Maharajah was beautiful, too. Yes, beautiful. That was the word for him. The rhythm and precision of his actions were a thing of sheer beauty.

He halted for a moment now, wiping the sweat from his forehead with a large silk handkerchief.

"Very good," he called out. "Bring up the Purdeys now, bearer. We'll see if they're as good as they look."

He took his stance again. The gun-bearer handed him the first of his new pair of Purdeys, which even Judy could see to be objects of marvellous workmanship.

Another flight of sandgrouse came in low over the lake, winging their way fast towards them. The Maharajah raised the gun, gracefully swung himself into the speed of the flight. One barrel went off with a subdued crack. Out of the corner of her eye Judy saw a bird drop from the swift-winging flight. Hardly had it begun to do so when the second barrel from the first Purdey brought down another bird just a little behind it.

Judy saw the gun-bearer, almost as adroit as the Maharajah himself, swing forward the second Purdey. The Maharajah caught it without the least deviation from his rhythm. It followed for an instant the flight of the birds above. There came a sharp crack. The bearer beside the Maharajah was already swinging forward with the next gun.

And then he stopped.

And then Judy realised that the whole swinging, swaying rhythm that was the Maharajah and his guns had stopped. It had been broken.

The Maharajah was falling away from the pattern he had established. His whole body was falling. And the crack of the Purdey. It had not been the subdued yet powerful sound that the two barrels of the first gun had made. It had been an explosion. A cracking, ugly explosion.

And now the Maharajah was on the ground. A great inert mass. And bloody. He was dead. Dead beyond any doubting.

Judy screamed. She screamed and screamed and screamed. Yet even as she did so, while there seemed to be no room in her head except for the ringing sound of her own voice, she was aware that nearby and farther away the sounds of gunfire were dying out. Before, it had been like being on a battlefield. Shots had come every few seconds, sometimes in volleys, sometimes as single sharp reports.

Then there had been that one report louder than the rest, perhaps masked by the noise all round to people not as near to the Maharajah as she was. And then she had seen that huge body fall, had realised that the Maharajah, one moment before such a picture of life, so graceful, and so active despite his great size, was dead beyond all possible doubting. So she had screamed. And others near, the gun-bearer, the loader, had shouted. And gradually everybody in the butts had realised that something terrible had happened. One by one they had ceased shooting and let the huge dark flocks of sandgrouse wing their way unmolested into the jheels. One by one they had turned to where the sound of shouts and screaming was coming from. One by one they had realised that tragedy had struck.

Judy stopped screaming.

"I'm sorry. I'm really so sorry," she said to no one in particular. "I don't know what . . ."

She felt an arm round her shoulders. A voice spoke.

"Judy, it's all right. Don't scream. It's all right now. You've had a terrible shock, but it's all right now."

It was James. Even in her fright and misery she felt a little tingle of pleasure. And at once berated herself for it.

"But—but he's dead," she said. "He is dead, isn't he?"

"Yes," James said. "I'm afraid he is dead. There can't be any question of that. What a terrible thing to happen. What an appalling accident."

He fell silent. Everywhere it was silent now. No one spoke. The only sounds to be heard were the thrumming of the wings of the sandgrouse still flying, thirst-crazed, to the water and from somewhere behind the song of another bird. An insistent, hammering song. Judy felt it gradually building up in her head in a nightmarish way. On and on. "You're ill, you're ill," it seemed to say. "You're ill, you're ill." And then it answered itself. "We know it, we know it." On and on. "You're ill, you're ill. We know it. We know it."

Later James was to tell her the name of the bird. The brain-fever bird. But at present the sound seemed less a birdcall than a terrible inward hammering.

Then she was aware of a commotion. A rapid movement on the ground not far from the huge slumped mound of the Maharajah's body.

It was the Maharajah's chief shikari, a lean, khaki-clad man, grey-haired and keen-eyed, the expert on all forms of hunting, on the flight of the sandgrouse, on the way to manoeuvre a massive tiger eight or ten miles across open country until at last it presented itself in front of the tree where a viceroy sat with his gun. The man had been on his knees, not beside his dead master but beside the treacherous Purdey that had exploded in his face and killed him instantly.

And now he had risen to his feet. The movement had been sudden, decisive, and purposeful. It had attracted not only her attention but also that of almost everybody else in the grim circle round the body. As one they turned to look at the lean, experienced old hunter.

"Maharajah," he said, turning to face Porgy.

There was a little shiver among the onlookers.

Yes, there was a new maharajah now. His Highness Maharajah-dhiraj Raj Rajeshwar Lieutenant Colonel Sri Sri Sri Sahib Bahadur Mahapundit Mahasurma Sir Albert Singhi, Grand Commander of the Order of the Star of India, Grand Commander of the Order of the Indian Empire, Doctor of Literature (Benares), Maharajah of Bhopore was dead. Long live His Highness Maharajahdhiraj Raj Rajeshwar Sri Sri Sri Sahib Bahadur Mahapundit Mahasurma George Singhi, Maharajah of Bhopore, known to his friends as Porgy, and no doubt to collect in due course a knighthood, membership of the Order of the Star of India and of the Order of the Indian Empire, an honorary lieutenant colonelcy, and an honorary doctorate from the University of Benares.

It seemed to take Porgy himself just a moment to realise it was he who was being addressed. But it was only a moment. Then he turned to the lean old shikari, and as he did so seemed to take on in an instant all that weight of honours that had been borne so lightly yet with such dignity by his father.

"Yes, Kishen," he said. "What is it?"

"Maharajah, I have looked at the Purdey. It was not an accident that made it explode."

Of all the silent circle round it seemed to be only Porgy, the new Maharajah, who grasped at once the meaning of what the shikari had said.

"Not an accident?" he repeated. "Then something was done to the gun. Was it that, Kishen? Was it that?"

"Ji, Maharajah. I have looked well at the barrel of the gun. Maharaj, into it someone had pushed something. I can tell even what that thing was, Maharaj."

Porgy's shoulders distinctly grew straighter at the old shikari's words. A look of fury, of cold fury, came onto his face.

"And what was it that had been put in the gun's barrel, Kishen?" he said in a voice of leaden weight.

"Maharaj, it was a piece of sapura bark. A piece of sapura bark was pushed deep into the barrel of the gun and then it was wetted, Maharaj. Of that I am certain."

VII

It was the Resident who spoke first. "Then it was murder," he said. "The Maharajah was murdered."

His words beat out in the silence like a judge pronouncing sentence. Even the brain-fever bird had stopped its insistent song. Only the faint sound of the wings of the sandgrouse could be heard, beating and beating overhead.

Judy realised then that deep down she had known all along. From the moment her reluctant eyes had traced the fall of the Maharajah's body, transformed in an instant from graceful movement to sacklike heaviness, she had known that the gun he had at that instant fired had not exploded in any accident. It could not have done. The Maharajah was too experienced a shot to have allowed any weapon into his hands about which he was not totally satisfied. His gun-bearer was too reliable for any mistake to have occurred. And the evening before they had had that warning when Henry Morton had told of his horrible experience as a young man. No, it was murder. The gun barrel had been deliberately blocked.

The others round seemed to have been thinking much the same thoughts because after the Resident had voiced the idea aloud there was a long pause. And then there came a buzz of questions and exclamations.

The quick muttering, person to person, questioning and replying, was stilled by the Dewan.

He stepped out of his place in the rough circle that had formed round the dead man's body and faced them all.

"Sir Arthur," he said to the Resident, "I have no doubt that what you have just told us is no more than the truth. His Highness could never have used a gun that had not been properly and carefully examined. Someone must have blocked that barrel. But that action tells us something more. Something that limits the circle of people who could have performed that act."

Eyes darted hither and thither. Eyes looking at those next to them in a new light. Suspicious eyes, probing eyes, thoughtful eyes, and perhaps evasive eyes.

They had all been ready to acknowledge inwardly that it had been murder. The logic of it all had been too strong. But no one, it seemed, had gone that one step further and had asked, "If it was murder, who then is the killer?" And now the Dewan's chilly words had made everybody think that thought.

And, worse, he had indicated that the killer was not just one person out of the thousands in Bhopore, not even just one out of the hundreds in the palace. He had indicated that the circle was a narrow one, a very narrow one.

"Well, Dewan?" Sir Arthur asked sharply.

"Your Excellency, you cannot have known, but yesterday His Highness, His late Highness, played a simple April Fools' Day trick that involved the use of sapura bark. I very much doubt, indeed, if you yourself know the properties of sapura bark."

"I can't say I do, Dewan. What is sapura bark? I don't think I'd ever heard of it till Kishen spoke of it just now."

"That doesn't surprise me, Your Excellency. There are very few sapura trees in India, and of them most are to be found in the remotest parts of this State. Occasionally on the normally thin bark of this obscure tree a knot of some sort gathers. And this knot of bark has a most curious property. Though normally very soft and easy to mould, or to push for instance down quite a narrow tube, once it gets into contact with a little water it hardens to an iron hardness. Yesterday, Your Excellency, in front of only a small audience, His late Highness had some of a piece of bark, which had been brought to him, as his right, only that morning, stuffed into the exhaust of Your Excellency's car."

"Yes, that's right, Father." It was Little Michael. Though he had been standing very quietly just behind the Resident, none of them had realised that he was there.

"It's really right, Father. The Maharajah played a trick on me. I didn't tell you because I thought you'd get in a bate. But he did. And I asked him for an elephant instead of the car and came all the way home on that."

"Michael," the Resident said sharply, "this is no place for you, my boy. Now I want you to go straight back to the car, and tell Ahmed to drive you home. Wait for me there."

"But, Father, I was telling you—"

"Enough, Michael. Remember, the head and the hoof and the haunch and the hump."

"Yes, Father."

Little Michael turned on his heel and walked away, a small white-clad figure under a large white topi in the open dusty country. No one spoke as they watched him make his way towards the place where the cars were parked.

When he was almost out of sight the Resident gave a little dry cough.

"Now, Dewan," he said, "perhaps you would finish explaining to me what you were saying when we were interrupted."

"Certainly, Sir Arthur. And in fact your son was doing no more than confirming the point I was making. Sapura bark is very rare. A piece was brought to the palace yesterday morning, the first for almost thirty years, and was in His late Highness's possession until he gave a portion of it to his personal bearer to put in the exhaust pipe of your car, Your Excellency. An April Fools' Day jape."

The Dewan shrugged his elegant shoulders.

"Now, the point I am making is this," he continued. "Very few people know about sapura bark. You yourself did not, Sir Arthur. But even fewer people saw that demonstration yesterday of just how effective the bark is when it is pushed into a narrow cylinder of any sort. The fact that the Maharajah's death occurred in exactly the same manner cannot be a coincidence. It cannot be so in any way."

Sir Arthur looked down steadily at the bulk of the Maharajah's body. Already there were a few flies buzzing round it.

"Yes, Dewan," he said. "I am inclined to agree with you."

He gave another of his little dry coughs.

"More," he added. "Giving the matter my full consideration, I cannot but feel that you are precisely right. The Maharajah's murder was a direct copy of that somewhat unfortunate joke yesterday. There can be no doubt of it."

"And can there be any doubt of the consequences, Your Excellency?" the Dewan asked.

"The consequences?" Sir Arthur said sharply.

"That the person responsible for the death of His Highness must have been one of those few who saw that joke take place. Little Michael, as he was telling you, in fact rather turned the tables in that affair. He requested, with considerable dignity, that an elephant be fetched from the hathikhana to convey him home. The Maharajah felt, I know, that he had been rebuked. It was very clear that no one was to talk of the incident again. You will remember that at dinner last night when he was recounting his April Fool successes of the day not a word was said about the incident with your car."

"Yes. Yes, that's quite right. I knew nothing at all of it. So what you are saying, Dewan, is that only those present then would have had the idea of putting this—this sapura bark into His Highness's Purdey?"

"Exactly so, Your Excellency."

Sir Arthur straightened his back, protected by its spine pad, just a fraction more.

"Very well then, Dewan. Name those names. I take it you are in a position to do so."

"Yes, Your Excellency. I am in such a position. Because I myself was there. So, first, I name myself."

The Dewan looked straight into Sir Arthur's cold eyes.

"Very good, Dewan. I note your name. And the others?"

"There were not many of us, Your Excellency. Most of His Highness's guests had not even arrived in the State at that time. Mrs. Alcott and Miss Alcott were still in their train. Mr. Henry Morton was still in His Highness's aeroplane. So there are left, I think, only four others. Or five, if one includes Little Michael."

"And that," Sir Arthur said, "I think one need not do. So, the four?"

The Dewan turned to Porgy, to the new Maharajah. He gave him a little formal bow.

"There is His Highness first of all," he said. "Of course it is unthinkable that . . . But nevertheless you were there, Highness, were you not?"

"Yes, Dewan, I was there. And it is right that you should include me on your list."

"Thank you, Highness."

The Dewan bowed again.

"And who are the other three?" Sir Arthur asked.

"There was Miss Brattle, Your Excellency. You know Miss Brattle, I believe?"

Sir Arthur sighed.

"Yes, I have met Miss Brattle."

From her place in the circle near Porgy, Dolly Brattle, platinum shingled hair bright beneath her protective hat, stepped back a quick half pace.

"I— I wasn't—" she said.

The Resident looked at her with cold contempt.

"You were not what, Miss Brattle?"

Dolly turned visibly paler under the deep shade of her wide-brimmed hat. Then she looked defiantly across at the Resident.

"I wasn't there," she said. "I wasn't watching the man put the whatever-it-is bark into your car. I don't know anything about it."

The Resident turned to the Dewan. He did not speak, but by the merest cock of an eyebrow asked the question, "Is the woman lying?"

The Dewan remained totally impassive.

"I think, Your Excellency," he said, "that Miss Brattle has become somewhat confused. Most naturally confused in view of the horrible circumstances in which we all find ourselves. She was not, of course, present when His Highness's bearer put the sapura bark into the exhaust of Your Excellency's car. But, of course, she was there with all the rest of us when the actual trick was played on Little Michael."

He turned towards Dolly.

"With all the rest of us, I'm sure you remember, Miss Brattle," he said.

Dolly gave Porgy beside her one quick glance. It was a look that said, plainly as if words had been spoken aloud, "Please, help me, Porgy. Please tell them I wasn't there, even though I was. Please get me out of this."

Standing tall where he had been when Kishen, the old shikari, had told him that his father had been murdered, Porgy looked straight ahead into the far distance, to where on the jheels still the sand-grouse in their hundreds were flying to the life-giving water.

Dolly reluctantly turned to the Dewan again.

"Yes," she said. "Yes, you're quite right, Dewan Sahib. I made a mistake. A silly mistake."

She tried to produce a girlish laugh. It was not a great success.

The Resident continued to regard her with the unblinking severity of a judge.

"Let us get matters quite clear, Miss Brattle," he said. "You were present when that trick was played on my son? You saw what could be done with sapura bark?"

"Well, yes, Your Excellency. That is— Yes, but—"

Tears sprang up in her eyes, those eyes surrounded by tiny wrinkles that each morning careful powdering sought to obliterate.

"Yes, I was there, Your Excellency. You know that. I said it. I told you. I admitted that. But— But I didn't understand what was going on. I promise you that. I don't understand lots that goes on in this country. And I didn't understand what was happening out there on the steps. Honest, I didn't."

The Resident winced visibly at those last words, a lapse into a more vulgar form of speech than Dolly generally managed.

"Very well, Miss Brattle," he said. "You have stated your position, and of course, we must respect it."

He turned to the Dewan again.

"And the others present at that display?" he asked.

"There was me," James Frere said. "I've a feeling I was rather brought out there to be an audience for the Maharajah's joke, and I must say I certainly caught on to what had happened. Sapura bark and everything."

"Thank you, Lieutenant," Sir Arthur said.

"There is one thing, though," James Frere added.

"Yes?"

"Well, I don't quite like to say this, but there was your driver there, sir."

"Ahmed?"

The Resident considered briefly.

"Yes," he said. "Ahmed must certainly have known what had happened to my car. He'd have had to get rid of that sapura bark somehow before I drove over to the Summer Palace last night for dinner. But I don't see how he could have got hold of the rest of the bark afterwards. The stuff doesn't soften up again, I take it, Dewan."

"No, Your Excellency. Once it has been wetted and grown hard it stays hard as rock, hard as iron ever afterwards. I am afraid Ahmed will have had to replace the exhaust pipe of your car."

"Yes, well, I daresay he did. He's a good man. Knows what he's about. But I think in that case we can rule him out as possibly having been responsible for this morning's dreadful business."

Joe Lloyd, dustily red-haired, wearing khaki that looked as if it had seen more and tougher service than a few well-organised shikar parties, stepped forward now.

"I guess, Sir Arthur, I'm the only other person who saw that trick performed yesterday," he said. "I remember thinking that they hadn't rustled up as many people to watch as the Maharajah would have liked. Though when that kid of yours upped and ordered his elephant, I suppose the old boy must have been pretty glad not too many people had seen."

"Dewan," Sir Arthur asked, "do you confirm that this was the whole extent of the audience on that occasion?"

"No, Sir Arthur. Mr. Lloyd has forgotten that Captain Ram Singh was there. Though, of course, he was—er—not able to be present this morning. So he, together with your driver and your son, cannot be taken into account. And that leaves His present Highness and Miss Brattle and Lieutenant Frere and Mr. Lloyd and, of course, myself."

Sir Arthur received this final list in silence.

Judy, gradually recovering from the first shock of witnessing so closely the Maharajah's death, realised now, as she stood there in the increasing heat of the sun, that the Resident must be going over in his mind a list of only five people. Five people who could have been responsible for the murder of the Maharajah. And it was a list, she realised, that was present, horribly present, in her own mind too.

A murderer. Was a murderer really standing just here, so close? Impossible. Yet there, equally close, was the body of a murdered man. And there were flies, quite a lot of flies now, circling and landing and rising again. Shouldn't somebody do something about the body?

Nobody seemed to feel the need. Porgy, who ought really to have given orders, was standing looking moodily at the ground, kicking at a tuft of grass from time to time and sending up small puffs of dusty earth. The Resident, a man for issuing commands if ever there was, was standing like a statue that happened to have been placed in this spot but that had nothing, absolutely nothing, to do with it. The Dewan seemed as lost in thought as Porgy.

But no wonder. There was a lot for him to think about, Judy realised. First, that, as he himself had admitted, he was a murder suspect. And more than just a suspect from having witnessed that awful, ironic dress rehearsal for the actual murder. By things James had said, she knew that relations between the Dewan and the dead Maharajah had been very strained of late. Indeed, she had seen as much for herself just in the way the Maharajah had spoken to the Dewan about Henry Morton's plans for bringing industry to Bhopore at dinner last night. So he seemed to have a motive as well as the opportunity which knowing the effect of sapura bark constituted.

But James. Thinking of all he had told her about life in the palace at Bhopore—and yesterday, only yesterday, she had thought it all so fascinating and so comically quaint—brought her to the realisation that James, too, was now a murder suspect. But that was ridiculous. Impossible. Laughable. And, even thinking of it just as logic, he didn't have any sort of motive. He couldn't have. Not in the way the Dewan did.

Or in the way, she added to herself, that Porgy did. Because from other things James had said she knew that Porgy and his father had by no means agreed on every subject. Porgy was modern: his father was a stickler for the rules of old. And nothing that he had said when he had been discussing the zinc-mining plan with Henry Morton—and hadn't there been something odd, something a little wrong, with the way he had talked about setting up factories here?—had made him really one little bit modern, as he had claimed it had.

And then Porgy had been quarrelling with his father, too, about Miss Brattle. Dolly. If what James had told her was right, Porgy wanted to marry Dolly and his father had very strongly objected. So there was a motive. A terrific motive when you came to think about it. And, of course, Porgy had that sapura-bark opportunity, too.

And so had Dolly. If the Maharajah, the old Maharajah, had been objecting to her marrying Porgy, that could have made her want to get rid of him. Because one thing was certain: if the old Maharajah objected to something, that something was not going to happen. He had been a person of power. Of rather horrible power. So Dolly, too, was on the opportunity-and-motive list. Especially if she really had understood after all what had been going on when the Maharajah had played that stupid April Fool trick on Little Michael.

Suddenly Judy felt a wave of weakness come over her. Was she going to faint? Because the last name on the list had come into her head. Uncle Joe. And at once she had known that he had a motive too. A hell of a motive. The Maharajah's blank refusal to let the dam, his darling dam, be used in the proper way. "Over my dead body," the Maharajah had said when she'd been so idiotic as to try and sweet-talk him into being sensible about the dam. Would Uncle Joe have made that body dead so as to get the dam used properly?

She thought that he very well might. He had that temper, that flaming Lloyd temper. She knew: she had her share of it too.

VIII

The funeral ceremony was over. It had gone well. There had been no difficulties, no awkward hitches despite the necessary swiftness of it all. It was now half-past eight in the evening. And, on time to the minute, the Resident had arrived in his car, the car that the dead Maharajah had played his doubly unfortunate trick on. He was flying his flag. He had come to see the new Maharajah.

Sir Arthur gave a precise five minutes to politenesses and condolences. Porgy felt that somehow the man must be able to see the watch on his wrist through the white linen of the arm of his suit.

Five minutes precisely. And then—

"Maharajah, I do not have to tell you that the situation is extremely serious."

"Serious, Your Excellency? Sad, I agree. It is tragic even. But I do not see in what way serious."

"Maharajah, the Viceroy is due to arrive in Bhopore in exactly thirteen days' time."

"Yes, I know. And I have already decided not to postpone the opening of the dam. But I have decided to rename it. It shall be called the Maharajah Albert Singhi Dam in honour of my father. However, I will not postpone the opening. My father would not have wished it. The dam meant a great deal to him."

"Of course, of course."

The Resident let a silence fall. While he counted—Porgy was sure of it—up to five, slowly.

"Yes, Maharajah, an excellent plan to name the dam in honour of your father. But, of course, the opening could not in any case have been postponed. It was included in the Viceroy's timetable."

"Yes, yes."

Porgy now let a brief silence fall. In tribute to the Viceroy's timetable.

"But I still do not see, Your Excellency, why you find the situation in Bhopore serious. It cannot be that you think the Thakur of Panna will attempt to rise after my father's sudden removal. He knows that I will have ascended to the gaddi at once, and the State forces are entirely loyal."

"No, no, Maharajah. That was not what I had in mind at all."

"Then what is it, Your Excellency?"

"It is the murder, Maharajah. The murder of your father and no certainty at all about who is responsible. The Viceroy cannot come to a State where that situation exists, where he might be put in the position of meeting a ruler who . . ."

Sir Arthur checked himself. But Porgy, in the privacy of his own head, completed the unfinished sentence. ". . . of meeting a ruler who turns out to be the very person who had murdered the previous Maharajah."

"But the Viceroy's timetable?" he said.

The Resident pulled a long face.

"If the worst comes to the worst," he answered, "there would have to be a cancellation. I suppose, some shikar somewhere could be arranged for H.E. But there would be difficulties. Such short notice. Almost insuperable difficulties. We would have to give him a minimum of a week's warning. A minimum."

"Yes, I see," Porgy said helpfully.

"So, Maharajah, there is only one course open to us. Open to you. As I see it."

"And that is?"

Porgy wondered what was going to come. Surely not abdication? It couldn't be. Whatever the Resident suspected about the murder, there was no one else to fill the vacant gaddi. Even poor dead Raghbir would have been hopelessly unsuitable. The Thakur of Panna? No, he had opposed Papa and the Resident in every way he could for years. So abdication was unthinkable. But then what?

Sir Arthur made his grave face even graver.

"I think you would agree, Maharajah," he said, "that in view of the peculiar circumstances, the very peculiar circumstances, an investigation into your late father's death by the State police is not a practical proposition. I have, as you know, the greatest respect for your cousin, the chief of the Bhopore police. The greatest respect for the way he maintains discipline in the force. But, of course, he could not . . ."

Porgy was on the point of asking what his cousin could not do.

But suddenly he realised. He could not carry out an investigation in which he, the new Maharajah, was perhaps the chief suspect.

He thought a sigh would be politic. He sighed.

"So what do you suggest, Your Excellency?" he asked.

Sir Arthur shook his head sadly.

"It is not a course I would normally have advocated," he replied. "Not in any circumstances. Not in any circumstances but these. However, I am afraid it is the only course open to us."

"And that is?"

"D.S.P. Howard. District Superintendent of Police Howard. From Sangabad, you know."

"Yes," said Porgy thoughtfully. "I have heard of him."

"Of course, he's an excellent officer. An excellent officer. A remarkable record of successes. Remarkable."

Sir Arthur fell silent.

"But there is . . ." Porgy said tentatively, after a little.

Sir Arthur sighed. A restrained, almost imperceptible sigh.

"Well, Maharajah, you know what it is," he said, doling the words out as if it hurt him to produce each one of them. "You know what it is. The fellow's country-born. The father was Indian Police before him, married perfectly reasonably, but they never sent the boy back home. And now, here he is, fellow of about forty-five, I suppose, never been out of India in his life."

"Yes," said Porgy. "Yes, I see."

He let the words weigh heavily, like stones each sinking a reputation yet deeper. Because he understood exactly what the Resident was saying in his roundabout way. He had learnt it in his time at Cambridge, if he had not known it subtly even earlier. To be "country-born," not to have been subjected, if by chance your actual birth had occurred somewhere in India, to the bracing climate of the mother country. That climate that was always thought of as being not simply physically bracing with its cold winds, its hard driving rain, its pure snows, but also as being morally bracing. Above all, morally bracing. A man who had not had that was somehow suspect.

Evidently encouraged by his ready agreement, Sir Arthur ventured to enlarge on what he had said.

"I suppose the mother must have begged the father not to send the boy home." He shook his head. "But it never does. It never does. They become—become attached. Nothing very evident often, but there gets to be some sort of link. With India. Yes, with India. Not a good thing."

Porgy nodded gravely.

"But, as I say," Sir Arthur continued lugubriously, "an excellent officer. Solved the Lampson case, you know. Fellow who shot his wife because he'd let himself go to pieces over some chee-chee girl and then tried to put the blame on the local Tahsildar's son. Bad business. Fellow might have brought it off, and then there'd have been a lot of talk. Wouldn't have done, wouldn't have done at all. But Howard sorted it out."

He sighed.

"So I'm afraid I shall have to ask you to call him in," he said. "As a matter of urgency."

IX

District Superintendent of Police Howard was driving towards the Summer Palace of Bhopore. It was still quite early in the morning on the day after the murder of the Maharajah. He had left his lonely bungalow outside the sprawling town of Sangabad in British India before it was light and had pushed the secondhand Buick he had hired from a somewhat dubious gentleman in Sangabad, one Bool Chand, as fast as it would go. He would have preferred to make the journey on horseback, to take one of his two sturdy Walers, horses imported from New South Wales, and approach Bhopore at his own pace and in his own way. He reckoned that from the back of a horse you could tell what was going on, if you had eyes to look for it. But in a car, even with the canvas hood down, you saw little and heard less.

But from a lengthy telegram he had received from Sir Arthur Penderevel, the Resident in Bhopore, he had learnt that the business that lay ahead was seen as being of the utmost urgency. And so, reluctantly, between tidying up a great many loose ends in Sangabad District, he had arranged with Bool Chand to have the car.

There was a great deal in Sangabad that he was loath to leave. Mr. Gandhi's "white caps" were particularly active in the wake of the recent gaol sentence on Vallabhai Patel, brother of the President of the so-called Indian Legislative Assembly. He would dearly have liked to stay on station until he was sure that none of them was going to make trouble in his district. There was a gang of dacoits, too, who had been impudent enough to have held up the Director of Land Records and Agriculture from the neighbouring district while he had been passing through, a person after all coming seventy-seventh in the Warrant of Precedence. That needed dealing with pretty quickly.

But the Resident in Bhopore had pulled his strings, and an order was an order. Yet he would have been a lot happier if there weren't apparently such damned urgency about the matter. Softlee, softlee, catchee monkey had always been the best way to go about things.

Ahead of him on the dusty, sun-bright road he saw a lone figure progressing steadily along under the shade of a large black umbrella. And something about the way the man was walking made him come to a sudden decision. It may have been the determination evident in every step the slight, skinny-looking figure took. Or it may have been the tiny, birdlike movements of the head which seemed to say that the determination was not just single-minded concentration on getting to a destination but an act of will that did not exclude the passing world. Whatever it was, D.S.P. Howard made up his mind in a moment and brought the Buick to a quiet halt just ahead of the plodding figure.

He leant out.

"Am I on the right road for the Summer Palace?" he asked, knowing the answer full well.

"Oh, yes, Sahib," the man answered. "Straight along. Only six miles more. I am going there myself."

Without hesitation D.S.P. Howard said, "Then hop in." The sharpness of the eyes in the thin and anxious face had decided him.

"Thank you very, very much, Sahib."

The determined walker carefully closed his large black umbrella, then grasped the handle of the back door of the car and began to open it.

"No, no," D.S.P. Howard said. "Come and sit beside me. Go round."

For a moment the man glanced at him with, behind a careful vacancy of expression, a look of mistrust. Was this going to be the prelude to some inexplicable, violent joke? Was the Angrezi Sahib with the expressionless face and hooded, impenetrable eyes going to knock him from the car's running board and abuse him for impudence?

But evidently he soon decided—his shrewdness could not be concealed—that the offer was no more than what it seemed to be. Or very little more.

Scuttling a bit, he rounded the front of the Buick, opened the door beside the D.S.P., leant in, carefully stowed on the floor his umbrella, which after all was respectably aged, and seated himself.

The D.S.P. let in the Buick's clutch and they set off.

"What takes you to the Summer Palace?" he asked, his voice casual as could be.

His passenger wagged his head.

"Oh, I am His Highness's Schoolmaster," he said. "Or, that is to say, until yesterday I most certainly held that position. Now all is in doubt."

"Oh, yes? And why is that?"

"Oh, Sahib, Sahib. Yesterday was indeed a most tragic day. Altogether most tragic."

"Tragic? How was that?"

But D.S.P. Howard's unvarying tone of polite interest seemed at this point a little to worry his passenger. For several seconds that casual question received no reply. Then the Schoolmaster spoke again.

"Sahib," he said, "may I most respectfully suggest that you are very well knowing the tragic incident that occurred by the jheels here in Bhopore yesterday A.M.?"

D.S.P. Howard shot out a sudden flick of a grin, scarcely more than a quick lift of his hooded eyes and a curling of the corners of his straight-set mouth.

"Sorry," he said. "I like to hear as much as I can in what you might call an unbiased way. So I wait as long as possible before revealing any interest that I may have."

"Sahib," replied his passenger, "would I be wrong to think that I have the honour of addressing District Superintendent of Police Howard, of Sangabad?"

"No. You'd be right. Though I'm a little surprised that everyone in Bhopore knows already that I've been called in."

"Oh, no, D.S.P. Sahib. It is not everyone who knows. It is only myself who is putting two and two together."

"Two and two being the murder of the Maharajah of Bhopore yesterday morning and an Englishman, even if he is in mufti, driving in the direction of the Summer Palace at just this time?"

"Yes, indeed, Sahib. Plus also the Sahib's reputation far and wide beyond the borders of Sangabad District."

"All right," D.S.P. Howard said.

And then after a lapse of a minute or so, while the Buick pushed steadily along the road, raising behind it a cloud of dust that lingered in the bright morning air, he turned once more to his unexpectedly perceptive passenger.

"You said that 'all is in doubt' about your position as the late Maharajah's Schoolmaster," he said. "Tell me, why is that? Does the new Maharajah not believe in education?"

"Oh, no, Sahib. His new Highness is a very, very progressive gentleman. That is well known. But, you would understand, I am engaged to instruct the various children of former His Highness who are yet too young to be sent to the appropriate scholastic establishment. So it is possible that new His Highness will be wanting to make other arrangements. Also . . ."

"Yes?"

"Also yesterday I was taken away from the schoolroom altogether. I was requested to act as guide and instructor to the European visitors to the palace."

A tiny little spark showed itself beneath D.S.P. Howard's hooded eyes.

"Oh, yes?" he said. "Are there some European guests there? Who are they? Do you know?"

The Schoolmaster, who had been staring intently at the dusty road as it was being eaten up under the Buick's tyres, turned his head for one instant in the direction of the D.S.P.

"D.S.P. Sahib," he said, very quickly, "I am thinking you are well knowing. Otherwise why would they be sending for you if it was some low-caste Indian fellow only they were thinking had murdered the Maharajah?"

D.S.P. Howard gave a little grunt that might have been a laugh.

"And I am thinking," he replied, "that you must have got it into your head that at least one of the people you showed round the palace yesterday could have been the person who killed the Maharajah."

"Oh, Sahib, I would not think a thing of that nature, not at all."

"You damn well would," D.S.P. Howard answered. "Now, let's hear. Or I'll stop and put you out to walk again."

For a little the Schoolmaster did not reply.

"It is still a long way to the palace," he said at last. "And I very much relish not having to make the journey on foot."

"So?"

"Well, D.S.P. Sahib, it is not in fact so much a guest that I had in mind as one who has been resident in Bhopore for some time."

"Oh, yes?"

Another silence.

"Do I have to stop the car?" D.S.P, Howard said.

"Oh, no, no, Sahib. It is a most relaxing way of travel. It is of Lloyd Sahib I am thinking."

"The engineer of the new dam, eh?"

"Sahib has heard of Lloyd Sahib?"

The D.S.P. took his eyes from the road for a moment.

"Oh, come," he said, "you must have realised that I did not set out for Bhopore without being very well instructed."

"Yes, Sahib. So Sahib will well know that Lloyd Sahib has been building the dam for many, many months. For more than three years. And that he is very, very proud of what he has done. And certainly the dam is a most beautiful and majestic construction."

"And?"

The Schoolmaster sighed.

"And Maharajah Sahib was not allowing all the water to be released by the dam so that the water levels in his jheels would not be altered," he said.

"Is that all?" the D.S.P. asked, sounding perhaps a little disappointed.

"Well, no, Sahib, there is one thing more."

"Then perhaps you'd better tell me it, Schoolmaster Sahib."

"Does the D.S.P. Sahib know the manner of the Maharajah's unfortunate death?"

"He does."

"Then does he know also that the sapura tree, from which the death-dealing bark came, is a very, very rare growth? That it occurs only in the most remote parts of Bhopore?"

"And? Come on, Schoolmaster Sahib."

"And that Lloyd Sahib, when he was first here in Bhopore, was making many expeditions into all sorts of jungly parts so as to be finding the best of all possible sites for his great dam?"

"I see. Well, if that's the limit of your suspicions, Schoolmaster Sahib, I think you'd better tell me what you can about the other visitors to Bhopore before we find ourselves at the palace."

"As you wish, D.S.P. Sahib."

"I certainly do wish."

"Then, may I ask, are you already in possession of the information that in order to kill the Maharajah in the manner in which he was killed it was necessary to have witnessed a certain practical joke being carried out the day before?"

"Yes, yes. A very great deal can be said in a telegram if it is being sent in code and at the expense of the King-Emperor."

"Very good then, D.S.P. Sahib. I shall confine my observations to those members of my tour party yesterday who were in that position."

"And push on with it, Schoolmaster Sahib."

"As the Sahib pleases. Number One, then, shall be Lieutenant James Frere, Indian Army. But really there is very little to say on the subject of Lieutenant Frere. He is altogether a most estimable young man, a guest in Bhopore these last two months. He was a friend in England of the Maharajkumar, now His Highness the Maharajah. But I cannot see at all that he should have any reason to wish to kill the Maharajah, unless it is that the Maharajah had beaten him at chess and, I understand, that the Maharajah is not always strictly adhering to the rules."

He cocked his head quickly sideways.

"Please," he added, "it is only a joke that I am making concerning Lieutenant Frere."

"Yes, Schoolmaster Sahib. Even I did not think that the young man would be driven to murder over a game of chess, however unorthodoxly played. So, go on."

"Well, that is the whole of the subject of Lieutenant Frere, except to be adding that already he has fallen most terribly in love with one of the American visitors, Lloyd Sahib's niece, Miss Judy Alcott, who is herself not to be included in any lists on account of late arrival."

"All right. So sentimental conjectures apart, what else can you tell me?"

Whether the Schoolmaster had noticed or not, the old Buick's speed had now been reduced by some fifteen miles an hour. But already they had passed the wayside shrine on which on his journey home on the day before the Maharajah's death the Schoolmaster, sharp-eyed, had registered the fact that a few new flower heads had been placed.

"D.S.P. Sahib," he said, "I fear we cannot set aside sentimental conjectures. Not at all. No, no."

D.S.P. Howard sighed, and eased his foot another quarter inch from the accelerator pedal.

"Very well then, conjecture on, Schoolmaster Sahib."

"It is very difficult for me, D.S.P. Sahib."

"Nevertheless, you're going to tell me. And *ek dum*."

The Schoolmaster squared his bony shoulders. Not for the first time in his life, caught between the devil and the deep blue sea, he plunged for one or the other and hoped.

"It is the Maharajkumar, now His Highness," he said. "And a certain person. A European. A visitor. A female visitor. Of considerable duration."

"Yes, yes. That would be Miss Brattle, Miss Dorothy Brattle. Go on."

Emboldened, but still keeping his eyes fixed on the unrolling dusty road before him, the Schoolmaster went on.

"The former Maharajah," he said. "He would never have given permission for any—ahem—matrimonial arrangement. It is known. It is well known. He would have prevented the Maharajkumar ascending the gaddi. But Brattle Memsahib, she is already not a young lady. That also is well known. It is necessary, necessary for her to secure the Maharajkumar in bonds of matrimony. Oh, D.S.P. Sahib, I am thinking she could very well stoop to murder to achieve her ends. My goodness, yes."

"Is that all?"

"D.S.P. Sahib, she was lying also. When Resident Sahib was saying, just after the fatal moment, that it was necessary for the perpetrator to have witnessed the incident of the sapura-bark joke, she was attempting to say she did not see."

"All right, Schoolmaster Sahib. Now let me add, to save you the pain of mentioning it, that there's an equal motive there for His present Highness himself. Enough said. Have you anything else to tell me?"

The D.S.P. brought the Buick to a halt. Already the outline of the Summer Palace, all domes and arches like a small mountain range, could be seen not far along the road.

"Sahib, there is the Dewan."

"Yes. There is the Dewan. Tell me everything you know. More, tell me everything you've heard."

"Sahib, it is like this. For many months now late His Highness has been distrusting the Dewan. Why that is, nobody is altogether knowing. But well they are knowing that there have been pieces of business which late His Highness did not at all tell the Dewan. Sahib, many people have said that it would not be long before Bhopore was seeing a new Dewan. Late His Highness was quick always to dismiss those he did not like. Sahib, A.D.C.s by the dozen have come and gone, like Captain Ram Singh at present, Sahib, whose father is the Thakur of Panna, and who was accused by late His Highness of attempting poisoning and at once imprisoned."

"Well, dismissing officials is not so unusual. Absolute rulers have always been fickle. The Dewan can't have counted on retaining his position indefinitely."

"Oh, but D.S.P. Sahib, with respect, yes. Yes, indeed. For many years has Sir Akhtar been Dewan of Bhopore, and, Sahib, it is well known that this is his lifeblood, the guarding in every way of the interests of the State."

"I see. And the new Maharajah, does he care for Sir Akhtar?"

"Sahib, already he has announced that he is to be his Dewan also."

"All right. Now, who else have you got to tell me about?"

"Sahib, there is no one. Each and every person who witnessed the incident of the sapura bark and who also was out at the shikar at the jheels, where in the darkness of the night they could have placed a further piece of bark in the barrel of one of late His Highness's guns I have spoken of."

"All right. Well, now, I think, Schoolmaster Sahib, you'd better hop out and make the last of your way to the palace on foot."

If the Schoolmaster was surprised or hurt by this abrupt dismissal he showed nothing of it. He stooped, retrieved his black umbrella, turned the handle of the car door with care, and stepped down onto the softly dust-covered road.

Only when he had done so did the D.S.P. add another word.

"It would never do, Schoolmaster Sahib, for anyone at the palace to know that you were my pair of eyes there. Much less my pair of ears."

The Schoolmaster did no more than offer the Englishman and his car a deep salaam. But there was a sharp twinkle in his eyes as he did so.

X

In the palace the Schoolmaster found that it had been decreed that this was another day of holiday for the late Maharajah's boisterous offspring. Once again he was deputed to entertain Porgy's guests by showing them yet more of the palace treasures while Porgy was learning from the Dewan the ways of his sudden inheritance. Or was he, he wondered, a sort of guard? There to make sure, in a thoroughly polite way, that the visitors could not attempt to leave.

Latish in the afternoon, when the guests had got up from their afternoon sleep— Had servants watched while they dozed? No doubt they had—he was in the palace Armoury with Judy and Mrs. Alcott and Lieutenant Frere. With them was a somewhat restive Henry Morton III, plainly unimpressed by the line of aged craftsmen sitting cross-legged, embroidering new velvet sheaths for the swords of the Maharajah's personal guards. This was hardly the sort of production line they had in America.

Nor did the weapons, both ancient and modern, arrayed all round the sails of the huge, almost darkened room impress the tycoon any more. Powder horns delicately carved in ivory, guns with their barrels chased in intricate patterns, designed to be fired from the backs of camels, long-barreled jezail muskets, curving-bladed tulwar swords, daggers with blades of gold and handles of crystal, none aroused in him the slightest interest.

"Yeah, yeah," he said, when the Schoolmaster displayed a powder horn made from the shell of a sea urchin. "Yeah, I guess it's pretty, all right. But did it hold all the gunpowder it could? A guy would be mighty upset in the middle of a fire fight to find he'd run out, no matter how beautiful the darned thing was."

"Very true, Sahib, very true indeed," the Schoolmaster said. "But on the other hand, if the said powder horn was shown to contain the maximum quantity of powder needed for any particular martial engagement, then perhaps the user might derive not inconsiderable pleasure in his off-duty hours from contemplating the workmanship of his horn. You know, Sahibs and Memsahibs, that an object like this might take as much as one year to make?"

"Oh, my, a whole year!" Elaine Alcott exclaimed.

"Yeah," said Henry Morton, "and if the guy who made it had been set to to make powder horns in tin he'd have turned out a couple of thousand in the year, enough to equip the whole darned army."

The Schoolmaster wagged his head.

"But, Sahib, if the whole army was already equipped . . ."

He saw that his was an argument that did not appeal to the American. Hastily he passed on.

"Now here, Memsahibs and Sahibs, we have a most interesting object."

Dutifully Judy, her mother, and James Frere peered at the object hanging from the wall above them. It seemed to consist of two dull chunks of iron, joined together with a leather thong.

"What is it?" Judy asked, still with enthusiasm.

She had seen so many marvels already in the palace, but her keenness was undimmed. From time to time the thought of the horrible event that had marred their visit to Bhopore rose up inexorably in her head. But for the most part the wonder of the place managed to overcome even that black notion. And what it was she feared about Uncle Joe was something that she forced herself to expunge from her mind altogether. Some things do not bear thinking about. Ever. At all.

The Schoolmaster gave his little lecture-beginning cough that secretly amused Judy every time he did it.

"What you are beholding, Memsahibs and Sahibs," he said, "are the very pair of tiger's claws, as they are named, which a former Maharajah of Bhopore wore on the historic occasion when he confronted his ancient enemy, the Muslim leader, Sheikh Allaudin. The two had been many years at war. Then a truce was arranged. Each leader was to come alone and unarmed to the place agreed. This they appeared to do. But then—"

The Schoolmaster allowed a long dramatic pause to hang in the dark of the huge weapon-decorated room.

James Frere gave Judy a little nudge. She put a hand to her mouth to stifle an irrepressible giggle.

"Then what, for heaven's sake?" Mrs. Alcott asked.

"Then, Memsahib, the Maharajah saw that beneath his cloak Sheikh Allaudin had concealed a small but deadly dagger."

"Was the Maharajah killed then?" asked Mrs. Alcott, the best listener the Schoolmaster could have wished for.

"Ah, no. Not at all, not at all." The Schoolmaster drew himself up to his full modest height. "When the Maharajah Sahib saw the Muslim's treacherous dagger, what do you think that he did? He embraced his foe. Yes, he put his arms round the man and embraced him in a deep hug. And it was then, then, that the terrible tiger claws of iron that he himself had had concealed in his hands dug fatally into the back of his enemy."

"Oh, how awful."

"Oh, no, madam, it was not in any way awful at all. The Maharajah had conquered his enemy. Do you not see? It is a Maharajah's duty to rule. For that, whatever he does is good."

It was then that Judy, glancing away, noticed a white-clad figure standing silently watching and listening as the lecture—it could not be denied that the Schoolmaster was inclined to drone on—continued. She recognised him as the District Superintendent of Police, to whom she had been introduced that morning.

He waited patiently while the little group round the Schoolmaster listened on. But Judy was sure that his hooded eyes missed nothing. Not the sense of strain that was apparent behind the darting birdlike movements with which her mother looked from object to object. Not the glances between herself and Lieutenant Frere. Not Henry Morton's impatient boredom.

Only when at last the party turned directly towards the archway and his figure must have been plain to them all, lit by the light coming in from an open stone window away to his left, did he speak.

"Good afternoon. We meet for the second time. And actually, if you don't mind, I'd like a word with you, Mrs. Alcott."

Elaine Alcott gave a gasp that could be heard clearly as if it had been a pistol shot in the silence of the dimly lit Armoury.

"But— But— Mr.— Gee, I'm sorry I've forgotten your name since we were introduced."

"Not at all. It's a name that's easily enough forgotten. Howard. District Superintendent of Police."

"Yes," said Elaine Alcott, as if that last piece of information were one that she did not in the least need reminding of.

D.S.P. Howard stood quietly waiting. The others looked at each other as if one of them were expected to give a cue before anyone could move. At last the Schoolmaster broke the silence.

"Memsahib and Sahibs," he said, "if you would be so good as to come this way."

"Yes, right, of course," James Frere said.

Judy held out a hand towards her mother.

"You'll be all right?" she said.

D.S.P. Howard gave the slightest of smiles.

"I assure you there's nothing to be afraid of," he said. "I just have a few more questions about what happened at the jheels to put to your mother, Miss Alcott. Since she was not shooting she may have seen something significant."

"Oh, I'm sure I didn't," Elaine Alcott said hastily. "I—I'm not a very observant sort of person, I guess. And the noise of the shooting, all that banging, I wasn't looking at anything really."

"Yes, yes. I'm sure there's very little you have to tell me. But I'd like all the same to have a word."

The D.S.P. moved slightly to one side. It was the smallest of gestures, hardly more than shifting from one foot to the other. But somehow it had the effect of bustling the others out of the dim Armoury and leaving him there alone with Mrs. Alcott.

"It's only a very small matter," he said to her as soon as the others' footsteps had begun to fade on the marble floor of the passageway outside.

"Yes?" Elaine Alcott said, her voice jerking suddenly up.

"It's the Maharajah's guns again," D.S.P. Howard went on. "Now, you were all shown the rack in which they were carried?"

"Well, yes. Yes, I suppose we were. But I didn't take too much notice of it. I don't care for guns and all, and I just looked and turned away."

"Very natural. But I wondered about the time when you had all arrived at the jheels and people were being shown to their various butts. That's what happened, wasn't it?"

"Yes," she answered, with the utmost caution.

"Good. Now, you had said, hadn't you, that you would not be shooting?"

"Yes. Yes, I had."

"Good. So you stood waiting, I imagine, while all that was going on."

"I guess I did. But—"

"Now, I'd like you to try and remember just as much as you can of that scene. There were lanterns, weren't there? Hurricane lamps?"

"Yes. Yes, I can see those now."

"Good. Now, can you remember seeing the gun rack then?"

Elaine Alcott dutifully closed her eyes. But from the expression she forgot to wipe from her face it was clear that she had no intention of remembering anything more than she absolutely had to.

"No," she said, after the briefest of pauses. "No, I don't think I exactly recall seeing that."

"No? A pity. But perhaps you remember your brother there? Where exactly was he when people were being shown where they would shoot from?"

An edge of steel underlined the question.

"My brother?" Elaine Alcott said, fluttery as an imprisoned bird.

"Yes. Your brother, Joe. Mr. Lloyd. Where was he?"

"I don't know. I really don't know. I wasn't with him."

"Well, I think you were, you know. If you remember. If what I've been told is correct, he was in the same car as you and your daughter on the way to the jheels. Isn't that so?"

"I– Yes. Yes, that was so. Yes, he was. I admit that."

"Good. Now you're beginning to remember things. And when you got out of the cars, what happened then?"

"Well, I guess– Oh, yes, I know. One of those what-do-you-call'ems, A.D.C.s, came up with a list. And, yes, he called out Joe's name. 'Lloyd Sahib,' he said. You know the way they have. And Joe just went off. He went straight to his place. Straight. I can swear to that."

"But it must have been still dark then, Mrs. Alcott," D.S.P. Howard said gently.

There was a long moment of stricken silence.

"Mrs. Alcott," D.S.P. Howard said, in a voice caressingly gentle as those of the pigeons that made their homes inside the huge palace. "Mrs. Alcott, you're afraid that your brother might have murdered the Maharajah, aren't you?"

"I– Certainly not. Why should Joe do a thing like that? What do you mean?"

"Oh, come. We all know why Mr. Lloyd might have taken it into his head to act against the Maharajah. I have heard all about that scene at dinner the night before the murder took place. Your brother was in a tremendous rage then, wasn't he?"

"No. No, he was not. Officer, whatever you are—"

"Just Mr. Howard."

"Well then, Mr. Howard, there's something you don't understand about my brother."

"Is there, Mrs. Alcott? Then please tell me. I'm here, you know, to find out the truth."

Soft and almost kind though the D.S.P.'s voice was, what he had actually said seemed to frighten Elaine Alcott even more than she had been before. She stood where she was, just beneath the innocent-looking little pieces of iron that had been the undoing of the would-be treacherous Sheikh Allaudin long, long ago, and she said not a word.

"Now, Mrs. Alcott, you told me that there was something I didn't understand about Mr. Lloyd. I'm sure there's a lot I don't understand about him. After all, I've scarcely met him. Just a few moments' formal talk with him while he told me what he'd been doing at the time of the murder, nothing more."

Elaine Alcott bristled.

"Well, if he's told you what he was doing, why did you have to ask me?" she snapped.

"Oh, I wasn't asking you about him in particular, you know. I was only trying to find out if you had happened to notice something that might be useful to me and then had forgotten it. I thought that probably you would remember what your brother had been doing at the time and that that would perhaps bring other things back to your mind."

She heaved a sigh of relief, a sigh so large it could not have escaped observation even from eyes a lot less keen than the hooded ones that now watched her.

"Oh, well," she said, "if that's all, I'll try to remember more about the jheels. I thought you were asking—"

She checked as abruptly as a horse rearing up at the sight of a cobra in the road in front of it.

"You thought what, Mrs. Alcott?" said that soft voice.

"I— I don't know. You'll have to forgive me, Mr. Howard. I'm kinda all confused. You know, I only got to India two or three days ago, and everything's so strange. And then a murder happening. A murder right in front of my eyes, almost."

"Yes, yes. I'm sure it has all been most distressing for you, especially feeling about Mr. Lloyd as you do."

"Yes, well, with him being always so—"

Again she checked. But this time as suddenly as if the cobra in the road had launched forward and struck.

"Mr. Howard," she said, in a voice in which the tears were not far away, "Mr. Howard, could you talk to me about this some other time? I guess— It's so hot here. And so strange. And I was telling you, we've only just arrived. I'm confused. I'm so confused I don't know what I'm saying."

"But, of course. I must apologise. I'm afraid I was thinking more of my duty than of your feelings. I well understand what you must have gone through. A murder is a damned unpleasant business even if it happens somewhere where one feels at home, but for you to be involved in it all here . . . Never mind, I'll talk to you another time. Tomorrow, perhaps."

"Oh, thank you, Mr. Howard, thank you. I daresay you think I'm just a silly woman, but, gee, you don't know how strange everything is here."

"I think nothing of the kind," D.S.P. Howard said. "And now can I make sure you can find your daughter and the others? Or would you rather go to your rooms and lie down for a little?"

"Yes, yes. I think I'll do that. If I can find the way."

"Let me show you. I daresay I can find someone to tell us, even if I'm not wholly acquainted with the palace as yet. Shall we go this way?"

For a little they walked together along the long corridor outside, going in the direction the D.S.P. had chosen, which was not the direction that the Schoolmaster had gone in.

It was not for almost two minutes that the D.S.P. spoke, and when he did so it was in the most conversational of tones.

"Oh, by the way, you were going to tell me what it was that I didn't understand about your brother."

"Oh. Oh, yes."

Elaine stopped and clutched him by the forearm.

"Mr. Howard," she said, putting all the sincerity she could into her voice, "you must realise this. Joe does get into rages. Well, no, that's not it. He seems to get into rages. Yes, that's what it is. He only seems to get into a furious temper and threaten all sorts of things. But he doesn't mean it. Why, he's never— Well, what I mean is: you mustn't put too much reliance on what people who don't know him tell you about him. He's really the meekest, nicest boy. He always was. Back home, you know."

"I see," said D.S.P. Howard. "And he never has done anything which might indicate otherwise? Never?"

Elaine Alcott dug the nails of each hand hard into their palms.

"Never," she said.

The D.S.P., happening at that moment to raise his eyes, spotted in the distance a servant. He called out. The man came hurrying up.

"Show the Memsahib to her rooms," the D.S.P. said.

He turned to Elaine Alcott.

"Thank you very much," he said. "You've been most helpful. Already. And tomorrow when you're feeling more like it I may come and have another chat? Thank you."

She walked away behind the servant, like a prisoner released.

And the D.S.P. glanced at his wristwatch and swore softly to himself. If only he had more time . . .

The Resident stared sombrely down at D.S.P. Howard.

"More time, Mr. Howard?" he said. "I'm afraid I cannot give you that. Far from it. If I have to cable the Viceroy and say that he must cancel his visit to Bhopore at as little as a week's notice, I shall hardly be in his good graces."

"No, sir. I understand that. But this is an extremely complex business you have confronted me with."

"I daresay it is, Mr. Howard. But it is also a business that must be cleared up. Must be. We cannot have a person on the gaddi of one of the greatest states in India who may have murdered his father."

"No, sir. I see that."

"Then get on with it, man. Get on with it, for heaven's sake."

"I am doing all I can, sir. But there are complications. To begin with, it's now perfectly clear to me that it was so dark out at the jheels yesterday morning that there is no possibility at all of finding out who among those who saw that April Fool trick might have approached the Maharajah's gun rack. The Maharajah's bearer had left it while he went with the Maharajah to his butt, and any one of those five could have got to it in the time he was away."

"You're sure of that?"

"I would stake my reputation on it, sir. I spent three hours first thing on my arrival here this morning talking to everybody who had been out at the jheels. None of the servants had occasion to be near the place where the gun rack had been left. All of the five possibilities had times when they were out of observation by anyone. It's a piece of the most damnable bad luck, if I may say so."

"We don't want bad luck, Howard. We want an answer. An answer as soon as may be. Five days from today I shall have to send that cable to the Viceroy. What precisely are you doing?"

"Well, sir, I have, of course, questioned each of the five possibilities you mentioned in your telegram about their movements at the jheels. Tomorrow I shall question them again in the hope that the guilty one among them may make some slip and betray himself. But I may as well tell you now, sir, that I have very little hope of succeeding there. It was a scene of some confusion at the jheels, as you will know yourself, sir. No one is very clear about what they did. Their stories are rudimentary. There's practically no room for any significant variation to show up."

"Hm," said the Resident sharply, as if that state of things had been arranged for the precise purpose of annoying him.

He gazed out balefully at the Residency tennis courts beyond the windows of his study, their chick blinds hoisted now that it was evening.

"Well, what do you mean to do about it then?" he asked.

"I hope, sir, to get at the answer through that piece of sapura bark."

"Damned ridiculous stuff."

"Well, yes, sir. It's hard not to wish it didn't exist. But it does, and it has at least one useful property."

"And what's that, if you please?"

"That stain it gives off, sir."

"What stain? What stain? Why have I not been told of any stain?"

"I suppose, sir, it didn't seem a relevant piece of information at the start of the affair."

"And why not? Why not, eh?"

"At the early stage, sir, I hoped that it might be a comparatively simple matter to discover what had happened to the remaining piece of bark from the moment that the Maharajah flung it over to Captain Ram Singh."

"Man's an idiot."

D.S.P. Howard sighed.

"Unfortunately, sir, that line of inquiry proved almost as much of a dead end as my inquiries about the gun rack."

"You seem fated to encounter difficulties beyond your capabilities, Mr. Howard."

"I encounter the difficulties that exist, sir."

"Hm. Do you? Do you, Mr. Howard? So what new set of difficulties are you about to encounter now?"

"A set that may not be insuperable, sir. It seems that Captain Ram Singh pushed the piece of sapura bark into his pocket. And there it stayed, sir, forgotten by him, until Lieutenant Frere carried out that search during the course of the dinner you attended, sir."

"Yes, and a pretty disgraceful business that was. I do not speak ill of the dead, Howard, but the late Maharajah's whims were often irritating beyond endurance."

"I imagine they were, sir."

"Well, go on, man. Go on."

"The piece of sapura bark was placed on the stool in Lieutenant Frere's bathroom, sir, in the course of the search. And when it was over Ram Singh, I gather, was so embarrassed by the whole thing that he simply crammed most of what he'd had in his pockets back in again and left a handful of rubbish there on the stool. A handful of rubbish that included the piece of sapura bark."

"Appalling carelessness."

"I daresay, sir. However, it occurred. And the sapura bark was there in Frere's bathroom. No one had occasion to go in there, sir. Frere's bearer was elsewhere. Anyone could have entered the rooms and abstracted the piece of bark. It's very noticeable, sir. A brilliant orange colour."

"And I suppose that none of the five I drew your attention to can account for their activities during the time after dinner?"

"They each of them could have got into Lieutenant Frere's rooms unobserved, sir."

"Hm."

Sir Arthur gave his tennis courts another scrutiny.

Then he swung round to the D.S.P.

"But listen to me, Howard," he said. "Someone like Sir Akhtar Ali does not wander into other people's bathrooms uninvited. Nor, for the matter of that, would I expect the Maharajkumar to have done so."

"No, sir. Except that he and Frere are friends. He might have had some occasion to drop in on him."

Sir Arthur's mouth pursed.

"Then you think . . ." he said.

"No, sir. Or by no means necessarily so. Because there is another factor that has to be taken into account."

"Indeed? And what might that be?"

"Monkeys, sir."

"Monkeys? Monkeys? Howard, are you—"

"Perhaps you don't know, sir," the D.S.P. broke in hastily, "but troops of monkeys are apt to go swinging along the palace corridors at any and every hour of the day or night. There were signs, Frere's bearer says, that some of them had been into his rooms that evening."

"And what then, man? What then?"

"Nothing is more likely, sir, than that one of them picked up a bright object like that piece of sapura bark and took it off with him. Then, when he found it was uneatable, he might well have dropped it in a passageway nearby. And there, sir, any one of your five might have spotted it, and would have at once known what it was, having seen it out on the palace steps that afternoon."

"You seem to make difficulties, Howard."

"They seem to be there, sir. However, as I said, sapura bark does have one quality that may be useful here."

"And that is?"

"It stains, sir. It stains so badly that a week's hard washing won't get the stuff off. The fingers and hands are marked bright orange. The late Maharajah's personal bearer, who carried out that trick on your Rolls, sir, has got two bright orange palms to his hands at this instant."

"And the five?" The Resident's eyes gleamed. "The five, Howard, which of them bears the telltale traces?"

"None of them, sir."

"None of them? None of them? But that's ridiculous."

"No, sir. It's perfectly to be expected, when you think of it. You see, all of the five heard quite clearly the Maharajah telling everybody that the stuff does stain like that, sir. And our culprit, if he's nothing else, is a person capable of calculating the odds. He would have taken damn good care not to get the stain on his hands, sir. He or she, sir. Damn good care."

"I see. Yes. Yes, I see. So that leaves us at another dead end."

Sir Arthur sighed. Heavily.

"Not quite, sir."

"Not quite? What do you mean 'Not quite'? It's perfectly clear to me that none of this staining business helps in any way."

"It may not do so, sir, true enough. But it's possible, you know, that the culprit was not the first to come across the bark. Anyone in the palace may have seen it lying in a passageway somewhere, and they may have picked it up. The person we want may have got it in some way from them."

"Yes. Yes, I suppose that's possible."

"So I intend to keep an eye out for a pair of orange hands, sir."

"Yes. Good man. But we'll do better than that. We'll have every damned man jack in the palace out on parade. Hands to the front. We'll pin this fellow down in no time at all."

"I think not, sir."

"Eh? What's that?"

"I did consider the idea, sir. But a parade of that sort would take a great deal of organising. Everyone in the palace would know all about it long before it happened. Our man would almost certainly take fright, and that would be the last we saw of him, sir."

"Yes," said Sir Arthur Pendeverel. "Yes, I suppose it would. But there are hundreds of people in the palace, Howard. Hundreds."

"Rather more than one thousand, one hundred, sir. The Dewan could not be more exact."

Sir Arthur Pendeverel actually groaned.

"Then it's going to take a long time," he said. "Why, it may be weeks."

"Hardly that, sir." The D.S.P. smiled his little bleak smile. "The stain of sapura bark probably does fade in about ten days."

"But the Viceroy."

"We shall just have to hope I'm lucky, sir. I may be. And I do have other lines of inquiry as well."

"Yes. Yes, I suppose so. Would you care for a knockup on the tennis court, Howard? One must not neglect one's fitness, you know."

"I can spare half an hour, sir. That's very good of you."

D.S.P. Howard beat Sir Arthur Pendeverel 6–4, 6–1. Sir Arthur took his defeat like a gentleman.

XI

At dawn at the palace gates three musicians, two young, one an old man, herald each new day with the reedy, fluting music of the shenai. The melancholy sound floats up into a pale sky tinged all over the far horizon with delicately descending tones of pink thickening near the earth's edge to first an orange and then red. Blood-red.

On the next morning after D.S.P. Howard's arrival in Bhopore his white-clad figure could have been seen standing quietly watching the two young musicians and the one older as they played. They, intent on the ritual of their music, saw nothing of him. But he saw them, noted after a few minutes the palms of their hands, nodded once to himself, and passed on.

The malis, the gardeners, whose first duty of the day it was to water the huge gardens, equally did not realise that a lone figure was observing them at their work. As they, bent-backed, brought their heavy, leaking, water-filled goatskins to the places assigned to each one of them, they little realised that their hands were being examined, checked off, and added to an already long list of negatives.

Through the back gates of the palace a procession of plodding humpbacked bulls made its slow way. Heavily dangling on each side of each beast there was a swollen bundle of washing. Their destination was the dhobi ghat, the assigned place on the lakeshore, where each item would be bashed and battered into cleanliness by a squatting dhobi, even now perched, bare ribs showing, on one of the bulls' backs. D.S.P. Howard, standing quietly where no one would notice him, watched them and entered one more tally of negatives in the invisible notebook in his head.

The syces exercising the horses in the palace stables while the day was still cool never knew that their departure was watched and that they all were logged as negative in the brain behind hooded, watching eyes. When to the Tea Pantry the bearers came to take away chota hazri for the sahibs still in their beds, their hands as they lifted their trays did not escape scrutiny.

A little later in the day the various male servants in the mardana quarter of the palace whose daily duty it was to sweep the endless marble-floored corridors with brooms made of a fistful of stiff twigs or tough grass little knew that their activities had been noted and more negative crosses added to lists in a mental notebook.

Where hard-working hands in the European-furnished rooms of the palace applied the daily ration of beeswax and rubbed and rubbed till everything shone, their freedom from any telltale orange staining was noted. Where the fresh odour of turpentine that had been used to clean marble niches and marble shelves struck the air, a sharp nostril smelt it and checked on its users.

Out in the gardens again the nine-year-old child whose task it was, when the mango trees dropped their heavy petals, to pick up each single one by hand was watched for just a few minutes by a white-clad figure until even her infant hands were exonerated.

But observation was not the only line of inquiry that D.S.P. Howard pursued that early morning. He was standing waiting just inside one of the arched side entrances to the palace, the one near where a flight of stairs led up to the schoolroom where the large number of the late Maharajah's children of teachable age were assembled, when the Schoolmaster came through it.

"Ah, good morning, Schoolmaster Sahib. What a piece of luck happening to bump into you."

"D.S.P. Sahib. Good morning, Sahib. I trust you are in the very pink of health?"

"Thank you, Schoolmaster Sahib. I'm not often ill. And you? Are you teaching your pupils today, or is it another day of being a tourists' guide?"

The Schoolmaster wagged his head.

"Nothing has been said, D.S.P. Sahib. So I suppose I am to go up to the schoolroom in the customary manner."

"Yes. I heard a lot of noise coming from there as I happened to go by just now, so no doubt they're waiting for you."

The Schoolmaster sighed.

"Late His Highness's sons are almost always in very, very high spirits," he said.

"I can imagine. However, I don't suppose anyone will complain of the noise."

"No. No, it is true that complaints about the behaviour of the boys are not well received."

The Schoolmaster refrained from sighing again, with difficulty.

"So, perhaps, Schoolmaster Sahib, you can spare me a few moments."

"I am at your service, D.S.P. Sahib."

"It might be an idea if we walked back along the way you came in, just for a little. I noticed that nobody except a few malis seems to come along that path."

"Yes, yes. It is altogether unfrequented."

Schoolmaster and policeman set off together into the gardens.

The sun by now was striking with some force. The Schoolmaster put up his large black umbrella. Holding it rather high, he was able to include the tall, white-clad figure of the D.S.P. in its shade, though not without some strain on his extended arm.

The noise in the schoolroom grew. Paper darts were made and thrown. A copy of Mowbray's *Junior Mathematical Problems* sailed through the air. Two fights developed, though they were quickly over.

Out in the gardens the tall white-clad figure and the lean, stoop-shouldered one holding the black umbrella paced up and down, backwards and forwards. Little by little D.S.P. Howard became acquainted not only with everything that the Schoolmaster had seen in the palace in the weeks preceding the murder of the Maharajah but with everything that he had heard about too.

It turned out that, in one way and another, not much that happened in the Maharajah's immediate circle failed to come to the Schoolmaster's ears sooner or later. If it wasn't his boisterous pupils gossiping among themselves, it was a word that the Dewan had had with him. If it wasn't a snatch of conversation between Porgy and Dolly that he had happened to overhear as he was passing nearby, it was some hint which a sly servant had told him trying to curry favour for whichever pupil it was who was his master.

So the D.S.P. eventually had in his mind an extraordinarily clear picture of what had happened on the evening before the Maharajah's death right from the time he had given his display of rifle shooting, under the guise of a little practice. It was a picture to all intents and purposes as complete as if he had been present himself throughout. The events of the dinner party on the Maharajah's last night alive, even down to the most trivial of remarks, were there recorded in his brain. Nor did conversations that might have been thought to have taken place in privacy escape. In India it is not the walls that have ears. It is the servants. So just what Joe Lloyd had said to his sister and what Elaine had said to Judy when they had been dressing for that last dinner, all of it was entered in the notebook in D.S.P. Howard's head.

"Schoolmaster Sahib, I'm afraid I've kept you from your duties."

"It is nothing, D.S.P. Sahib. Nothing. In any case I am able to get into my pupils only the minimum quantity of useful and edifying information, I am sorry to say. They are refractory, you understand, decidedly refractory."

"I daresay. But I mustn't keep you anymore."

"Very well, D.S.P. Sahib. I expect I may encounter you again before very much time has elapsed?"

"I expect you will, Schoolmaster Sahib. I expect you will."

The black umbrella hurried jerkily back towards the side entrance to the palace, and the white-clad figure made its way quietly about the gardens for a little longer.

He watched three servants hauling a cart from the old icehouse with on it a great block of ice, sawdust sticking to it, already melting fast. Although there were refrigerators in the palace in these modern days, the ancient icehouse was still in use. The D.S.P. walked over and had a few words with the servants. No, there was no special time for fetching ice. When it was needed they were sent. He noted the fact. And he noted their clear hands.

He surveyed the jogging, bouncy perambulator procession returning to the cool of the palace now that the sun was getting hot. Not one of the tall Sikhs pushing the late Maharajah's last offspring had hands that betrayed any brilliant orange staining.

Prowling still, he came to the kitchen quarter. Servants crosslegged on the grounds were picking over rice. There were, he counted, seventeen of them in a long row, all hard at work. Nearby others were scouring with sand at cooking vessels, great toppling heaps waiting to be attended to. He noted a great many hands here. None of them showed any sign of orange staining.

In the palace again, the lonely secretly wandering figure scooped up yet more pairs of hands. Those of the pigeon boys, small imps in neat green uniforms, their heads dwarfed by large orange pagris, elaborately wound, whose continuing duty it was to scare the multitude of pigeons and prevent them roosting in any of the small, convenient holes in the stone screens which separated zenana from mardana. Nothing so unlucky as to be splashed by bird droppings.

From room to room the white-clad figure wandered, from suite to suite, from the wide roof gardens down to the stinking dungeons. Underneath the hooded eyelids the eyes missed nothing. The Moti Mahal, the Pearl Room, its many mirrors set in pearly silver-grey frames, was empty. The Manak Mahal, the Ruby Room, deep-glowing in colour, its alcoves rich with glass and porcelain, was empty too. The Chini Mahal, the Chinese Room, bright yellow with tiles brought over the mighty Himalayas, glinting and glittering with a hundred and more tiny mirrors inlaid in its walls, was equally unoccupied. But in its emptiness a large punkah flapped to and fro with a thunk at each flap. It was operated by a rope through a hole high in one of the walls. D.S.P. Howard prowled round a little more. He found the punkah-wallah, one of scores in the palace, sitting cross-legged in an airless stone-walled corridor, eyes shut, lost in his rhythmical work. His hands were stain-free.

And into lesser, and odder, places the D.S.P. went. The Dispensary, where the Maharajah's physician, Dr. Sen, sat. The D.S.P. had a long chat with Doctor Sahib. And left satisfied that the death of Raghbir at least had been accidental, however sudden. That it had been no more than a herald of what had been to come.

Along the long, long passages prowled the white-clad figure. Sometimes disturbing pigeons the pigeon boys had failed to move, sometimes sending a small troop of monkeys whooping and swinging and chattering their way to the nearest open window and the trees outside.

He stopped once where the palace mason was at work replacing a section of stone that had fallen away from the base of one of the hundreds of pillars in the palace. He waited long enough to see that the man's hands, though stone-dust-covered, were in no way orange and then he moved on.

At eleven o'clock precisely, however, he was waiting outside the Maharajah's study. Porgy had given him an appointment for that hour. He was not a minute late.

A servant came out, salaamed, murmured that His Highness was ready to see him. He went in. Porgy was seated at the enormous leather-topped desk, on which were still scattered various papers that he had apparently been going through with the Dewan. But he was alone now, and as the D.S.P. came in he swept aside all the batches of papers into one jumbled heap.

"Mr. Howard," he said, "please sit, please. Make yourself comfortable. Will you drink some whisky? I have some King George IV here. It is very good, you know. One of the best brands. What is it they say in the advertisements in the English magazines? 'Contains every nutriment value of the ripe grain in its most virile form.' That's it, I think. And we are all of us in need of virility. Isn't that so? Isn't it?"

The D.S.P.'s hooded eyes hardly lifted. But they took in, besides this uneasy stream of inconsequent chatter, the way in which Porgy's right hand played and played with the heavy gem-set rings on the fingers of his left.

"No, I won't take anything, if you don't mind, Maharajah," he said. "I don't like to imbibe before the sun's over the yardarm."

"Very good, very good. A most sensible way of life. And one that I make a point of sticking to myself. I learnt it in England, you know. When I was up at Cambridge. At Trinity, you know. Yes, I'm a Trinity man."

He jumped up suddenly, strode over to a large cupboard against the wall behind him, opened one of its doors, and came back to his desk with a bottle of King George IV whisky and a couple of glasses on a tray.

"Think all the same I will have a spot," he said. "Feel somehow a bit down this morning. My father's death, of course. A terrible blow to me, terrible, terrible. You're sure you won't change your mind and join me?"

"No. Thank you, Maharajah."

Porgy waited no longer but poured a generous slug into one of the glasses. A little of the amber liquid even swirled up and spilt on the green leather of the desk.

"Soda? Soda?" Porgy said.

He looked vaguely round, but apparently there was no bottle of soda water on hand.

"Oh, well, never mind. Daresay it works better this way."

He lifted the glass to his lips, took a careful sip, and then abruptly flung back his head and drained all the glass's contents.

Unmoving in the chair on the other side of the desk, D.S.P. Howard watched him.

"Well now, Mr. Howard, what exactly can I tell you? More about the circumstances of my father's death? I'm afraid I won't be able to be any help. To tell you the truth, my mind's absolutely blank about what happened out there by the jheels. Shock, I suppose. But I really hardly remember a thing."

"Then perhaps you can tell me about your relations with Miss Brattle?" D.S.P. Howard said flatly.

Porgy gaped. His jaw dropped and his mouth stayed wide open.

"Come, Maharajah, you must have expected to be questioned about Miss Brattle."

"I—I did— I mean, what business is it of yours whether I— Or what?"

"Maharajah, I've been brought here to attempt to find who murdered your father. There can be no doubt at all that he was murdered, and you yourself heard Sir Arthur Pendeverel say within minutes of the death taking place that, owing to the peculiar manner in which it was contrived, only those people who knew about the trick your father played the day before with that piece of sapura bark can be suspected of the crime. Maharajah, you were one of those people, and your relations with Miss Brattle are plainly an important factor."

"Yes," Porgy said.

He looked like a dog that had been taught, with measured severity, just how it should behave.

"Very well, Maharajah, I put my question again. Just what are your relations with Miss Brattle?"

"You won't believe this," Porgy said.

"Perhaps I shall not. But let me be the judge of that."

Porgy licked his lips, darted a glance at the empty whisky glass.

"I am not going to marry her," he said. "I know it seems ridiculous when everybody knew that I had had more than one fearful row with my father over just that. And I did want to marry her. I did. I was in love with her. I think I still am. Perhaps I'm not. I don't know."

"But you now no longer contemplate marriage?" The D.S.P. put the question in a voice devoid of any feeling at all.

"You think I'm just trying to prove that I didn't have a motive for killing Papa," Porgy burst out.

He clenched both his fists and beat them on the leather surface of the desk in a sharp little tattoo.

"But that's not so," he said, his voice loud and ugly. "I— I didn't know until after Papa was dead that I was going to feel like this. It was just— It was when I found that I was the Maharajah of Bhopore that I knew I couldn't marry Dolly. She's— She's very sweet, you know. And she's been— Damn it, she's been marvellous to me. Marvellous. But she just can't be the Maharani of Bhopore. I see that now. I saw it almost the moment Papa was dead."

"But until your father was dead you continued to believe that you wished to marry Miss Brattle? You continued knowing that your father was adamantly opposed to the match?"

Porgy hung his head.

"Yes," he answered. "Yes. So I had a motive. I had a motive. But, Mr. Howard, believe me, I did not kill Papa."

"Yet I have only your word for it, Maharajah," the D.S.P. said, apparently no more affected by Porgy's near-sobbing declaration than he would have been by the announcement of luncheon. "Can you produce some evidence that makes it clear you had nothing to do with your father's death?"

"I can't. You know I can't. But— But, well, there are others, aren't there? Have they all proved that they couldn't have done it? Have they? Have they?"

"I am not at liberty to disclose the progress of my investigations, even to you, Maharajah."

"There's Sir Akhtar," Porgy said, his voice rising up again. "He's someone with a hell of a motive."

"Your father had disagreed with the Dewan certainly," D.S.P. Howard replied, in a quietly argumentative tone. "But, then, remember, you and he had had a disagreement every bit as profound, perhaps more so."

"Well, that's where you're wrong, Mr. Howard. That's where you happen to be bloody well wrong."

"Indeed?"

The D.S.P. seemed to be expressing only the mildest interest.

"Yes, indeed. Yes, this proves it. Yes."

"Well, suppose you tell me just what it is, Maharajah."

"I bloody well will. I'm not going to keep quiet about it any longer. Not when my bloody life's at stake. No, too bad. He'll just have to put up with it if he hasn't known all along. Or anyhow since that appalling dinner party."

"I'm afraid, Maharajah, you have me at a disadvantage."

"What? What's that?"

The smallest of smiles lifted the corners of the D.S.P.'s eyes for one instant.

"I don't know what you're talking about, Maharajah," he explained.

"What— Not— Oh, I see. Yes. Yes. Well, it's perfectly simple."

Porgy sat back in his huge desk chair for the first time.

"Yes," he went on, "it's perfectly simple. You know that Papa— that my father, His late Highness, had a certain fondness for practical jokes?"

"Maharajah, the whole affair depends on that unfortunate taste of your father's."

"Quite so, quite so. Well, this is what it's all about. My father was playing a joke on the Dewan. A really tremendous joke."

"What joke, Maharajah?" D.S.P. Howard asked patiently.

"A joke about that American, Mr. Morton, Henry Morton the Third, as he calls himself. You see, Mr. Howard, all that business about zinc mining in Bhopore—you know about that, do you?"

"I know."

"Well, the whole damn thing was just being got up by Papa to tease the Dewan. He'd absolutely no intention of allowing that man to set up factories and everything and turn Bhopore into a second Chicago or wherever it is. It would have been anathema to Papa, anything like that. He'd have died first. But he knew Dewan Sahib would feel, if anything, even worse about it. So he got that chap Morton to come here, and he pretended he was going ahead with the scheme. Perhaps he hoped Dewan Sahib would resign. He was fed up with always being told what was best for the State, and how he shouldn't be splashing out on his pet projects, like shikar, but should be building more roads and things all the time. He was absolutely fed up with all that, and if Sir Akhtar had resigned he'd have been pleased as Punch."

"And you think Sir Akhtar realised what trick had been played on him and killed your father in a fit of fury? Is that it?"

Porgy looked suddenly crestfallen.

"Well, it could have been, couldn't it?" he muttered.

"Maharajah," the D.S.P. said, almost as sharply as if he had been speaking to one of his own police constables who had been guilty of some minor breach of orders. "Maharajah, have you any reason for believing that the Dewan knew that all this business was no more than a joke on your father's part? Have you?"

Porgy picked up the empty whisky glass, put it down with a clunk on the leather of the desk.

"Well, no," he said. "No, I suppose, I haven't. Not any absolutely definite reason. But— Well, he could have, couldn't he?"

Then a thought seemed to strike him.

"Listen, Mr. Howard," he said, with urgency. "Listen, please. Whatever you do, if Dewan Sahib doesn't know, don't tell him my father did that. I mean, he would be hurt, deeply hurt. And I wouldn't want that. Not at any price. Please, Mr. Howard, can I rely on you for that?"

The D.S.P.'s face was impassive.

"Maharajah," he said, "it will be my duty to ascertain if I can whether the Dewan did or did not know your father had played this elaborate joke on him. But, insofar as I can, I will take steps to find out discreetly."

"Thank you," Porgy said.

D.S.P. Howard, who had risen from his chair in front of the big green-topped desk, made the Maharajah a short bow as he stood near the door. But before leaving he spoke again.

"Maharajah," he said, "I am happy to take your word that your father put forward the zinc-mining plan only as an elaborate joke. As to whether Sir Akhtar realised this before your father's death, I retain an open mind."

He put out a hand and felt for the doorknob.

"As equally, Maharajah, I retain an open mind about when and why you decided that you were not going to marry Miss Brattle."

And before Porgy could get in another hot denial the door had opened, the white-clad figure had stepped in an instant through it, and the door had closed again.

Porgy, Maharajah of Bhopore, sat there gasping like a landed fish.

XII

Outside the study, here and there in the long corridors and the many different rooms of the palace, those hooded, observant eyes resumed their hunt. They watched for a little the two telephone orderlies who sat in the little wooden cubicle devoted to housing the mysterious instrument, waiting for the ring-ringing of its bell, ready to lift the tube of the receiver from its hook, to ask respectfully and in very reasonable English, "Who is speaking, please?" and then to hurry off in search of whichever sahib it was that the call was for. But when it was clear that neither man's hands bore giveaway orange marks the watcher moved quietly on.

Another, and very different, means of communication also recieved its few minutes of scrutiny. All along a corridor not far from the Armoury sat the palace scribes, laboriously copying out manuscripts and records as their fathers and their grandfathers and their great-grandfathers had done before them. The sound of their quills scratching on parchment was unceasing. But though hands here were ink-stained, none was orange-marked. With a thoughtful nod D.S.P. Howard passed onwards. He numbered the unmarked scribes with the unmarked syces in the stables. He added them to the unmarked mahouts in the hathikhana looking after their great grey lumbering, yet strangely graceful charges. He added again the dozen carpenters working solidly all day, day after day, repairing and renewing, whose work was never done. To these again he added the A.D.C.s, the A.D.C.s' servants, the A.D.C.s' servants' servants. And more, and yet more. But never one bearing the startlingly bright sign that he sought.

It was during the afternoon, when almost everybody in the vast building was lying flat, lying on well-stuffed mattresses if they were sahibs, lying on the interlaced cords of charpoys if they were lower in the scale, lying on the cool corners of floors if they were the lowest of the low, it was at this hour of heat-smothered sleep that the still prowling figure encountered one of the few in the palace to be wakeful.

"Good afternoon, Schoolmaster Sahib. I see you are not sleeping!"

"Good afternoon, D.S.P. Sahib. You also are defying sleep."

"I have work to do, Schoolmaster Sahib. And much too little time to do it in."

"And I have a book to read, D.S.P. Sahib. And at last a quiet hour."

D.S.P. Howard gave a little smile, the merest twitch of the corners of his straight mouth, the tiniest lifting of his hooded eyelids.

"Then I will not disturb you, Schoolmaster Sahib."

"No, no. Please, D.S.P. Sahib." The bony-shouldered Schoolmaster scrambled to his feet. "Please, consider my time is yours."

Again that smallest of smiles.

"Then sit again, Schoolmaster Sahib. And I'll sit beside you for a few moments, and take a little rest."

This time it was the Schoolmaster who smiled. But so discreetly that the expression on his face changed no more than had the policeman's.

"D.S.P. Sahib," he began, diffidently, once the policeman had settled himself on the out-of-the-way marble bench chosen for its quietness. "D.S.P. Sahib, I have been thinking very much about the murder of late His Highness. As who could not fail so to do? When a person like His Highness, a man of such importance, and also of so much vitality—so much a man—when he is untimely snatched from this world by impious murder, then one cannot cease from speculation."

"About what exactly, Schoolmaster Sahib?" There was an unconcealed impatience in the D.S.P.'s tone.

The Schoolmaster sighed.

"It is the question of the sapura bark, D.S.P. Sahib. How, after all, was that fateful snippet obtained?"

"A good question, Schoolmaster Sahib. And one to which I have been devoting most of my time."

"Indeed, Sahib? And may one ask with how much success?"

"With no success so far, Schoolmaster Sahib. As you already know, there was, of course, only one piece of sapura bark available, the piece that was brought to the Maharajah early on the morning of the day before his death by the tribesman who found it."

"Yes, yes. That is certainly so. I happened to have a few words with late His Highness's bearer and he was altogether clear about that."

"A few words, Schoolmaster Sahib? Did you?"

For a moment or two the D.S.P. was silent, and there was a faint twinkle to be observed under the hoods of his eyes.

"Very good," he resumed. "Now we have several witnesses as to what happened to the other half of the piece after the Maharajah played his trick."

"It was thrown by His Highness to Captain Ram Singh," the Schoolmaster said decisively. "I was talking, by chance, to Captain Ram Singh only this morning, congratulating him on his release from durance vile, and he mentioned the matter to me."

"Did he indeed? I wonder how that happened to enter the conversation."

The Schoolmaster did not rise to the bait.

"Very good," D.S.P. Howard continued. "Now we have the bark in one of Captain Ram Singh's pockets. But do you know what happened to it next?"

"D.S.P. Sahib, as it happens, I can inform you about that. I was having a few words with Lieutenant Frere yesterday after I had shown him some of the beauties and interesting aspects of the palace, and he informed me that the piece of bark came to light when Captain Ram Singh was being searched, on His Highness's orders, in Lieutenant Frere's bathroom. The piece, together with a few other tiny unconsidered trifles, was apparently not taken up again by Captain Ram Singh when that search was concluded, and it continued to lie on the stool in Lieutenant Frere's bathroom."

"But," said D.S.P. Howard, "when Lieutenant Frere's bearer looked into the bathroom next morning to make sure that all was in order for Lieutenant Frere's bath the sapura bark was not there. Did you happen to talk with Lieutenant Frere's bearer?"

"Yes," said the Schoolmaster, "I chanced to meet the fellow and we exchanged a few words."

"And from those few words did you discover how very easy it would have been for anybody to enter Lieutenant Frere's rooms during the remainder of that evening and to take away the other half of the sapura bark?"

"Yes, D.S.P. Sahib. The bearer mentioned that the rooms were deserted for all that time. However, it would surely be a most unlikely circumstance for Miss Dorothy Brattle to enter the rooms of Lieutenant Frere."

"A good point, Schoolmaster Sahib. But it does not take into account one very simple fact of palace life."

The Schoolmaster sat in silence for a little. You could almost hear the facts of palace life, so many and so various, being put through the mill of that busy mind.

At last, with a cross little contraction of his mouth, he turned to D.S.P. Howard again.

"Please, what fact of palace life?" he asked.

The D.S.P.'s almost hidden eyes glowed in brief triumph.

"The monkeys, Schoolmaster Sahib," he said.

The Schoolmaster slapped his thigh in vexation.

"You are perfectly right, D.S.P. Sahib. And, dropped somewhere by a thieving monkey, anyone could have picked up that little bright object."

"That, I think, is the situation, Schoolmaster Sahib. It is a situation that does not make my life in any way easier. Except for the fact that that person very likely has orange-stained hands. Perhaps that's something you might care to remember, Schoolmaster Sahib."

The D.S.P. pushed himself to his feet from the cool marble of the bench. He stood for a moment making up his mind where next in the palace he would go.

"I'm sorry to have disturbed your reading, Schoolmaster Sahib," he said.

"Not at all, not at all, D.S.P. Sahib. What you have been telling me is very, very much more interesting than the pages of any detective story."

"You're reading a detective story?"

"Yes, indeed, D.S.P. Sahib. The newest work of Mrs. Agatha Christie, *The Seven Dials Mystery*. Present His Highness was kind enough to lend me the volume. He invariably obtains the latest detective stories from the emporium of Messrs. Harrod in London."

"Does he?" said the D.S.P. "Does he indeed?"

And he turned on his heel and stalked off into the great labyrinth of the still sleeping palace.

When the least privileged of the many, many inhabitants of the huge building began to stir their activities came under scrutiny once more. The two men whose duty it was each day to wash a large supply of small coins and put them in velvet bags, ready for the Maharajah to distribute to such poor people of Bhopore as he might encounter, were watched for a few minutes and duly noted as having clean hands. The fifteen servants who, in spite of the recently installed electricity and its throbbing generator, spent a large part of each day in cleaning and filling the many oil lamps that were to be distributed at dusk here, there and everywhere throughout the massive pile, were observed too and found to be free of orange stains.

D.S.P. Howard, substantial ghost in neat whites, flitted on.

The new Maharajah did not, as his father had done, require the presence of his Dewan reading the newspaper during the hot afternoon, if only with a decorum-preserving screen between them. So the D.S.P. was able to find the administrator of the State in his own office.

"Dewan Sahib, I trust I am not disturbing you? I realise you must always be busy."

The Dewan, who worked at a large, low table sitting cross-legged on a plump white cotton-covered cushion, carefully put aside the document he had been reading, a wide sheet of paper covered with intricate, beautiful Persian-style penwork.

"Mr. Howard, yes, I am busy. True, I am almost always busy. But I recognise that some things must come before others, and that the reason you are here in Bhopore is a matter perhaps more urgent than any other one whatsoever. Please, be seated. Take as much of my time as you need."

The D.S.P. sat himself on the plumply firm cushion on the opposite side of the papers-covered table. He had no difficulty in assuming the cross-legged posture necessary.

"Dewan Sahib," he said, "I have been spending a great deal of time since my arrival in seeing what goes on in the palace. So I have acquired already a considerable knowledge of its ways. May I say that I have been very much impressed by the manner in which things are run?"

The Dewan could not quite conceal his pleasure in the compliment.

"Mr. Howard, even before there was any question of your coming to Bhopore, I had heard a good deal about Sangabad District and the man who policed it. So to have won his approval for my own small efforts to keep affairs in the palace running in an orderly way is to have gained approval indeed."

"Please believe, Dewan Sahib, what I have said was no idle compliment. I am not a man for idle compliments."

"No. I suspect, Mr. Howard, that you are not a man for idleness of any kind. So, enough politeness, however gratifying. Now, what can I do for you?"

The D.S.P. acknowledged this directness with a small, sharp smile.

"One thing in particular, Dewan Sahib," he said. "There is one aspect of this whole matter that I am not altogether satisfied about, and I think you can assist me."

"If it is in my power—"

"Oh, I am sure, Dewan Sahib, that it will be in your power. I don't imagine there is very much in the State of Bhopore that is not in your power."

The Dewan raised a deprecating hand.

"No, there, Mr. Howard, you are wrong. There is a very great deal in Bhopore that is not in my power. There is a very great deal that could be done to make life for the people of Bhopore better in many, many ways. The dam that His Excellency the Viceroy will open, inshallah, in eleven days' time is only one step in a large programme of necessary improvements."

"Ah, yes. The dam. Tell me, Dewan Sahib, who exactly was it who proposed building the dam, yourself or the Maharajah?"

The Dewan smiled.

"That is a question almost on a par with 'Have you stopped beating your wife?' Mr. Howard," he said. "If I say that I was the prime mover in getting the dam constructed, you will think that the Maharajah was opposed to the plan and there was enmity between us because of that. If, on the other hand, I say that the plan was the Maharajah's, you will say that he wanted that and that only, and that I may have felt that other necessary plans were being neglected. So, shall we leave the matter undecided? Let me hear instead what it is that you believe it is in my power to assist you over."

It was the D.S.P.'s turn to smile now. But the twitch of his straight-set lips might have been mistaken for almost anything but a smile.

"Yes, Dewan Sahib," he said, "perhaps I put things a little badly earlier on. I am well aware that there must be many things you would like to see done in Bhopore that you cannot have put in hand. I know that money is not always to be had, and that sometimes when money has been available it has been used for odd purposes. And I know, too, that a man of your sort has to fight often against engrained attitudes and rules. But, when I spoke about the power you have, it was information that I wanted from you, and that I think you will be able to give me."

"What information, Mr. Howard?"

"About Captain Ram Singh, Dewan Sahib."

"Ah, Captain Ram Singh. The unfortunate Captain Ram Singh. What can I tell you about him?"

"It's quite simple. His late Highness ordered Captain Ram Singh to be detained at the end of dinner on the night before he died. I have no doubt such an order would be obeyed, to the letter."

"It would indeed."

"But there is something I have asked myself about it."

"And what might that be?"

"It occurred to me to wonder if say a guard charged with watching over a man His Highness had thrown into prison came to know that His Highness would be dead before very long, whether then he might not be so careful in carrying out his duties."

The Dewan smiled again.

"I can see that no possibility in this matter is going to escape you, Mr. Howard," he said. "That is as I had expected. And in a way you are right to have had that thought. I would not have been altogether surprised, if Captain Ram Singh had remained at liberty, to hear that he had made an attempt upon His Highness's life."

"No? I have scarcely met him. He seemed at first to be outside the scope of my inquiry. Yet I wouldn't have thought, frankly, that he was intelligent enough to have murdered the Maharajah and got away with it."

"Well, perhaps he is not," the Dewan answered with a smile. "But that does not mean he would not try. Captain Ram Singh must have been a very desperate man when he arrived back in Bhopore from visiting his father, the Thakur of Panna, you know. After all, consider. He had been sent on the express orders of His Highness to secure from his father certain money that ought long ago to have been paid. He was returning not only empty-handed but with not even polite promises. Now, the position of A.D.C. to the Maharajah is one that many young men of good family aspire to. It promises later high office in the State, such a position, for instance, as chief of the State police. Captain Ram Singh must have seen all his hopes about to crumble over his head. And he knew, all the while, that the then Maharajkumar regarded him with the greatest friendship. If the Maharajah were to die his prospects would be turned about in an instant."

D.S.P. Howard held the Dewan in his eyes.

"But you doubt that he was responsible for the death?" he said.

"I do indeed. Not, mind you, that he was incapable of it, and even in the manner in which it eventually happened. The sort of really quite simple trickery involved is very much—what shall I say?—Captain Ram Singh's style. Indeed, for that very reason as soon as I realised what exactly the situation was, that the killing was, if you like, a sort of carbon-paper copy of what had happened with the Resident's car the day before, then the thought came at once into my mind 'Captain Ram Singh.'"

"And yet?"

"And yet he was in prison, Mr. Howard. You have taken leave to doubt it. I too doubted it. So immediately I made the very strictest inquiries. Something of the same notion that you had entertained had entered my head. Could Captain Ram Singh have been released by someone expecting the Maharajah would soon no longer be there to punish any laxness over his orders? And the answer was 'No,' Mr. Howard."

"Beyond doubting?"

"Mr. Howard, you were good enough to say just now that it was in my power at least to know what was happening anywhere in Bhopore. I quite simply agree to that. It is in my power. And I tell you that Captain Ram Singh did not leave his prison cell until long after the old Maharajah was dead."

"Thank you, Dewan Sahib."

D.S.P. Howard rose from the firm white cushion he had been sitting on. He was about to take his leave. But the Dewan halted him with a gesture.

"Mr. Howard, while you are here and we are alone, there is something that I would like to say to you."

The D.S.P. lowered himself skilfully onto the cushion again.

"Yes, Dewan Sahib? I am at your disposal."

The Dewan drew in a long breath.

"Now that I am face to face with it, I find it somewhat difficult to begin."

"You can only begin, Dewan Sahib."

"Yes. Yes, that is so."

But the Dewan did not begin. Instead he sat looking down at the papers neatly piled in front of him, some typewritten in English, more handwritten in flowing Persian-style script. He sat looking at the papers but not seeing them.

At last D.S.P. Howard broke the silence.

"Let me tell you what I think you will have to say to me, Dewan Sahib."

The Dewan looked up. There was a glint of something in his eyes. Perhaps suspicion. Perhaps even fear.

"Very well, Mr. Howard."

"I think that you have a confession to make."

"A confession?"

Again that little flick of the straight-set lips that might have been a smile appeared on the D.S.P.'s face.

"A sort of confession," he said.

He was answered by what was quite plainly a smile from the Dewan.

"Yes, Mr. Howard, a sort of confession. And it is absurd, really, that I should have made such heavy weather of it."

"Then cease doing so, Dewan Sahib," the D.S.P. said, with open impatience.

"Very well. It is simply this then. I wish to confess, if that is the word, not, of course, to the murder of the Maharajah, but to being the person you must think murdered the Maharajah. I wish it to be plainly understood between us that I am the one who, when you carefully examine the situation, is most likely to have committed that crime. There are five of us only in a position actually to have carried out the deed. Very good. Of those five, it is, first, patently ridiculous to suspect an English visitor like Lieutenant Frere."

The Dewan paused and looked at the D.S.P.

The D.S.P.'s face remained inexpressive under his hooded eyes.

"Dewan Sahib," he said, "I am still in the course of my investigation. You must not expect me to comment on any aspect of it. Not even the most apparently obvious."

For a moment the Dewan looked puzzled. Then he gave a little shrug.

"Very well, D.S.P. Sahib. You must permit me then to state that Lieutenant Frere is dismissed from consideration. And so, I venture to add, is Miss Dorothy Brattle. Yes, yes, I know that she must be seen to have a motive, and a powerful one. The Maharajah stood between her and any possibility of a marriage with his son, and plainly Miss Brattle needed to make that marriage. She is—what shall I say? —not as young as she was. If her liaison with the Maharajkumar was never to be more than that, her chances of then securing herself a comfortable alliance would surely be slim indeed."

"There, Dewan Sahib, I can agree with you. But if you are going to add nevertheless Miss Brattle as a woman could not have committed the crime, then that is a matter on which I reserve judgment."

The Dewan shrugged.

"Very well, if you choose, Mr. Howard. But let me say that I myself have no doubts on the matter. I cannot see Miss Brattle putting that piece of sapura bark into the barrel of one of His Highness's Purdeys. I cannot see her adding a little water. She is not, surely, a practical person. But there it is. You reserve your judgment: I will believe what I believe. And that leaves me with just two other people."

"It does."

"Mr. Lloyd then. Yes, he would certainly be capable of that business with the bark. No doubt of that. But what about his motive? Oh, yes, I know that he was heard to utter very direct threats against the Maharajah. But, Mr. Howard, ask yourself this: Does a man who shouts threats of that sort invariably act upon them? I say that, in fact, he never acts upon them. I say that Mr. Lloyd is one of those men who only breaks the law in words, never in deeds."

Again the hooded eyelids moved in what might have been a smile.

"Your question is one that I have asked myself, Dewan Sahib. And have answered to myself."

"Very good. So we are left face to face with His present Highness."

"If you say so."

The Dewan brought the tips of his fingers together in a pyramid.

"Mr. Howard, I am well aware that there would seem to be every motive for His Highness to have murdered his father, and, needless to say, the method of the murder is well within the abilities of His Highness. More, in the history of India he would not be the first son to have attained the gaddi by murder. No. Nevertheless, I put it to you that this was not what happened. It could not have been what happened."

"I am listening, Dewan Sahib."

"Mr. Howard, you are unfortunate in one thing in this matter."

"No, Dewan Sahib. In many things." The hooded eyes momentarily lifted up.

"If you say, 'In many things,' so be it. But in one thing in particular you are most unfortunate. You were not here in Bhopore before the murder took place. Not in just the few days before the murder, but in the many, many months before. Because if you had been here, as I have, you would have known what the real relations were between His Highness now and his father. He loved his father, Mr. Howard. He loved him. There is no more to say than that."

"Very well, Dewan Sahib. You have made out excellent cases why none of the four people you have discussed could have murdered the Maharajah. And that leaves, of the five, only yourself. And yet you tell me you did not kill the Maharajah."

The Dewan's eyes clouded.

"No, Mr. Howard, I did not kill him. But I want it clearly understood that, of the five, I am the one who ought to have killed him. My time as Dewan of this State was coming to its end. None knew that better than I. Gradually the Maharajah and I, once so close, had been drifting away from each other. I had begun to have larger ambitions for Bhopore than the Maharajah could ever have had. And he was becoming with increasing age more and more determined to stick to the old ways. Mr. Howard, Bhopore and its life mean everything to me. It has become my life. I would sacrifice my life for Bhopore. You must see me as your chief suspect."

D.S.P. Howard's straight mouth curved this time into a clearly recognisable smile.

"Yes, Dewan Sahib," he said. "Be clear about that. I do regard you as the chief suspect."

XIII

The Resident looked at D.S.P. Howard.

"Have you time for a game of tennis?" he asked. "Out on the court we can be rather more sure of not being overheard. None of my ball boys has much English."

"Yes, certainly, Sir Arthur."

Down on the Residency's beautifully marked-out No. 1 court, there were two ball boys in smart uniforms, who even if they were a good deal older than what is generally understood by "boy" were guaranteed to know only English words connected with their duties: "Ball!" and "Good shot, sir," and "Advantage, Resident Sahib." In shorts and white flannel shirts now, D.S.P. Howard and Sir Arthur Pendeverel exchanged a few words over the tightly stretched net.

"Well, Howard, any orange-stained hands?"

"No, sir. Not a sign so far."

"I see. Well, you have only four days until I must cable the Viceroy. It isn't very long, Howard."

"I am well aware of that, sir. But, as I hope you've come to see, the affair is a good deal more difficult than it looked at the outset."

"I suppose it may be. I suppose it may be. But nevertheless it remains simply a matter of finding out which of five people is responsible for murdering the Maharajah. Please remember that."

D.S.P. Howard made no reply. A short silence ensued over the well-stretched tennis net. It grew longer.

"Shall we play?" the Resident said abruptly.

He lost to the D.S.P., 6–4, 6–4.

It was time for cocktails once again. There were fewer people in the palace drawing room to take them than there had been when the Resident had come to dine. Tonight dinner was to be simply for Porgy's guests and a handful of courtiers. But the service was as assiduous as ever.

White-jacketed Goan bearers went soft-footed through the huge room, skirting the white marble fountain that softly splashed in its centre, moving from one island of back-to-back richly brocaded Empire sofas to the next. On their trays tonight were not only the sugary cream-topped Alexanders that the old Maharajah had so delighted in, but many another concoction as well: lime-tinted gimlets, faintly rosy pink gins, darker green glasses in which green Chartreuse or crème de menthe predominated, gin and orange as well as whisky awaiting the bubbles of the soda-water bottle beside it.

Under the high arched ceiling of the long room, divided into two by the fountain and the two immense carpets on either side of it, there were not many to make their selection from the bearers' silver trays. There was Porgy, resplendent in a blue brocade sherwani. There was the Dewan, in black silk. There was Captain Ram Singh, tall, impossibly handsome, his moustached face bearing a faint contented smile, as if never in his life had he seen the stinking inside of one of the palace dungeons. There was Mrs. Alcott, in a deep ruby-red dress that had been splendid in Wisconsin but somehow here was no longer so splendid. There was Judy, in simple white, simply pretty. And, beside her—where else?—there was James Frere, in dress uniform, his crest of fair hair soft under the light of the three six-foot-high chandeliers that hung from the high ceiling. There was Joe Lloyd, whose white boiled evening shirt-front once more had popped a stud. There was the scarred figure of Henry Morton III, puffing hard at a large cigar and eyeing Porgy almost all the time with a look of open calculation.

Two people who might have been expected to be there were not, though whether they were missed by the others it was impossible to say. Certainly Porgy ought to have been conscious that his Dolly was not present, the Dolly who until a very short time before had been the figure his eyes strayed to again and again when they were in any crowded room together. But Porgy seemed totally absorbed, talking pigsticking with Captain Ram Singh and James Frere, with Judy as an eager listener.

And who among them all was fighting to keep out of mind the fact that D.S.P. Howard was not there? Who was wondering where those eyes, which seemed always to be so hooded that they could see nothing but which nevertheless still gave the disquieting impression of seeing everything, were looking now?

Porgy raised the forefinger of his right hand in a tiny gesture. A bearer was at his elbow within moments. Porgy murmured an instruction. The bearer glided past tables crowded with silver-framed photographs—not a few of them of European royalty, flourishingly signed—and reached the gramophone cabinet where it stood in a corner, all gleaming mahogany. He opened the heavy lid, selected from the mahogany rack beside it the record Maharajah Sahib had ordered, wound the machine, placed the record on the spindle, carefully lowered the head of the moving arm so that the thick needle found the outer grooves of the record, released the brake lever. Music twanged on the air. "Alexander's Ragtime Band."

Faintly the jaunty little tune came to D.S.P. Howard up on the floor above, wearing evening dress but still pacing and peering and calculating.

And then another sound was added to the tiny jangle of the music in his sharp ears. It was scarcely louder. But it made him pause at once, think for an instant, then glide forward noiselessly on the white marble floor of the long corridor.

He moved, quiet as any of those thieves of India who can enter a sleeping white sahib's room, remove the tick-ticking watch from the teapoy table just a foot from his ear, and vanish again unheard. Along the remaining half of the corridor he glided, and at its end he flattened himself against the cool plaster of the wall. Then half inch by half inch he eased himself round the corner there.

The small smile that was hardly a twitch of straight-set lips appeared on his face. He had seen more or less what he expected to see.

At the head of a narrow staircase, not far along the intersecting passageway, a staircase that led to a less frequented part of the palace and on to the gates through which the dhobi-wallahs and their washing-laden bulls went each morning, was the tall platinum-crowned figure of Dolly Brattle. She was dressed in outdoor clothes and was carrying a suitcase.

A white woman carrying her own suitcase, and nor was it a lightweight one. D.S.P. Howard drew his conclusions.

Rapidly, his feet striking echoing taps now on the marble floor, he went along the intersecting corridor towards the stairs and Dolly. At the sudden sound she turned, gasped, put her free hand to her half-open mouth, and then turned again and set off down the stairway, swaying a little from the weight of her heavy suitcase.

"Miss Brattle."

The two words stopped her again decisively as if an iron bar had dropped across the stairs in front of her.

"Good evening. I was hoping to have a word with you. It's D.S.P. Howard. We met, you remember."

"Yes. Oh, yes. Yes, of course. But— Well, you see— Well, I was just going somewhere."

D.S.P. Howard, standing now at the head of the stairs, only a foot or two above her, looked down at the heavy suitcase tugging her right arm straight as if it were simply a strand of thick rope.

"Yes, I see you're on your way somewhere. But, you know, I think we had better talk. Your rooms are just along here, if I've got my geography right. Let me carry that case for you."

Dolly Brattle found herself back in the rooms she had thought hardly two minutes before that she would never see again. An air of disorder was startlingly evident. The doors of the tall almirah were wide open. The drawers of the dressing table gaped. A few small discarded cosmetic items lay on its surface, rolling uselessly.

"May I sit?" said D.S.P. Howard.

He perched on a corner of the bed, the bed that Dolly had seldom slept in during her stay at the palace. Dolly herself realised that, thank goodness, there was a little armchair just behind her. She let her jellylike knees go limp.

But through the haze in which she sat a cuttingly clear voice was asking a question.

"Well, now, what was all that about? This suitcase you were hefting all on your own? Hefting very dashingly, but on your own?"

"I— Well, I— Oh, damn it, it's no good. I was going, leaving. Running away, if you must know."

"But I asked you what it was all about. I could see you were departing, and without so much as letting a single servant know. What I asked was: Why?"

Tears were not far from her eyes now. She straightened her back in the little low armchair and forced herself to look hard at the man in evening dress sitting coolly there on the end of the bed.

"I suppose you've a right to ask?" she said, with a little spurt of weary defiance.

"Certainly I have. You know quite well that I've been called in to investigate the murder of the Maharajah. You must know, too—you heard Sir Arthur Pendeverel state it, so I'm told—that anyone who both saw the late Maharajah play that April Fool trick with sapura bark on Little Michael and who also had access to the Maharajah's gun rack at the time of his death is under suspicion. So, yes, I have a right to ask where you were going just now."

"It's not that. It's not what you think."

"And what do I think?"

"That I killed the Maharajah and was trying to escape. God, I'd have liked to see him dead all right. That great elephant with his bloody ideas of tradition and the age-old rules and who could be a maharani and who couldn't. Yes, I'd have liked him out of the way, I don't mind telling you."

"But you're telling me that you did not one way or another come across a piece of that sapura bark, that you did not take a lesson from what happened when the driver tried to start the Resident's car, that you did not push the sapura bark down the barrel of one of the Maharajah's guns so that it would explode and kill him, the way a gun had once all but killed Mr. Henry Morton. You're telling me all that?"

"Yes, I am."

"And you're expecting me to believe it? Just to take your word for it?"

"Well, what else can I do? I didn't kill him, even if I would have welcomed him being out of the way. So all I can do is to say I didn't."

"No. It is not all you can do."

"What can I do then?"

"You can tell me why you were trying to leave the palace in secrecy."

She sat and looked at him. She saw square shoulders, an absolutely upright back. A level, uncompromising mouth. Two hooded, expressionless eyes.

"It's not something I'm very proud about," she said.

"I daresay."

No help, no hint of sympathy, in the tersely uttered words.

"It's Porgy, of course. I mean the Maharajkumar. Well, he's the Maha—"

"I know very well who Porgy is."

"Yes. Yes, I suppose you do. I suppose you know that he wanted to marry me too?"

"Of course I know. It's my business to know things like that. But you said 'wanted.' Do I understand he no longer wants to marry you?"

"Yes."

Her eyes, which she had been forcing herself to hold steady on his, dropped. The tears came into them again. Careless of everything, she sniffed like a horse to keep them in.

"Yes," she repeated, muttering rather now. "Porgy's the Maharajah now, and suddenly he wants to marry whatever daughter of some damned princely house his father had lined up for him or was all set to have lined up for him. Porgy's the Maharajah, and suddenly I'm not the one he worships anymore."

She looked up again now. Her eyes were bright. But no longer with tears. With, instead, sudden rage.

"I thought I was going to do it," she said. "I was as near pulling it off as 'damn it' is to swearing. Porgy loved me. He did. He was mad about me. Mad about me. A future Maharajah. And he'd have married me. He bloody well would. We'd have gone off to Bombay. Or even to England, or Scotland, to Gretna Green, if we'd had to. And in the end I'd have been the Maharani."

She jumped up and stood in front of him, eyes blazing now.

"You know what I was, do you?" she said. "You've probably heard. In the chorus at the London Pavilion. Porgy didn't bring me out here, you know. I came out to get married. Married. I thought I'd done all right then. Chap I met while he was on leave. Told me he was a tea planter, running a huge estate. Big career in front of him. Had to go back before we could get the licence in England. But he paid my passage. And then when I got to Calcutta, what did I find? He was only a skinny little box-wallah. Stuck in an office there, just half a hand's-breadth above the blacky-whiteys. I'd have had a worse life there than if I'd stuck it out at home."

"So you ditched him?"

She flopped back in the little armchair again.

"So I ditched him. I thought I could make it on my own out here. Lots and lots of men, Englishmen. And damned few women, if you don't count the chee-chees and the natives. But I had a hard time of it, I can tell you. I got myself over to Bombay. But I'd precious little money. The police got on to me. Do you know what a D.E.W. is?"

"A Destitute European Woman. There are funds to provide passages to England for them rather than have a white prostitute on the streets."

"Exactly. Well, that's what I was threatened with. I was warned. And then . . . Then I had my stroke of luck. I was blowing my last few chips on dinner at the Taj Hotel. I was ready to say I'd go next day. And along came Porgy. He picked me up, you know. I wasn't the one to make the running, not at first. Honest, I wasn't."

"All right, I believe you."

"Well, that was it. From damn nearly the mire, right up to the top. Come and stay. Live with me. We'll get married. To hell with Papa and his objections, I'll marry you in spite of everything. Till that business out at the jheels there. Bang, you're dead. And do you know? When I saw that great fat body lying there, I could have sung aloud for joy. Yes, I could. Sung aloud. There's nothing to stop us now, I thought. Nothing to stop us at all. I was even going to say something to Porgy there and then. Out at the blasted jheels. Not exactly tactful, but I thought he loved me. I thought he was mad, mad, mad about me. But he just didn't want to know I was there."

She smiled now, a twisted smile.

"I ought to have picked up one of those guns and put a bullet or whatever it is through my head there and then," she said.

"But instead you hung on for a little?"

"You're bloody right. Hanging on it was. Trying to convince Porgy when all the time I knew it was hopeless. Trying to blackmail him into doing the decent thing, if you must know. But I should have realised that once you're a blasted Maharajah you don't have to play by any rules anymore. I should have gone the moment we all got back from the jheels."

She peered across at the D.S.P. as if willing him to utter just one word of encouragement.

He rose from the end of the bed.

"You had better unpack and come down to dinner," he said. "I'm afraid I require you to stay here."

D.S.P. Howard came into the drawing room in time to take one whisky before everybody went into dinner. Dolly Brattle did not come down until the meal had begun. Under the cap of her shingled platinum hair her face was a dead-white which no amount of rouge could conceal.

Dinner was not a cheerful meal, for all that nothing was spared in luxury.

XIV

Some time after dinner that night Elaine Alcott and Judy were to be seen coming up together onto the enormous flat roof of the palace, a garden almost as verdant as the well-watered lawns and shrubberies of the grounds all round. Here there were not flower beds but urns and huge earthenware pots. But they were as full of marigolds and zinnias as the neatly ranged beds. And there were, too, statues and fountains and long colonnades of marble pillars. Above, the huge stars of the Indian night pulsated in the deep-blue velvet sky.

"What is it, Mother? Why this sudden 'Come with me, dear'?"

"I'll tell you. But not yet. Not just yet."

"Mother, why not, for heaven's sake?"

Mrs. Alcott stopped and looked behind her at the small domed building which covered the head of the stairs leading up to the roof. In the soft, scented darkness there seemed to be not the least movement there.

"I wanted to speak to you, Judy," she explained, in a whisper that was rather more penetrating than her ordinary voice.

"I know that, Mother dear. But what do you want to say? And why do you have to bring me all the way up here to say it?"

"Come over here, dear."

Sighing in muted exasperation, Judy followed her mother along a colonnade, the sweet scent of the jasmine twining its pillars delicate in their nostrils. At the far end Mrs. Alcott came to a stop. She looked round carefully. She looked back along the colonnade.

But she failed to spot a figure in black evening dress. She had failed to see him when he had emerged from the stairs as soon as her back had been turned. Now, quickly inferring her coming action from what he had detected of her movements in the darkness, he had stepped back into the deep shadow between two of the pillars at just the moment she turned for her final inspection of the colonnade.

D.S.P. Howard counted slowly to ten in Urdu. Then he slipped out of his temporary hiding place and made his way on silent feet nearer to where Judy and her mother now stood.

"Mother, you're behaving like a villain in an old movie. What on earth is all this about?"

"Servants," Elaine Alcott hissed.

Judy looked round, but perfunctorily.

"No, dear. Not servants here. That's just why I insisted you come up to the roof. Judy, I've found out you can never be sure."

"Sure of what, Mother?"

"Sure there are no servants standing just around the corner flapping their black ears when you're having a private conversation. Judy, when I think what I let your Uncle Joe say to me in my room the other night I shiver. Yessir, I shiver."

"Mother, what was that? What is this? You're getting me confused."

"Judy, you know perfectly well. Your Uncle Joe let rip with the most terrible remarks about the Maharajah the very night before the man was murdered. I didn't know about servants then, but I've found out since. I've caught them standing there."

"But, Mother, they're only waiting to see if there's anything they can do for you. It's different in India, Mother. They just want to make sure that you have everything and that you don't have to do a hand's turn for yourself. It's what they feel is their duty. James told me all about it."

"James," said Elaine Alcott.

"Mother, don't you dare say a word against James. Why, he's the sweetest, the most upright guy I've ever met. Or that I ever hope to meet in a thousand years."

"Judy, listen to me."

"Mother, I have been listening. I've been listening and listening, but I'm darned if I can make out what all this is about."

"Judy, am I your mother or am I not?"

Judy laughed. A little soft giggle in the darkness.

"Don't laugh, Judy."

"I'm sorry, Mother. But when you ask me if you're my mother or not it always means just one thing."

"And what's that? Haven't I brought you up? And looked after you? And cared for you? And this is all the thanks I get."

"Now, Mother, don't be silly. Don't you know I think everything in the world of you? Don't you know that I appreciate what a hard time you've had ever since Dad died? You know I do."

"Well, I daresay. You're a sweet girl, Judy, though I say it. But that only makes it harder for me."

"Makes what harder, darling? You know you really are being mysterious tonight."

"If I'm being mysterious, honey, it's because I believe it to be necessary, I assure you. Judy, you don't realise just what sort of a fix we've gotten ourselves into."

"A fix? A fix, Mother? But we haven't. Honestly, we haven't. Hell, I know it's pretty terrible the Maharajah being murdered like that. He was our host an' all. And Porgy's our host now, I guess, and I suppose it's possible that he did kill his father. James says that things like that aren't unknown in India. But, Mother, we are only guests. It's none of our business really."

"Isn't it, dear? Isn't it?"

Suddenly Mrs. Alcott put out a hand and held tight to her daughter's forearm. A grip sharp with anxiety, even dread.

"Mother, what is it?"

"Judy. Judy honey, this isn't going to be easy for me to say. But I must say it. And, Judy, it's what I brought you all the way up here to say. Where I can say it and know that no one, no one at all, has heard a single word."

"Mother, darling. Has something happened?"

"No. No, it hasn't. Or, well, yes, it has. Something's happened. But not something to me. Not something in the way you meant. Judy, can't you guess what I'm going to have to say?"

Judy was silent for a moment. In face of her mother's evident state of alarm she felt there was nothing else she could do but stay silent. At last she spoke again.

"Mother, now you must tell me. I'm sure it's not so bad as you think. However bad it is, we'll be able to do something about it. Uncle Joe will know what to do. James will know—"

"James. James. James. Judy, can't you see? It's James I've got to talk to you about. You say you don't know what's happened. But you do. You do. James has happened. James has happened to you, hasn't he?"

"Well, yes. Yes, I guess. Mother, I didn't want to say anything. I mean, he hasn't said anything. We've only known each other just four days. But we don't need to say anything. Mother, we both know, and I'd have told you as soon as there was something— Well, something more definite to say."

"I know you would, dear. I know you would. And you wouldn't have had to tell me either. I may be an old woman—"

"Mother."

"Well, I may be a woman who's getting on just a little, but I can see what's right in front of my eyes. It's not you saying nothing, Judy dear."

"Then, Mother, what is it? Is it Uncle Joe? Are you worried that he's— Mother, you aren't thinking, are you, that Uncle Joe really did murder the Maharajah?"

"Honey, how can you think that? I know my brother, for gosh sakes. I tell you, if he'd wanted to kill any Maharajah he'd have upped and killed him and no fussing over pushing bits of Indian bark into guns. No, Judy, it's not Joe. It's not Joe. It can't be."

"Then who? Or what? Mother, I still don't understand."

"Judy. Judy, I want you to promise me one thing."

The gripping hand on her forearm, which had scarcely slackened its grip, dug now like frenzied claws.

"Mother, what? What?"

"Judy, don't ask me why. Don't ask me anything. Just— Just do as I'm going to ask you."

"Of course I will, Mother. Only tell me. Make it plain. I can't do anything if I don't understand."

"Judy, I want you to treat— Well, just to treat Lieutenant Frere as a friend, just a friend. Just someone you happen to know who's friendly."

"A friend? But—"

"No, Judy. Don't ask me anything. Don't beg and demand. Just do this one thing I've asked. Just that."

"But—"

"Judy, no buts. Judy, will you promise?"

There was a long, long silence. In the sweet-scented night a listening figure strained to hear every least telltale sound, a figure waiting still as the white stone statues of absurd nymphs which Porgy's grandfather had had imported from Europe to decorate the palace roof. Only this figure was not of white marble but clad in black evening dress.

"Mother." Judy's voice was trembling. "Mother, I can't. You mustn't ask me. It's too much. You know it is."

"But, Judy, I do ask you. I have to ask you."

"But, why, Mother? Why?"

"I can't say. I'm not going to say. But, Judy, I beg you, for your own sake, to do what I ask. I'm not going to say another word now. Not one."

Suddenly as a polo player changing direction to outwit an oncoming rider, Elaine Alcott swung round and walked, almost ran, along the long colonnade towards the stairs leading down into the vast honeycomb of the palace below.

But that black-coated figure had eased deeper into the shadows between two pillars, had drawn his jacket lapels across his stiff white shirt-front well before she was anywhere near him. In the deeper darkness D.S.P. Howard quietly nodded to himself.

If dinner that evening had been a subdued occasion, breakfast next day was, in the end, anything but subdued. It was the first time since the murder that Porgy, now Maharajah of Bhopore, had joined his guests for the traditional meal of hot or cold cereal, of eggs in whatever way the guests chose to order them, of liver or kidneys or smoked haddock, of toast and Oxford marmalade or honey. Previously he had been already closeted with the Dewan, even at that comparatively early hour, busy taking up the reins of government. Busier than any of those who had known him before his father's death would have thought likely.

But this morning, perhaps feeling that the essentials were now fully in his grasp, he appeared in the breakfast room punctually at nine and after polite good mornings sat himself at the head of the table. The others at their places waited while the assiduous bearers, neatly white-gloved, inquired whether they would take porridge or cornflakes. Only James Frere opted for porridge.

But, when he made his now customary joke to Judy about his choice, to his surprise she returned only the briefest and most polite of smiles. He decided she must be feeling out of sorts, was on the point of inquiring, realised that any question might be tactless, and busied himself over his porridge, waving away both cream and sugar in true Scottish style and helping himself only to a liberal sprinkling of salt.

Porgy was helping himself to nothing, and after a moment or two Elaine Alcott noticed this. She had no inhibitions about putting a question on a possibly delicate subject and no longer any qualms about addressing a Maharajah by his familiar name.

"Why, Porgy, you're not eating. What's the matter? Hangover or something?"

Porgy smiled.

"Not at all, Elaine. It's simply that on religious grounds I am not able to eat at the same time as—shall we say?—people from over the black waters."

"That's us? We're from over the black waters? What are the black waters, for heaven's sake?"

Again Porgy smiled.

"Oh, the black waters are nothing more terrible than any of the seas that surround Hindustan. Many of my countrymen consider that crossing them is tantamount to death."

"Hindustan?" Elaine inquired tirelessly. "That's India, is it?"

"Yes, it's the old name for India. The land of the Hindus."

James Frere joined the conversation here.

"But, Porgy," he said, "you never used to object on religious grounds to eating with fearful foreigners. What's made you change your mind?"

For a moment Porgy looked particularly serious.

"James," he answered, "I suppose you'll find this difficult to believe. After all, you knew me at Cambridge when, I regret to say, I broke almost every rule that my religion imposes on me. But the truth of the matter is that since— Well, since I became Maharajah I find I look on things in a rather different light."

James was instantly respectful.

"Yes, I see," he said. "I suppose in a way I might feel the same if I unexpectedly inherited the family estates. I mean, I wouldn't start going to church. Well, actually I might. But what I mean is all sorts of rules and things which up to now I haven't paid all that much attention to would suddenly seem to mean more to me."

"Thank you, James," Porgy said, still very serious. "And actually that makes it easier for me to tell you all something I think you ought to know."

"Whatever's that, Maharajah?" Elaine asked.

It was the first time she had called Porgy by his new title. The word seemed to make an acknowledgment by them all that he had stepped into a different world now, a world of power.

Porgy paused a moment before answering the question.

"It's just this," he said at last. "I'm untouchable."

The first of them to react was, a little unexpectedly, Henry Morton III. He had been pretty silent ever since the Maharajah's death. It was plain that only one thing interested him: whether he would be able to get a deal on his zinc-processing plan. And it was that now which was clearly still uppermost in his mind.

"Untouchable?" he said. "Does that mean you can't do business?"

Porgy turned to him gravely.

"No, no," he assured him. "I am perfectly able to handle any business that has to be done. It's only that when anyone passes any papers to me, or anything like that, they have to put them on a table and wait for me to pick them up. I'm afraid it's what the priests say has to be done."

Henry Morton looked as if he wanted to growl out that this was no way to conduct business. Wall Street could hardly run if no one was able to push a telegram or a strip of ticker tape into someone else's hands. But he managed to restrain himself, just.

Instead he gave Porgy a cautious look.

"How long's this going to go on?" he demanded.

"Oh, it's only for today," Porgy assured him. "Every now and again the pundits calculate from the stars that it's one of my untouchable days as Maharajah, and there's nothing much I can do about it."

"You could ignore the lot of them," said Joe Lloyd.

Porgy was so surprised by this uncompromising statement that he could scarcely get out any sort of answer.

"Well, I don't think— Well, I suppose I— It's— It's just that . . ."

Eventually he managed a smile.

"Mr. Lloyd," he said then, "you must just accept that it's different for you Americans."

But this did not seem to appease Joe. He glowered hard.

"Hell, now," he exploded at length, "that's what's wrong with this country. Superstition. Always obeying a lot of stupid rules for no good reason."

"Joe," Elaine begged, as if he were still her boy brother and was saying something impolite at a coffee party for old ladies back home.

Joe shot her an angry look.

"No, I will not keep my big mouth shut," he announced. "There was too much of that in the old Maharajah's day. Well, it's time now that somebody spoke out. And yes, by heck, acted out too."

He pushed back his chair and marched up to the head of the table, where Porgy sat before his empty plate.

"Now, listen, Maharajah," he said, "I expected an order to go out yesterday at the latest for the dam to be put into full operation. It hasn't gone out, has it?"

Porgy looked distinctly embarrassed.

"Well, no," he muttered. "No, that's quite true, Mr. Lloyd. We have not actually given any orders."

"We? We? Who's we?"

Porgy looked yet more embarrassed. He picked up the spoon laid in his place and turned it bowl side down. Then he turned it up again.

"I suppose 'we' is me," he said. "Manner of speaking, you understand."

"No, I do not understand," Joe thundered back, standing towering over Porgy. "I do not understand why that order has not been given."

Porgy sighed.

"Well?" Joe shot out.

Porgy sighed again, more deeply.

"Mr. Lloyd," he said, "believe me, I have considered this matter most carefully."

"Hell, there's nothing to consider," Joe said. "I built that dam so's it would irrigate the maximum feasible area. I was all set to release the first of the water when somehow or other word got back to your father about just what places would be flooded and how deep. And he realised that his precious jheels would get a few inches higher than they customarily are. So what did he do? He slapped a darned unnecessary order on me forbidding me to have the dam do its proper task. Well, all I want is for that order to be rescinded."

"I know you do, Mr. Lloyd. But—"

"But what?"

"But it is difficult."

"It's damn well not. There's nothing to prevent the extra flooding going right ahead. No damned logical reason whatever. So where's the delay?"

Porgy looked up from his much turned-over spoon and stared Joe straight in the eyes now.

"Mr. Lloyd, I will tell you," he said. "It was my father's wish, my late father's wish, that the water levels in the jheels should on no account be raised. Mr. Lloyd, I feel that that is a wish I must respect."

"But, damn it, only a few days before the Maharajah died you told me yourself that you agreed with me. It was damned wrong to let people go hungry next year just so's to get some good shooting when the damned Viceroy comes."

"Yes, I said that," Porgy admitted. "But, Mr. Lloyd, consider. That was, as you yourself point out, a few days before my father died. Now he is dead. The situation has quite changed."

Joe Lloyd clenched his teeth in impotent anger.

"But I'm telling you it hasn't changed," he stormed. "It hasn't changed one bit. The dam's still there. It's still capable of irrigating a bigger area by far than it's doing now. You've only got to give the word. Give it right now. And then when the Viceroy cuts his ribbon that water'll flow the way it's meant to flow. It'll all be done before you've finished your damn breakfast."

Porgy smiled, though rather shakily.

"Mr. Lloyd, I'm not having breakfast."

"All right, all right. You choose not to have breakfast because of your religious taboos, that's okay with me. You're the only one to suffer. But when you start making taboos for yourself which cause hundreds and thousands of innocent people to suffer, then that's a damned different matter. Now, are you going to give me that order?"

"Mr. Lloyd, I very much regret it, but I am not."

"Because your father was pigheaded enough not to give it himself?"

Porgy shrugged.

"If you like."

"Well, I don't like. I don't like one little bit. And I tell you what I'm going to do about it."

Still Joe Lloyd stood, red hair bristling, looming over Porgy.

"Maharajah," he said, "if you don't give me that order now, on the spot, straightaway, I'm going—I'm going to touch you."

There was a gasp all round the table at this. Elaine gave a little moan of exasperated despair. Judy, whose morose self-communing had gradually been broken in upon by the loudness of her uncle's voice, looked suddenly near to tears. The Dewan half rose from his chair, his face showing clear signs of outrage. Captain Ram Singh still kept his customary vaguely smiling expression, but it was clear that it had been left on his features only from forgetfulness. Henry Morton, though he could be seen to sympathise with Joe, still looked as if his fellow citizen's threat was going a good deal further than he would have gone himself. Even Dolly Brattle, who had been plunged in self-misery yet more deeply than Judy, looked up in something like horror, and James Frere's open fresh face was plainly stamped with that feeling.

Only one person round the table sat quite unmoved. D.S.P. Howard. But his hooded eyes had not missed the tiniest movement, the least change of expression.

"Well," Joe demanded again, "are you going to give the order to let the waters run or aren't you? I've warned you."

Porgy, Maharajah of Bhopore, decreed by the rules of his pundits to be that day untouchable, sat unmoving as one of his grandfather's roof statues.

"No, Mr. Lloyd," he said, his voice terribly quiet in the shocked silence. "No, I am not going to rescind the order that my father gave."

Joe Lloyd leant forward and placed his thick, hairy hand squarely on Porgy's slim brown one as it rested on the white cloth of the table.

XV

The Schoolmaster was taking a geography lesson. They were doing the rivers of India. They had been doing them for two and a half weeks. But they had by no means finished. Dinning the names and the lengths in miles together with the sources and discharge points of India's major rivers into the heads of each and every one of his pupils was a slow business. They were still on the rivers of the Punjab, the Jhelum, the Chenab, the Ravi, the Beas, and the Sutlej. But none of the pupils had managed to get them in the correct order from west to east, and several still had failed to get even the names into their heads.

"Jhelum, Chenab, Ravi, Beas, Sutlej," the Schoolmaster chanted as loudly as he could in order to overtop the buzz of chatter at the ranks of school desks. "Now, after me, repeat."

"Jhelum, Chenab, Ravi . . ."

But at this point the chorus, which had never been complete, broke hopelessly down.

The Schoolmaster sighed.

"We will now take a break," he announced.

He left the room with what dignity he could muster.

Outside a motionless white-clad figure awaited.

"Good morning, Schoolmaster Sahib. I take it that you have no news for me."

The Schoolmaster tried, rapidly as he could, to adjust from one world to another, from turbulence to controlled quiet.

"Ah, it is you. Good morning, D.S.P. Sahib. No, I have seen nothing in the way of orange hands, I regret to state."

"You're taking a break?" the D.S.P. inquired, in the manner of a question expecting, very definitely expecting, the answer "Yes."

"Yes. Yes, a short break. Concentration is what is chiefly lacking there. Yes, concentration. That is the problem. So from time to time I take a short break. Then we resume with renewed vigour."

"With renewed vigour, good," said the D.S.P., his voice studiously neutral.

Without further consultation, the two of them abandoned the hub-bub behind the closed schoolroom door, descended the narrow staircase nearby, and went out into the gardens. There was a long walk, partly shaded by high masses of red-flowered bougainvillaea. They set off, without a word, along it.

After a little the D.S.P. spoke.

"That business at breakfast," he said, confidently as if he had seen the Schoolmaster in the breakfast room with his own eyes.

The Schoolmaster wagged his head with gravity.

"Not at all a good business. To touch a person who is untouchable, it can only have the most serious results."

"Oh, yes. The results will be serious enough, all right."

The Schoolmaster sighed.

"It is not as if Lloyd Sahib is altogether a newcomer to India," he said. "An individual who could not be expected to understand the customs. But that is not at all the case. Lloyd Sahib has been in Bhopore for more than three years. And let me add this, if I may. Never in that time until now has he shown disrespect for the native customs of the country."

"Lloyd Sahib is a man with a lot on his mind," said the D.S.P. "Nevertheless, it was good of His Highness to take it as well as he did."

"Well, what else could a gentleman do? He could only rise from his place, offer the company a bow, and leave the room altogether."

Again the D.S.P. did not feel the need to comment on the almost photographic accuracy of the Schoolmaster's description of a scene at which he had not been present. There had been other observers, six or seven white-gloved bearers at the least. By now that scene would be photographically inscribed in many more heads in the palace than that of the Schoolmaster.

The two of them paused and watched a twirling-winged flight of green parrots swing down over the masses of bougainvillaea.

"D.S.P. Sahib," said the Schoolmaster, "may I most respectfully inquire how the course of your investigation is proceeding?"

The D.S.P.'s straight line of a mouth twitched in an ironic smile.

"You may inquire, Schoolmaster Sahib," he replied. "But I shall not give you an answer, and you may draw what conclusions you can from that."

The Schoolmaster sighed.

"At least you have learned one new thing today," he said.

The D.S.P. gave a sharp little grunt.

"A new thing? That Mr. Joseph Lloyd is capable of breaking the rules? I hardly needed that extraordinary business in the breakfast room to tell me that. You don't get a dam the size of the Maharajah Albert Singhi Dam built in three years in this country without being capable of action as well as of hotheaded words. I knew that."

"Nevertheless," said the Schoolmaster after they had walked a dozen paces more. "Nevertheless, you have something in the nature of oracular proof now, D.S.P. Sahib."

Again the D.S.P. gave his little dissatisfied grunt.

"Proof that Lloyd Sahib is capable of breaking a rule, yes," he said. "Even of breaking a rule that he knows to be of importance, however much a matter of mere airy belief it may be. Proof, if you want to stretch a point, that he might be capable of breaking the rule that says, 'Thou shalt not kill.' But proof of murder, Schoolmaster Sahib? Proof that he is the murderer of the Maharajah? I'm a long way from that. A long, long way."

The Schoolmaster sighed again.

The long morning wore on. Most of the many, many inhabitants of the palace occupied the time in exactly the same way they occupied it every other morning. At the dhobi ghats, under the burning sun, the barebacked dhobis knelt or squatted, bang-banging at all the many, many soiled garments the life of the palace produced, and when they had battered them into cleanliness they laid them out in the hot sun to dry. Outside the kitchens, in a long strip of deep shade, there squatted the row of seventeen maidservants who spent most of their life in picking over huge mounds of rice. They were busy as ever removing with deft fingers tiny stones, little dried bits of grass, fragments of twig. In the stables the many syces carefully groomed the horses and ponies in their charge, working steadily in the dung-smelling dimness. Out in the gardens the nine-year-old whose task it was at this time of year to pick up every single heavy fallen mango-tree blossom moved from one thick petal to the next, squatting and shuffling.

Only the Maharajah's guests were unoccupied and whiled away the time and the heat as best they could, since Porgy was not there to entertain them and he had forgotten, too, to detach the Schoolmaster from his usual duties and make him a temporary guide-lecturer.

But D.S.P. Howard was by no means idle. Assiduously he added to his tally of hands surreptitiously inspected. And quietly he flitted, too, from one suspect to another, listening uninhibitedly to any conversations that he could. Had not the Resident, in advocating that he be called in, indicated that, country-born as he was, he was not "quite the thing"? So he felt himself, in the pursuit of his calling, perfectly free from the restraints of the true British code of conduct.

When he saw Dolly Brattle pause and listen outside a door and then quietly turn the knob and slip inside, he did not hesitate, un-British though it was, to go up to the door after her, making scarcely a sound on the marble corridor floor despite his heavy shoes, and to listen there as she had done.

After a little he decided that she was no longer in the room immediately on the far side of the door. He grasped the knob, waited for a moment or two, and then began to turn it. He turned it a great deal more cautiously and expertly than Dolly had done, and when it was fully turned he waited again as long as it would take to count in Urdu up to five before he began to ease the wide door open.

When it was open perhaps three inches he was able to see that there was now indeed no one on the far side. He slipped into the room and took as much care in closing the door as he had in opening it. The room was, as he had expected, merely a lobby with three other doors leading off it. Two of them were shut. The third was ajar.

D.S.P. Howard stood quite still and listened. From the other side of the slightly opened door there came small sounds. The sounds of a person with sharp European high-heeled shoes slowly moving to and fro. The faint inbreathing of an occasional sigh.

D.S.P. Howard moved noiselessly across, gently swept the door farther open, and fixed himself there in the doorway.

The room in front of him he recognised at once for what it was. One of the Maharajah's clothes rooms. The other two doors behind him, he knew now, would also be where the Maharajah's clothes were kept. When there are particular colours and particular types of garments that are reserved for use on one special day of the year only a great many outfits will be needed, as it might be the black sherwani with the black and gold turban that was kept solely for Diwali, the feast when Lakhsmi, goddess of prosperity, is honoured with fireworks of all sorts and myriad tiny lamps placed along the roof lines of houses great and small.

So he saw coats in materials of every sort from the richest brocades to the plain whites kept, with plain khaki turbans, for funerals. They hung in long lines from racks running across the wide room, pinks and greens and reds and blues and violets and magentas and purples and fine yellows. And on the walls were deep shelves with the appropriate trousers for each sherwani. And there were racks for all the many turbans, with beside them six glossy top-hats, four neat bowler hats for London wear, shooting caps, trilbys, and flat straw panamas, each with a different club ribbon.

Dolly Brattle was walking slowly up and down at the far end of the room, past all the gorgeous lines of hanging clothes. Occasionally she put out a finger and drew it along the pattern of a particularly fine brocade.

"I think you're ill advised, Miss Brattle," D.S.P. Howard said quietly.

She gave a huge start. He saw her pale face turned towards him, the mouth with its vivid outline of lipstick slightly open.

"Oh," she said, after a little. "It's you."

"Who else did you think it would be?"

"I— I don't know. I suppose it wasn't likely to be anyone else really. Not if they'd spoken to me. It wouldn't be anybody but one of the servants sneaking about like that."

Her voice had developed an edge of bitterness, a desire to wound. But the D.S.P. was unmoved.

"A policeman is like a servant in many ways," he said. "It's his duty to watch his masters, to note what needs to be done and, when the right time comes, to do it."

"And you enjoy that? The spying? And the hunting? I suppose you must."

He did not answer immediately.

"The hunting, yes," he said at last, as if he had been giving her jibes deep consideration. "Yes, I enjoy the hunt when I can see my quarry for what he is. Out after a gang of dacoits when they have just held someone up, there is a thrill of the chase. I have never gone in for riding after jackal all dressed up in a red coat and calling it 'pink,' but I admit to the passion for hunting something."

Dolly Brattle came towards him, thrusting aside as if it were a curtain a magnificent sherwani in deep gold encrusted with embroidery of thousands of fine pearls.

"But you don't actually enjoy this particular sort of business, eh?" she asked, the sharpness gone.

"No, I don't enjoy it."

"Yet you do it. You go on and on doing it, Mr. Howard."

"Yes, of course. It's my duty."

"Duty? And do you ever think of anything else?"

"Not when I'm on duty, no. Or not so far as I can help it."

She was standing in front of him now.

"Well," she said, "you advised me not to go mooning over all these clothes that Porgy may have altered for him, if he doesn't have the whole lot made new."

"Yes. That was perhaps going beyond the bounds of duty."

"All right."

She stood in silence. Behind her the rainbow array of fine cloths, of silks and satins, hung stilly.

"Thank you," she said.

"I wish I could tell you that by tomorrow or the next day you will be free to go. But I can't."

"No, I suppose not."

Again she stood there saying nothing, quite still from the helmet of her bobbed platinum hair to the spiky points of her heels. But gradually a look of calculation came onto her face.

"Mr. Howard."

"Yes?"

"You've given me some advice. Would you think it daft if I gave some to you?"

"I'm always prepared to listen. To anything anyone says to me."

"Oh, yes, I'm sure you're that. I saw you from one of the windows not long ago, walking about out in the sun with that tatty little schoolmaster the old Maharajah kept for his bastards."

"You had some advice for me, I think."

"Yes, perhaps I did. Perhaps I have. You see, you're not the only one who's been thinking about the murder."

"I'm sure I'm not. Someone here in the palace, someone you yourself know, has doubtless been scarcely thinking of anything else."

"Yes. Well, that's not me, you know."

"No. You are only one of the possibilities."

"The famous five possibilities. The suspects. Just like one of those bloody detective stories Porgy always used to like so much."

"Used to like?"

"Yes. He's gone off them now. And that's not the only thing he's gone off."

"I'm waiting to hear your advice."

"And getting all ready to laugh at it behind those damned deep eyes of yours."

"No. I hope I shall listen. And then make up my mind according to what I hear."

Again Dolly was silent. D.S.P. Howard patiently waited.

"All right then, I'll tell you. Not because it's my duty, mind. But— But just to get you off my bloody back, if you must know."

"I'd prefer the advice itself to your reason for giving it to me."

"I daresay. All right then. The famous five suspects. Has it occurred to you that you might have counted wrong?"

"We won't concern ourselves with what has or has not occurred to me."

"No? All right. Always play your cards close to your chest, don't you?"

"I do. And so, it seems, do you."

"Oh, no. I'll tell you all right. I'll tell you. What about that bloody Yank then? Have you ever considered him?"

"And which 'bloody Yank' would that be?" the D.S.P. asked levelly.

"Oh, not Joe Lloyd. He's on your famous list, isn't he? No, how about Mr. bloody Henry Morton the Third?"

"Who did not arrive in Bhopore till long after the late Maharajah had demonstrated how sapura bark could be used."

"Oh, I don't mind about that. I don't really understand it, in spite of you telling me so often that it makes me the one who killed the old boy. No, it's why he could have done it that I've been thinking of."

"Indeed?"

She glared at him suddenly.

"Indeed, indeed, indeed," she mocked. "Don't you ever say anything straight out?"

"Very seldom."

She stood there then, thickly lipsticked lower lip thrust out mutinously, as if she had almost made up her mind to go no further with what she was on the point of telling him. But at last she thought better of it.

"Look," she said, "do you know that the old devil of a Maharajah brought that chap all the way to bloody Bhopore just as a joke?"

"Yes, I know that."

"I suppose you would, Mr. Spy."

D.S.P. Howard said nothing. After a little Dolly began again.

"All right. Well, put yourself in his place. You're a big American tycoon. A ruddy millionaire, I daresay. You're used to people yes-sirring you left and right. America may be the land of the free and all that, but I can't say as I've ever noticed any rich American who didn't expect to be kowtowed to just as much as if he was a lord."

"I'm imagining all this."

"All right. Well, imagine it then. You come here expecting some big deal that's going to make you another fortune, and then you find out it's all nothing more than an April Fools' Day trick. So what do you do? You damn well kill the fellow, that's what."

The D.S.P. looked at her from under his deep, hooded eyes.

"Yes," he said at last. "Do you too read the detective stories His Highness gets sent from Harrod's, Miss Brattle?"

"I don't waste my time with that sort of thing."

"No. And neither do I. I'm a policeman. I have to deal in plain and simple facts. Such as the times things happened and who could have known what. I think if you give this notion of yours a little more thought, you'll see that it doesn't really fit all the facts."

"The sapura bark," Dolly said resignedly. "Well, I suppose I knew really that he would have had to know about that. So we're back to your famous five. Five including Dolly Brattle. Well, it was worth a try."

"Oh, yes. It was worth a try. I found it all most instructive."

"Damn you, damn you, damn you," Dolly Brattle shouted.

The Resident came over to the palace before luncheon to see D.S.P. Howard. He came under the guise of a courtesy call on Porgy. But he made that last just as short a time as was decent, and before it began he sent a palace servant to tell the D.S.P. that he would like a word with him. Perhaps they could meet at the palace steps and walk in the gardens?

The D.S.P. was under no illusions about that. The palace gardens were the one place where they could be sure of being able to talk without being overheard. He was under no illusions either about what the Resident would have to say to him. "Mr. Howard, there are only three days now till I have to send that cable to the Viceroy."

"Mr. Howard," the Resident said as they strolled slowly away from the broad steps in front of the palace, where his Rolls stood waiting in the shade of the neem trees as it had done on the day of the Maharajah's most unfortunate April Fool joke, "Mr. Howard, there are only three days now till I have to send that cable to the Viceroy informing him that a visit to Bhopore would not be propitious at the present juncture. Have you any news for me?"

"Very little, I'm afraid, sir."

"Howard, how many of the people in the palace have you succeeded in inspecting for stains on their hands?"

"Eight hundred and fifty-four, at the last count, sir."

Such precision seemed to worry the Resident. He gave the D.S.P. a sharp glance, as if he suspected that just possibly the fellow was trying to make some sort of joke. But the D.S.P.'s entirely serious, closed face reassured him.

"That many?" he said.

"Yes, sir. I keep a careful count. It's necessary. Of course, as I explained to you, I don't know exactly what total I'm aiming at. No one can tell me that. And, again, there are all the inhabitants of the zenana. They come within the Dewan's count, but naturally I am unable to see them. On the other hand, all but a few of the mamas there are unable to come into the mardana, so they can safely be left out of account."

"Yes. Yes, I see. So, in fact, your general inspection must be nearing its end?"

"I'm afraid it is, sir."

"Afraid? Afraid?"

"Since I haven't seen the least trace of any orange staining on any pair of hands so far, sir. It means that this line of inquiry is petering out."

"Yes. Yes, I suppose so. But have you other lines? I mean, time is running out, Howard. Time is running out."

"Yes, sir. I know it is."

They had reached one of the many artificial ponds that dotted the grounds. The Resident came to a halt at its edge and peered into the shallow, often renewed water. A few fat golden carp could be discerned, swimming to and fro with calm slowness.

That's just about the way this fellow's going about the business, the Resident thought to himself furiously. Mooning here and there, and getting nowhere.

As if in answer to that thought, well concealed behind features of schooled impassivity though it was, the D.S.P. broke the silence.

"It has been suggested to me, sir, that Mr. Henry Morton killed the Maharajah in a fit of rage at being called to Bhopore on something of a fool's errand."

"That American."

The Resident sounded as if he were flirting with temptation. Then, resolutely, he put it behind him.

"No, Howard, it won't do. The chap wasn't even in Bhopore when that ridiculous business with my car took place."

"Exactly so, sir."

"Well, haven't you anything better to suggest?"

"Oh, yes, sir. I shall continue to find out all I can about all the possible suspects. Something will come of that, sooner or later."

"I daresay it will, Howard. But I strongly suspect that it will be a great deal later than sooner. A great deal too late."

The Resident turned away from the pool and its slow-moving carp in an abrupt gesture of rejection. He strode towards his waiting car without another word.

One of the few places D.S.P. Howard had hardly visited in the sprawling palace was the hathikhana. As he wandered slowly through it, past the sixty or so great grey-backed elephants whose home it was gently swaying from side to side in their stalls, his eyes picking out a pair of hands here and pair of hands there, he became aware that he was being looked at. Up in the gallery of the massive echoing building Henry Morton III was morosely watching one of the elephants being got ready for some minor ceremonial. But the scarfaced tycoon seemed uninterested in the process of painting the thick, crinkled grey skin.

Perhaps the frivolity of it repelled him. Perhaps only the feeling of latent power that emanated from the huge stalled animals as they rocked from side to side was what had brought him to the hathikhana.

D.S.P. Howard climbed up and placed himself quietly beside the American.

"It must be irritating for you, Mr. Morton, hanging about here waiting till the Maharajah has time to complete your business deal," he said.

The scarred face turned towards him.

"Complete the deal? I'm beginning to wonder if the guy's any more intention of doing that than his stick-in-the-mud father had."

The D.S.P. stiffened slightly.

"The Maharajah playing hard to get?" he asked casually.

"I'll say. Damn it, the guy seemed one hell of a forward-looking individual. Everybody I talked to said 'progressive.' And there couldn't be a more progressive scheme for a hole-and-corner, backward place like this than what I have in mind."

"I gather you want to establish large zinc-processing plants here, using local labour, and so forth?"

The tycoon's eyes hardened.

"Gather?" he said sharply. "You been talking to the Maharajah? Or that what-d'you-call'im, that Dewan?"

The D.S.P. put a smile on his face.

"Oh, no, not at all. No, I've had some exchanges with His Highness, of course. And with the Dewan. But strictly only about my business, Mr. Morton. Not yours."

The American grunted.

"Thought you might have learnt something," he said. "Hell, Mr. Howard—it is Mr. Howard, isn't it?—I can't wait here day after day till the guy says he's ready to talk. Time's money, you know."

"So I've often heard it said."

The D.S.P. let the conversation lapse. After all, he had succeeded in positioning himself in such a way that the American would not find it easy to squeeze past him in the narrow gallery. He could put any questions he might have at any time.

He watched the business of the elephant being got ready for the ceremony. A painter was standing up on an ancient chair with a pot of gold paint in his left hand. He was applying the liquid to the elephant's face with a long brush, making the second of two large circles round the beast's little glittering eyes.

"How far had you got with your discussions with the former Maharajah then?" he asked the American, almost idly.

"No way at all. The guy said he didn't want to talk business first of all. Said the evening was for amusement or something. Well, I reckoned one evening more or less wouldn't make much difference, even though he'd cabled me in London and fixed for me to come at just that time."

"But he did talk business with you in the end?"

"Yeah. Suddenly at dinner. Started rattling off about the whole plan. I tell you, Mr. Howard, I wasn't one hundred percent pleased."

"You don't like to have your affairs discussed in public?"

"Too right, I don't. But there's no holding a guy like the old Maharajah, you know. He didn't seem to have any idea of the rules, the way business should be done. Made up his own damned rules as he went along."

"I can see it must have been difficult for you. Why do you think he changed his mind and started to talk business at dinner when he'd said he wouldn't?"

For a moment or two the American considered. D.S.P. Howard breathed in the rich aroma of elephant dung.

"D'you know what?" Henry Morton III said at last. "D'you know what? I think he was doing it just to rile that Dewan guy. Yes, sir. I think he suddenly took it into his head to rile the fellow, and my business was the easiest way he could think of to do it."

"Indeed? But that seems appallingly casual, even for the Maharajah. I mean, to make a sort of joke out of a business deal that must be worth hundreds of thousands of pounds."

"Millions of dollars, Mr. Howard. Millions of dollars. Why, if this thing still goes through it'll bring millions and millions of dollars to little old Bhopore."

"Millions of dollars," the D.S.P. said, his voice suitably awed. "So surely the Maharajah wouldn't have joked over that?"

In the interior dimness of the hathikhana he watched the American's face with all the intensity of a mongoose watching a cobra.

Henry Morton shrugged.

"Well, I wouldn't have expected anyone else to joke about that many million dollars," he said. "But I'm pretty sure that's just what the guy was doing then. He was using my deal to rile that Dewan."

"Well, perhaps you're right. Certainly from all I hear the Maharajah liked his little jokes. Do you think that the Dewan realised what he was doing, by any chance?"

Henry Morton shrugged.

"Hard to tell," he said. "That guy'd make a darned fine poker player."

"Yes," said the D.S.P. with the faintest trace of a smile. "I expect he would."

"Still, I'd rather deal with him than the old Maharajah," Henry Morton added. "Gee, you should have heard the way that guy went on and on at dinner about all the crazy tricks he'd played that day. Like a kid."

The scorn, even the fury, with which the American pronounced these last words rang through the huge hathikhana. The mahout on top of the elephant having the gold circles painted round its eyes looked up at them. But the patient beast under him did not seem to have been disconcerted by the sound.

Again D.S.P. Howard let the conversation lapse. Henry Morton seemed content to be standing there looking down at the line of slowly swaying crinkled grey backs. Presumably he had nothing better to do until he could inveigle Porgy into a face-to-face discussion of his proposition for Bhopore. And certainly the sight of all the huge beasts exuding patience must be calming to even the most pushful of people.

"So what's next for you?" the D.S.P. asked after their companionable silence had lasted long enough.

The painter had finished the elephant's second eye and was lowering a careful leg from the chair.

"What's next? A session with the new Maharajah's next. I've got to get that guy on his own and hammer some sense into him."

"It has to be the Maharajah, does it?" D.S.P. Howard asked, continuing on a casual note. "You know the Dewan's got a great deal of power in the State. More than ever now."

"Yeah. From what I've managed to learn from that young Lootenant Frere, I reckon that's so. Only there's just one bad thing there."

"Oh, yes? And what would that be?"

Down below the painter had begun on the elephant's toenails. He was painting them red. A slanting ray stealing in from the sun outside just illuminated the yellowish brick floor by his hands.

"I guess the Dewan isn't too keen on having industry come to Bhopore," he said. "I approached him when I'd discovered what the situation was from young Frere, and, boy, was that man cold."

"He took your proposition seriously though?"

Henry Morton shot him a glance that had more than a spark of anger in it.

"You bet he took my proposition seriously," he flared. "It's one hell of a serious proposition. All that labour, and not one of'em ever so much as heard of a union. The Maharajah behind me, and they'll work till they drop. Those damned union bosses back home'll laugh on the other side of their faces then, I can tell you."

"I'm sure they will."

Henry Morton gripped the wide flat wooden rail of the balcony in front of him.

"So why the hell won't the Maharajah see me?" he demanded.

The D.S.P. had at last satisfied himself that the smears on the elephant painter's hands could not possibly be concealing any startling orange. He gave a little shrug.

"I can't imagine why he won't see you, Mr. Morton," he said, and abruptly descended the gallery's narrow ladder.

"So, Schoolmaster Sahib, you've finished your Agatha Christie?"

The Schoolmaster looked up from the cool stone bench he liked to sit on while all the rest of the palace slept through the worst of the afternoon heat. He scrambled to his feet.

"D.S.P. Sahib. You are not sleeping?"

The little tic at the corners of the D.S.P.'s hooded eyes that passed for his smile came and went.

"I don't sleep all that often, Schoolmaster Sahib. Not when there's an investigation needing to be worked on. But sit down, man, sit down. Don't let me keep you from your new book."

The Schoolmaster resumed his seat. But he put down the new book—it was one of the three that constituted his private library, much reread, Emily Brontë's *Wuthering Heights*—only taking care to lay it face down so that he could resume his reading when the D.S.P. Sahib had finished talking to him.

"I see that they're painting one of the elephants in the hathi-khana," the D.S.P. said, dropping onto the cool stone of the bench.

"Yes. It would be for the Maharajah's visit to the temple at Kalimpat Village. It takes place every year on this day, but it is not at all an important event. One elephant only."

"But the new Maharajah is going?"

"But of course, D.S.P. Sahib. He is the Maharajah now. It is his duty."

"Yes, of course. Tell me, Schoolmaster Sahib, have you met the

American, Mr. Morton? I happened to see him in the hathikhana just now, looking at the animals."

"Oh, yes, D.S.P. Sahib. I had the honour of showing Morton Sahib together with other guests some of the objects of interest within the palace walls."

"Ah, yes."

A short silence fell. It was broken by the Schoolmaster.

"A somewhat impetuous gentleman, Morton Sahib," he ventured. "But I understand from my study of Mrs. Agatha Christie that such is often the nature of American millionaires."

"Yes, I think in this case Mrs. Christie's notion of the typical American millionaire would be confirmed."

The Schoolmaster gave a little apologetic cough.

"It is a good thing for him, then," he said, "that he had not arrived in Bhopore when late His Highness was demonstrating an unexpected use for sapura bark. Otherwise a man of such impetuosity would have at least what Hercule Parrot Sahib calls the temperament for the murder."

"If only Monsieur Poirot were here now, Schoolmaster Sahib. Then, with a few quick discoveries in the matter of temperament, all our troubles would be ended."

The Schoolmaster sighed, with voluminously breathy sympathy.

"Yes, indeed, D.S.P. Sahib. But we ordinary mortals must content ourselves with the discovery of facts only."

The D.S.P. did not challenge this assumption of a Holmes-Watson relationship. Indeed, he encouraged it.

"A curious chap, Morton," he said. "He doesn't seem to be able to think of anything but his deal with the Maharajah over the zinc under the salt lakes."

The Schoolmaster patted both his cheeks in dismay.

"Oh, that would be a thoroughly bad business," he said. "What would become of Bhopore if everybody was made to work in mills processing zinc? That is not at all a proper sort of life. It would be worse than the cotton-mill wallahs in Bombay or the jute-mill coolies in Calcutta. I sincerely trust present His Highness will have nothing at all to do with that scheme. I am altogether certain that late His Highness would never have done."

"Yet he was the person who summoned Mr. Morton to Bhopore, you know."

"Yes, yes. I was having a small chat with one of the telephone orderlies who despatched the cable. I know that the invitation was sent. But, D.S.P. Sahib, I have my own ideas as to its purpose."

"Oh, yes, Schoolmaster Sahib?"

The Schoolmaster's eyes twinkled.

"D.S.P. Sahib," he said, "it is my understanding and belief that the whole arrangement for Morton Sahib to come to Bhopore from London by aeroplanic conveyance was for the sole object and purpose of late His Highness playing yet one more April Fools' Day trick."

"Indeed, Schoolmaster Sahib. And who would he have been playing this trick on?"

"Oh, Sahib, I singularly fear it was upon Sir Akhtar Ali, Dewan of this State."

"Is that what you singularly fear, Schoolmaster Sahib? So, tell me, has Sir Akhtar ever realised that the trick was played on him? Nothing was said at the dinner that night, was it? Not if your account to me of that occasion was accurate."

"Sahib, one thing I am promising. Every word that I recounted to you concerning that occasion, and indeed all others, is fully and completely correct."

"Yes, I should think it would be, Schoolmaster Sahib. So what's the answer to my question, eh? Did the Dewan Sahib know the Maharajah had played a trick on him about zinc mining in Bhopore? Has he learnt of it since?"

The Schoolmaster pulled a grave face.

"D.S.P. Sahib," he pronounced after what he considered a proper time to have devoted to deep concentration. "D.S.P. Sahib, I think I can say without fear of contradiction that the Dewan Sahib most certainly did not know that he was the victim of late His Highness's joking at the dinner that night. And indeed I very much doubt if he is yet aware of that fact."

"And so, Schoolmaster Sahib," said the D.S.P., "Sir Akhtar believed that the Maharajah was all set to launch Bhopore on a policy of brutal industrialisation. He must have been convinced of that fact on the night before the Maharajah was murdered."

"Yes, D.S.P. Sahib, I am sadly afraid that that is a conclusion we must come to."

XVI

It was in the palace pinball room that D.S.P. Howard found Joe Lloyd. The old Maharajah had developed a taste for playing pinball machines some ten years earlier on a visit to Europe. In London he had ordered twelve of them. He was accustomed to order in dozens, and once when in Calcutta he had ordered a dozen huge chandeliers and the owner of the shop had rashly queried whether he meant to buy quite so many he had retorted by purchasing the entire contents of the place. There was a storeroom in the City Palace still filled with them all, packed in their wooden crates just as they had been transported from Calcutta.

But the twelve pinball machines had been brought into immediate use when they eventually arrived from the London supplier. Harrod's had expressed their willingness to obtain them, but they were not an article they stocked at the time of the Maharajah's descent on them, and so his A.D.C. at that period—he was the seventh before Captain Ram Singh—had had a busy morning tracking down a place where the Maharajah could see before buying. Eventually the London Rolls, with its enormous coat of arms on the rear nearside door, had come to an impressive halt in a side street at the far end of the Edgware Road and then a flashy gentleman with a narrow moustache and an ill-concealed Cockney accent had experienced the oddest afternoon of his life.

In the room now the machines, which the Maharajah had ceased to use a month after their installation, were squeaky inside when their spring triggers were pulled back owing to the long accumulation of Bhopore dust. But they were still polished every day by the servant who originally had been deputed to carry out this duty. Sadly, his ministrations had almost obliterated the names on the headboards of the various games the machines offered. Still, a vigorous tug of the trigger would yet send a heavy steel ball, only a little rust-tinged, rattling round the bouncy pegs and notching up, with yet more protesting squeaks, the gaily coloured numbers on the headboard, and some sort of a notion of success or failure could be gained.

Under the intricately painted ceiling, an elaborate affair depicting Krishna and Radha in an amorous scene surrounded by a deep frieze of some forty or fifty precisely repeated dancing milkmaids, Joe Lloyd was at play, his large feet squarely planted on the smooth Persian carpet. The repeated twang of the spring trigger he was tugging was what had eventually led D.S.P. Howard to his quarry.

"Ah, Mr. Lloyd. A happy chance. I trust I'm not interrupting?"

Joe Lloyd turned his weather-tanned face under its unruly tangle of greyish-red hair towards him.

"Interrupting? You can't interrupt boredom, Mr. Howard."

"Yes. Boredom. I suppose you must be pretty bored cooped up here. I'm sorry I've had to ask you to stay on."

Joe Lloyd looked at him, much as if he were assessing the load-bearing limits of a concrete pillar.

"I guess it'd be no use me just telling you I didn't murder the Maharajah?" he said.

D.S.P. Howard's almost nonexistent smile flicked into place and went again.

"I wish my task were that simple. To go round to the suspects in a case, ask them whether they had committed the murder, yes or no, and get their truthful answers. But I'm afraid it's not like that."

"I guess not."

"No, what I have to do, Mr. Lloyd, is to ask question after question. To ask the same questions again and again. And, provided the person I'm putting them to has nothing to conceal, then I expect the same answers again and again. But if, on the other hand, I'm questioning someone who is having to invent certain of his answers, then I can always hope the moment comes when—what shall we say?—a discrepancy occurs."

"Seems a pretty tedious way of going on, almost as bad as endless pinball games on machines with the name of the game rubbed out."

The grunting sound which the D.S.P. produced in response to this might have been a laugh. Perhaps he was amused simply by Joe Lloyd's picture of himself. Or perhaps Joe's comparison had struck him as a particularly apt description of his own task. It was a matter for doubt.

"Then I assume," he went on, his voice steadily level, "you'll have no objection to abandoning these machines and answering the few questions I'd like to put to you?"

"Questions I've already answered, eh?"

"Some of them, perhaps."

"Go right ahead. I guess it's what I'm here in the palace for. I'm the guy who more or less threatened the Maharajah's life in public after all."

"Oh, yes. Undoubtedly you have a motive for the murder, Mr. Lloyd, although whether it's a motive that would be sufficient in your particular case is something I cannot necessarily know."

"I could tell you that, much as I hated that old tyrant's guts, I never considered bumping him off?"

"I think we can take that statement for granted. In any case it's not motive but means that I'd like to ask you my few questions about."

"Means?"

"Yes. Means. I haven't read many detective stories, Mr. Lloyd. Indeed, only one of Agatha Christie's, I think, when I was laid low with malaria once and it was the only book in the dak bungalow where I chanced to find myself. But their old trio of motive, means, and opportunity has a certain amount to be said for it, you know."

"If you say so. You're the expert. And what are the means in this case, anyhow?"

"Oh, come. You know that."

"Do I?"

The D.S.P. did not answer. He stood just inside the ornate arched doorway of the room beside the first of the pinball machines and looked steadily and intently at Joe Lloyd. A tension developed.

"Well, I guess you must mean that sapura bark," Joe said at last. "That was what actually killed the Maharajah, I suppose."

"Yes, that was what actually killed the Maharajah."

Again the D.S.P. fell silent, and continued to regard Joe unblinkingly. Joe half turned back to his game on the machine behind him. And then thought better of it.

"Weren't you going to put me through it?" he said abruptly. "Questions. Questions about the means used for the murder."

"Yes, Mr. Lloyd. What do you want to tell me about that?"

"Me, want to tell you? Hell, I— Well, it was the sapura bark, wasn't it? What more's there to say about it? One of the five of us who saw how the bark was used must have pushed it into the Maharajah's gun barrel. Or six of us, if you count Ram Singh, but he was locked up when we were out at the jheels. Well, that's it then. The sapura bark was the means. What more's there to say?"

"You could suggest how the bark came into the hands of the person who pushed it down the Maharajah's Purdey."

A look of caution came into Joe Lloyd's eyes.

"Yeah," he said, "that's a thought. Last I heard about the bark it was in Jim Frere's bathroom, after he'd taken it off Ram Singh."

"In Lieutenant Frere's bathroom? Yes. But tell me, Mr. Lloyd, how did you happen to know that?"

Joe grinned then. A sudden wide-splitting grin crinkling his reddened, weather-beaten face.

"Can't catch me there, pal," he said. "I didn't know where the bark was till long after the Maharajah was good and dead. Matter of fact, that schoolmaster guy told me. Came up to me and started talking in that way of his, you know, on and on. And pretty soon he got to the murder. I guess I tried to give him the push, but he wouldn't take no for an answer. And then he started on about the sapura bark, and he happened to mention that Jim Frere took it off Ram Singh."

"Did he indeed?" said the D.S.P. And he looked, for just a moment, irritated.

"Yeah, he surely did. And that was when I remembered seeing the Maharajah throw a piece of it to Ram Singh, just after that kid of the Resident's had made Maharajah Sahib look a damn fool."

"I see. And you didn't enter Lieutenant Frere's rooms that evening after dinner?"

"I did not."

"Perhaps you'd care to tell me what you did do?"

"Once again?"

"Please."

But Joe Lloyd's detailed account of how he had spent the time between the breakup of the dinner on the eve of the Maharajah's murder and his falling asleep that night did not differ in the least from the previous occasion he had accounted for the period to the D.S.P.

And it was plain that he knew as much.

"So, would you like me to tell you once again what I did in the morning, Mr. Howard? Right from brushing my teeth?"

"I don't think that will be necessary. Thank you very much."

D.S.P. Howard turned away. But, just as he had got through the archway out of the room, he stopped.

"What about the other piece of bark?" he said, turning and looking hard at Joe.

"Other piece of bark? What other piece?"

Joe's face seemed to be expressing merely bewilderment.

The D.S.P. produced his minimal smile.

"Didn't you get hold of some sapura bark in the jungle?" he said. "When you were assessing the water table for the dam?"

"No, Mr. Howard, I did not. How did you come to think I did?"

The D.S.P.'s face was expressionless once again.

"Oh, someone told me, I think," he answered.

"Someone? Who?"

Joe Lloyd's face had darkened with anger.

"Oh, I don't know. I think it may have been that schoolmaster of the Maharajah's. Yes, I'm pretty sure it was him. You know how he talks and talks at the least opportunity."

"He'll talk on the other side of his face before I've finished with him."

It took the D.S.P. a good many hours of negotiation before it was arranged for him to have an interview with First Her Highness. He had had as a preliminary to apply to Porgy. And Porgy had been extremely reluctant to help.

"But, look here, Mr. Howard, I can't see what you can possibly want to see First Her Highness about."

"In pursuit of my inquiries, Maharajah."

"Well, yes, I know. But what inquiries exactly? I mean, I thought at least the whole basis of the thing was cut-and-dried. I mean, there are the five of us. The ones who saw my father play his trick on Little Michael and who were also out there at the jheels. You aren't suggesting that First Her Highness was out there, too, are you?"

"No, Maharajah, I'm not. I know the purdah ladies sometimes go out by car to watch shikar, from behind properly smoked windows, of course. But I'm not suggesting that First Her Highness was anywhere near the jheels at the time herself."

"Then what are you suggesting?"

"I'm suggesting nothing, with respect, Maharajah. All I am asking is to have an interview with First Her Highness."

"But what about, for heaven's sake?"

"Maharajah Sahib, I don't wish to have to remind you of the difficulties of the situation we both find ourselves in. But perhaps I should point out that I was called in to Bhopore at the suggestion of the Resident."

Porgy's full, pouting mouth took on a look of barely stifled rebellion. Relations between a British Resident, officially no more than an adviser, and an Indian ruler, in all but such matters as foreign affairs in theory an absolute monarch, had never been easy. It was clear always, though nowhere written down, that a Resident's "advice," provided he avoided such subjects as religious observances, was pretty much an order. Although a maharajah, or even a lesser rajah, could disregard it, were he to do so more than very occasionally some good reason would be found to remove him from his gaddi. And that was something which the presence of British troops under a Resident's ultimate command made it perfectly easy to do.

So, perhaps for the first time, Porgy faced the classical dilemma of his kind. Was he to do what he wanted, which was to keep D.S.P. Howard's steel claws as far away from his mother as possible? Or was he to obey in advance the very plain "advice" he would get from the Resident at once if the D.S.P. were to go to him?

"Oh, all right then. I'll talk to Her Highness and we'll see."

But it was not until next morning that the interview took place. When ladies live always in such a state of seclusion, the laws of purdah being so strict, that should they fall ill the doctor has to prescribe for them as it were at second hand, then a great deal of negotiation has to go on before one of them can submit to interrogation by a police officer. A police officer is in any case a man, and further in this case a white infidel.

The doctor manages by speaking from the far side of a screen. From there, as necessary, he calls out instructions to the lady's trusted maid. "Put your hand on Her Highness's stomach." "Jee, Doctor Sahib." "Do you feel that it is distended?" "Nai, Doctor Sahib." "Press with your fingers." A sharp groan. Is that appendicitis?

But the dentist, when a toothache makes his presence necessary, is unable to operate through another person. So for him a discreet square opening is cut in a draped cloth partition. Through this he plunges his forceps or his drill.

Meanwhile, in times not of sickness, the inhabitants of the zenana live their secluded lives. They see no men but their husbands, their brothers, their sons, and young boys of the family. They have little to do, nothing much more than to consider what different sari they will wear, what jewellery to put on with it. They order meals. They eat them. They consume sweetmeat after sweetmeat. They pray. They gossip. Occasionally there is an outing. Sometimes this, if the rules permit it, is in a purdah car with darkened windows or by train in a purdah carriage equally dark. On arrival a curious canvas corridor is stretched out between train door and waiting car. Or there is for local travel the closed palanquin, bumpy on the shoulders of four strong servants, close confined and hot inside its enveloping curtains. Sometimes there is a trip to a different part of the palace to witness some particular religious ceremony. Then it is a matter of being led by trusted eunuchs through dark and narrow stone passages, cleared if necessary of any intruding male. Up narrow stairways they go and down others, with only the sound of swishing silk and faintly jingling bracelets. Up various mysterious ramps, all sense of direction lost, they continue until at last a gallery, specially built long ago with screens of pierced stone, is reached. From there the ceremony for which this special outing has been undertaken can be discreetly watched.

It had been agreed, then, that D.S.P. Howard might speak to First Her Highness in an anteroom that lay between zenana and mardana, with access from both. A heavy wooden screen was to be put in position not far from the zenana entrance. Behind this would be placed Her Highness's seat. On the other side, at a little distance, a chair would be put for the D.S.P. He could sit there and announce his questions. They would echo out into the tall-ceilinged room with its odd items of half-discarded furniture, its couple of differing sofas, its one or two trophies and photographs hung here and there on its walls. First Her Highness would hear clearly. She would consider. She would utter her reply. No doubt the D.S.P. would be able to hear. An interview would be conducted.

The D.S.P. insisted in his quiet voice, which seldom met with opposition, on carrying out an inspection of the anteroom well before the hour set for the meeting.

"I'm afraid I'd better, Maharajah. Supposing I've been put to sit where I shan't be able to hear First Her Highness. I don't suppose she's accustomed to bawling out everything she has to say. And I don't want to have to ask to go through all this again."

Porgy sighed.

"Oh, very well, Mr. Howard."

So before the D.S.P. saw First Her Highness he had opportunities for other inquiries. He found Lieutenant Frere in the palace roller-skating rink. Roller-skating had been an enthusiasm of the Maharajah's, acquired only two years before in England. Harrod's had had no difficulty in supplying a dozen dozen of roller skates. The pastime was popular. Back in India, some of the Maharajah's courtiers had had a little difficulty in acquiring the art. But that had only enhanced the whole business in the Maharajah's eyes.

The rink had been designed by a German interior decorator who had been making the rounds of a number of princely states in India constructing various adjuncts to palaces, swimming baths, barrooms, guest suites, all in the very latest style. He had left behind him a great trail of smooth-contoured bulbous furniture, of wall mirrors in pinkish petal-shaped glass, of chromium-topped bars with tall tubular bar-stools, of bedheads in plain ebonite decorated with three severe lines of polished steel, with behind them tall murals depicting scenes such as a naked, vaguely winged girl riding a tiger through a landscape of clouds while wielding a long tubular spear held in an unlikely balance.

The Maharajah's roller-skating rink had been executed in fine tilework. The tiles were orange and two shades of green, eau-de-Nil and what the architect had called "ze *echt Dschungel* colour." It might otherwise have been described as bottle-green. The building had a flat glass roof, divided into rectangular panes of different sizes. Since no servant had been allocated the duty of preventing debris collecting on them, and the Maharajah had not entered the place for some eighteen months before his death, the roof now had lost its strictly symmetrical qualities and the semi-opaque glass showed silhouettes in various leaf-shaped clusters. James Frere was skating idly to and from beneath them.

"Ah, Frere. What luck. I'd one or two little things I wanted to ask you."

James Frere came to a halt in the middle of the smooth black surface of the rink. The cessation of the noise of his skates—the pair he had unearthed from a rink-side cupboard could have done with a spot of oil—came like the sudden ending of a shrieking storm scene in a movie when the film abruptly breaks. The noise had been what had guided D.S.P. Howard to the rink and James Frere.

"Mr. Howard. What can I tell you?"

The D.S.P. smiled. But it was doubtful whether the little movement of his eyelids would have reached James across the black expanse of the rink.

"Same old questions again, I'm afraid," the D.S.P. said. "About when you actually last saw that piece of sapura bark. All that sort of thing. It's a bore, but it's got to be done."

"Of course, sir."

James Frere's description of his movements from the time he had searched Captain Ram Singh in that embarrassing incident until he had at last dropped to sleep that night did not vary in the least from the account he had previously given. When the D.S.P. had exhausted every variation on his questions that he could think of he thanked James and prepared to go.

"Mr. Howard."

"Yes?"

James's open face wore an expression of perplexed anxiety so obvious that it was almost ridiculous.

"What can I do for you, my dear chap?"

"Mr. Howard, I hope you won't think this is frightful cheek."

"If I do, I shan't hesitate to tell you."

James looked up quickly at the D.S.P. His face, with its ever hooded eyes, betrayed no indication of whether he was joking or serious.

"I mean—" said James.

He began again.

"I mean, I don't want to teach you your job or anything, sir. Or, no, not that. What I mean is I didn't want it to look as if I'm trying to teach you your job."

"Very well."

"Oh, gosh. I'm sorry, I'm making an awful mess of this."

"You are."

James swallowed hugely.

"Look, sir," he said, "the zenana."

"What about the zenana?"

"Well, listen. I mean, I know, sir, you're awfully experienced and all that. I mean, I've heard a lot about you. Well, from the Resident here and all that."

"Let's assume I can imagine what the Resident will have said about me."

Into James's mind at once, with these words, there flashed what the Resident had actually said in his hearing about D.S.P. Howard.

His comments had not at all been what he had meant to refer to when he had said, choosing his words so badly in his embarrassment, that he knew about the D.S.P. He had meant to convey that he had the highest respect for his work. But the chief thing the Resident had said was that the fellow was country-born. And that implied that, however white you were, you were somehow too Indian. You were too much on the Indians' side. You were touched with that mysterious attraction to India which it was all right to recognise, from an always well-kept distance, but which it was fatal to succumb to.

"I'm sorry, sir," James said again. "I seem to be getting off on the wrong foot every time. What I meant is, sir, I know you're an enormously experienced police officer. But your work's naturally been in British India, and you may not have had as much experience— That is, sir, well, I've been at the palace here for quite a time, two full months, and I—er—know Porgy Bhopore pretty well really, sir, and he's told me a lot. And, well, sir, have you really considered that this whole thing might have come from the zenana, sir?"

The D.S.P.'s face remained altogether impassive.

"You mean that First Her Highness or Second Her Highness may for some reason have arranged the Maharajah's death? Is that it, Frere?"

"Yes, sir. Yes, that is it exactly. I mean, you see, sir, they, either one of them, would quite likely know all about sapura bark, wouldn't they, sir? And I daresay they might get hold of some somehow. Send someone out to the jungle with bribe money, for instance. Or even have a sort of kidnapping arranged when that chap was bringing it to the Maharajah from wherever he found it, sir."

"Yes, Frere. I would say that your hypothesis, so far, merits at least consideration."

"Gosh. Thank you, sir. I mean, it's been worrying me, sir, ever since the idea first came to me, sort of in the night, sir."

"In the night. I see."

The D.S.P.'s eyes, for all their drooping eyelids, held James as if he were between the steady fingers of two hands, firmly but never pressingly grasped.

James tried to shift his right foot. But the heavy skate on it made the movement impossibly clumsy.

"There is— Well, there is another thing, sir," he said.

"Another thing?"

"Yes, sir. Look, I'm not making an utter ass of myself, am I? I mean, please say if I am."

"Go on, Mr. Frere. I'm most interested."

For a moment it seemed as if what the D.S.P. had said must have struck James as being the very opposite of what his words actually were. He stayed silent, as if he had been sharply rebuked.

"Well?" the D.S.P. said.

James gathered himself together.

"Well, sir, it's motive," he said. "I know this is frightful cheek, sir, but what if First Her Highness knew just how bad things were between Porgy and his father, sir? Well, I mean, you know, they were. Bad, that is. Just about as bad as can be, from what Porgy confided in me."

"Indeed?"

In the green and orange tiled entrance to the rink the figure of the D.S.P. was statue-still. Yet somehow to James he gave the impression of being intensely energetic, of a mind seizing on every word he was saying, checking it, assessing it, and filing it rapidly into place.

"Well, sir," he went on, tumbling the words out, "you know that First Her Highness is tremendously fond of Porgy, sir. And she was absolutely determined he would get the gaddi. He told me all about that even when he was up at Cambridge. Well, sir— Well, I mean, it all follows, doesn't it? I mean, if she saw the Maharajah as being on the point of disinheriting old Porgy and thought there was only one thing to do about it, sir?"

His voice trailed away.

The D.S.P. stood where he was, like a robot with only the internal mechanism in operation, for a second or two longer. Then he turned away.

"Thank you, Lieutenant," he said.

James stood where he was, feet anchored by the cumbersome skates, and watched him go.

But at the last moment the D.S.P. turned round again.

"Oh—er," he said, with uncharacteristic hesitation. "Er, you haven't seen Miss Alcott, have you? Er—Judy?"

A blush, sudden, unexpected, and unstoppable, hurled itself up into James's face. For a moment he was altogether unable to reply.

"Jud— Miss Alcott," he stammered out at last. "No. No, I don't think I have seen her. Not— Not for some time."

"Ah."

The D.S.P. turned away again.

"I thought that you and she . . ." he murmured.

Then once more he swung round. He said nothing this time. But he looked keenly for an instant at James's expression of hurt bewilderment, an expression he longed to be able to bury deep within him but could not.

"And I'll thank you to keep your damned thoughts to your damned self," Joe Lloyd concluded.

The Schoolmaster looked down at his toes.

"Oh, Lloyd Sahib," he said, "I am most very, very dismayed altogether. Believe me, Sahib, I do not in any way at all recollect having made any such suggestion as you speak of—"

"You're not calling me a liar, are you?"

Joe Lloyd's heavy fist was openly clenched.

"Oh, no, no, sir. Not at all, not at all. Not by any means. Sahib, I fear only there has been some altogether appalling mistake made. But not by you, Sahib. No, no. By some other individual altogether."

"So you're calling D.S.P. Howard a liar now, are you?"

"No, no, no, no. No, no. I would never do that, Sahib. I have the greatest respect for D.S.P. Howard, Sahib. The very greatest respect."

"Well, see you keep it then. Understand?"

"Oh, yes, Sahib. Very well I am understanding. Very well. I think."

And, certainly, an extremely thoughtful look was left on the Schoolmaster's face as Joe Lloyd marched away.

A servant showed D.S.P. Howard into the room in which in an hour's time he was to interview First Her Highness. He salaamed and stood by the doorway waiting until the D.S.P. had made his inspection.

The D.S.P. gave a sharp order in Urdu. The man salaamed again and left.

The D.S.P. looked slowly all round. There was little enough to see, only the heavy wooden screen, near which he was careful not to venture, the two sofas in the far corners, the one window through which a strong but diffused light came. The D.S.P. strolled over and looked out.

The window gave onto a small courtyard in common with a row of windows in the zenana quarter, each impenetrable behind its stonework screen. Down below in the bright sun, a syce was exercising a magnificent horse, magnificently caparisoned. To the man's quiet but sharp words of command the splendid creature showed off its paces, galloping in decreasing circles, twisting in figures of eight, coming in sudden hoof-shrieking halts, rearing up, pawing at the stones of the yard.

The D.S.P. nodded in sudden understanding. A display for the zenana ladies to look at through their pierced stone windows, doubtless their daily entertainment.

He turned from the window and stared inwards, blinking his hooded eyes after the impact of the blazing sunlight. Then he nodded, to himself, in much the same way, again.

He crossed the wide room, went up to one of the photographs hanging on its walls—it was a portrait of the King-Emperor George V and Queen Mary—took it from the haphazard nail by which it hung, and set it on the floor at his feet. He gave a quick glance towards the door through which the servant had shown him in. It was safely closed.

He reached up, grasped the nail, and twisted with all his strength. The nail resisted. Then with a tiny squeak it came loose. He pulled it out, glanced back at the light from the window, moved a yard to his left, examined the plaster of the wall carefully, found the sort of spot he was looking for, put the point of the nail at it, and pushed hard on its head with his thumb.

Slowly as he wriggled his thumb round in a semicircular motion the nail penetrated the soft plaster. At last it seemed to be far enough in. Quickly the D.S.P. hung the photograph of the King-Emperor and his consort on it. Gently he eased away the hand taking the picture's weight. The picture hung firm.

The D.S.P. stepped rapidly back to where the chair awaiting him had been placed, at a scrupulously calculated distance from the heavy screen. He dipped down onto it. He gave a quick glance at the picture with its reflecting glass. He nodded in satisfaction.

A moment later he was standing in the middle of the big room. He clapped his hands loudly once.

Immediately the door opened. The servant who had shown him in stood there, salaaming respectfully.

"You can take me back to the Maharajah now," the D.S.P. said. "I must tell him I find everything in order."

"Very good, huzoor."

XVII

It was a considerable time after D.S.P. Howard's interview with First Her Highness had begun before he arrived at the point of putting any questions to her. First, when a low but clear voice from the other side of the heavy carved screen had intimated that his subject was present, he had thanked her for allowing him to see her. Urdu is a good language for a certain floweriness. Then he had commiserated with her on the death of her husband and praised the Maharajah a good deal. A phrase or two from Urdu poetry, all Persian elegance, had crept into his discourse.

But then at last he judged that the time was getting near. He risked a quick look at the photograph of the King-Emperor George V and Queen Mary to check his assessment.

It was a quick look only. If in the reflecting glass of a photograph that happens to be hanging at a certain point on a wall it is possible to see someone seated on the far side of a screen, it is equally possible for that person, should they chance to be looking upwards and in that direction, to see you. And then, perhaps, they may recall that the photograph has not always hung in quite the position it is in today.

The D.S.P. had used his convenient little arrangement only once so far. As he had heard the faint sound of slippered feet approaching on the marble of the floor on the far side of the screen he had assumed a questing, listening look, which just happened to focus his eyes on the picture. In it, seating herself on a low, padded brocade stool and waving a hovering maidservant away, he had seen a figure of unmistakable regality dressed in a sari of widow's white without any jewellery whatsoever. Once when a maharajah had died his widow would have unhesitatingly thrown herself onto a burning pyre in the act of suttee. Now it was the custom only for her to shave her head, dress in simple white, abandon jewels, and break the gold ankle chain which it was the privilege of a maharajah's first wife, the Badamaharani, and no one else, to wear.

In the second quick glance the D.S.P. now took into the King-Emperor's photograph he saw First Her Highness sitting composedly on her stool, looking thoughtfully downwards, but apparently undisturbed by the awkward conversation so far. If she felt grief for her late husband, she was not showing it. On the other hand, if the Maharajah's death was no grief to her at all, she was showing no sign of that, for all that she believed herself to be quite unobserved.

"But at least Your Highness can rejoice that your son is safely on the gaddi," the D.S.P. said.

"I can, Howard Sahib."

"There must, if I may respectfully say so, have been times when you perhaps feared for that outcome?"

Out of the corner of his eye he caught a glimpse of movement in the photograph's glass. A quick, and even angry, straightening of the back.

No answer came floating out into the room from behind the ornate carving of the impenetrable screen.

"Your Highness, you must excuse me if from time to time I put a question or a suggestion to you that on any other occasion would be altogether improper. But, you must know, I have been summoned here, on your son's own orders, to conduct an investigation into the death of the late Maharajah. There can be no question, you know, that his death was anything other than deliberate murder."

"You are quite right, Howard Sahib. Whatever you ask I will answer, and answer with truth."

"Thank you, Your Highness."

He made himself not look up at the picture.

"Then, may I ask you again, were there times when you feared your son would not come to the gaddi?"

"There were."

A silence in the large, airy room. From outside the clear sound of distant birdsong. It was a coppersmith bird, its single repeated note going on and on like the sound of a hammer tap-tap-tapping at a sheet of metal into frail beauty somewhere in a coppersmiths' bazaar.

The Badamaharani resumed.

"My son and his father did not agree always, true. But my son had been confirmed, solemnly, as heir to the gaddi. My husband would not have altered that."

The voice was definite, cool and definite. D.S.P. Howard gathered his thoughts for a moment before replying.

"And yet, Your Highness, I have heard suggestions—"

"What suggestions?"

In the mirror picture he caught again a quick, sharp lift of the head.

He cursed inwardly. He had hoped that his artfully abandoned sentence would be enough to jolt the Maharani into a long denial, in the course of which she would give away more than she intended.

"Your Highness, I must repeat that I find myself in a situation where it is my duty to refer to matters which, in the normal way, I would never for a moment voice aloud."

"You have said that, Howard Sahib."

The voice on the far side of the screen was chill as air from the earth-buried ice wells that still served the palace.

The D.S.P. sighed.

"It may prove to be my duty, then, Your Highness, to repeat suggestions that I have heard, mere rumours only, which in the ordinary way I would not even allow myself to listen to."

"What suggestions, Howard Sahib? What rumours?"

She was not making it in the least easy for him.

He took a short breath.

"Your Highness, it has come to my ears—I shall not say in what manner—that there was a time when the late Maharajah was ready to declare that the baby born to you when the birth of the Rajkumar was announced was not a boy at all but a girl. He was prepared to say that the Rajkumar was born to some concubine in the zenana and was substituted for your girl child so as to make certain of the succession."

"Untrue, Howard Sahib. Untrue."

He did flick a glance at King George and Queen Mary now. In the glass, clear against the sepia of the photograph, he saw that the Maharani was sitting upright on her stool as if she were on horseback. On horseback and commanding an army, as more than one rani of old had done.

"I daresay that it is untrue, Your Highness," he said with calm levelness. "I daresay it is the most baseless gossip. But you do understand that, if there is any hint of truth in it, it considerably alters the situation I have found in Bhopore?"

For answer there came from behind the heavy screen a single ringing slap of palm on palm. A moment later there was the flip-flap of bare feet on marble.

"Fetch the book of the Maharajah," he heard First Her Highness order.

Apparently no need was felt for further explanation. Bare feet hurried away into the inner parts of the zenana.

A silence fell in the anteroom. Only outside the insistent hammering of the coppersmith bird went inanely on and on.

But the silence did not last very long. Soon, flap-flapping on the stone of the floor, came the sound of the servant returning.

"Maharani," the D.S.P. heard her murmur.

"Is there a mama there?" came First Her Highness's sharp question.

A mama. One of the aged retainers allowed to appear outside the zenana. The D.S.P. realised why one had been summoned. To come round the screen and hand him this book of the Maharajah, whatever it was.

He wondered for a moment whether the woman who would appear would be the selfsame person who, he had heard from the all-knowing Schoolmaster, had been sent the day before the Maharajah's death to the city and was there said to have bought a quantity of diamond dust, most trusted of poisons.

There was a shuffling on the other side of the screen, a quick command, and then the old woman came into sight. She certainly did not look appetising, the D.S.P. thought. Old, sloppily fat, with hair falling raggedly about her shoulders. Yet nevertheless she bore herself with an air of assurance. It indicated, surely as could be, the trusted servant. Here was one who had seen so much, had done so much, that she was now above all rebuking.

In her hand she carried a formidable bound volume with the Maharajah's name on it in prominent gold lettering. She thrust it out.

The D.S.P. took the book, glanced at it, found that the old mama had instantly and with some contempt shuffled back into the depths of the zenana.

"Your Highness," he said, raising his voice a little, "I have the volume you sent for."

"That book, Howard Sahib, is a record of every dalliance my husband has had with concubines in the zenana. The dates are all there. The beginning and the end. It starts before our marriage. It finishes with his death. You know the reason such a book is kept?"

The D.S.P. thought for a moment.

"Yes, I think so," he answered. "It's plainly important to know just what children are born to a maharajah, or to a rajkumar. The best way of doing that is a book such as this."

"Perfectly so. Now you will look up the period nine months before the birth of my son. You know how old he is?"

It had been one of the facts he had learnt from the Schoolmaster.

"Yes, Your Highness. I shall be only a minute or two."

Again a silence in the empty anteroom. But two sounds now. The tap-tap-tapping of the distant, bell-clear, damnable coppersmith bird and the rapid rustling of the thick paper pages of the Maharajah's book.

"Your Highness?"

"I am here."

"There can be no doubt in my mind now that your son is the true heir to the gaddi."

"Thank you, Howard Sahib. You may leave the book on your chair."

It was a dismissal.

But the D.S.P. did not wish to go yet. There were things about First Her Highness's son, and about her dead husband too, which even the Schoolmaster would not know. And if he were able to keep the conversation with the Maharani going for some time longer yet he might with luck get to find out some of them.

"There is one more thing, if Your Highness permits?"

A sigh, clearly audible on the other side of the heavy screen.

"Yes?"

"Raghbir, Your Highness."

"Raghbir? What of that boy? If you want to know anything about him, and I cannot see why you should, you must talk to his mother, to Second Her Highness."

"Perhaps I had better do that," the D.S.P. said slowly and with significance.

Now it was a quick indrawn breath he heard on the far side of the screen.

"What is it you want to know about Raghbir? Why do you want to know anything about him?"

"There were two sudden deaths in the palace within hours of each other, Your Highness."

"What if there were?" The hidden voice snapped with anger again.

"What if there were? The boy died of ptomaine poisoning. Ask Doctor Sahib. Ask Resident Sahib. Even he was satisfied."

"That it was simple death by ptomaine poisoning, and not by the administration of some poison? Something like diamond dust, for instance?"

A second gasp in the big, silent room. Then a steely voice.

"No, Howard Sahib, not diamond dust. Whatever . . . No, not diamond dust. Do you know how a man, or a child, dies from having eaten diamond dust? Ask any who saw Raghbir die. He did not die like that. He happened to die by chance. And that is all."

"But the Maharajah did not die by chance."

"No. And are you any closer to finding out who took his life, Howard Sahib? Any closer than when you first came to Bhopore?"

"Yes," said the D.S.P., very quietly and quite confidently. "Yes, I am nearer. There may be a long way to go yet. But I am nearer, Your Highness."

He let a tiny pause hang in the air. In the ornately framed photograph he saw that the Maharani was sitting on her low stool gazing quietly downwards at her lap.

"Your son and his father quarrelled," he said. "You have told me that you had no fears about your son coming to the gaddi, and I accept that. I accept that you had no fears that young Raghbir might be chosen instead."

A tiny stamp of a foot on the far side of the screen. His words had been a home thrust then. No doubt it had been lucky for that imperious lady who believed she was at this moment unobserved that poor clumsy Raghbir had died by chance, by chance-caught ptomaine poisoning. Before another death came to him.

He resumed.

"You yourself had no fears about your son's succession, Your Highness. But what of your son himself? Had he begun to doubt that he would come to the gaddi after all?"

"No, Howard Sahib, he had not. He had no doubts at all."

"Yet he had heard his father declare that he would not suffer a white maharani in Bhopore, after him, and he very much wants to marry Miss Brattle."

A sound of sheer contempt came from behind the heavy screen.

"Oh, come, Your Highness. Too many people have told me of his behaviour with Miss Brattle. I have heard his very words to her repeated."

"Servants' gossip."

"Perhaps. But servants' gossip has a way of being true, or half true at worst."

"I tell you my son has no intention of marrying that white whore."

"Strong words, Your Highness." The D.S.P. put a touch of steel into his voice now.

"But true words," the Maharani flared back. "Wasn't she sleeping with him? Night after night."

"And if she was, doesn't that mean that he was in love with her? Wouldn't he have done anything to have made her his wife?"

"My son has no intention of making that woman his wife. You can take that from me, Howard Sahib."

"Very well, I will accept that."

A sharp contented little sigh in the big room.

"I will accept that, Your Highness, as being the state of affairs now. Now that your son is Maharajah of Bhopore. But I do not at all accept it as being the situation before he came to the gaddi."

"But my son loved his father."

The cry rang out. It was almost as if the harsh tones had brought down the heavy carved-wood screen.

The D.S.P. waited till the last faint ringing note of them had died utterly away. Then he spoke quietly, and almost sadly.

"But love can turn to hate, you know. The stronger the love, the stronger the hate. You must know that that is so."

"Yes, Howard Sahib, I know it."

And the undertone of unadmitted fear was clearly to be heard on the far side of that screen.

D.S.P. Howard's next interview was conducted in very much simpler conditions. It took place in the palace Trophy Room. But only because it was in the Trophy Room that he last tracked down the next person on his list. In the notebook that did not bulge any of his pockets but lay instead, always ready, always open, in the back of his mind, he was able now to put one more tick.

The Trophy Room was large, though luckily there was no one else in it when he entered except the person whose name was on his list. All around the high walls skins hung. There were the striped skins of tigers, the spotted skins of panthers, and more densely spotted, the skins of cheetahs, fastest runners of them all. Here and there there was the tawny skin of the Indian lion. Under each skin, fixed to the pale green walls, was a brass plate. The plates had been polished so well and so often—it was a servant's daily task to do this and nothing else—that with all except the latest ones it was hardly possible to read them. But each was inscribed with the name of the Maharajah who had brought this particular beast down, the date of his triumph, and the exact measurements of the kill, measured carefully between pegs hammered into the ground at the site and stretched only so far as the rules of the game permitted.

Between and above the hanging skins were the horns and heads of various other kills over the years. There were the massive horns of bison, the delicately curling antlers of antelope and gazelle. At the far end of the room a huge rhinoceros head hung as if it were on the point of charging, red-rimmed eyes ferocious, down the whole length of the chequered marble floor to the tall and stately double doors.

It was through these doors, quietly opening one leaf just wide enough to allow him to slip in, that the D.S.P. had come. And there, looking with fascinated distaste at a row of shaggy ugly, fiercely tusked wild boar heads, was Mrs. Elaine Alcott.

"Ah, Mrs. Alcott. Good evening."

She wheeled round with a gasp.

"I'm sorry. I startled you."

"Well, yes. Yes, you did, Mr. Howard. I guess I'm jumpy. To tell you the truth, I just wish I was out of here. I wish I was out of India altogether."

"I'm sorry to hear that. India's an astonishingly beautiful place, you know."

"I daresay it is. To you. But no one can appreciate all those beautiful places and things if they're darned scared from the time they wake up in the morning till the time they go to bed at night. No, I'm wrong. For most of the time they're in bed at night too."

She came quickly across the wide empty floor towards him, the heels of her shoes clicking out.

"Mr. Howard, last night just outside my window there was someone coughing. I lay awake and listened. He'd cough. And then there'd be silence. And then, when I just convinced myself there was no one there, that cough would come again. Mr. Howard, who was it? Who could it have been?"

The D.S.P. smiled. It was a more noticeable smile than that usual infinitesimal twitch of straight-set lips or hooded eyelids.

"There's no need whatsoever to be alarmed, Mrs. Alcott," he said.

"It was almost certainly one of the chowkidars, the watchmen. They are there for your protection, you know, though I must admit they're inclined to go to sleep when they should be awake. And they will smoke bidis, Indian cigarettes. And those are very strong and give the people addicted to them permanent bronchitis as often as not."

"Well, it's kind of you to explain. But I guess it doesn't make me like India any more. There's snakes, too."

Again he smiled.

"Have you seen a snake, Mrs. Alcott? In all the time you've been in India?"

"I guess not. But I haven't been here long. If I stay another week, and I hope to goodness I shan't, I'm sure I'll not only see one, I'll get bitten by the darned creature."

"I've been in India all my life, you know. And I've never been bitten by a snake. Come to that, I haven't seen a great many of them."

"It's no use your talking, Mr. Howard, though I know it's meant kindly. But I'm not going to like India. I'm just not, and that's all there is to be said to it."

"But what about your daughter? Doesn't Judy like it here?"

Elaine Alcott drew up her thin, nervous frame.

"She likes it far too well," she said. "And someone she's found in India she likes even better."

"Lieutenant Frere?"

"Lootenant Frere."

She pronounced the words as if she were reciting the Latin name for the most venomous snake to be found in the whole vast peninsula.

"Oh, come now, Mrs. Alcott. Frere isn't a bad fellow. I'd even say he was somewhat of a catch. His people back home are very well off. A good deal of land, I gather, and retired Indian Army. You can't do very much better than that."

"Oh, yes you can. You can find a decent, clean-living all-American boy."

"And is that why you've forbidden Judy to have anything more to do with young Frere?"

"You knew that? How did you know that?"

Again the D.S.P. smiled. But this time it was that little, faintly sardonic lifting of the corners of his straight mouth.

"Now, Mrs. Alcott, I know you haven't been in India many days, but I'm sure you realised long ago that there is always a servant somewhere nearby wherever you are. And that servants listen."

"That's another thing I just don't like."

"It's something one gets used to. One gets so used to it one often forgets completely that it happens. But not when one has been in the country only a short time. Then one remembers."

"What— Just what do you mean by that?"

Another tiny flick of a smile.

"Oh, simply that if one wishes a certain thing to be known there's no better way of making sure it is than by speaking of it loudly and clearly where a servant will hear."

"I don't understand."

She swung on her heel and went, trying to walk with calm dignity, across to where the huge rhinoceros glared down at the scene. She leant forward and peered at the brass plate beneath it. But the D.S.P.'s quiet voice inexorably came to her.

"You know, I think you do understand, Mrs. Alcott. I have a feeling—correct me if I'm wrong—that you wanted the impression to get about that you somehow believed that Lieutenant Frere, who after all is one of the people who both learnt from the Maharajah how to use sapura bark to deadly effect and was out at the jheels when it was used, that you wanted it known you somehow had reason to think poor young Frere murdered the Maharajah."

She wheeled round. There was a desperate look on her strained face now.

"Listen, Mr. Howard," she said, "I had to protect my daughter. A mother has a duty, you know. She has a duty."

"To protect your daughter from Lieutenant Frere?"

"Yes. Yes, exactly. That's what I had to do."

"Because you knew that Lieutenant Frere murdered the Maharajah? Is that what you're telling me?"

"Yes, I am. Don't you see? I couldn't let a daughter of mine have anything to do with him. I couldn't. Mr. Howard, isn't there any possibility of us leaving? Leaving tonight? All three of us? Judy, me, and Joe. Joe could see us at least to Calcutta. And couldn't we get a ship from there to the West Coast?"

"You want your brother to go with you, Mrs. Alcott?"

"Yes. Yes, I do. It would be better, wouldn't it? I mean, neither Judy nor I have much idea how to get about in India. And Joe's been here so long. He'd have to come with us."

"To Calcutta, Mrs. Alcott?" the D.S.P. asked in his quiet voice.

"Yes, yes. Just to Calcutta. Only to Calcutta."

"Not on with you to America?"

She took a step backwards.

"To America? Why should Joe want to go to America?"

The D.S.P. looked at her steadily out of his hooded eyes.

"Perhaps," he suggested, "so that you could get him into hiding somewhere?"

"Hiding— Why should— I don't know what you mean."

"You do, of course. You know very well. You've known what I've meant from the very beginning, haven't you? You knew that I meant that I have perfectly well understood why you wanted it to come to my ears that you had some good reason to suspect James Frere. So that I should not suspect Joe Lloyd."

"But— But, no."

She came towards him again now, tottering a little on her high heels.

"Mr. Howard," she said, "you have got to believe this. You've got to. I do think James had something to do with it. I did believe that. Honest to God, I did."

He was looking at her.

She could tell nothing from his face. It reminded her—in a sudden flash of comparison like a lightning stroke passing between two heavily charged clouds—of some of the statues she had seen in her brief time in India. Impassive faces, lost in worlds of their own, unreachable.

"Mr. Howard," she said again, "you can't think I'd play with my daughter's happiness like that. My own daughter."

"Mr. Lloyd is your own brother," he answered. "And one of whom you've been very fond ever since you were children. Aren't I right?"

"Well, yes. Yes, I guess. But— But, listen. Listen, Mr. Howard, I do really think James Frere must know more than it seems. I do truly. I did truly."

"Very well, suppose you tell me just what you know about him that I don't."

She drew breath. But she plainly did not find it easy to begin.

"Could we— Couldn't we sit down?" she asked at last.

"Of course."

There was a couch against one of the walls, a small modern European couch in mottled-green moquette. It stood just underneath a pair of gigantic swooping elephant tusks resting on small brass brackets. They walked over. Mrs. Alcott had the slumped look of someone who has run a long race and lost. The D.S.P. walked half a step behind her, contained and wary.

They sat down.

"You— You haven't got a cigarette, have you?" she asked.

He produced his case. It was old and battered, in gunmetal. He flicked it open. She fumbled with sweaty fingertips to get a cigarette out and managed it only after some time. She pushed the cigarette into her mouth without bothering to tap the tobacco down. The D.S.P. pulled out a box of matches and struck one. He held its small flame close to her, steadily as if it had been gripped in an iron clamp.

She got the cigarette to it, jerked it back half lit, pulled at it hungrily.

The D.S.P. waited. He seemed to have all the time in the world.

Mrs. Alcott had smoked the cigarette half down its length in big fast-burning drags before she spoke.

"Look, I don't know anything—anything, well, like evidence," she said. "I mean I didn't pick up a cigarette end in his rooms or anything."

"No, I'm sure you didn't. There's nothing like that to be found. Of that much I'm certain at least."

She turned to him quickly, eyes burning.

"But you aren't certain of anything else?" she asked. "You still can't name a name?"

"My dear Mrs. Alcott, it would be my duty not to tell you if I could."

She blinked and frowned.

"I'm not sure I understand what the hell that means," she said.

"It means I cannot tell you anything about the course of my investigation. It's quite simple."

"I suppose. Well then, but listen, Mr. Howard. James Frere. Look at him. He can't be as innocent as that. All those others, the four of them, why, they've each got a good reason to have killed the Maharajah, haven't they?"

She peered across at him. There was nothing to be told from his features.

"Well, they have," she went on. "Everybody knows that. You've only got to listen. Even— Even Joe had a good motive."

She gave a proud little tilt to her insignificant bosom at the daringness of what she had just managed to say.

"Yes, Mrs. Alcott. On the face of it your brother had a strong motive for murdering the Maharajah. On the face of it he still has a strong motive."

"Yes, but don't you see, that's all the more reason for knowing he didn't do it?"

She brightened as she produced the theory. A sharp little smile appeared on her rather faded face. It did not look in place.

"Don't you see?" she repeated urgently. "If— If Joe had really wanted to kill—to kill the Maharajah he wouldn't have done it the way it was done, or at the time it was. He would have known he'd be the first to be suspected. So he couldn't have done it, could he? And I guess the same goes for the other three."

"And that's your reason for suspecting James Frere?"

"Yes." It was a single word of defiance.

"Or, shall we say, that is the way you managed to convince yourself that you did not need to think whether your brother had really killed the Maharajah, Mrs. Alcott?"

"No."

But there was nothing of defiance in that single word. It was a whisper only. A whisper of admission, of defeat.

XVIII

In the cool of evening, with the sun fast dropping below the horizon, the Schoolmaster, later than his customary exact hour, was making his way homewards. He walked slowly, using his now furled black umbrella as a stick.

He had had a hard day. Not that the late Maharajah's sons by his various concubines had been particularly unruly. But they were seldom other than noisy, inattentive, and misbehaved. And weighing on him too was the thought that he had let down the Angrezi D.S.P., whose conversations with him he had valued so much.

Had it been wrong of him to have dallied in the palace gardens well after the hour for the end of lessons had come hoping to hear a voice say, "Good evening, Schoolmaster Sahib"? His pupils had long gone. As usual, they had abruptly decided they had had enough of schooling some quarter of an hour before the time officially set for the end of their day. But that he had minded today less than he might have done. The rivers of the Punjab had been finally and completely mastered by every single one of his charges. There was that modest triumph to mull over.

But its taste was as ashes in his mouth. Was he never to have another comfortable, interesting, private chat with D.S.P. Sahib? Yes, it had really been wrong to have lingered so long within the palace walls.

He hardly had eyes now for any of the small wayside sights that in the ordinary way enlivened his twelve-mile homeward trudge. His ears, normally almost as acute as his eyes, were insensitive now to the little sounds there were to be heard, the occasional songs of birds —an insistent tap-tap-tapping coppersmith bird, the repeated "You're ill, you're ill, we know it, we know it" of the brain-fever bird—the occasional bray of a distressed bullock, the unending interwoven pattern of squeakings and chirrings from the insects everywhere.

Nor did he hear, until it was almost at his back, the soft sound of the hooves of a horse thudding on the dust of the road. And, before he had really taken it in and begun to turn to see who it was riding at a hard canter behind him, a voice called out.

"Schoolmaster Sahib, good evening."

"Oh. Oh, it is you, D.S.P. Sahib. Good evening."

The Schoolmaster glanced up at the D.S.P. astride the horse he had been lent from the palace's huge stable. Then he turned and looked steadfastly at the dust-matted road in front of him, winding vaguely onwards in the direction of the city. He began trudging forwards again.

But if he had expected the D.S.P. to touch his spurs to his mount's sides and resume his vigorous canter, his gloomy foreboding turned out at once to be quite unjustified. The D.S.P. let his horse's reins fall loose on its back, and the animal began to walk slowly along beside this trudging human.

"I'm surprised to see you now, Schoolmaster Sahib," came the voice from high up beside him. "I thought you left the palace a good deal earlier than this."

"Already you have learnt our times and routines, D.S.P. Sahib."

The Schoolmaster hoped that this compliment would serve as an acceptable substitute for the truth it would be exceedingly embarrassing to tell.

There was silence from above. In the cooling air there were only the sounds of the busy insect life, the distant monotonous birdsong, and the dust-softened clopping of the horse's hooves.

But at last the D.S.P. spoke again.

"Yes. Yes, I suppose I have learnt a good deal of the pattern of things here."

And the Schoolmaster understood that this response was in fact a way of saying that the reason he himself was later on his way home than usual was perfectly plain to the D.S.P. And that any small indiscretion he had committed before was now to be forgotten.

"D.S.P. Sahib," he said, "may I respectfully ask: now that you have established the pattern of palace life well in your mind, can you see upon it perhaps that one ragged end which is a significant difference?"

A grunt of a laugh from above.

"Schoolmaster Sahib, you must stop reading those books of Mrs. Agatha Christie's."

Tramping along beside the gently walking horse, the Schoolmaster sighed.

"Yes, D.S.P. Sahib, I suppose life is not like that."

But, to his surprise, there came again from over his head a grunt of laughter.

"You're wrong there actually, Schoolmaster Sahib. What happens in those books? Or what happened in the one of Mrs. Christie's that I've read? A puzzling murder occurred. The Great Detective arrived. He displayed his eccentricities for a little, those unlikely moustaches, those too well-polished shoes, that egg-shaped head with its contents of little grey cells. Then he made some inquiries, conducted a few interviews, and then, getting towards the end, he went away somewhere and had a great think."

"Yes, yes, Sahib. That is exactly the traditional course of events."

Another quick grunt of a laugh.

"Well, Schoolmaster Sahib, here we are in real life. Here is a simple District Superintendent of Police busy keeping dacoity down in his corner of India. He gets invited to a princely state because a murder has been committed. Or perhaps, to stick a little more closely to the truth, because a Viceroy is expected. And what does he do? He makes some inquiries, he interviews a few people, and then, damn it, he feels the need to go away and brood. So he borrows a horse, thinking he'll have a good long ride, get some exercise, and perhaps find that an answer, which has seemed to be stuck in the back of his mind like a pomegranate seed lodged in a back tooth, will of its own accord come to the fore."

The Schoolmaster turned, as he plodded along, and looked up into the D.S.P.'s face. But the hooded eyes were as uninformative as ever.

"Yes, Sahib," he said. "You have acted very much in the tradition of the Great Detective. Except, if you will excuse me, that you have not shown signs of any interesting eccentricities."

"No. No, I don't think I quite go in for eccentricities."

The Schoolmaster had turned his head to face the way he was going again. He exhaled a breathy sigh.

"Sahib, I am very much afraid that my humble person, occurring in the way as you rode, has prevented the customary course of things taking place. The Great Detective was going to, as you said, brood. But instead he has conversed."

"Yes. Yes, he has conversed, Schoolmaster Sahib."

"I am altogether most apologetic, D.S.P. Sahib. Perhaps if you cared to ride on now . . ."

Another grunt of laughter from above. Another.

"No, Schoolmaster Sahib, I do not care to ride on."

A very puffed-out sigh from a height of rather less than five feet from the softly dusty ground.

"No, I see, D.S.P. Sahib. The train of thought is broken. The process of brooding, if I may so describe it, has been totally ruined."

"It ought to have been, Schoolmaster Sahib, yes."

"It ought to have been?"

The Schoolmaster twisted his head round and upwards. The D.S.P.'s face betrayed no more than it ever did.

"It ought to have been, Schoolmaster Sahib. But life has a touch of ironic humour, I often think."

"Yes, yes. Indeed so, Sahib. I have frequently had just that idea, if I may say so."

"Yes, a touch of ironic humour, Schoolmaster Sahib. You see, scarcely had I got up on this very decent horse of the Maharajah's, all ready for a good long ride with plenty of healthy exercise thrown in, than—click—up into the front of my mind popped that elusive thought."

The Schoolmaster stopped dead in his tracks. But the D.S.P.'s horse, encouraged perhaps by the slightest tensing of the D.S.P.'s knees, continued to amble onwards. The Schoolmaster jerked to life, ran a few awkward, waddling steps forward until he had actually outpaced the D.S.P. by a couple of yards, and then wheeled straight round to confront horse and man.

"D.S.P. Sahib," he charged, "you know?"

The hooded eyes moved not a flicker.

But the horse did come to a stop now.

"Let's say it was a curious idea that popped into the front of my mind. A notion that things do not always have to be the way they seem. Something like that."

"But, D.S.P. Sahib."

The Schoolmaster's protest was quite involuntary. Curiosity for once had totally conquered politeness and discretion.

"Yes, Schoolmaster Sahib?"

The Schoolmaster swallowed.

"D.S.P. Sahib," he said, with more caution now, "might I ask what is the nature of this discovery of yours? Might I ask that much?"

The tiniest of twitches appeared at the corners of the D.S.P.'s straight-set mouth.

"Let me give you something to think about, Schoolmaster Sahib," he said. "What Mrs. Christie, I suppose, would call a clue. A clue or two. Or perhaps a red herring or two."

"Yes, D.S.P. Sahib?"

An avid desire to know was stamped on the Schoolmaster's mild face like a heavy postmark disfiguring every delicate line of the engraver's art beneath it.

"You know, I daresay, that Miss Brattle was thinking at one stage of leaving the palace?"

"Yes, yes, D.S.P. Sahib. Her bearer, a fellow I happened to have some conversation with, mentioned that you—ahem—persuaded her that it would not be a good idea to leave."

"Yes. You're quite right, as usual. Well, she had been on the point of going. She was carrying her own suitcase, even. And it was a good, heavy case. Remember that, Schoolmaster Sahib."

"A good, heavy case." Puzzlement was chasing curiosity away on the Schoolmaster's face. "And that is what I am to remember, D.S.P. Sahib?"

"It's just something you might like to think about, Schoolmaster Sahib. Keep you away from Agatha Christie."

"But there is something else? There is more, D.S.P. Sahib?"

"If you like."

"But what? What is it, D.S.P. Sahib? Please?"

"Oh, well. Here's a small thought for you. Murder is evil. I think you'd agree to that?"

"Oh, yes, D.S.P. Sahib. Murder is altogether most evil."

"Yet murder is not always done from an evil motive. What would you say to that, Schoolmaster Sahib?"

"Not always done from an evil motive." The Schoolmaster repeated the words with care, as if by saying them sufficiently slowly a meaning which had altogether escaped him on first hearing might after all emerge.

Evidently nothing did emerge because he looked up at the D.S.P.'s impenetrable face again.

"And something else?" he begged almost piteously.

"That's quite enough to keep you thinking, Schoolmaster Sahib. Quite enough."

The D.S.P. picked up the loose reins on his horse's back and gave them a small, decisive flick. At once the animal jerked into rapid motion.

"D.S.P. Sahib," the Schoolmaster shouted as horse and rider moved lungingly past him, "D.S.P. Sahib, what is it you are going to do?"

The D.S.P. turned as he trotted fast away.

"Oh, I have a plan, Schoolmaster Sahib. I have a plan."

The horse was cantering now. Between the D.S.P. and the Schoolmaster a cloud of dust sprang up, soft, enveloping, choking.

It was at the hour for cocktails that D.S.P. Howard announced his plan. Once more beneath the immense, glittering chandeliers of the drawing room the Maharajah's guests and a select handful of courtiers were gathered. Once more the discreet, white-jacketed Goan bearers were circulating with their heavy silver trays on which were arrayed in sparkling appropriate glasses, creamy-topped Alexanders, pale lime-coloured gimlets, amber whiskies from bottles of King George IV (containing every nutriment value of the ripe grain), the deep green of crème de menthe, the sharp pale pink of gin touched with angostura.

As usual the Dewan, thin and elegant in his black sherwani, was sipping nothing more alcoholic than a bright red tomato juice. Joe Lloyd, the front of his boiled shirt for once complete with its full quota of studs, none of them burst, was drinking whisky. And drinking it rather fast. Next to him, his sister had at least conceded to India the chocolaty Alexander, that Western import. She, before the cocktail hour had very much advanced, had begun sipping at her second.

Lieutenant Frere, on the other hand, a whisky man, was keeping very strictly to his rule of one only before dinner. Yet as the bearers, soft-footed, passed by him with their loaded trays, he could be seen to be casting glances at the array of drinks on them that were not without envy. And, if no one else noted this, two pairs of eyes certainly were aware of it. One pair, of course, was hooded. The other belonged to Judy. She was sitting in the opposite half of the long, high-ceilinged room, on the far side of the gently splashing white fountain in the centre. It was a place she had chosen deliberately.

Yet she had too, equally deliberately, chosen to sit on a richly brocaded Empire chair that gave her a clear view of the tall, straight-backed figure of James Frere.

Two others of the small party had also contrived to put the white marble fountain between them. In one half of the heavily furnished room Porgy, Maharajah of Bhopore, resplendent in a pale green brocade coat heavy with minutely embroidered red roses, was as rapid with his whiskies as Joe Lloyd. In the opposite half of the room, Dolly Brattle sat by herself and drank a gimlet, savouring it as if it might be her last. Earlier, Judy, seeing her on her own, had threaded her way past the little tables with their displays of silver-framed photographs and the many richly coloured armchairs and had tried to engage her in conversation. But she had been rebuffed.

"You don't have to talk to me, you know, dear."

Judy had blinked.

"Oh. Oh, but I want to. Yes, I want to."

"You do?" A quick, bitter little smile on the heavily made-up lips. "And what do you want to talk to me about?"

Judy had floundered. She had cursed herself and wished with all her might that she could have thought of some interesting subject which would draw out this taut-faced, plainly miserable Britisher. But nothing had come.

For a little Dolly had let her mutter incoherently about India, and it all being so exciting, and that there must be a thousand things she wanted to know though she couldn't think of one of them right now. And then she had shaken her head a little.

"All right, dear. You've done your best. You've been the Lady Bountiful. You can go off now. Why don't you go and talk to James? He wants you to, my dear."

Judy did rise to her feet at that. But she did not leave.

"I don't have to talk to anybody just because he seems to want me to talk to him," she said stiffly.

"Have it your own way, dear. Cut off your pretty little nose to spite your face. You can afford to. You've got plenty of time on your side."

Judy almost sat down again on the sofa beside Dolly then. But Dolly stopped her with a gesture.

"No, dear. I can look after myself. Don't you worry. I've done it long enough, I can go on doing it as long as I have to now."

Judy had wanted to offer some kind of apology. But what, she had thought, can I apologise for? For her having been ditched in such an obvious way by the new Maharajah? For her so plainly being dangerously old now for a young woman? For my own lack of the right words?

She compromised by making a vague gesture towards that still bright cap of platinum hair. A gesture which tried to say, "I'm sorry for you, I wish I could help," but which only said, "I don't know how."

She made her way back to the chair she had originally been sitting in, the one from which she had a good view, from a safe distance, of the crown of fair hair on James Frere's head.

Just behind her she could hear Henry Morton III in conversation with Captain Ram Singh, the two of them, for all their difference of appearance, age, and nationality, somehow out of the same mould, uncomplicated men.

"Listen, Captain, I've got to get to see the Maharajah."

"Oh, but Mr. Morton, you are seeing him now. He is there. Over there, you see. At present he is talking with the Dewan, Sir Akhtar Ali."

"Captain, I know who the Maharajah is. For gosh sakes, he was friendly enough before the murder. A fine progressive man, I put him down as. But now . . . Now he won't let me see him."

"Ah, it is talking with him you are meaning. Now I understand. Yes, yes. But if you are wanting to talk, that is very easy to do."

"It is? You surprise me, Captain. But I'm happy to believe you. What do I have to do?"

Captain Ram Singh slowly blinked his luminous brown eyes. He felt as if an open polo goal lay straight in front of him, as if his mallet were raised and the ball just far enough ahead of his pony, but with a sneaking suspicion in his head that it was not after all going to be so easy. The goalposts might suddenly shrink inwards, or his pony bend at the knees.

Yet there was nothing for it but to play the shot.

"You must walk over to where the Maharajah is standing, quite near to the gramophone, you see. And then you . . . Well, you must talk."

A look of rage, barely contained, appeared on the American tycoon's scarred face. He took in a deep breath.

"Yes, Captain," he said. "I quite understand that I could go over to the Maharajah and engage him in conversation about the weather, or about pigsticking or polo or some damned such nonsense. But I want to talk to him. Talk. Talk business. Business, you get it?"

"Oh. Ah. Business. Yes, business, I see. I am afraid, you know, I don't know a great deal about the box-wallah side of life. I am rather more of a sporting man myself. Now, if you wanted to discuss with His Highness pigstick— Or polo . . . Well, if you wanted to discuss any sort of sport, I could help you. I mean, I could come with you and explain to His Highness what it is you are wanting. But business. No. That is something I do not understand."

"I'll say you don't. And neither does anybody else in this damned country. Listen, man. I have a big deal I want to put to the Maharajah. You understand what a big deal is?"

"Oh, yes. Yes indeed. A big deal. Yes. Many lakhs of rupees, crores of rupees even. Yes, I understand."

"Captain, I don't think you do. I don't know exactly what a lakh—is it?—of rupees is, or a crore of'em for that matter. But I guess it's a whole lot less than a million dollars U.S. And it's more than a million dollars U.S. that I'm talking about, a whole lot more."

"Oh, yes?" said Captain Ram Singh, with great politeness. "Most interesting. That would be a very great amount of money."

He began to turn away.

"Captain!"

"Yes? Oh, yes, Mr. Morton? Another drink? Bearer! Bearer!"

"To hell with another drink. Listen to me. I want to get to talk with the Maharajah. To talk business. I've asked and I've asked and I've gotten just nowhere. Now I'm asking you. Can you fix it? Yes or no?"

"Oh," said Captain Ram Singh. "No. Quite definitely no."

"Why the hell not? You're his A.D.C., aren't you? Isn't that some sort of damn secretary? Or personal assistant? Well, it's the job of a personal assistant or secretary where I come from to fix up appointments for their boss. And that's just what I'm asking you to do for me."

Captain Ram Singh's handsome moustached face wore now an expression of pain.

"But, Mr. Morton," he said, "if the Maharajah already has said no, then what can I do?"

Henry Morton III shook his head in sadness.

"Captain, let me explain to you the fundamentals of business dealings," he said. "It's plain enough neither you nor anyone else in this hell of a country has any idea of'em. 'No' isn't 'no' when you're in business, not if you mean to get anywhere, it isn't. 'No' is just the opening move. It's just a signal you get to tell you you've got to hustle some. See?"

"Well, no," Captain Ram Singh said with caution.

The American gritted his teeth.

"Listen, man. Someone says 'no' to you, it means he's not accepting your first offer. Get it? It never means he doesn't want to do business. Who the hell never wants to do business?"

Captain Ram Singh gave a little cough.

"Mr. Morton," he said, "I think I can give an answer to that question. It is the Maharajah who does not want to do business."

The American's face darkened.

"Mr. Morton, Mr. Morton," Captain Ram Singh hurriedly explained, "it is not at all your fault that he does not. It is the Viceroy's, Mr. Morton."

"The Viceroy's? What the hell—"

"But, Mr. Morton, surely you cannot have forgotten. The Viceroy is coming."

"Well, what if he is? He's not coming for eight or nine days yet, is he? Why can't the Maharajah see me now? Why can't he see me at nine o'clock tomorrow morning?"

The handsome A.D.C. shook his head in sadness.

"Mr. Morton, you are not at all understanding. When the Viceroy is visiting a Maharajah, it is not a matter of 'Would you care for a cup of tea, Your Excellency?' It is a matter of protocol, Mr. Morton. It is a matter of precedents. What did the last Viceroy to visit the State do? What happened at the last State which the Viceroy visited? The Maharajah is not going to allow a ruler with fewer guns in his salute to take more of His Excellency's time than he will himself. He is not going to make the mistake of going to greet His Excellency one step nearer than a mere eleven-gun wallah. If His Excellency has bagged a ten-foot tiger on the visit before ours, he's jolly well going to get an eleven footer when he comes to Bhopore even if we have to press down the measuring peg every four inches to lengthen the cord enough to make it."

"But that's nothing but darned fiddling. It's bowing and scraping made ridiculous. And it's all standing in the way of a deal worth millions and millions of dollars. Why if I—"

But what Henry Morton III would have done had he been ruler of

Bhopore, or Viceroy of India, was never to be known. Because at that moment D.S.P. Howard chose to make his announcement.

It was the Maharajah himself who silenced the buzz of desultory conversation from the little clumps of guests and courtiers here and there all over the huge long room. He did it by clapping his hands. At once a respectful hush fell.

"Ladies and gentlemen," Porgy said, "you all of you know, I'm sure, why we have Mr. Howard staying with us. You all of you must be as damned keen as I am to have the horrible business of my father's death properly cleared up. Well, in connection with that there is something Mr. Howard wants to say to all of us now."

He turned to the still, dinner-jacketed figure beside him.

"Mr. Howard," he said.

By that time everyone in the big long room was on their feet and had moved to points where they could be sure of seeing the figure of the D.S.P. Nor did he have to raise his ordinarily quiet voice when he spoke. No one was going to make any sound that would stop them noting every least shade of meaning.

"Ladies and gentlemen, I suppose in the course of my career in the Indian Police Service I have investigated well over a hundred cases of murder. Of course, when I say 'investigated' that is perhaps overstating the matter somewhat. Rather more than ninety of those cases have been simply a matter of making sure that the person or persons who have committed that murder are arrested as quickly as possible. But there have been a few affairs where it has been necessary to make a number of inquiries, and even to solve something of a mystery."

No one in that long room beneath the tall, glittering chandeliers moved as much as one half inch. The D.S.P., who had paused to take a long, slow look round at them, went on.

"But even those mystery cases, ladies and gentlemen, were not really very difficult to unravel. Yes, the murderers had tried to cover up what they had done. One had even tried on one occasion to throw the blame onto someone else. But their efforts really were not very convincing, and once the exact facts of the affair had been brought to light, what had happened was really perfectly clear. But the murder of the Maharajah has proved to be a very different matter."

Now there was movement among his listeners. A stir of interest, of apprehension, that had been impossible to keep in check.

The D.S.P. waited patiently until it had run its course.

"Yes," he said then, "this very sad business has proved to be by no means everything that it seemed. And I'm afraid that it took me quite some time to realise what the exact nature of the case was."

Again he paused. And while he did so, with a scarcely perceptible movement of his head he allowed his hooded eyes to roam carefully over every face in the room. The quiet marble fountain at its centre seemed suddenly to be noisy and insistent as the roaring of a waterfall.

"Indeed," the D.S.P. resumed at last, "it was only this evening, while I was out riding to clear my mind a little, that I realised that I had been making a fundamental error about the whole nature of the case. You know, I think most people who have talked to me about the murder have fallen into much the same trap. We all assumed—correct me if I am wrong—that, since the Maharajah died from the effect of the barrel of one of his guns exploding, the heart of the matter concerned, first, a somewhat unfortunate practical joke he had played with a piece of sapura bark and, then, the short period in the dark of early morning out at the jheels when someone could quite easily have got at the Maharajah's guns in their locked rack."

Here and there in the big room people were glancing at one another now with puzzled frowns. Quietly still, the D.S.P. went on.

"But I am going to suggest to you that those events were not at all the key to the affair. I am going to suggest to you—or rather, perhaps, inform you—that the key to the affair lies altogether in another event."

Porgy stepped forward now.

"Yes," he said, his face clearly betraying excitement, or possibly some other feeling. "Yes, Mr. Howard was telling me—"

"Your Highness."

Porgy came to a sudden stop. He turned towards the D.S.P.

"Your Highness, if I may respectfully suggest it, this rather complicated matter is perhaps best dealt with by just one person."

"Of course, of course, Mr. Howard. You must forgive me for breaking in on what you were saying. The truth is that it's so jolly astonishing to me that I simply longed to tell someone else."

The infinitesimal twitch of the lips that served D.S.P. Howard as a smile came and went.

"I quite understand, Your Highness. And I assure you that you will have plenty of opportunity to discuss it all in just a few minutes."

"Thank you. Thank you, Mr. Howard. Do please carry on."

"Thank you, Your Highness."

The hooded eyes moved to examine the wider audience again.

"Yes, ladies and gentlemen, as I was saying, the key to this affair, I realised only this evening, does not necessarily lie in that incident with the sapura bark and the Resident's Rolls-Royce out in front of the palace. It lies elsewhere. It lies, in fact, unless I am very much mistaken, in the dinner that took place on the night before the Maharajah met his sad end."

Faces turned from one to another. Nobody seemed to understand this. There were even one or two subdued questioning sounds.

The D.S.P. gave a short, sharp cough. Silence fell again instantly. Only the gentle sound of the fountain could still be heard.

"In view of my discovery, ladies and gentlemen," the D.S.P. continued, "I have just a few moments ago consulted His Highness and he has been good enough to agree to a plan I put to him."

Porgy looked gratified.

"What I have asked His Highness to do is this," the D.S.P. went on. "I have asked him if he can arrange for tomorrow night a dinner party that will reproduce as exactly as possible the one that was held the night before the late Maharajah died. Just before I came in for drinks here, His Highness sent an invitation to Sir Arthur Pendeverel to attend this—er—reconstruction, just as he attended the first dinner party."

He allowed a slight pause here, perhaps in tribute to Sir Arthur. Captain Ram Singh took advantage of the silence.

"Excuse me, Mr. Howard," he said, his voice rather too loud. "Excuse me, but do you mean to say that I've got to— Well, damn it, have I got to go through all that business of being arrested again? I mean, it's perfectly plain I never had any intention of murdering His Highness. I mean, you know, I was—er—locked up at the time that the sapura bark was put in the Maharajah's gun."

"Oh, yes, I know you were locked up, Captain Ram Singh. And, of course, that means that you could not possibly have tampered with the Maharajah's guns. I'd certainly like that very clearly understood."

"Thank you, Mr. Howard. But then, if I may ask, what's all this second-chukka dinner party about then?"

The hooded eyes looked steadily at handsome Captain Ram Singh, who, in just one moment, abruptly looked a lot less handsome and a lot more hangdog.

"I was only—er—just asking, you know."

"Of course. And it was a good question, Captain Ram Singh. You see, it draws attention to the whole question of the Maharajah's behaviour that night. The question of his unusually extravagant behaviour."

"Yes, ladies and gentlemen," Porgy broke in once more. "You see, really Papa—my father was behaving unusually even for— That is, he was behaving most unusually that night. And, you see, Mr. Howard has, most cleverly, discovered the reason for that."

The silence in the long room was yet more intense. The tiny quiet splash of the water in the fountain seemed to grate on nerves as irritatingly as if it were some Chinese water torture.

But the D.S.P.'s voice when he took up his account was, if anything, even less emphatic.

"Thank you, Your Highness," he said. "You have put your father's actions that night in a light which it might have been impertinent for me to have done. Yes, his behaviour was extravagant. And it has occurred to me to ask what made it so."

He paused and looked slowly round the assembly.

"It has occurred to me," he repeated, "to ask what substance affected the Maharajah that night. Was it, I asked myself, such that it could have made the Maharajah himself put sapura bark into the barrel of his own gun, not knowing what he did?"

XIX

The writing paper was very large and very thick and very, very white. It was headed by a large and very impressive crest. The typewritten words on it were very, very black.

Sir Arthur Pendeverel regrets that he is unable to accept the kind invitation of His Highness Maharajahdhiraj Raj Rajeshwar Sri Sri Sri Sahib Bahadur Mahapundit Mahasurma George Singhi, Maharajah of Bhopore, to dinner. His Excellency does not accept invitations at short notice.

"I say," said Porgy, Maharajah of Bhopore, after D.S.P. Howard had finished reading the note next morning in the Maharajah's study, "will it actually matter all that much? I mean, I don't suppose you're going to arrest the Resident for putting a drug in Papa's food during this tamasha tonight, are you?"

"No, Your Highness, I shall not be doing that," the D.S.P. said.

"Well then, that's all right. And we'll just go ahead without His Excellency."

D.S.P. Howard shook his head in slight negative.

"No, I don't think so, Maharajah," he said. "You see, it's very important that at the dinner everything will be as exactly as possible as it was on that night."

Porgy looked very serious.

"Well, yes, I see that of course, Mr. Howard. It's vital to have things just the same. Yes, of course. I mean, that's why I've spoken specially to Dewan Sahib and made it clear that the cooks have got to produce just the same dishes as we had then, and we're going to have the same wines and liqueurs and everything."

"Excellent, Your Highness. I really would like things reproduced right down to little items like the liqueurs, if that's possible."

"Of course it's possible, Mr. Howard. What does one have servants for but to do things like that? But there is just one snag, if you'll excuse me saying so. I mean, of course, one snag besides this letter of the Resident's."

"And that is, Your Highness?"

Porgy, who had been standing on the far side of his wide, leather-topped desk, looked down anxiously at a large crystal paperweight standing on its immaculate surface.

"Well," he said, in evident embarrassment now. "Well, it's just, you see . . . What I mean is, Mr. Howard . . . Well, damn it, Papa, my father—er—can't be there, you know."

"Yes, I perfectly understand that, Your Highness." The D.S.P.'s face was unmoving. "But may I point out that I, too, was not at that dinner party. I had no idea then that I was ever to come to Bhopore. So what I simply propose—if this is all right with you, of course?—is that I should sit in your father's chair. Is that all right?"

It was clear that it was not. The expression on Porgy's face was a look of appalled horror. That anyone should sit in Papa's place. That anyone should sit in the seat customarily kept for the Maharajah of Bhopore. That an Englishman, a person from over the black waters, should do so. It was unthinkable.

Yet mingled with this look of horror was another, one of constricted sheepishness. How was one gentleman to explain this to another? How was a thoroughly progressive chap to put it to someone from the West—even if, of course, he had been born in India and had never left it—how was he to put it to him that this idea was somehow out of the question?

He was spared coming to an answer.

"Of course, Maharajah," D.S.P. Howard said, "I quite understand that the idea will have come as a shock to you. But let me assure you, it's absolutely necessary. I would never have suggested it unless it were. You'll realise that?"

"Oh, yes. Yes, of course. Of course, I never thought that you would propose such a thing unless . . . unless it was, well, you know —er—necessary."

"It's more than necessary, I assure you, Maharajah. It's vital. Quite simply vital."

"Oh. Yes, of course. Vital."

"You see, it's of the first importance when things are as I've suggested they are that absolutely every circumstance be reproduced as accurately as possible. So I'm afraid there's no question of you occupying your father's chair or anything like that. "

"Yes, I thought I was going— That is, of course I absolutely understand. Everything the same. Just as it was then. With— With you—er —acting as Papa. That is to say, with you sitting where my late father sat. Of course."

"Thank you, Maharajah. And that's why it's important, too, you see, for the Resident to attend, just as before."

The Resident, Sir Arthur Pendeverel, was standing in his study, the chick blinds excluding every last ray of the Indian sun though not every last sweat-producing degree of the Indian heat, looking down at the small figure of his son, Little Michael, neat as ever in white shirt, white shorts, and white socks, well pulled up. Michael had just made a request. The Resident was giving it his consideration.

"No, Michael," he said at last. "I think not."

"But, Father, you said Mr. Howard was the best police officer in all India. Why can't I see him when he comes to see you? That may be the last time."

"Because I say not, Michael."

"But—"

"Michael."

It looked as if the Resident were about to order his son to bed on the spot. At the very least he would repeat the memorable lines of Rudyard Kipling, "Now these are the laws of the jungle, And many and mighty are they, But the head and the hoof and the haunch and the hump is Obey." Yet at the last moment he relented.

"Let me try and explain, my boy," he said, with a sigh. "Mr. Howard is, in my opinion, the finest police officer in India. As such it would be, certainly, very good experience for you to meet him. There is, however, a complication."

The Resident paused. He was giving himself plenty of time to put the complication in its clearest light. It was a habit he had. Whenever there was anything complex or difficult to be said he would pause, arrange it to the best order in his mind, and then, when he was quite ready, pronounce. It was a habit that did not make him popular. But perhaps it had been responsible for his steady rise in the exclusive ranks of the Indian Political Service, those thousand or so dedicated men, called "the heaven-born," who under the Viceroy ruled a subcontinent.

"Michael," Sir Arthur began again, "are you acquainted with the term 'Domiciled European'?"

It was characteristic of him that he put this question in such a way that he might as easily have been expecting from Little Michael the answer "Yes" as the answer "No."

"No, Father. What does it mean, please?"

Sir Arthur sighed. Really the material coming up for service in India nowadays was not what it had been.

"A Domiciled European, Michael," he answered, "is a person, a white man, or a white lady, come to that, who has been born in India and who has no place of residence to return to at home."

"I see, Father. Yes. And, please, is Mr. Howard a Domol—" A great breath taken. "A Domiciled European, Father?"

"Yes, my boy. That's precisely the trouble. You see, while Mr. Howard is plainly a gentleman—there can be no question of his not being that, of course—he is nevertheless clearly Not One of Us. You understand, my boy?"

"Yes, Father."

"So, on the whole, it's a good deal better if you don't see too much of him. Follow?"

"Yes, Father. Thank you, Father."

"All right, my boy, cut along now."

"Yes, Father."

"Well, Mr. Howard, I trust you've sought this interview for the purpose of letting me know at last who was responsible for the murder of the Maharajah."

"I'm afraid not, Your Excellency."

The Resident stood on the other side of his desk, which was smaller than that of the Maharajah of Bhopore but in distinctly better taste, and in silence gathered together the material for a rebuke.

D.S.P. Howard stood in front of him, impassive of face, oddly still of body, with the stillness not of a soldier standing tensely to attention but of a motionless jungle animal, all relaxation.

"Mr. Howard, I caused you to be summoned to Bhopore for one reason only. That I considered you the best person to deal with an extremely awkward situation. Your task was simple. To find who had murdered the Maharajah and to report your findings to me. Yet now you request an urgent interview and tell me you still have no idea who was responsible."

"Yes, sir."

"Then may I ask, Mr. Howard, why you have chosen to waste my not unvaluable time in this manner?"

"Yes, sir. I came to ask you to accept the Maharajah's invitation to dinner this evening."

Again the Resident drew up an internal memorandum of the terms of his reply. Again D.S.P. Howard stood still and waited.

"Mr. Howard, I gathered from the private note which the Maharajah included with his singularly peremptory invitation that you were the instigator of this curious notion."

"That is correct, sir."

"And that the purpose of the occasion, a particularly tasteless purpose, was to reproduce, for some reason I have failed altogether to fathom, the dinner which the late Maharajah held on the night before his death. Is that so, Mr. Howard?"

"Yes, sir. It is."

"And do you intend to enlighten me on the object you had in mind? Can you, indeed, enlighten me or anybody else on such an extraordinary idea?"

"Yes, sir. I think I can."

"Then perhaps you would be good enough to do so. I am a busy man, Mr. Howard. The Viceroy is due in Bhopore in eight days' time unless I cable him tomorrow. There are a great many preparations to be made."

"I understand perfectly, sir. And may I say that I hope by means of this reconstructed dinner party, something I would not ordinarily have had recourse to, to make as certain as I can that the question of who killed the Maharajah is satisfactorily cleared up tonight."

"Do you indeed? Then I must tell you that I still see no reason whatever for my attendance there."

"No, sir. I quite understand that you would not. That's why I asked to come and see you."

"Suppose you explain then. And as quickly as may be."

"Yes, sir."

D.S.P. Howard drew in a slow, careful breath.

"It's like this, sir," he said. "I've come to the conclusion that the business isn't quite as simple as we thought at first."

"Not as simple? What do you mean? It's simple enough to me. One of the five people who both saw the Maharajah play his sapura-bark trick and who could also have put a piece of the bark into the barrel of that Purdey down at the jheels is the murderer. And that's that."

"I'm afraid, sir, that I have come to the conclusion that that isn't exactly the situation. The circle of possibilities is a little wider than that. Unfortunately, however, this doesn't lead beyond doubt to knowing who the person responsible is. And it's for that reason I would like you, sir, to go through with what really is somewhat of a charade."

"A charade? I am not following you, Howard."

"Yes, sir. A charade. I let the new Maharajah and the others believe that I have discovered that the old Maharajah was somehow suffering from the effect of a drug of some sort that night, and that this was the cause of his death, sir. A sort of induced suicide. Of course, that was nothing but nonsense."

"I was about to observe as much."

"Of course, sir. But, you recall, the problem all along has been one of time. Given plenty of time, I could have asked enough questions, discovered enough small discrepancies to begin to get some idea of the truth of the matter. But with only twenty-four hours now before you must warn off the Viceroy, obviously that approach will have to be abandoned."

"There is hardly time for the sort of approach you are using with me now, Howard."

"No, sir. I'll try to be as brief as I can."

"Please."

"Very good, sir. Well, deprived of the possibility of the methods I favour, I have come to the conclusion that, since I have some idea of the general lie of the land now, I must force the pace. Force it as much as I possibly can. And that's where this reconstruction business comes in, sir. In the atmosphere that an exact repetition of that dinner would generate, I think I can count on learning what I finally need to know."

"And you want me particularly to be present?"

Quite slowly the Resident sat himself at his desk. The spine pad attached to his back kept him formidably upright.

"Howard," he said, "I am not misunderstanding you, am I?"

"I think you must be, sir," the D.S.P. answered quietly. "There cannot, of course, be any question of the pressure that I hope to bring being brought to bear on yourself. I know, of course, from all that I have learnt in the palace that the late Maharajah must have exasperated you, sir, on many an occasion indeed. But that could never be a reason for you wishing to murder him. You could have had him removed from the gaddi easily enough, had you had any strong reason to wish him gone."

"I am glad to hear you say that, Howard," the Resident said.

And the words, very clearly, implied that if he had not heard the D.S.P.'s disclaimer he could as easily have arranged for him no longer to be District Superintendent of Police, Sangabad, as he could have arranged for the removal of a Maharajah of Bhopore.

Once more the Resident stayed silent. A whole flurry of memoranda were evidently being passed from one department of his brain to another, small, sharply pointed minutes were being made in their margins, initials were being appended. At last the process was complete.

"Very good, Howard. I shall send a note straightaway to the Maharajah telling him that, with the unexpected cancellation of a previous engagement, I shall be able to accept his invitation for this evening."

With much of the palace, it seemed, a-bustle with preparations for a second huge formal dinner within such a short time, it was more important than ordinarily to keep the rout of the old Maharajah's male offspring out of trouble's way in the schoolroom. Which made it all the more curious that a conscientious man like the Maharajah's Schoolmaster should have abandoned his charges in the middle of the morning. But there he was, making his way hither and thither, up and down the long passageways of the palace, stopping frequently to engage anyone he saw in idle chatter, preventing them often from getting on with the work of preparation.

And, for all that the Schoolmaster seemed eager to linger in aimless conversation, his eyes, sharp as a bird's, never seemed content to rest on whoever it was he was talking to. Constantly they darted towards the far end of long passages, and especially so when on a distant marble floor the sound of footsteps in heavy European shoes was heard.

Suddenly now, in the very middle of a vigorous gossip with the second of the telephone orderlies who had just come off duty and was making his way back to the little dark hut within the palace servants' quarters that was his home, the Schoolmaster turned and started off towards the light pouring in from a far archway.

The telephone orderly stood, his mouth agape, listening to the rapid flip-flop of the Schoolmaster's sandals as he quickly vanished into the distance. Then, just as the retreating figure reached the archway, he heard the echo of a voice speaking in English.

"Why, Schoolmaster Sahib, I didn't think to see you hereabouts at this time of day."

The remark caught the Schoolmaster distinctly at a disadvantage.

"Well, yes, D.S.P. Sahib, it is true that in the customary way at this hour I should be in the schoolroom with my pupils. But—" Inspiration came. "But, you know, today is not an ordinary day. Tonight there is this great and unexpected dinner party. By your request, I understand, D.S.P. Sahib. And in consequence not one of my pupils will attend to a single word that I say."

"Lack of discipline, Schoolmaster Sahib. Very wrong in the classroom."

But at each corner of the D.S.P.'s straight-set mouth there was a tiny upwards-curling tilt. And by now the Schoolmaster could read the signs on that impassive face.

"D.S.P. Sahib," he said with sudden frankness, "I have been greatly pondering the remarks you left with me yesterday, and also what I have heard since about this dinner party that you have requested and the reasons for it. And . . ."

"And, Schoolmaster Sahib?"

"And I do not at all understand."

Again that tiny tilt of a smile.

"And what exactly do you not understand, Schoolmaster Sahib?"

The Schoolmaster looked up into the D.S.P.'s face anxiously. Then, more anxiously, he looked all round the small inner courtyard to which his hunt for the D.S.P. had brought him.

Satisfied at last that there were no eager listening ears within range, he broke out with what he had to say.

"D.S.P. Sahib, this matter of a drug."

"What about the drug, Schoolmaster Sahib?"

The look of pain there had been on the Schoolmaster's fleshless cheeks became yet more pronounced.

"Sir," he said, "there is no such drug as the drug that is supposed to have done such terrible things to late His Highness."

"Indeed, Schoolmaster Sahib? You are sure of that?"

Indecision raged on the Schoolmaster's face. On the one hand, there was all he had read, all he had learnt, in the English books it had been his life's business to pore over and master. On the other hand, there was this statement that had been made before witnesses by the D.S.P. Sahib himself. The D.S.P. he had come to trust and to admire. Every exact word of what he had said when he had made his announcement had come back to him from one servant to another. He could not doubt its correctness.

But at last the D.S.P. put him out of his misery.

"You're quite right, of course, old chap. There isn't any such drug. Though I rather think the Maharajah believes there is, despite all he should know that tells him better. And certainly Mrs. Alcott, and her daughter, and her brother too, and Lieutenant Frere all believe it now, or at least half believe it. And certainly Captain Ram Singh believes it as fervently as he believes every word of the Holy Grantha."

"And the Dewan, D.S.P. Sahib?" the Schoolmaster asked.

"No. I don't suppose Dewan Sahib believes my little fairy tale, not in the least. But he's much too clever to let anyone know."

"And Brattle Memsahib, she believes?"

"Yes, she's too much absorbed with her own problems to question anything."

"So of the five who saw the sapura-bark trick and were also at the jheels," the Schoolmaster summed up, "four certainly do not know the real reason for this—I believe it is called a reconstruction?"

"That is so, Schoolmaster Sahib. None of them knows. And the Dewan, does he actually know the real reasons for this rather dramatic notion of mine? He may well not. He may only be able to guess. As you can, Schoolmaster Sahib. And I wonder if you guess right."

The Schoolmaster felt like an untried youth who, running hard through the jungle, is suddenly confronted with a deep stream. He must make up his mind in an instant. To dive and see if he can swim over in safety? Or to turn away and never reach the end of his journey?

He plunged.

"D.S.P. Sahib, you do not know who it is you are looking for. That much you told me yesterday. But you know something. You know now the pattern of it, I see that. And time is your enemy. The Viceroy is coming in eight days from now. You must find an answer for the Resident very soon. So you must put fear into some person's heart. You must create—what shall I say?—a monsoon atmosphere, D.S.P. Sahib, heavy and brooding and electric also with tension."

He risked a glance up to the D.S.P.'s face. The hooded eyes were still.

He was in the stream. He had surfaced. He was striking out all right. But the far bank was by no means within grasping distance yet.

He straightened his shoulders.

"And there is something else, too, I believe, Sahib. It is a question of what exactly happened after dinner that night. It is a question of how the person, whoever it is, whichever one of those five, obtained that piece of sapura bark which Lieutenant Frere found on the person of Captain Ram Singh and left by chance in his bathroom. Perhaps it was as you suggested, D.S.P. Sahib, and a troop of monkeys did happen to move that little piece of deadly stuff. But if they did, no chance passerby picked it up. I think we can be certain of that now. No one in the palace has orange-stained hands. So perhaps one of the five did enter that bathroom by chance, or by mistake even in the unfamiliar palace, saw the bark, and realised how it could be used. This is what you also hope to discover tonight, D.S.P. Sahib. Is it? Is it not?"

"Shabash, Schoolmaster," said the D.S.P. softly. "Well done."

The Schoolmaster's face beamed with delight, like a schoolboy praised by a demanding schoolmaster.

"What shall we say?" the D.S.P. went on. "Eight out of ten. No, nine. Nine out of ten, Schoolmaster Sahib."

"Nine only?"

The smiling schoolboy was transformed instantly, comically, into the downcast schoolboy.

D.S.P. Howard grinned, almost a full-mouthed grin.

"Yes, nine only, Schoolmaster Sahib," he said. "You see, there is one thing you haven't cottoned onto. You remember I told you that, just before I came upon you in the road yesterday while I was out riding, an idea had suddenly come into my mind, an idea that altered the whole picture I had had until then?"

"Yes, Sahib," said the Schoolmaster with caution.

"Well, you haven't spotted that idea. Have you?"

The Schoolmaster was silent for a little, thinking desperately. Then at last he gave a little sigh.

"Nine out of ten, D.S.P. Sahib," he acknowledged.

The D.S.P. laughed. His usual grunt that was an apology for a laugh.

The Schoolmaster looked up at him, almost piteously.

"D.S.P. Sahib," he said, "may I not know?"

"Oh, yes," the D.S.P. said, "you may know. I want you to know. Knowing, you may be able to be very helpful to me."

"Sahib, what I can do I will do."

"Good man."

For a moment or two the D.S.P. was silent, gathering his thoughts.

"It's like this, Schoolmaster Sahib," he said at last. "All along, people have been telling us that the murderer of the Maharajah must be one of five possibles, the five who knew about sapura bark and who also had the opportunity to put a piece down the barrel of one of the guns the Maharajah had announced he was going to use."

"Yes, Sahib?"

"But, think, Schoolmaster. That circle was not as small as everybody has been telling us. Was it? When you look at it hard?"

The Schoolmaster looked hard.

Then he looked up at the D.S.P.

"No, Sahib," he said.

But his face was not that of a schoolboy who has at last hit on the answer to a difficult problem now. It was the grave face of a man who sees something deeply disturbing but inescapable in front of him.

"No, Sahib, you are right. The circle is bigger than anyone up till now has said."

XX

Everywhere in the smoothly run palace now preparations were afoot for the great event that evening. And everywhere, it seemed, a quietly moving figure dressed in whites watched through always hooded eyes. Watched and recorded. And hoped that his watching would be reported back and back.

Standing in courtyard somewhere in the obscure back parts of the huge sprawling edifice he looked through barred windows at the palace bandmaster, his gorgeous uniform on his back but unbuttoned now, putting his men through their paces. The oom-pah, oom-pah of the gleamingly polished brass euphonium blared out a version of "Dance, Dance, Dance, Little Lady." The bandmaster's high, cracked voice chanted the beat, "Tum. Tum. Tum-ti-ta. Ta-tum." Sweat in the stuffy atmosphere poured down the faces of the bandsmen as they tootled, blew, and thumped.

"Now," shouted the bandmaster, the moment they had come triumphantly to an end all on the note. "Now, 'Yes, Sir, That's My Baby.'"

In the parts of the palace gardens, where flowers were grown, not neatly arranged in beds to make the best show, but in thick lines to provide blooms for cutting, the malis were methodically working. Flower after flower they picked. Dextrous fingers nipped tall red canna lilies, lush pinky oleanders, elegant roses, white, pink, and red. Tonight they would appear on the long dinner table. Others would go into the many huge vases that every day decorated chosen spots in the palace and every day were carefully inspected to see where the least signs of wilting marred the whole.

For a few minutes the watching white-clad figure looked at the stooping brown bare backs, at the baskets being rapidly filled. Then D.S.P. Howard moved on, happy at the quick little glances he had seen being exchanged by those under his observation.

Down at the dhobi ghats by the lakeside he watched dozens of

pairs of cotton gloves being beaten into new whiteness, ready for the
hands of the dozens of bearers who would wait on the guests at the
long table. He watched too as the huge white tablecloths, of best
Irish damask as supplied by Harrod's of Knightsbridge, were equally
thwacked and battered spotless by teams of kneeling dhobies at the
water's edge.

There was a moment of alarm as a mugger, swimming just at the
lake surface, approached with slow, evil intent. But yells and shouts
of alarm and a volley of stones set all to rights before long and the
quietly watching figure moved on.

Indoors, in an obscure room off an obscure passageway, skilled
lean fingers were twisting pieces of brightly coloured crepe paper
round elegant little bottles of perfume imported from a certain bou-
tique in the Rue Saint Honoré, Paris. If the ladies who had attended
the dinner given in honour of the newly arrived guests by His
Highness Maharajahdhiraj Raj Rajeshwar Lieutenant Colonel Sri
Sri Sri Sahib Bahadur Mahapundit Mahasurma Sir Albert Singhi,
G.C.S.I., G.C.I.E., D. Litt. (Benares), had received gifts of Parisian
perfume, the ladies attending tonight's dinner must have just the
same gifts again. Even though Sir Albert Singhi's large body was
ashes now and scattered far away by priests on the waters of the
Holy Ganges.

Through the open archway D.S.P. Howard watched for just a few
minutes, long enough to see one present beautifully wrapped and
work on the next begun. Long enough to be sure that he himself had
been seen.

At the Residency preparations for dinner at the palace were also taking place, if not on the same furiously busy level. But the Resident's
bearer was working on the undress uniform he wore at the last dinner and would wear again tonight. An iron, heated over a little dung
fire, was applied to the trousers, making sure the creases in them
were knife-sharp. The long, curving ceremonial sword sheath had already received its loving and careful polish.

Little Michael, wandering here and there in the big house, familiar
with every servant there, as easy with them in Urdu as he was with
his father in English, and perhaps more so, had seen the preparations. And evidently they had troubled him a little.

At luncheon, which he and his father took together, one seated at either end of the large table, each served by a different bearer, he broached the subject.

"Father, Naresh was ironing your undress uniform just before lunch. What was that for?"

Sir Arthur frowned.

"Lunch, Michael? Lunch?" he said. "What is that word?"

Little Michael blushed, a deep rosy-red.

"I mean 'luncheon,' Father. Just before luncheon."

"Well, what about just before luncheon? And, Michael, there seems to be something left on your plate."

"Well, it's a piece of rather awful fat, Father."

"Eat it up, my boy."

"But, Father . . ."

"You have to set an example, Michael. If you waste good food, what will the servants learn from that?"

"To waste things too, Father."

"Exactly. So let me see your plate empty."

Little Michael squared his shoulders. He cut the piece of fatty meat in half. He speared the smaller part with his fork. He looked at it. He took his knife and pushed the piece of yellowy fat off the fork. He pursed his lips in an expression of determination that almost brought tears to his eyes. He stabbed the larger fatty piece with his fork, brought it swiftly up to his mouth, crammed it in, chewed.

Now there were tears in his eyes. But before they spilled he took a heroic swallow. The piece of fatty meat went down.

Michael lowered his fork.

"I said all of it, Michael."

"Yes, Father. I will. I really will."

"Then do it, my boy. When a duty lies before you there is only one course to take."

"Yes, Father. Father, is that why you're going to the palace tonight? You are going, aren't you, Father? I mean, that's why Naresh was getting your undress uniform ready, wasn't he, Father? I mean, you only wear that here when it's for a dinner party at the palace."

"Michael, are you attempting to evade your duty?"

"No. No, Father. Honestly. I really wouldn't, Father. It was just that I wanted to know what—"

"Michael."

"Yes, Father."

Little Michael stabbed the remaining piece of meat. It was the fattier part now that he came to look at it, even if it was not the bigger that he had determined to get down first. He pushed the gobbet into his mouth. He began to chew. The piece did not yield as easily as the first had done. He chewed harder, tried to swallow. He failed to get it down.

His face grew redder and redder instant by instant. He chewed like a madman. The slippery little lump seemed to resist everything his teeth could do.

He tried to swallow again. And failed as signally.

Now it seemed he would never be able to get it down. He looked up at his father. Sir Arthur, his plate empty before him, was sitting looking magisterially down the length of the big table. At him.

He chewed till his jaw ached. He tried a swallow.

"If you have something in your mouth, Michael, that cannot be eaten, you may put it out. Provided you do so with your fork, and in a discreet manner."

The fork was up at his lips in a moment. The manner of the disposal of the half-chewed gobbet was reasonably discreet.

The Resident signalled to the bearers that they could take away the plates.

"I shall not be taking any dessert, Michael," he said. "If you will excuse me, I have an extra burden of work this afternoon."

"Yes, Father," Little Michael said, his voice reduced to a whisper by his exertions.

Sir Arthur rose from his place. The bearer scuttled to open the door for him. He sailed towards it.

"Father."

Sir Arthur appeared not to hear.

Michael, despite the fact that he was actually being served with the fruit salad that constituted dessert at the Residency luncheon that day, slipped from his chair. He ran to the doorway through which his father had just gone.

"Father, please."

Sir Arthur turned. It was not his habit to make any move or any gesture lightly. When he turned he turned. He faced a new direction, and he made it clear that to have asked him to do that was to have asked a lot.

"Well?"

Little Michael actually turned a shade pale.

But he did not flinch.

"Father," he said, "I've got to know. Are you going to the palace tonight? Have you been made to go to dinner there? Is the new Maharajah just as bad as the old one?"

A quick frown appeared on the Resident's high forehead.

"Bad?" he said. "As bad as the old one? Michael, I am afraid I do not understand you."

And this time the quelling tone did quell. Tears sprang into Michael's eyes. He put his head down and charged past his father, up the wide staircase that was a central feature of the big house that only in India is called a bungalow. Into his bedroom he ran and flung himself face down on his familiar bed to sob all that he wanted.

Sir Arthur sighed. He clapped his hands. A servant at once appeared.

"Send Ayah to Michael Sahib's room," he said. "The boy is not well."

Porgy, Maharajah of Bhopore, summoned D.S.P. Howard to his study.

"Some jolly good news," he said.

"Indeed, Maharajah? I should be happy to hear good news."

"It's the Resident. He's changed his mind. Or, well, I mean he's sent me a note saying that a previous engagement has fallen through and he'll be glad to join us at dinner tonight."

"That is good news, Maharajah."

"Yes. I thought so. I thought I'd better let you know at once. I mean, to have that dinner exactly as it was. It's what you said you wanted, isn't it?"

"It is. Thank you for telling me."

"Jolly good."

Porgy looked down at his huge desk. He looked up at the ornately decorated ceiling high above him.

"Er—" he said.

"Was there something else you wanted to tell me, Maharajah?"

"No, no. Not at all. No. Er— Look, yes. Look, have a drink. I've got some George IV whisky here. Jolly good stuff. Made from the natural . . . Oh. Believe I mentioned that to you once before. Well, never mind, have a drink."

"It's a bit early for me, Maharajah."

"Early? Oh, yes, I suppose it is."

"But perhaps a small one."

"Oh."

For several seconds Porgy made no attempt to do anything about getting the D.S.P. the drink he had so unexpectedly agreed to. Then at last, with an "Oh, yes, of course," he hurried over to the well-stocked cupboard and came back with whisky bottle, glasses, and bottle of soda water on a tray, already set out. He poured two drinks. Neither of them was small.

He raised his glass.

"Your jolly good health," he said.

"Yours, Maharajah."

The D.S.P. took a token sip from his glass.

"Look," said Porgy, Maharajah of Bhopore.

He said nothing more.

"Yes, Maharajah?"

Porgy looked down at the wide surface of his desk again. He did not seem to find inspiration there. He looked up again.

"Listen," he said.

More seconds went by.

"I am listening, Maharajah."

"Well, damn it, Mr. Howard. Damn it, this is what I don't understand."

"You don't understand? Forgive me, I'm not quite sure what you're asking."

"No. Yes. No, this is it. The Resident. Why is it that it's so dashed important that he has to be here tonight himself? I mean, before I got his note saying he'll come I was thinking about it, and I couldn't really see at all why it had to be him in that chair at the table and no one else. I mean, it would be just the same to have someone, someone who wasn't there at the time, to just—er—well, do what the Resident did. Say what he said, as far as anyone can remember it. I mean, I could have found some chap quite easily."

"I'm sure you could have done, Maharajah."

"Yes. Well then, why? I mean, why is it such good news that the Resident himself will be here after all?"

The D.S.P.'s mouth twitched in what must be a friendly and reassuring smile.

"Oh, it's very simple, Maharajah," he said.

"Is it? Is it? Well, I'm damned if I can see it, Mr. Howard."

"Let me try to explain."

"I wish you would."

"It's simply this. There's some question, you know, of just how the piece of sapura bark that was pushed into the barrel of your father's Purdey got there at all. Of how it fell into the hands of whoever put it there."

Porgy concentrated.

"Yes," he said. "Yes, I hadn't really thought of that. But I suppose it's true. Yes."

"It is true, Maharajah. And it may be a very important factor in tracking down the person I'm after."

"Good. Yes. I follow that. I read quite a few detective stories, you know. Or at least I used to. They don't seem quite so—quite so important nowadays somehow."

"I can see that. But if you have read detective stories, then you'll see my point at once."

"Yes," said Porgy, not convincingly.

"It's like this, Maharajah," the D.S.P. went on. "The piece of bark which was the only available piece in the palace or anywhere around was thrown by your father to Captain Ram Singh out on the palace steps. And then, when your father had Captain Ram Singh searched by Lieutenant Frere at dinner that night, the piece of bark was just left in Frere's bathroom as being of no account."

"Yes. Yes, I see that. Quite natural in the circumstances."

"Oh, yes, Maharajah. Perfectly natural. But, you see, either someone went in there, saw the bark, realised that with it the Rolls-Royce trick could be repeated to deadly effect or, less possibly, the bark was moved from the bathroom, say, by a monkey that got in there or something, and the person who used the bark found it elsewhere."

"And so," said Porgy, Maharajah of Bhopore, triumphantly, "it's vital to know where everyone actually was after dinner that night. And that's why it's so important for the Resident himself to come."

"Exactly, Maharajah."

Porgy looked pleased. And then he didn't.

"No," he said.

"No, Maharajah?"

"Well, look, I mean I still don't understand."

"No, Maharajah?"

"No. No, I don't. I mean, look here, the Resident didn't know about sapura bark, did he?"

"No, Maharajah. I think we can be sure of that."

"Well then, it can't be a question of knowing where he went after dinner, can it? I mean, he wouldn't have picked up the sapura bark even if he had gone into James's bathroom. And I don't see why he should have wanted to do that anyhow."

"No. No, the Resident would hardly have gone into Lieutenant Frere's bathroom."

"Well then?"

"Well?"

"Well, I mean, why's it so important to have him here tonight?"

"You can't see, Maharajah?"

"No. I'm afraid I damn well can't."

"It's not because of what the Resident did that night, Maharajah. It's because of what anybody might have done while the Resident wasn't at the Residency or elsewhere to see them. If the same conditions prevail tonight, I shall be able to deduce what might have happened then."

"Oh. Oh, yes. I see. Or, well, I think I do. Thank you, Mr. Howard. Thank you very much."

The D.S.P. bowed, as custom dictated, and left the Maharajah's presence. Porgy, Maharajah of Bhopore, looked a very puzzled man.

Even during the hottest middle part of the day, when sleep is the only answer, preparations for the great dinner at the Summer Palace did not entirely cease. The huge quantities of rice that was to be cooked and coloured in a dozen different ways still had not been totally picked over. So, sitting cross-legged in whatever shade they could find, the women servants from the kitchens continued bent over the big dull white mounds. Quick fingers obeyed sharp eyes as every tiny stone and piece of foreign matter were spotted and discarded. Soon the cleaned rice was taken to be boiled in the scores of carefully scoured cooking vessels, the cleaning of which had occupied servants by the dozen all morning.

In a room near the kitchens which was solely devoted to storing all the chutneys consumed in the course of a year the chutnai-wallah selected the best of his guarded treasures to appear on the long white-cloth-covered table that night. For a few moments, at the open door, D.S.P. Howard watched him at work. He asked him three or four questions, appeared satisfied with the answers he got, moved on. In a few moments, he knew, the door of the chutney store would be carefully closed and the chutnai-wallah would slip away to tell his friends some news.

In the cellars where there were stored wines, spirits, and liqueurs, imported from London not by the crate of a dozen bottles, but by the dozen crates, the D.S.P., taking advantage of the coolness but not lingering a moment longer than was necessary, asked more questions. He examined the carefully sealed tops of half a dozen different bottles, nodded, noted, and gave nothing away under the hooded lids of his eyes.

The tinfoil-sealed packs of a dozen different brands of cigarettes with their London stamps still on them he also looked at as he went. The big tin boxes of biscuits, every variety that could withstand the chocolate-melting heat, received too their rapid scrutiny. As did the crates of hair shampoo, the crates of Christmas crackers, the crates of toothpaste, the big crates of scented lavatory paper that came from France.

As the worst of the heat passed by and preparations in the kitchens mounted in fury, none of the work escaped its few seconds of inspection. The four cooks trained in the European cuisine—one had been taken to Rome once, to absorb the secret of Alessandro's lasagne—were watched as they concocted the numerous hors d'oeuvres, the potato salad and the cucumber salad, the garnished beans and the garnished tomatoes, the cleverly arranged olives and the equally artistic anchovies. Delicately tiny beetroots had their centres sliced away and delicately the hole thus made was stuffed with capers. Only the tins of smoked salmon and the tins of oysters remained, awaiting the last possible moment before they were exposed to the heat-swamped Indian air.

D.S.P. Howard picked up one of each, turned and twisted it, eyes unyielding, and replaced it exactly where it had been put.

He moved on to watch for a little the five Hindu cooks, Brahmins to a man, who prepared the Indian dishes. Through a hole in the wall of their kitchen, constructed some hundred years before, the Muslim cook, who alone knew the exact ingredients and the exact method or preparation for certain of the dishes, was calling his instructions to the pure Hindu hands within. Beside him, for a little, for long enough, the white-clad figure of the D.S.P. stood.

A few minutes later he was watching the sweetmeats that would be served at the end of the gala dinner being wrapped each one in the thinnest of layers of gold foil, the process watched in turn by the official whose hereditary task it was to supervise the use of the delicate layers of gold and to account in his turn to a yet higher official in a train of order that would end eventually with the Dewan himself. Again, ultimately to the Dewan, on whose shoulders the smooth running of palace and State depended, there would go the record of the items of goldware that had been taken that afternoon from the palace strong room, the process noted by a pair of hooded eyes, the gold covers for champagne bottles, the gold crumb scoops, the gold epergnes, the gold vases and bowls, the many, many items of gold cutlery.

And before his prowling vigil was done that afternoon, the D.S.P. had overseen, too, the drawing up of the table plan for the night on the ingenious board specially constructed for this purpose with strips of elastic running down its length so that cards with guests' names on them could be held in temporarily assigned places until later consideration caused them to be moved, upwards or downwards.

He had seen the result taken to the palace printing shop by an anxiously running orderly, there to be laboriously letter by letter set into type and at last run off in enough copies for one to lie in each guest's place. He had watched, too, the envelopes addressed to those gentlemen who were to have the honour of escorting ladies into the banqueting hall having each one his card inserted with the name of the lady to be accompanied written on it. He had watched a few of those names being written in fine flourishing copperplate English by a scribe, seated on the floor, his desk resting on the knees of his crossed legs, his open bottle of black ink beside him.

And finally, and perhaps most important of all, if news of his activities was to get back to the ears he intended, the D.S.P. examined carefully the great gold platter with its high-domed gold cover and its gold padlock, on which the late Maharajah's last dinner had been served on the night before his murder. He had talked, too, with the late Maharajah's personal bearer. He had followed the platter every inch of its way from the safe where it was normally kept. He had seen at last the bearer squatting patiently beside it as it awaited the pretasted food which would be served to the nonexistent Maharajah at the head of the table that evening.

XXI

So at last there arrived the hour for that dinner, the grotesque replica of the luxurious formal meal that had been the culmination of the Maharajah of Bhopore's last day on earth. In keeping with Porgy's instructions, issued at the behest of D.S.P. Howard, everything that evening was as close a repetition as possible of the previous events.

Once more the many guests, each one of whom had been there on the former occasion, assembled for predinner drinks. And again there were only champagne cocktails and the chocolaty cream-topped Alexanders that had been His Highness's favourites. Once more the atmosphere soon became lively. Only now it was not the prospect of an unsurpassable day's shooting on the jheels on the morrow, with the Imperial sandgrouse already mad with thirst from their exclusion from every source of water for miles around, that was causing the excitement. Instead it was the evening itself that all present were just embarking upon. They were so many unknowing creatures driven to this moment of final revelation by a shikari every bit as cunning, in his own way, as the lean-faced fellow who, under the late Maharajah's own guidance, had supervised that massive kill of birds on the day the Maharajah himself had been killed.

Now Porgy suddenly brought the excited, questioning buzz of conversation to an end by loudly clapping his hands.

"Ladies and gentlemen," he announced, "you all know what is the purpose of this evening. At the request of District Superintendent of Police Howard, whom I have asked to Bhopore to solve the appalling mystery of my father's death, we are reconstructing as closely as we can the events of his last evening upon earth."

Some of the lesser courtiers, hovering on the edges of the big drawing room, here thought it their duty to offer a subdued wail or two in memory of Porgy's father. A quick look from their new lord immediately put an end to the noise.

"Ladies and gentlemen," Porgy resumed, "in response to this request from Mr. Howard a servant is soon to come in to announce the death of my half brother Raghbir, just as he did to my father, as you will remember."

At a push from the Schoolmaster just outside, the same servant who had informed the Maharajah of Raghbir's sudden ominous end, licking his lips in anxiety, now entered. But he did not go up to Porgy. Instead, casting nervous glances all round, as if wondering whether the audience for the little play he was enacting would be as hostile as he expected, he went up to D.S.P. Howard.

But, confronted with the D.S.P., any words that he had been going to utter completely deserted him.

"It's all right," the D.S.P. said to him in quiet Urdu. "I know what your message was going to be. It is as if you had given it to the old Maharajah himself now. So, go. Go back just as you did before."

"Huzoor," said the servant with a deep salaam.

Watched by a now totally silent assembly, the poor fellow made his way out, fumbling so badly with the doorknob that the Schoolmaster, who had been listening through the tall teak panels of the door to everything that had gone on, had to open it for him before he could get out.

"Now," the D.S.P. announced, "at this point, so I understand, the Maharajah left to go and inquire how the death of Raghbir had come about. You will remember he returned quite soon and had Captain Ram Singh go round explaining that, sudden though the boy's end was, it was nothing sinister but only the result of simple ptomaine poisoning. As indeed it was."

He looked round at them all for an instant.

"Very well," he said. "I shall leave now just as the Maharajah did and return in due course. Will you all please carry on as you did then?"

He left, not making the impressive exit which the Maharajah had done, despite the disquieting news he had just received about Raghbir, but slipping out quietly and quickly, almost as if he had never really been there amid all the cocktail chatter and clinking of glasses.

Outside, he spoke at once to the Schoolmaster.

"Excellent. Well done. Just as it was before. That should start the ball rolling nicely. Now, you know what you've got to do next?"

"Yes, D.S.P. Sahib. Now comes my watchkeeping. When the guests go into dinner, I am to be your eyes and ears outside. To patrol everywhere, to make sure that no unexpected arrival enters the palace, however seemingly insignificant. Those were your instructions."

"They were, Schoolmaster Sahib. To the letter. Thank you."

D.S.P. Howard returned to the crowded drawing room, in his persona as the Maharajah, in exactly quarter of an hour. And, as the Maharajah had done before him, he went at once to Captain Ram Singh.

"Now, Captain," he said, "I am telling you that Raghbir's death is no more than an unfortunate occurrence due to ptomaine poisoning."

Captain Ram Singh's large brown eyes clouded in misunderstanding.

"But, Mr. Howard," he said, "I already knew that. The Maharajah himself told me. Late His Highness."

"Yes, yes, Captain. And now I am repeating what the Maharajah said that night."

"Yes, I know, Mr. Howard. But you are not telling me anything I did not know already. As I have just explained to you."

The D.S.P.'s face expressed nothing.

"Yes, Captain," he said. "I know that you know. But perhaps you don't remember: this is a reconstruction of that dinner. I am taking the part of the Maharajah. That's why I'm telling you about Raghbir."

"Ah, yes. Yes, of course." Captain Ram Singh's face brightened behind its formidable defences of curling moustaches. "Yes, you are the Maharajah. I have got it all straight now. And from here on it's up to me to go round telling everybody about Raghbir."

"Good man. That's it. Just carry on."

But again the A.D.C.'s eyes clouded in sudden bewilderment.

"Excuse me, Mr. Howard," he said.

"Yes? Yes, what is it?"

"It's just this." The A.D.C. struggled for a moment to get things sorted out in his mind. "Yes. It's this, Mr. Howard. What will happen if the people I tell about Raghbir, that is, of course, the people I am only pretending to tell, well, what happens if they think I am really telling them? I mean, they'll think I'm some sort of a bloody fool."

"I don't think that's likely to happen, old man," the D.S.P. said. "You try it, and you'll see."

"Oh. You're sure? Right then, I'll carry on."

Captain Ram Singh braced his broad shoulders, swung a metaphorical polo pony round between his sturdy legs, and faced the goalpost.

He found the Resident, his first victim, without difficulty. But the sight of the tall Englishman, standing aloof and stern-faced, gave him pause. Eventually he came to a halt in front of that august figure and said not a word.

At last Sir Arthur spoke.

"Good evening, Captain Ram Singh. I understand you are meant to be taking part in this—eh—unfortunate charade. You are to tell me, if I understand correctly, that the boy Raghbir died of ptomaine poisoning."

"Yes," said Captain Ram Singh. "Yes. But how did you know that already, Sir Arthur? I mean . . . I mean, I was meant to be breaking the news to you."

Sir Arthur sighed.

"I think that will do, Ram Singh," he said.

Captain Ram Singh could understand a dismissal easily enough. Dismissed, he turned, frowned for an instant as he tried to remember who was next on his list, found that he was almost face to face with Mrs. Alcott and her brother, Joe, realised that it had been the two of them that he had encountered at almost this exact spot on the night when he had really been charged with the duty of explaining Raghbir's death, and broke into a broad smile.

"Raghbir died of ptomaine poisoning," he said.

"What— What—" Elaine Alcott stammered, seemingly tumbled from a precarious calm by this sudden statement.

She turned to the stocky, dustily redheaded form of her brother.

"Joe? Joe? Has somebody else died? God, I want to get out of this place."

"Hush, honey. It's all right. That was only this reconstruction. And you'll get out. You'll be able to go tomorrow, I guess. You and Judy both, if you really want!"

"Oh, Joe, will we? But— But what about you? Joe? Joe, they won't keep you here, will they?"

"Honey, I've said. I've got to be here for when the Viceroy comes. I've got to show the old buzzard the whole dam, explain it all."

"And that's why you're staying on, Joe? Only for that? You'd tell me if there was any other reason, wouldn't you? You would, wouldn't you?"

"Sure, I would. But what other reason could there be? The dam's all built. I'm finished here, soon as the Viceroy's seen it."

"Yes, Joe, yes."

But doubt was written large in every anxious line on her face.

Captain Ram Singh had left, almost as bewildered as Elaine Alcott. Luckily, he spotted the Dewan, and, although on the night he had first made his announcement the Dewan had not chanced to be the next person he had informed, he made a beeline for him now. This would be a straight shot at goal, surely.

"Dewan Sahib, I have to inform you that the death of Raghbir was caused by ptomaine poisoning only."

"I am much relieved to hear that, Captain Ram Singh," the Dewan said gravely.

For a moment the A.D.C.'s barely won self-confidence faltered again. But evidently the Dewan saw what had happened.

"As far as I remember, Captain," he said, "the last time that you gave me this information you added that this was the clear diagnosis of Dr. Sen."

"Ah, yes. Yes. Dr. Sen Sahib assured me that this was so."

"Good, good. So now, Captain, you have shortly to go through the unpleasant business of being arrested on the Maharajah's orders once more. An arrest, whether justified or unjustified, is always an experience to be avoided."

"Yes," said Captain Ram Singh. "Yes. Well, I must tell the others also. Thank you, Dewan Sahib."

"Thank you, Captain Ram Singh," the Dewan said, grave and courteous and unfathomable as ever.

Captain Ram Singh went to look for Porgy, the next on his list. But as he did so, at the back of his lustrous brown eyes a faint lack of comprehension made itself apparent. The Dewan, just what exactly had he said? Or what had the words he had uttered meant?

"Your Highness— That is—er—Rajkumar Sahib. I mean, Porgy, old boy."

"Yes, yes, my dear chap. Let's take it as read, shall we?"

Porgy, formerly Rajkumar of Bhopore, now Maharajah, seemed to Captain Ram Singh a great deal more tense than he usually was.

"Yes, yes," he said hurriedly. "As read, as read. Only of course I'm not reading. Er— Ha, ha. Got to remember it all, you know."

Porgy made no answer, but stood teeth scraping and scraping at his lower lip, hands hard-clenched.

"Miss Brattle, it is my duty to inform you, at the request of His Highness, that the unfortunate death of Raghbir has proved to be due to ptomaine poisoning. A sad and sudden occurrence. But His Highness has specially requested that we will not let it spoil the enjoyment of this evening."

Dolly Brattle, face carefully made up beneath her cap of shingled platinum hair, barely succeeded in nodding acknowledgment.

"You do know," Captain Ram Singh went on, "that when I say 'this evening' I do not mean 'this evening' but—er—that evening, and when I say 'His Highness' I do not mean His Highness but—"

"Oh, for God's sake, shut up."

Captain Ram Singh's eyes widened as if just at the moment when he was about to plunge his pigsticking spear into the side of a particularly weighty wild boar it had changed into one of the Maharajah's Rolls-Royces.

"Oh, yes," he said. "Yes."

He turned and fled the field. There are some things a chap should never be asked to face.

"Oh, my God, James. James, I'm glad it's you."

"Well, I'm glad it's you, old chap. But why in particular?"

"James, never have anything to do with that Brattle woman."

"Yes. I see what you mean. Bad luck, old boy. Real dragon we've turned into since Porgy got the gaddi. Still, can't say I blame her. I mean, it must be pretty rotten having to hang on here after you've been told you've got the jolly old push."

"Yes. But why?"

"Why what, old boy?"

"I mean, why has she got to hang on in Bhopore? If I were her, I'd have beetled off to Cal or somewhere days ago."

"Not allowed, old boy."

"Not allowed? Why not? I mean I'm sure His Highness would be only too delighted if she did pack up and go."

"He would be, I'm sure. But she's to stay. D.S.P.'s orders, old boy. She's a suspect, you know. And until this business tonight's over, when I gather he'll know everything, she's got to stay like all the rest of us."

"Like you, James? But surely . . ."

James Frere grinned.

"Yes, like me, old boy. I'm one of the ones who saw His late

Highness play that trick on little Michael Pendeverel and was also there at the jheels next morning, you know. One of the five."

"Yes, I suppose you are. I say, old man, you— No. No, you can't have done."

James smiled again.

"I assure you I didn't, old boy," he said. "But you'll just have to take my word for it."

And then, from outside on the lawn, the band abruptly brought "Dance, Dance, Dance, Little Lady" to a halt in midnote and instead there came loud and clear the old bugle call, "Roast Beef."

Time to dine.

The atmosphere at the long table with its immaculate white cloth, its miniature railway line in pure silver circling the whole, its glittering crystal candelabras, its gold dishes piled high with fruit—they were item for item exactly the same as those that had appeared on the night before the Maharajah's death—its crystal and gold vases filled with flowers, was curious, to say the least. At the lower end, where the lesser courtiers had not been much concerned with the events that had preceded the Maharajah's death, conversation soon became general, if subdued. No real attempt was made to recall the previous dinner. But at the upper end, where the dinner-jacketed, contained figure of D.S.P. Howard occupied the thronelike chair on which, on the previous occasion, the enormous frame of the ebullient Maharajah had rested, things were very different. At times the guests would attempt to talk to each other as if this were simply a dinner party to which they had been invited to enjoy themselves. Then abruptly they would recall that it was not and would fall silent. Next they would attempt to reproduce the conversation that had taken place at the earlier dinner.

But, though with servants trained to remember the least detail it is not too difficult to place the exact pieces of fruit on the exact bowls which they occupied before, it is by no means so easy for dinner-party guests to remember just what they said and did at that same table even on that ever memorable night.

The D.S.P., however, was remarkable in his ability to help them, especially considering that at the time of that earlier dinner he had been peacefully in his bungalow in Sangabad planning how to outwit the latest band of dacoits.

"Mrs. Alcott, I believe at about this time the Maharajah explained to you about this train on the table here in front of me."

"What? Oh. Oh, yes. Mr. How— That is, have I got to say 'Maharajah'?"

The D.S.P.'s tiny twitch of a smile appeared.

"If you find it difficult, Mrs. Alcott, don't let it worry you. All I want to do is to establish as closely as we can the sort of thing that was said that evening. I want to check what's been told me with other people's recollections."

"Yes, I see."

Elaine Alcott looked apprehensive nevertheless.

"So was the train mentioned at this point, more or less? Do you recall?"

"I— I'm not sure. Gee, does it matter about the train, a toy like that?"

"It may matter, Mrs. Alcott, yes. Even the smallest trifle may turn out in the end to have considerable significance. So if you can remember?"

"Yes, but I don't want to say, if it's going to be important. I mean, you may be going to hang someone on what I say. You do hang murderers here, don't you?"

"Yes," said the D.S.P. levelly. "In all of British India hanging is the penalty for murder. Of course, this murder will come under the Bhopore administration, and the murderer might even be trampled to death by elephants."

He looked quickly up and down the length of the table nearest him. A silence had fallen.

It was broken by the Resident.

"I think, Mr. Howard, I can answer the question that Mrs. Alcott feels unable to. Yes, the subject of the Maharajah's toy train did arise at this point."

"Thank you, sir."

The D.S.P. closed his eyes in thought for an instant.

"Then, if I've been told right," he said, "you, Mr. Morton, made some comment about the length of time it would take for the train to get round the table if everybody stopped it to help themselves from the trucks?"

"Yeah, I could have said something like that. And then the Maharajah got his laugh by pointing out that none of those guys at the bottom end of the table will dare to touch the train. Yeah, that'd be it."

"Thank you, Mr. Morton. I hoped I could rely on a businessman's attention to detail."

"I'd be better pleased if this businessman was allowed to attend to business," the tycoon growled.

The D.S.P. flicked his almost imperceptible smile at him.

"Well, perhaps tomorrow, Mr. Morton, the matter of the Maharajah's murder will have been disposed of and His present Highness might feel more free to devote time to you and your problems."

The tycoon's eyes hardened.

"You think it will be cleared up tonight?" he asked. "Can you promise that?"

"No, I'm afraid I can't promise American hustle, Mr. Morton. But let's say there's a good chance. A good chance."

Again an awkward and sudden silence fell at the top end of the table.

After a little the D.S.P. recalled that the Maharajah had described the delights of Delhi Week to them at much that point of the meal before. The white asparagus soup was eaten and the plates removed.

Judy, as this conversation was recollected piece by piece, began to feel hot surges of dismay mounting up into her cheeks. In another few minutes would come the time she had so stupidly tried to influence the dead Maharajah into allowing Uncle Joe to use the newly built dam to the full. A move which had led to that terrible outburst of his. Had the same thing got to happen again tonight?

It had.

"Yes," said D.S.P. Howard with sudden decisiveness, "and now, as the Maharajah, I turn to you, Mr. Lloyd, and I say, 'Mr. Lloyd, have you been teaching your niece to put the view to me that the dam should be used to its fullest capability? I have told you already: it is over my dead body that the water level in the jheels will rise one inch above what it has always been.' Are those the words, more or less, that he used, Mr. Lloyd?"

"They are," Joe said.

"And what did you reply, Mr. Lloyd? As nearly as possible the same words, please. "

"Yeah, I can give it to you straight. I said what I said, and I meant what I said. And, damn it, I'll stick by that now."

Joe Lloyd took a deep breath and began.

"Your Highness, I never put a word into Judy's mouth. I'd scorn to do that. But I'll tell you this: you're wrong, darned wrong, not to let the dam work to the full. What you're doing is nothing short of murder. You're murdering poor guys whose land's going to go dry when it damned well need not. That's murder, in my book. Then or now."

He fixed his gaze not on the D.S.P. in the old Maharajah's chair at the head of the table but on Porgy.

And once more it looked as if a clash were about to take place that could result in anything. But, once more, as had happened on the previous occasion, the cool, calm voice of the Dewan cut in.

"It was I who said then, and I can only repeat it now, 'Mr. Lloyd, you are not taking all the facts of the matter into account. You know it is just as much a fact what the peasants of Bhopore are prepared to do for their Maharajah, present His Highness equally with late His Highness, as any of your calculations of water flow.'"

"Yeah," said Joe Lloyd, slumping back in his chair in just exactly the way—Judy remembered—as he had done when the Dewan had calmed the situation before. "Yeah, I remember what you said, and I can see the point. But I still think it's crazy to have a dam that could irrigate a hell of a lot more land than it's evidently going to be allowed to do."

The D.S.P. leant forward in the Maharajah's chair at this point.

"And very soon, Dewan Sahib," he said, "the dinner came to the point where there was a clash between yourself and late His Highness over unwarranted expenditure, was there not?"

The Dewan smiled.

"I should prefer not to call it a clash," he said. "But certainly I did point out to His Highness that there are worthier ways of spending his revenues than those he was embarking upon. And I am glad to say that my views now are being taken into consideration."

He leant back a little and looked challengingly round. There could be no doubt that he was saying, without a word spoken, "Very well, I stood to gain by the Maharajah's death. I have gained. I am here in charge at Bhopore still when I might very well have been dismissed in disgrace."

The D.S.P. looked at him steadily from beneath his hooded eyes.

"And soon afterwards, Dewan Sahib, if I have learnt the facts correctly, the Maharajah began to discuss with Mr. Morton here his project for bringing American methods of exploitation to Bhopore?

Am I right in thinking this was something that you had never been told about before?"

The Dewan was silent for several moments before answering.

"Yes," he said at last. "That was the first I knew of the plan. And it is a plan, needless to add, which I oppose totally."

He looked from the American tycoon to the new Maharajah with haughty disdain.

By now the roast meats, just the same ones as before, had been disposed of and the "Second Course," the caviar or the rice pilau with curry was being served.

"I don't think we need reproduce everything Mr. Morton told His Highness about his proposals," the D.S.P. said. "No doubt he hopes to repeat what he put forward then to the new Maharajah in due course. Nor do I think we need worry now if the conversations we are reproducing do not fall at exactly the same point in the meal as before. The main thing is that as much as possible that was said then should be remembered now. And I think that we have managed quite well so far."

There was a general murmur of agreement.

"So we come next," the D.S.P. went on, scarcely raising his voice above the subdued hubbub coming from the far end of the table, "to another important conversation, though short, in which you featured, Mr. Morton."

The American tycoon lowered the piece of caviar-covered biscuit he was about to put into his mouth.

"Yes, I guess I know what you mean, Mr. Howard," he said. "I was unhappy enough to refer to the accident which produced this."

He laid three fingers for a moment on the huge scar which disfigured one whole side of his face.

"Exactly," said the D.S.P. "Do you recall what you said at all?"

"Yes, I think so. I told the Maharajah that I wouldn't come on his what-d'you-call-it, shik—something—"

"The shikar at the jheels next morning."

"Yeah, that's it. I said I had used to like hunting till something got jammed in the barrel of a gun I'd got and exploded, with me only escaping with my life by a miracle."

"Thank you, Mr. Morton."

The D.S.P. turned to the others.

"The importance of that scrap of conversation," he said, "can hardly be exaggerated. It must have been what put the idea for the murder into the murderer's head."

At the head of the long table round him face turned to face. Eyes, hardly bothering to conceal suspicion—or taking care to assume it—looked at other eyes.

"Mr. Howard," Elaine Alcott jabbed out, her voice almost a scream, "do we have to go on with this?"

"Yes," said D.S.P. Howard. "We do."

XXII

The various courses of that long, luxurious meal, the exact repetition of the Maharajah of Bhopore's last dinner on earth, had come and gone. The point had been reached when the Maharajah himself ate. Into the huge banqueting hall, carried with ceremony by the Maharajah's own personal trusted bearer, came the enormous gold platter from which the Maharajah had always taken his food. Its high-domed gold cover was in place. The gold-covered padlock that kept the food inside safe from any poisoning hand was locked.

The bearer set the platter down in front of D.S.P. Howard, that slight quiet figure in the big chair at the head of the long table.

Even the chatter at the low farthermost end of the table was hushed now. Had the Maharajah really been murdered by a poison which would cause him to commit suicide being put in his food? Very few people up and down the length of that table were able to-tally to discount the notion.

"Unlock the dish," the D.S.P. said to the bearer.

From the folds of his cummerbund the bearer extracted the key. He inserted it in the padlock. He turned it. He opened the dish.

Inside was a replica of the enormous pile of goodness-stuffed rice topped by three chickens that the Maharajah had been served with. The D.S.P. put out his right hand towards it.

Heads everywhere craned forward.

"Now," said the D.S.P., "if you remember, the Maharajah did not eat as soon as the food was set before him. Instead he began to recount his April Fools' Day feats. Am I not right?"

"Yes. Yes, you are right," said Porgy, Maharajah of Bhopore.

There were globules of sweat on his forehead underneath his rich sulphur-yellow turban, the identical one he had worn before.

"Yes," said the D.S.P. "Well, I don't intend to go over each of those incidents again. I don't think there's any need to. But there is one thing I must get established, one very important thing."

There was no need for him to pause so as to get attention. Every single person up and down the long table was listening hard as they could.

"And that, of course," the quiet voice continued, "is the matter of the joke the Maharajah played on Sir Arthur's son, Michael. The joke that used sapura bark. Now, will you all confirm to me, please, that in his long recital of tricks the Maharajah made no mention whatsoever of that particular incident?"

There was silence. No one, it seemed, wanted to be the first to speak. At last the Resident, professional taker of responsibilities on behalf of the huge British Empire, spoke up.

"I am perfectly ready to affirm, Mr. Howard," he said, "that that rather infantile business was in no way mentioned at dinner that night."

That was a mutter of complete agreement.

"Good," said the D.S.P. "I felt it was most important that no one should have any doubts about that."

"So that means it is one of us, us five?" James Frere said, blushing a little as he spoke.

"No, Mr. Frere. It isn't."

"It isn't. It's someone else? But I don't see . . ."

"It may be one of you five, as you put it. But the circle was never as small as that, you know."

James Frere frowned.

"Well, I don't see how it was bigger," he said. "I mean, there weren't so many people there to watch the Maharajah's trick that one couldn't remember them all perfectly."

"Agreed."

"Then I don't understand. I just don't understand."

"There were the people who watched the trick," the D.S.P. said quietly. "But there was someone else there, too, someone besides the Resident's driver, whom we've eliminated to our complete satisfaction."

"Someone— I don't see who—"

James Frere abruptly stopped. He had seen who.

"Yes, Mr. Frere," said the D.S.P. "There was Michael Pendeverel there."

Now all eyes were fixed on the Resident. He sat there, unmoving, looking into the far distance. A waxwork out of Madame Tussaud's exhibition in London.

The D.S.P. spoke yet more quietly.

"Just a child, Mr. Frere, yes," he said. "But consider what was necessary for the act that killed the Maharajah. Simply to push a soft piece of bark down the barrel of one of the guns he was bound to use and then to wet it a little. And Michael, remember, has begun to learn to use a gun. Now, one of the first things one is taught when one begins to handle a firearm is that the barrel must always be perfectly clear, that it must be well cleaned before use. Isn't that so?"

"Yes," said Sir Arthur Pendeverel. "That is so."

His voice might have been that of some ingenious mechanical talking device.

"But why?" James Frere persisted. "Why, in heaven's name? It can't have been revenge for the trick played on him. I've got to know that lad quite well since I've been in Bhopore. The thought wouldn't have occurred to him."

"No, Mr. Frere. It would not."

"Well then, why? Why?"

"Let me put this to you. You are young. Only nine. Your mother has died. You are alone here in a remote part of India with your father. You worship that father, don't you?"

It was not the Resident who answered. It was James Frere again.

"Yes," he said. "Little Michael worshipped his father."

"Well then, think," the D.S.P. went on. "The Resident and the late Maharajah by no means saw eye to eye. There were numerous occasions when the Maharajah, with his exuberance—if I may put it like that—must have caused considerable annoyance to the Resident. Annoyance only, of course. Sir Arthur would not let himself go beyond that. But he must often have given signs of it in the privacy of the Residency, even if he said not a word. And a worshipping nine-year-old is more than capable of reading such signs and of thinking they are much more serious than in fact they were."

"Yes," said James Frere heavily. "Yes."

Again everyone turned to look at the Resident.

"However," D.S.P. Howard said, "more than motive is needed for murder. There is the question of means. How would Little Michael have got hold of that piece of sapura bark? Very easily, in fact. He had only to creep out of his bed when his father had left for the palace here, perhaps saddle his pony and make his way to the palace with the intention of begging that piece of useful bark from Captain Ram Singh, whom he had seen putting it in his pocket."

"But I never," Captain Ram Singh burst out. "I mean, I swear I never gave the boy a thing."

"No," said the D.S.P. "He would not have needed to beg it from you in the end. It was lying in Lieutenant Frere's bathroom. Or perhaps it was lying in one of the passageways of the palace where a stray monkey had left it."

"Then it is Little Michael," Captain Ram Singh said.

"It may be," said the D.S.P. "It may well be. Which is why I wanted proof and was so insistent, Sir Arthur, that you come here tonight."

"I see," said the Resident.

His face was ashen now.

"Which is why, too," the D.S.P. went on, "that I asked my friend the Maharajah's Schoolmaster to keep a particular watch this evening."

He lifted his head a little and called:

"Schoolmaster Sahib."

At the doorway at the far end of the room the Schoolmaster at once made his appearance. A dowdy figure in his skirtlike white dhoti among the peacock finery of the dinner guests, the brocade atchkans, the many-coloured turbans, the glittering jewellery, he marched ploddingly all the way up past the length of the long, long table. In the silence the sound made by each of his sandals in turn as it flapped on the marble floor was clear as a bell stroke. The dust on their soles left a set of smudged imprints in his wake.

"Well, Schoolmaster Sahib?" said the D.S.P. when at last the bedraggled dhoti-clad figure had reached the Maharajah's chair.

"He is not on his way, D.S.P. Sahib," the Schoolmaster said. "As instructed, I requested one of the telephone orderlies to inquire at the Residency. The boy is asleep in his bed."

"And on the night before the murder?"

"I have carefully asked each chowkidar who was on watch in the grounds tonight as he was on that night, D.S.P. Sahib, and I am satisfied beyond doubt neither the boy nor anyone else came into the palace."

"Thank you, Schoolmaster Sahib. Perhaps you would like to wait now. "

The Schoolmaster plodded over to the corner near where the Maharajah's personal bearer was standing waiting and joined him there.

"So it's down to five again, the five of us," said James Frere.

"Mr. Frere," the D.S.P. replied, "in an affair of this sort, you will understand, nothing ever must be taken for granted."

But it was not James Frere who answered. It was the Resident.

"Yes, Mr. Howard," he said. "I understand that."

"Thank you, sir. And now, perhaps, I ought to point out that we are, in fact, no nearer finding the solution which we all hoped this evening would provide. But perhaps I can clear up certain misconceptions by saying a few words about each of those Lieutenant Frere called just now 'the five of us,' namely Frere himself, Miss Brattle, Mr. Lloyd, Dewan Sahib, and, of course, His Highness."

If nerves had been tight-stretched up at the top end of the long dinner table before, they were at snapping point now. Even the ever calm figure of the Dewan was affected visibly. His long, lean fingers had gripped the gold dessert knife at his place tightly, as if it were a weapon he was going to need at any moment in a fight for his life. James Frere, too, up till now a model of relaxed politeness, was staring straight in front of him, seeing nothing and no one, least of all the pretty face of Judy Alcott. Porgy, in his gorgeous finery, looked simply like a ridiculous dummy, so lacking in presence he was now. Dolly Brattle, for all her careful makeup, looked an old woman, older even than the age she tried so desperately to conceal. Joe Lloyd had both his thick boxer's hands down under the level of the table. They were holding on to the sides of his chair. At any moment, it was clear, they might shoot up, clench into fists, and lash out.

"Oh, there's one thing," the D.S.P. said, appearing abruptly to recollect some small task he had to perform.

"What— What's that?" Elaine Alcott shot the words out, almost as a scream.

The D.S.P.'s little flick of a smile moved the sides of his straight-set mouth for an instant.

"Nothing to worry about," he said. "It's just that, surely, at this point the Maharajah made his somewhat unfortunate accusation against Captain Ram Singh. Wasn't that so?"

Captain Ram Singh's handsome face took on a look of fierce sullenness. But he did answer.

"Yes, it was now. But I should have been standing beside the Maharajah before this."

"Oh, I don't think we need go into every detail," the D.S.P. answered easily. "We all know that you did not put anything into the Maharajah's food, Ram Singh. But I would like the episode to be gone through again, if you don't mind. It's important to establish timings, you know."

"Do you mean I have got to go and be searched?" the A.D.C. asked. "I promise you I have not got a piece of sapura bark in my pocket now."

"Yes, I would like you to go with Frere to his bathroom, and perhaps between you, you could find something to represent the piece of bark and just leave it on the stool the way the bark was."

It was said in a light enough tone. But it was an order. There could be no doubt about that. Captain Ram Singh and James Frere got stiffly to their feet and walked out.

They were away not much more than five minutes, a definitely shorter time than they had been absent when James Frere had searched Captain Ram Singh so conscientiously on the night the Maharajah had made his accusation. But D.S.P. Howard did not seem put out when they returned.

"There's something left in your bathroom, Frere?" he asked.

"Yes. Yes, we put a cigarette packet there. A packet of Abdullas."

"That should be excellent. And now one more thing before I begin my perhaps rather tiresome remarks. The Maharajah's silver train. I think this was the moment he set it in motion, wasn't it?"

"It was," said the Resident, biting the words off.

"Good. Then I think I'd better do the same thing, and I'd like you all, if you would, to do whatever you did on the previous occasion. Stop the train by lifting one of the sweet dishes or the liqueur bottles on it, and take whatever it was you took before. I'm sure you'll all remember."

Nobody said anything.

The D.S.P. leant forward and tapped sharply on the silver button in its elegant silver mounting which stood just in front of the Maharajah's place. The silver train, correct in its every detail, gave a little toot and started off on its journey.

"You won't forget to take some nuts?" the D.S.P. said to Mrs. Alcott.

"No, no, I won't. I remember. That's what I did."

As the train rounded the corner of the table and approached Elaine Alcott's place, the D.S.P. leant back a little in the Maharajah's thronelike chair.

"In many ways," he said, his voice slow and easy, as if he were telling a leisurely story, "it is most unseemly for me to discuss His

Highness here in front of his subjects and while I am, quite irregularly, occupying the seat he should be occupying now, the seat in which his late father sat. Nevertheless, the possibility that His Highness murdered his father is one that, owing to the extraordinary nature of the murder of the Maharajah, has come before the public in an inescapable manner. So it is right, I feel, that I should say what I have to say about His Highness in this public manner."

His lidded eyes flipped up momentarily to look at Porgy. The present Maharajah seized one of the glasses in front of him and, without any consideration of what its contents might be, white wine or red or whisky or brandy, drained it to the dregs.

"The question all along here has been simply this: What exactly were the relations between father and son? Everybody knew that they were strained. His present Highness, as Mr. Henry Morton has often pointed out, is a man of progressive views. His late Highness was a stickler for tradition, though apt to have sudden unexpected ideas such as his plan with Mr. Morton to bring American methods of processing zinc to Bhopore. But underneath all their differences one thing was certain. The son loved the father. Now we all perhaps know that sometimes love can turn to hate. But if this happens, it can clearly be seen to have happened. The love is gone, the hate is there."

Again the hooded eyes flicked up to look at Porgy.

"It has been quite plain to me," the quiet voice went on, "from the very beginning that this had not happened, that the son loved the father after he was dead and had loved him, despite all differences between them, in the days immediately before his death. It was for this reason that I never seriously considered His Highness as the murderer."

Porgy's face was suddenly wet with tears. For a few moments those nearest him looked at the spectacle, fascinated. Then they turned away. The silver train came chugging slowly up to him, and through his curtain of tears he reached out and lifted the bottle of port from it, bringing it to a halt.

"Now let's consider what might be called a patent sight of hatred," the D.S.P. said.

And everybody, at once, knew that he was talking about Joe Lloyd.

"No one," the D.S.P. went on, his voice reflective, as if he were considering the merits of the excellent claret he had been served with earlier, and which remained untouched in the glass at his elbow. "No one can have any doubts that Mr. Lloyd here had very strong feelings about the Maharajah. He repeated them tonight. He considered, rightly or wrongly, that His late Highness was a virtual murderer. So presumably he might well feel entitled to execute him. The only question that faces us is this: If he killed the Maharajah, would he have killed him in the way he was killed?"

Joe Lloyd's two ham fists came suddenly up from where they had been holding on and on to the sides of his chair. The chair itself began to go backwards with an ugly scraping sound as the tough engineer rose to his feet.

"That will do, Mr. Lloyd," the D.S.P. snapped.

For a moment it looked as if his words had been the final insult and that next second Joe's fist would crash into his face. But it was for a moment only. Then the broad-shouldered engineer sank back into his seat.

"Perhaps Mr. Lloyd's action just now proves my point as well as anything," the D.S.P. said. "He is a man of action. No doubt in the course of his life he has more than once behaved with foolish impetuosity. No doubt this was what his sister has all along feared in his nature. But there can be no doubt either that the Maharajah was not killed impetuously. Mr. Lloyd did not kill him."

Elaine Alcott shook her head from side to side as if she could hardly believe the words she had heard uttered, the reprieve.

Far down the long table now the Maharajah's silver toy was chuntering merrily on its way, undisturbed by any minor courtier.

"But if Mr. Lloyd, who could certainly have managed the business of putting the sapura bark into the Maharajah's Purdey, did not kill him because that was not his way, we must ask ourselves now about a person who has all along claimed that the simple business of blocking that barrel was altogether beyond her. Miss Brattle."

Dolly Brattle at once stirred in her chair. Her eyes flashed fire.

"It damn well was beyond me. And nothing you can do or say will prove otherwise."

The words were almost a shout of defiance.

In answer to them the D.S.P.'s minimal smile appeared and disappeared.

"You know," he said, "I think that's just what I can do, Miss Brattle. Or if I cannot perhaps prove beyond doubt that you have the ability to do more than behave in a ladylike and thoroughly impractical manner, I can certainly show to my satisfaction that you are a very able lady. And I can do it out of your own actions."

Dolly Brattle did not challenge the D.S.P. now. It was clear that she, at least, knew exactly what he was talking about.

"Yes, Miss Brattle. We met, did we not, when you were leaving the palace, by a back way that you had carefully ascertained existed, and carrying with you, quite unaided, a rather heavy suitcase. No, I don't think you are at all an impractical person underneath. Nor do I believe you would have any difficulty over realising what sapura bark can do and putting it into the barrel of the Maharajah's gun out there in the darkness of the jheels."

"But I didn't. I didn't. I tell you I didn't."

"No," said D.S.P. Howard, "I don't think you did. Not for a moment. And it was precisely your attempt to get away from the palace that showed me you did not. You were not at the end of your resources then, however depressed you may have been. You knew in your heart of hearts all along that if you did not succeed in marrying His Highness here, you would survive somehow, somewhere. You did not absolutely need to murder the Maharajah, and you are not the person to have done that except at the end of your tether. Are you?"

"No," Dolly Brattle said with dignity. "I am not."

The little silver train, so pretty and so ridiculously costly, had made its way round the great bend at the far end of the long table and had begun to head for the area where it could be stopped with impunity.

"So, if Miss Brattle never really had a motive for the murder," the D.S.P. said, "we ought perhaps next to consider someone who avowed to me, and to others perhaps, that he did have a motive, that he was—to use a crude phrase—Suspect Number One."

He turned and looked levelly at the elegant, yet tense, figure of the Dewan.

"Motive, means, opportunity," he said. "Dewan Sahib, as he freely admits, has them all. It is very possible that under His late Highness he would have lost the office that, with its opportunities to improve the life of Bhopore, means everything to him. Sapura bark he could possibly have obtained, with the power at his disposal, even if he had not had it so near at hand in Lieutenant Frere's bathroom, only a few yards from where we are now. And to put it in the gun barrel and wet it and wait, that would have been easy enough for him. And, as I have said before, murder does not have to be committed for an evil reason."

Quite suddenly the Dewan's tense fingers gripping the gold dessert knife relaxed. The heavy little object fell to the table with a soft clunk.

"But, no," said the D.S.P., "Dewan Sahib did not murder the Maharajah. He is, I have no hesitation in saying it to his face, a good man. A very good man. A man too good for that particularly painful and horrible way of removing an obstacle from his path."

"Yes," said the Dewan, speaking as quietly as the D.S.P., "you are right, Mr. Howard. I could not have killed the Maharajah in that way."

The little silver train chugged happily onwards.

The D.S.P. turned to the last of the five. James Frere.

"Lieutenant Frere," he said. "Look at him, the decent young man who had no possible motive for murdering the Maharajah."

Fifty pairs of eyes looked at the decent young man. Who sat straight as a die in his chair, straight as if he were facing an enemy firing squad, prepared to die.

"The decent young man," the D.S.P. repeated, "who had no possible motive for murdering the Maharajah. And that, ladies and gentlemen, simply says it all. He had no possible motive. Why should he murder the Maharajah? He did not murder the Maharajah. There was never any possibility that he had."

"Oh, James. James."

The cry was wrung from Judy. Nothing could have kept it back, the sudden upspringing of joy and hope, hope for a future she had not dared in these last few days to contemplate.

What her mother would have said at this unseemly outburst, or what others might have whispered, was not to be known. At that moment the D.S.P. spoke sharply again.

"The train," he said. "The train."

All attention focussed on the absurd little toy with its ridiculous cargo of nuts and sweets, port and the dark crème de cacao liqueur that the dead Maharajah had loved.

"Miss Brattle," the D.S.P. said, "be ready to stop it. The Maharajah asked you to take some port, I believe. Take some, please."

Dolly Brattle did as she was told.

But as the little silver train came to a halt with the port decanter lifted from its truck, another voice was heard. A voice that, if the dinner had gone completely strictly to the pattern of the earlier one, should not have been there. Captain Ram Singh should have been languishing in one of the Maharajah's dungeons. Instead he was standing at the back of the room, not far from where the Schoolmaster was. And now he broke in.

"But, Mr. Howard, you have gone through the whole list. You have cleared every one of the five. Who is the murderer of the Maharajah then?"

"Yes, Ram Singh, we must come to that," the D.S.P. answered.

Then his attention was momentarily distracted. The ridiculous toy train had started on its journey once again.

"Mr. Morton," he called, "don't forget you stopped the train next. You took crème de cacao."

"As if I could forget," the American tycoon growled. "The damned trick the Maharajah played on me. Shooting that stuff all over my jacket."

He reached forward and lifted the crème de cacao bottle gently up from its truck. The little silver train came to a prompt halt. The spring underneath the crème de cacao, as it had done when the Maharajah had ordered it, flicked powerfully up. A stream of sticky, chocolaty liqueur shot all over Henry Morton III's jacket.

"Hell and damnation," he yelled. "What bloody fool set that up again? Howard, didn't you tell the damned fools not to release that damned trick spring?"

People up and down the long table were laughing. Some almost uncontrollably. The tension until a few seconds before had been almost unbearable. Now it was released.

"Your Highness," the D.S.P. said to Porgy, raising his voice a little, "would you as before take Mr. Morton to wash?"

Porgy had already leapt up. Now he took the American by the elbow and began leading him off.

"What did you say to him as you went, Your Highness?" the D.S.P. called. "Say it again, please. As accurately as you can."

"I don't know, I don't know," Porgy answered. "How can I remember when someone's done this stupid thing once again? As far as I can remember, I said something to Mr. Morton about my father's way of playing tricks. I said—"

He came to a full halt.

"Yes," called the D.S.P. "What did you say?"

"I'll tell you," Porgy answered, still holding tight to Henry Morton's elbow. "I'll tell you, damn it, word for word. I said, 'He does the same thing every April the first. Why, only this afternoon he put a piece of something we call sapura bark into the exhaust pipe of the Resident's car. He ruined that machine.' Those were my words, Mr. Howard. And I went on to explain the whole joke in full detail, and then I took Mr. Morton to the nearest bathroom, Lieutenant Frere's."

"Yes," said the D.S.P. "That's what I had come to think, thanks to the report of the dinner I had from my friend the Schoolmaster here. You were quite right, Schoolmaster Sahib. Mr. Morton knew about sapura bark before the Maharajah was murdered, even though he was not even in Bhopore when that famous trick took place. And he knew, too, after that dinner that the chances of getting the zinc concession, a concession that meant everything to him with all his union troubles in America, from someone as capricious as the Maharajah were almost nil. So he decided to bet on the Maharajkumar. The progressive member of the family."

Henry Morton III broke from Porgy's grasp and began to run. But there were green-uniformed, magenta-turbaned Sikh guards at the doorway. He got no farther.

It was next morning. Preparations for the imminent visit of the Viceroy to open the Sir Albert Singhi Memorial Dam in Bhopore were already at fever pitch. But along the dusty road from the palace a car was driving, a secondhand Buick, the property of a dubious gentleman in Sangabad called Bool Chand.

Soon its driver spotted, trudging along towards him, a figure clad in a sagging white dhoti with, hoisted above his head against the rays of the already powerful sun, a large and ancient black umbrella. He brought the car to a halt.

"Good morning, Schoolmaster Sahib."

"Good morning, D.S.P. Sahib."

"I'm glad I had the chance to say good-bye. I want to get back to Sangabad as soon as I can. There's a nasty little dacoity there I must get cleared up."

"Oh, yes, D.S.P. Sahib. I can understand that. And I too have a task awaiting me."

"Oh, yes?"

"The Maharajah's children," the Schoolmaster explained, with a touch of reproof in his voice. "They have yet to acquire the names of the rivers of the Ganges Basin. It is something that they ought to have locked into their memories."

"You're right, Schoolmaster Sahib. Very important."

The D.S.P. turned back to the Buick's dashboard.

"D.S.P. Sahib," said the Schoolmaster, "may I say, in parting, that to have been, however humbly, a collaborator of the renowned District Superintendent of Police Howard will be till the end of my days a treasured memory for me? Howard Sahib, if ever to my tally of four daughters there is added a son, I tell you this. That boy, please God, shall become a police officer."

"Well, thank you," said D.S.P. Howard, looking suddenly more pleased than he had ever looked during the whole of his stay in Bhopore. "Thank you indeed, Mr. Ghote."